THE WIDOWER'S WIFE

ALSO BY CATE HOLAHAN:

Dark Turns

THE
WIDOWER'S
WIFE

A THRILLER

Cate Holahan

**CROOKED
LANE**

NEW YORK

Published in the United States by Crooked Lane Books, an imprint of The Quick Brown Fox & Company LLC.

Crooked Lane Books and its logo are trademarks of The Quick Brown Fox & Company LLC.

Library of Congress Catalog-in-Publication data available upon request.

ISBN (hardcover): 978-1-62953-765-8
ISBN (ePub): 978-1-62953-778-8
ISBN (Kindle): 978-1-62953-779-5
ISBN (ePDF): 978-1-62953-780-1

Cover and book design by Jennifer Canzone

Printed in the United States.

www.crookedlanebooks.com

Crooked Lane Books
34 West 27th St., 10th Floor
New York, NY 10001

First Edition: August 2016

10 9 8 7 6 5 4 3 2 1

For Poppy

Part I

Term life

An insurance policy that provides protection for a
limited period of time.

1

November 16

Ryan Monahan liked liars. Not the three-times-a-conversation fibbers, who prettied up the truth to appear less pedestrian at parties and would swear to God they'd had *just one*, *Officer*. Those average assholes weren't even trying. No, Ryan liked the real deal, the kind of folks who weaved falsehoods into the very fabric of their lives until they wore their fictions like fine-knit sweaters, feeling safe and warm, wrapped in their bullshit. They were the challenge.

He didn't yet know if Tom Bacon was his kind of liar. But the man was definitely hiding something.

Tom hadn't invited him inside his French-styled starter castle, despite the unseasonably cold weather. Instead, the guy had greeted him on the driveway apron wearing a ski jacket. He'd carried a shovel in one gloved hand, a bucket of salt in the other, neither of which he'd set down for a handshake. Ryan had lingered at the curb after introductions, watching Tom spread ice melt over slush, waiting for a welcome indoors while Mother Nature's slick hand probed beneath the back vent in his pea coat.

Tom had asked about the death benefit as though it were a fait accompli, as though Ryan might have popped by to deliver a jackpot-sized certified check. No need for a discussion. Certainly no reason for Mr. Bacon to explain how his healthy, thirty-one-year-old wife had suffered a fatal accident on a cruise. Ryan had suggested that they'd both be more comfortable inside.

3

He stood in Tom's kitchen, socked feet on the hardwood floor, looking for a suitable spot for an interrogation. A pair of extra-large packing boxes sat stacked atop a pedestal table, the side flaps of the top crate sticking straight up so that they touched the chandelier above. Printouts littered a massive marble island. Ryan recognized the Insurance Strategy and Investment policy among the documents, broken into sections with multicolored sticky notes. Someone was doing his homework.

Tom pulled a chrome barstool from beneath the island. He half-leaned onto the metal seat. The stance was faux relaxed, a staged paparazzo snapshot awaiting a caption.

Ryan walked toward the chairs, his gate slow and stiff. He hated his inability to move from point A to B without broadcasting his injury like a fouled basketball player. People didn't limp without good reason, and at thirty-nine, he was too young for arthritis.

He placed a hand on the curved back of a stool and shifted his weight to his good leg. Bending the knee intensified the pain. Better to stand for this conversation anyway.

"Moving?"

"What?"

Ryan pointed to the kitchen table. "The boxes."

"Oh. Maybe."

Ryan couldn't tell whether Tom was curt or distracted. People suffering the loss of an immediate family member sometimes lacked focus, as though their loved one's death trapped them between this life and the next, unable to be present in either. But Tom didn't seem grief-stricken. He'd even shaved. And in Ryan's experience, a few months in, most guys resembled reality-show survivalists.

People handle grief in awkward ways. Ryan reminded himself of this as he continued to assess Tom's attitude. There'd been that lady last year who had giggled while bawling over her dead husband, as though she'd grasped some divine punch line in her spouse's fatal car accident but still knew that the joke was on her.

4

"Where are you thinking of going?"

"Not sure. I'm more cleaning up." Tom shrugged. "There are things I don't need anymore."

Ana's things? The ghost of Mrs. Bacon called out from decorating details: dried lavender on the windowsill, a wall calendar with notes in a woman's tight cursive, a kitchen towel draped over a faucet to display the phrase "Home is where Mom cleans."

On television, Tom had promised to "never give up hope" that his wife was alive. Eighty days later and he was shipping his beloved's belongings to long-term storage. Time didn't take long to murder belief in miracles.

There was little chance of finding Ana Bacon alive. She'd disappeared in the open ocean—at night, no less. Odds of surviving a fall off a cruise ship stood at 21 percent. Those chances dropped to near zero if a rescue didn't occur within twelve hours. There'd been one case of a guy surviving seventeen hours in the Gulf of Mexico after tumbling overboard, blackout drunk, but he'd been a young, ex-army paratrooper. And if Ana had washed ashore in the Bahamas after a day in the water, somebody would have reported her appearance. Her picture was all over the news.

Ryan cleared his throat. "Sorry about what happened." He offered the platitude with legal precision. No mention of death or loss. Any confirmation on his part that a policyholder was deceased could be considered evidence that the company should start processing a claim.

"Thanks." Tom's tone was flat. He folded his arms across his chest. "So what's the status of the benefit?"

"That's what I'm here to discuss."

He'd come specifically *not* to pay the benefit. Insurance Strategy and Investment hadn't stayed in business for five generations by doling out multimillion-dollar settlements. The bosses wanted a ruthless investigation. Ana's policy contained a so-called double indemnity clause, meaning it paid double if she perished from a sudden mishap—ten million, to be exact. And the policy was still in the two-year contestability period, so suicide was not covered.

Ryan's statistics-laden subconscious told him that Ana's death was no accident. His intuition might also have fingered "the husband." When a woman died violently, her intimate partner was the cause more than a third of the time. But Tom had a solid alibi. He'd been at the pool when his wife had gone overboard, and he'd been seen by a couple vacationers and a striking redhead. The woman had wallpapered the news with her guilty admission that she'd been chatting up a married man at the exact time that the guy's wife had fallen overboard. Bad girl.

With Tom out of contention, the most probable culprit was Ana herself. But Ryan would need to prove it.

"As you can imagine, ISI has a certain due diligence process in cases without—"

"Daddy?"

Ryan turned to see a young girl enter the kitchen, a pretty kid with eyes befitting an anime character. He recalled the photos of Mrs. Bacon. The child took after her mother.

"Not now, Sophia." Tom's mouth pulled into a tight smile. "Daddy is talking."

The child tilted her head like a confused puppy and considered Ryan. He gave a little wave. She stepped back into the adjoining room before returning her attention to her father. Ryan had never been good with kids.

"I want a snack," she said.

"After I finish."

The skin beneath the child's eyes pinked to the color of a pinched cheek. Her bottom lip crumpled. "Where's Mommy?"

Hadn't Tom told her? Maybe she was too young to grasp the finality of death.

Tom rubbed his fingers into his forehead. He shot his kid an exasperated look before heading to an open door beside the stove and dipping inside. Items rustled. He reemerged with a package of peanut butter crackers and offered her the plastic pouch like a tissue.

Little hands curled into fists. "It's not—"

"Sophia. Just take it. Daddy needs to talk right now."

The girl's mouth opened in a silent cry. She accepted the package, unsure of what to do next. Ryan recalled when Angie had been that young. Kids could break apart plastic dollhouses, demolish wooden furniture, and pop childproof caps, yet simple vacuum seals left them stymied.

"You need to open it for her."

Tom lowered his head and pulled apart the plastic. Sophia's face relaxed. "Okay? Please go watch your shows until I finish."

The girl scurried from the room, her bare feet flashing beneath a long princess nightgown. It was past noon.

Tom raised his eyebrows in Ryan's direction. "You were saying?"

"ISI has a review policy in cases without remains."

"What's to review?" Tom lowered his voice. "The court issued a death-in-absentia declaration. That's the same as a death certificate."

"Unfortunately, it's not." Ryan scratched at the wavy hair hitting the nape of his neck. The move was a nervous habit and a tell of liars everywhere. Men clasped the back of the neck when stressed. Women tended to trace the suprasternal notch, that delicate triangle between the collarbones. Ryan wasn't lying, but he did feel anxious. Since the incident with his leg, confrontation made him jittery.

Tom scratched at nonexistent stubble. "How is it different?"

"There's no cause of death."

"As I'm sure you know from all the media coverage, my wife drowned in the Atlantic. Her cause of death was well documented."

The ship's security cameras had caught Ana Bacon's fall. She'd been filmed hurtling through the air, grasping a lifeboat for a moment, and then, ultimately, losing her hold and dropping into the ocean. Unfortunately for Mrs. Bacon, the cameras had not yet been upgraded with sensors capable of alerting the crew when a large object went overboard. And, unfortunately for Mr. Bacon, a few seconds of fall footage wasn't enough to prove the circumstances of his wife's demise. A well-documented death needed a full timeline of the moments leading up to the last breath and the aftermath. It needed a body with a DNA-confirmed identity. Most importantly, it needed a coroner's report with one of four words printed in the center: accidental, homicide, suicide, or natural.

"Her disappearance has been established."

"Like hell—" Tom raked his hand over his mouth, blocking the profanities that undoubtedly wanted to follow. "Let's just cut the nonsense. My wife is dead and your company wants to stall payment for as long as possible." He looked at the ceiling, as if imploring his dead wife to intercede. "I have a three-year-old who is never going to see her mother again." He pointed to the ISI policy on the countertop. "I purchased this coverage to ensure that she would always be well taken care of, should anything happen to one of us. I already had to wait for the court to issue the absentia ruling."

Ryan felt a rare twinge of guilt. Dependent beneficiaries were the worst part of the job. He tried not to think about them, to focus on the puzzle instead of the pieces. Find fraud. That was his job. Find the fraud.

Ryan recalled an omission from the Bacons' application. Neither had listed current employers, though they had each included former jobs under recent work history. Normally, the lack of gainful employment would have been a red flag, but the actuarial models showed that people with seven-figure former paychecks paid their premiums. Lots of ex-traders lived off investments these days.

"Are you working?" Ryan asked.

"What has that got to do with anything?" Tom's chin jutted out. His biceps twitched. The micromovements answered Ryan's question. Tom wasn't employed, at least not in any capacity that he could list on a tax return.

Money problems could lead to suicide. Ryan made a mental note to press for details later. Too many questions about the Bacons' finances could encourage Tom to end their interview. "These are just standard questions." Ryan gave Tom a beat to breathe. "What was your wife's mood before she disappeared?"

Tom squinted at him. "Her mood?"

"Yes. How was she feeling?"

"We were on vacation."

"Was she having a good time?"

"Sure." A dark blush crept from Tom's hairless neck into his cheeks. Ryan sensed he wouldn't get too many more answers.

"Was there any reason she might have been feeling upset?"

"You mean, was she depressed and jumped, right?" Tom scowled. "It was an accident. I know you don't want that answer, but that's what happened. It was just a horrible accident."

"So no reason she—"

Tom slapped the counter. "My wife was pregnant, God damn it, and she had Sophia. To suggest that she'd intentionally leave her family . . ."

Ryan debated whether to fire another question. When people overflowed with anger, the truth could spill out. On the other hand, too much fury could drown out conversation. Better instead to first repent and then follow up in a friendlier fashion. Quick ways to establish a rapport: common interests and flattery. "I'm sorry. You two must have been excited about a second kid. I only have the one."

Ryan withdrew his cell from the front pocket of his suit pants and flashed it in Tom's face. Angie graced his home screen, bow mouth tied into a smile to hide the spaces vacated by baby teeth. The late fall sun shimmered on the blond in her browning hair. She was six in the photo. He'd taken it last year on a trip to the Bronx Zoo, before she and her mom had moved clear across the country.

Tom's expression changed from cross to careful. He had to know Ryan was only playing at good cop. But he also had to be aware that the insurance company wouldn't pay if he didn't at least try to cooperate with its investigator.

"Pretty," he said.

It was the only response when kid pictures were passed around. Anything other than some approving murmur was an insult, even if the darling daughter had horns, a cleft lip, and a tail. Still, Tom's rote compliment was agreeing to a truce. And if Ryan did say so himself, Angie's face would make most fathers join the NRA.

"Were you looking forward to a new baby?"

"I . . ." Tom drummed his fingers against the marble, as though working out where Ryan was headed with his new round of niceties. "You know, now isn't the best time for this."

"I don't have too many more—"

"My daughter is waiting." Tom stood. He pressed a palm on Ryan's shoulder, as if they were friends at closing time. Ryan winced at the sudden contact. "Let me grab your coat."

"A list of family and friends would be helpful." Ryan trailed his host to the mudroom. Salt crystals whitened a slate floor. A child's jacket hung beside his own, above a built-in bench.

"Why is that necessary?"

"Medical history." A half lie. It was routine to check the deceased's family for conditions that might have led to a denial of coverage, but Ryan already knew he wouldn't find anything. Ana didn't have medical problems. Her parents hadn't had a record of any hospitalizations. What he really wanted was for other people to attest to Ana's mental state.

"Sure. Fine." Tom handed over Ryan's coat with one hand and opened the side door with the other. "I'll find time to put that together."

Cold air kicked Ryan in the chest. He jammed his feet into his boots and shoved his arms through wool sleeves.

Tom waited with his hand on the door. "Let's not drag this out. My daughter and I have been through enough."

Ryan could feel Tom watching as he limped down the gritty driveway to the Dodge Charger parked at the curb. Sizing him up. Tom probably thought he was a rent-a-cop with a bum leg, some ex-grunt who'd stepped on an improvised explosive device before returning to school with GI cash. Not a real detective. Certainly no more of a threat than the Bahamas Maritime Authority, the rubber-stamp cruise police to which the FBI and Coast

Guard had willingly passed jurisdiction after rescue efforts had failed to turn up a body.

He slid into his car's front seat, turned the ignition, and cranked the heat.

Tom no longer watched from the doorway. Wooden slats barred the front windows, blocking the view inside. Good window treatments make good neighbors. Unfortunately for Ryan, shutters made shitty witnesses.

He put the car in drive and rolled past the silent house, thinking of his unanswered questions. What had happened behind those blinds to make a young mother desperate enough to jump ship?

2

"So I'm worth more dead than alive."

The words stuck in the silence separating me from my husband. Tom sat on the opposite side of the concrete dining table, one hand dangling from the back of his chair, the other gripping a wine glass. His body language declared victory. But this wasn't a fight. My husband loved me. He knew how hard I worked chasing after Sophia and keeping the house, especially now with the job on top of it all.

He reached for the slender neck of the bottle between us and poured. Bruise-colored liquid trailed down the sides of his glass. Light from the chandelier above reflected through the olive bottle, tinting his face.

He returned the wine bottle to the tabletop. A red teardrop dangled from the mouth before drooling onto the table's gray surface, seeping into the millions of microscopic holes in the honed material. I snatched my cloth napkin from my lap, dabbed it in my water glass, and pressed it to the stain.

"You really should have chosen a better table."

I glared at the spot rather than my husband. I didn't have the energy to justify the table's purchase. Besides, I couldn't. When I'd bought it, I'd thought only of its beautiful lines and grand size. The parties we'd have gathered around it. I'd never considered what it took to maintain. *A living finish*—that was what the furniture company said when I'd called to ask why water, let

12

alone wine, stained a four-thousand-dollar tabletop. Europeans relished the character, according to the New Jersey saleswoman. I'd explained that, as an American, I needed something capable of retaining its original appearance. She'd explained their final sale policy.

I blotted the stain. "I just don't understand what you're saying. You mean—"

"Ana, you're getting upset. Don't get upset."

He said my name in the same tone I used to scold our daughter. *Sophia, don't rock the chair.*

His glass clinked as it connected with the tabletop. Wine lapped at the sides of the crystal. I should get him a coaster. One thing at a time.

"Well, sorry for taking it the wrong way, but you're telling me that some life insurance policy would be worth more than me."

A smile twisted the corner of Tom's mouth. He wiped it away with his palm. "I'm not saying that. I'm—"

"Just saying that I'd be worth more—"

"Babe, there's no need to get emotional over facts. I just looked it up, okay? People in their thirties without health problems can get five million in coverage for less than the cost of a car payment. Think of it in terms of ROI. You make, what? Seventy K a year? If you work until you're seventy-five, you'll still only make a bit over three million. That's before tax."

"My salary will increase."

Tom snorted. "Yeah, with inflation." He reclaimed his wine glass and gestured toward the spiral staircase behind him. It led to the second floor and the bedrooms—to Sophia. The handheld monitor hummed beside me. Our daughter lay in her bed, arms stretched above her head. Three years old, yet she slept like a baby in the starfish position: on her back, completely vulnerable.

"Admins top out at a hundred fifty thousand dollars a year, even at a hedge fund," Tom said. "By the time you get there, Sophia's college will probably cost that each semester."

I'd taken for granted that we would pay tuition for our little girl and any siblings to come, though we'd never set aside money for it. The house, the cars, nursery school, ballet lessons, sending cash to my struggling parents—all had seemed more pressing than saving for something fifteen years into the future. We'd put away enough for a rainy day, but not a deluge like this.

Tears threatened my eyes. I, of all people, knew circumstances could change in an instant. Why had I not prepared for the worst?

Tom didn't share in my sadness. Two imploding stars shone beneath his brow, each radiating a hot, blue fire that belied my husband's casual body language. Tom hated the boss who fired him after he made half a billion dollars for clients in six years. He hated the buddies at competing banks who refused to open their doors. He hated the friends we'd entertained with Cabernets and crudités for slinking away. Sometimes I thought he hated me for bearing witness to it all.

I poked at my plate of cubed chicken. Gravy-laden brown rice stuck to the meat like the feathers of a sea bird caught in an oil slick. No wonder Tom would rather drink than eat.

He gestured toward me with his glass. "Point is, even if you managed to bring your salary up by ten percent a year, we're talking far less than five million dollars, and the tax man can't take any of the insurance."

"I don't even know why we're discussing this. Term insurance only pays when you die. You can't borrow against the policy, so what does it matter if we could get a huge dollar amount?"

"We have Sophia to think of."

"We have so many other bills that we can't pay, honey. We don't need another one."

Tom pinched his chin, creating another wrinkle to match his furrowed brow. I told myself that I wasn't the source of his anger. Tom had been the breadwinner; now his stay-at-home wife supported the family—poorly in comparison. He was disappointed, mostly in himself.

I softened my tone. "It will be okay. You'll find another job soon."

"Yeah, well, million-dollar-a-year jobs aren't a dime a dozen—not like admin positions."

I continued moving the mess of General Tso's chicken with my fork. Sauce seeped from the meat to the rice pad below, staining the white rusty orange. I should have ordered pizza. Cheap pizza topped budget Chinese.

His thick hand covered my wrist. "Listen to me. We have to stop pretending we'll just get through this. I am not getting a job before the next house payment is due. We can't live like this on a secretary's salary."

The touch felt like the man I'd married, though Tom no longer quite looked like him. The chandelier overhead cast deep shadows beneath his eyes, accentuating puffiness from stress and lack of sleep. The stubble on his jawline made the bottom half of his face appear fuller, less boyishly handsome. But still attractive. It would take more than a rough year to dull Tom's good looks.

"I know we can't keep the house." The words burned like whiskey. I chased them with a hard swallow. "I spoke to Stacy. She said she'd list it for a discounted fee, three percent."

"We'll never get close to what we paid."

I blinked away more shame. To think I hadn't even worried when the housing market dropped 40 percent. I'd been so confident in Tom's ability to make the payments. The house was our home, not an investment.

"The bank owns the house," Tom went on. "We won't get a dime back."

"So we'll downsize for a while. There are good towns farther from the city with solid schools. I'll just need to commute a little longer."

"And stick me with the kid."

I pictured Sophia gazing at him with those giant brown eyes, waiting for him to acknowledge her with more than a pat on the head, to give her something—anything—to do for him, like an overattentive waitress at a fancy restaurant. No one was ever stuck with Sophia, especially not her daddy.

"Our daughter goes to daycare until nearly four and I'm always home by seven. You could try to enjoy the three hours in between: throw a ball in the yard or read a book to her."

The lines between Tom's eyebrows deepened. Parenthood confounded my husband, though I couldn't blame him for it. His own folks had died when he was barely a preteen, leaving him without any strong memories of what parents did.

"You think I don't want to just enjoy our kid? I can't here. It's such a fucking rat race. No matter how much you make, you always need more: a more expensive house in a higher-ranked school system so your kid can compete or a better car so the neighbors know you belong or nicer clothes to look the part and—"

"None of that matters. We don't have to care what our neighbors think."

"Others determine our fate, babe. We must *always* care what they think."

One of Tom's hands rested beside his wine glass. I stretched my arm across the table. My fingertips grazed his knuckles as though testing a plate of hot food. Since losing his job, Tom could interpret even an encouraging gesture as patronizing.

"We don't need other people," I said. "We have each other. We'll get through this."

Tom's hand fled my touch. I left my palm outstretched on the table, a sign that I was there to support him. He offered a sheepish smile in return, an apology for recoiling. Glance and gesture are the language of the long-term couple.

My husband sighed. "It's just not easy."

His eyes flitted to his empty wine glass and the bottle destined for the recycling bin. He stood and strode around the table to the butler's pantry, where the light from the chandelier didn't quite reach and where we kept the hard alcohol. His half-lit form opened the overhead cabinet and dipped inside. Glass tapped against glass. A new glass meant Scotch.

"We'll just have to find a more middle-class area," I said.

He pulled in his bottom lip as the tumbler returned to chest level, licking the last drop of liquor. "No. We should leave the U.S."

"We can't just up and move to another country. We don't have work visas or speak other languages. Where are you even thinking?"

"Someplace in South America. Maybe by your folks, where the money will stretch further."

"You want to raise our daughter near favelas? Do you know how violent—"

"Don't be stupid. I want to raise her someplace where we are the wealthy people. Where we can give her everything without killing ourselves." His finger flew to his chest like a soap opera protagonist making a point. "Without *me* killing *myself.*"

He'd called me stupid. My tongue pressed against my teeth. I couldn't let our argument, or whatever this was, devolve into a schoolyard shouting match.

"I don't even know if we can get jobs there."

Tom scoffed. The sound erupted as a half giggle, half gasp. "I don't want to get a job there. I want to retire. You should see the mansions you can buy on the southern coast for just over a million."

Was this the alcohol talking, or had the year of unemployment pushed my husband over the edge? Retire? At thirty-four?

"Tom, what are you talking about? Our savings are near gone."

The conversation had become ridiculous. We'd have to eat humble pie for a time. My husband would have to swallow it. I collected the empty wine bottle and my full plate. Might as well scrape it into the garbage.

Tom grabbed my arm as I headed into the kitchen. Too rough. The wine bottle and my plate toppled to the floor. Orange sauce splattered on the hardwood and across the cabinet. A spot landed on the edge of his white shirt. How the heck would I get that out of linen?

"Damn it, Tom."

A chicken chunk rested atop his bare big toe. His nose wrinkled as he shook it off. "We're not done talking."

"Well, I was done eating."

He relinquished my arm. I grabbed the paper towel roll beside the farmhouse sink. Hands wrapped around my waist. Liquor-scented breath whispered by my ear. "I'm sorry about the plate. I didn't mean—"

"I need to clean all that food before it stains the floor." I yanked several sheets of two-ply off the roll.

Tom rested his chin on my shoulder. "I'm just trying to talk to you."

I wanted nothing more than to wipe up the food, take the trash out to the garage, and call it a night. The clock above the microwave flashed 9:58. I needed to leave in eight and a half hours to get to work before the head trader came in. But I could hear the need in my husband's voice.

I faced him. My long bangs fell into my eyes as I turned. "I'm listening."

For the first time all night, the lines between Tom's brows faded. "All the pressure in that job, trying to make enough to give you and Sophia everything and support your parents—it was too much. I can't work like that anymore."

I reached up to scratch the back of his head, the way I did with our daughter when she needed comfort. Oily strands slipped through my fingers. Tom's Ivy League haircut, always neat in the back, had devolved into an unwashed grunge style. "You don't need to. It will be okay. I'm working again and—"

"You can't make enough. Just look around." His arms opened wide to indicate our massive kitchen. Calacatta countertops. Gleaming white cupboards with matching paneled fridge and dishwasher. Stainless steel range. Built-in espresso maker and microwave. An island topped with a marble slab big enough to require a special cut at the Italian quarry.

Crying over things is a waste of tears. Still, my eyes welled. I stood in my dream kitchen, in our dream house. We'd been spoiled. I could never provide this. Short of winning the lottery,

I would never be able to afford to live in a decent public school district, let alone the best school district in the state. I would never be able to pay for all the extras we'd planned on giving our child: ballet lessons, art classes, tutoring. I wouldn't be able to send much money, if any, to my parents. And with both of us working—eventually Tom would have to do something—we wouldn't even be around to give Sophia the parental attention that we'd both agreed kids needed.

I gazed at the ceiling's embedded lights, little on-demand suns in a Venetian plaster sky. I'd agonized over the paint finish. My first-world problems. What I wouldn't give to have them back.

"How can I help any more than I am?" The question slipped out along with my tears. "I work ten hours a day, twelve with the commute. I'm pretty much the only one taking care of Sophia, not to mention the cleaning and the cooking." I choked out a sob. "I'm sorry that I can't go from being a stay-at-home mom to making millions overnight. But I am trying."

Tom watched me cry as though I were a wounded animal and not his wife. Anger overwhelmed my sadness. How could he just stand there? Helpless. I threw up my hands. "What more can I do?" I shouted. "Really, Tom, what else do you need me to do?"

He grasped my forearms. "It's not you. Okay? I know you're doing everything you can. I'm trying to talk to you about what I can do."

He cupped my cheek with his palm. The gesture warmed like a good memory. I wanted to lose myself in it, spend time in *before*, when we were happy.

My eyes closed a moment longer than a blink. When they reopened, Tom was staring at me, jaw set tight.

"I want to take out a life insurance policy," he said. "Then I want to fake my death."

3

The traffic light switched from green to yellow. Ryan slid his foot off the gas and let the Dodge slow to a roll. He could have gunned the six-cylinder engine and, in all likelihood, made it through the intersection before the light turned red, but he didn't take idle risks. Twenty-five percent of accidents resulted from running a red. Another 23 percent were blamed on weather conditions like the tire-stamped slush on the road.

Goons gambled with their safety. And though many of the investigators that Ryan had met were little better than goombahs with gun permits, he wasn't one of those. Ryan was a numbers man. Part detective, part mathematician. He prided himself on his ability to make informed decisions, to calculate the odds of potential outcomes, drawing from the encyclopedia of stats that he recalled with such ease. He figured he had a touch of Asperger's syndrome, though he'd never been tested. He *did* have the symptoms: fixated interests (statistics), an inability to read body language (a problem he'd solved with countless hours researching and analyzing behavior), and relatively low empathy (very much an issue, if you asked his ex-wife).

The light flipped red. Ryan scanned the sights of downtown suburbia as the car idled. A sprawling two-story school building extended from the side of a modest church. A café sign hung above a converted train station beside snow-packed tracks. Not much to see—just as with his case.

Tom hadn't given him anything to indicate that Ana had been depressed, and probably wouldn't if he could help it. Ryan needed to find someone without a financial interest in Mrs. Bacon's psychological condition.

Ana's parents in Brazil might know if she'd been suicidal. But they also had too great a stake in the insurance benefit to come clean about it. Though Sophia was Ana's primary beneficiary, Anna had set aside a small portion of the death benefit for her parents' care. Moreover, Ana had made her folks Sophia's secondary guardians. If anything happened to Tom, then Ana's parents would gain control of the ten million and Sophia. Still, Ryan would have to talk to them, if only to check a box on his report.

A horn interrupted his thoughts. The light had changed. In his rearview, a woman gesticulated as she yelled. Ryan pressed his foot on the gas, a touch too hard. The Dodge lurched into the intersection and then skidded several feet on the icy ground. Distracted drivers caused more than 40 percent of accidents. He flipped on his right blinker and turned into town.

Gray snow, piled a foot high by plows, pressed against the curb separating the tracks from free street parking. He stepped out of his car and into an unavoidable inch of salty slush. Boots already wet, he took the direct route to the café's side door, clambering over the snow median and limping through the accumulation on the abandoned railway.

A bell jangled when he entered the coffee shop. Two women were eyeing a row of pastel macaroons behind a display case. Ryan asked if they were in line. His question wrested the slightly taller woman's attention from the sweets. Although she wore what appeared to be gym clothes, thick navy eyeliner encircled her dark-blue eyes. Her forehead was near reflective, a sign of too much Botox. She mumbled something affirmative and pulled her companion a few steps closer to the register.

When it was his turn to order, he requested coffee, skim milk, no sugar, the way Leslie had gotten him to order it after years of nagging. He pushed the thought of his ex-wife out of his head and looked for a spot to sit. The women ahead of him had taken their drinks to one of two bistro tables pressed against a picture window. As good a thinking spot as any.

He paid and brought his drink to the empty table. Silver light struggled through a chalky film covering the glass. It would snow later. He'd need to get back on the road before it started.

Ryan plopped down on the stool and then pulled his cell from his pants pocket. He opened his e-mail and started a new message. His own address went in the *to* field. The subject: Ana Bacon.

Suicide wouldn't be easy to prove. It was rare for women to take their own lives. Only about five in one hundred thousand American females killed themselves each year, and most of those were either terminally ill or recently divorced. Still, suicide was more likely than the alternative. Of all the unfortunate ways to die, falling off a cruise ship was one of the unluckiest. The odds? Exactly 1 in 2.31 million. A person was twice as apt to be struck by lightning. Plus, nearly all "accidental" falls were due to intoxication. As a pregnant mother, Ana hadn't been drinking, at least not according to her husband.

Tom had blamed illness for Ana's death. He'd told news crews that his wife had suffered from a bad combination of morning and motion sicknesses. On the day that she died, he'd left her sleeping in a lounge chair on their balcony to go to the pool (where he'd been seen by multiple people). She'd been exhausted from vomiting on and off all afternoon, leading Tom to believe that Ana must have gotten sick over the side of the boat and lost her balance. Fellow vacationers had supported his story, claiming that Ana had been ill during dinner. Tom's alibi and the anecdotal comments from cruise-goers had been all the BMA had needed to claim "no evidence of foul play."

Ryan sipped from his coffee cup. He tapped the sides of the cardboard, pounding out the pins and needles from his thawing fingers as he tried to imagine the scenario Tom had envisioned. He pictured the attractive woman in the news photos leaning over the railing, her thin frame, made thinner by the inability to keep down food, extending too far over the side of the boat in a vain attempt to avoid splattering the boards beneath her with sick and then, somehow, tumbling over the forty-two-inch railing.

Ryan pressed his eyes shut. It just didn't make sense, and it would never fly with his bosses. His job was to get ISI out of paying ten million dollars, not explain how a five-foot-seven woman could, from the force of vomiting alone, propel herself up and over a large wooden bar set just below her sternum.

He typed "suicide" into his notes. To prove it, he'd need to know more about the Bacons' finances and marriage—especially their marriage. Men took their lives because of money problems. Women did so because of relationship issues. If he could prove both existed in the Bacon household, even better.

Where to start? Investigating rule of thumb: people grumbled about work at home and about home at work. He would speak with Ana's old coworkers at Derivative Capital. If the Bacons' relationship had been on the rocks, Ana was more likely to have complained to an office pal than to a neighbor.

Ryan took a long sip of coffee and stared outside the salt-splattered window. The street was as empty as a Hopper painting, though there were surely people in the shops. Ryan noted nail salons, hair salons, Pilates studios—establishments catering to well-to-do women. A less affluent suburb might have fast food restaurants, but here, if both parents worked, they probably employed a housekeeper or a cook.

Tom Bacon didn't appear to have help. But he didn't come across as a stay-at-home-dad type. The guy didn't even know how to get his kid a snack.

Ryan typed himself an instruction to track down any current or former workers in the Bacon home. Nannies. Housecleaners. Service people are great sources. Stay-at-home moms confide in their staff, as they are typically the only other adults around during the day. Women who work in others' homes are also experts at blending into the background when needed, enabling them to witness arguments.

Tom wouldn't just volunteer the name of any mommy's helper, not if she'd seen anything relevant. Ryan had his work cut out for him. He looked up at the women beside him, now chatting between sips. "Excuse me, misses."

Botox Queen liked his choice of prefix. She smiled at him, blank face prepared for a compliment.

"I recently came to the area. Are there any cleaning services that either of you could recommend?"

The edges of her plastic smile pulled in without crinkling the skin. "Did you buy in town?"

He ignored the question. "If we wanted someone to clean a large home . . ."

"Sorry. My nanny cleans while the kids are in school."

The friend sat up straighter. "We're thinking of getting a service to come in once a month." She turned to her gym buddy. "I think Madeleine straightens up more than really scrubs, you know? And the kids are always tracking in the salt from outside. It's ruining the floors."

"Which service are you thinking of?" Ryan asked.

"Robomaids. Everyone in town uses them. They come to your house like an army with mops and brooms. Done in a few hours, then on to the next house. And they're like the mailman," the woman giggled. "Neither rain nor sleet nor nor'easter."

"Well, the problem with having an army is you don't know who is really in your house." Ryan imagined that Botox Queen would have frowned at her friend's suggestion, if her muscles hadn't been paralyzed. "A lot of these services are staffed with illegals, so if they steal something, they can just disappear."

The other woman waved off her criticism. "They have so many clients. I can't imagine they have a problem with things going missing. Reputation is everything."

Ryan smiled broadly and thanked them before rising from the table. He took his coffee with him. Now that he'd opened the lines of communication, the women might want to chat. He'd enjoy the drink more in the car. Besides, he had work to do.

4

August 11

The lap pool beckoned at the edge of the property, a sapphire sparkling in the darkening sky, set in a square of tarnished grass. Blades crunched beneath my bare feet as I crossed the lawn to my oasis. My escape from my husband.

I couldn't argue with him anymore. The alcohol had been talking, not Tom. I'd said as much when he'd tried to outline his ludicrous plan to collect on an insurance policy that we didn't even have. *You're insane right now. Go sleep it off.* My swimming would give him time to stew and then simmer down. Once sober, he'd realize how silly he'd been. He'd apologize.

My black racing suit hugged my curves as I strode to the pool. Too often, clothing hung from my narrow frame, bypassing the inset of my waist to make me appear as rectangular as a Lego figurine. But the Speedo accentuated my hips. I wondered whether Tom was watching me from the kitchen window. Would he find me sexy? Did sex even cross his mind anymore, or was he too despondent from his job loss?

Prickly grass gave way to smooth stone. I dipped my toes into the water. It was cool, not cold. Still, shivers ran down my back as I lowered myself into the pool. I submerged my face, an ostrich burying its head in the sand. I screamed.

Yelling is silent underwater. I could wail until my face turned blue and all anyone would see was a tiny disturbance on the surface when, beneath, a furious sea fizzed around my eyes and nose. How could Tom just fall apart like this? I understood that for type-A men, losing a job was akin to the death of a loved one. I'd expected the anger and despair, even the drinking. But irrational fantasies?

Lack of air squeezed my temples. I tossed back my head and gasped. I felt sick. Screaming wasn't good enough. I needed to swim.

I grabbed the silicone cap that I always left to dry at the edge of the pool and tucked my hair inside. I pulled the goggles from my scalp onto the bridge of my nose. Ready, I scrunched like a spring against the cement wall. My thighs shot forward. My right arm extended straight, fingers flat. I pulled my hand in. Pounds of water pushed behind me.

I owed Tom for this release. If not for fear of losing my fiancé to baby bulge, I would never have dragged myself to the YMCA in the first place. I wouldn't have started swim classes and learned to shed tension in the water.

The lane line beneath me turned into a T. The wall loomed within a stroke's length. I folded at the waist. My legs flipped over my head. My feet hit tile. I propelled forward, kicking the water into froth. Swimming, rather than sniping, drained my anger. Tom needed an outlet other than drinking.

Without warning, my right leg seized. Lights exploded in my vision as my calf contracted with labor-like pain. I thrashed in the water, trying to rub out the cramp while floating. Too much lactic acid. Not enough water. Tom's fault. Had he not gotten me so upset, I wouldn't have wasted precious hydration on tears.

I drilled my thumbs into the spastic muscle. After an excruciating minute, the pain subsided. Aftershocks ran through the leg. I pulled myself up onto land and extended the injured limb above the water.

A minute later, I limped to the gate. Tom leaned on the other side of the iron finials. A frown, highlighted by the lights beneath the shimmering water, drew down his face. "You okay?"

"Yeah. Charley horse. How long have you been there?"

Tom shrugged. "I brought you a towel." He tossed the white, fluffy fabric over the fence. It waved like a flag of surrender in the air.

I caught it. "Thanks. I forgot to bring one down."

"Are you coming to bed?"

"Right after I rinse off."

The night air no longer felt warm as I rubbed the towel over my extremities. I pulled off my cap and shook out my hair, trying to look like a swimsuit model, trying to make my husband want me.

Tom's eyes glazed. He watched something in his mind, a scene from the past or hope for the future.

"Are you okay?" I asked.

"You're not going to tell anyone about what we discussed?"

Our ridiculous dinner conversation hardly qualified as a discussion. "No. Of course not."

"Good." Tom turned toward the house. "You coming?"

"I'll follow you up right after I shower."

"I'm tired. I'm going to bed."

"I love you."

My words trailed him as he marched back to the house, stamping a path into the brittle remains of our once lush lawn. He didn't seem to hear me. He didn't look back.

5

November 17

The phone rang in Ryan's ear, a mechanical tone that had twice before ended with a machine. The woman sitting perpendicular from him at a broad mahogany desk cast a scolding glance over her shoulder. She clearly didn't think it appropriate for visitors to Derivative Capital to chat on their cells while waiting for her boss.

There was little cause for concern. He knew Robomaids wouldn't answer his calls. If they'd intended to discuss a former client with an investigator, they would have returned his voicemails by now. He regretted not pretending to need a quote when he'd first phoned. Now he'd need to harass their answering machine until they called to make him stop.

A familiar Spanish accent picked up. "You have reached Robomaids. Out with the stains, in with the sparkle." The woman spoke the line as though she read off a card, with difficulty. "Please leave a message with your home's square footage, number of beds and baths, days you require the cleaning, address, and a contact number and we will call you back with an estimate."

For the third time, he explained that he investigated Ana Bacon's disappearance and needed to know if she'd been a client. The secretary stared at him the whole time he spoke. When he hung up, she finally relaxed into her chair, leaning back and angling her torso so that the boss behind the glass wall had a prime view of her improbable breasts.

The plaque on the woman's desk read administrative assistant, but her outfit advertised an altogether different profession. Cleavage popped from the plunging neckline of her white button-down, which couldn't have closed if she'd tried. Her black skirt barely covered her upper thighs when seated.

The outfit embarrassed him. He averted his gaze and fidgeted with the lock on the briefcase in his lap, feeling as though he was about to interview for a job above his pay grade. At times like this, he missed his NYPD badge—the way it forced people to stand up straighter, show respect, and above all, share information. Without it, he was just an employee of a private company, begging the favor of a conversation.

Ana's old boss, Michael Smith, had agreed to a meeting, providing that Ryan "kept it brief." No one would have dared say that to him when he'd been in the Financial Crimes Unit.

"Mr. Smith will see you now."

Ryan turned to see the blurry image of a man waving behind a frosted glass door. Michael stood from his desk as Ryan entered. He wore a smug smile that advertised his wealth as easily as his custom suit and the thick, silver hair that fell low on his forehead.

The banker leaned across his desk to dole out a salesman's shake, which Ryan returned with some awkwardness. Michael remained standing after his hand dropped to his waist, as though this last-minute meeting was keeping him from heading out the door. He cleared his throat. "So I understand that you have some questions about Ana Bacon."

"I do." Ryan pulled out a chair in front of the desk and settled in. He set his briefcase on the floor and removed a notepad. Michael's eye twitched as he brought out the pen, a whistleblower spooked by a recording device. Ryan waved the pad. "Helps me remember."

Michael's mouth drew into a line. He glanced at a wall clock and then resumed his seat in a wide captain's chair. "I've got a meeting soon."

"I understand." He did. He just didn't care. "When did Ms. Bacon start working here?"

Michael's eyes rolled toward his forehead, as though struggling to remember something years, not months, before. "I guess it was the beginning of February. She came in for an interview in late January and I hired her soon after."

"She was your secretary?"

"My administrative assistant." Michael gestured toward the glass wall and the woman sitting just outside it. "I need someone to keep my schedule, answer the phone, get coffee, that sort of thing."

The mention of coffee alerted Ryan to the stale scent of java lingering in the air. It mixed with a musky cologne that Ryan could only assume wafted from Michael.

"Was she good at it?" he asked.

Michael's self-satisfied smirk twisted at the edge, turning sheepish. "I hate to speak ill of the dead."

"So she wasn't good at it?"

"Well, you know . . ." He shrugged. "What can I say? Clients liked her."

Ryan bet they had. Judging from the photos on the news, Ana Bacon was a good-looking woman with large, downturned eyes, a tawny complexion, and a straight, narrow nose. Nice figure. Pretty smile. The kind of woman most men enjoyed having around.

"But you didn't like her?"

Michael rubbed the back of his neck. A tell, for most people. Smith was probably about to lie, maybe to avoid trashing a former employee. "I wouldn't say I disliked her. She was nice. *Very* friendly." Had he winked, the suggestion that Ana's behavior had bordered on inappropriate could not have been clearer.

"Flirty?"

Michael tilted his head as if to rhetorically ask, *Aren't they all?* A thick, platinum band glinted below the knuckle on his left ring finger. By age forty, about four-fifths of Americans had married. Roughly two-fifths of those got divorced. Ryan had never wanted to join the latter statistic.

"Was Ana's *friendliness* an issue for you?"

Michael shook his head. "No. No. I didn't care. Again, she was fine. Competent, for the most part." He leaned forward. "Truth is, her husband was the real problem. He wasn't working, but he couldn't even remember to pick up the darn kid from daycare. She'd end up running out all the time to get her daughter."

Ryan wrote *family emergencies* in his notepad. Below it, he scrawled, *Tom = Depressed?* "Do you have the name of the daycare?"

"Not sure. I think once I heard Apple something-or-other."

"I guess the Bacons didn't have a backup sitter?"

"I don't see how they could have afforded one. We paid Ana well, of course, but she was just an admin, and she'd been out of work for a few years prior, so it wasn't like she commanded top dollar. Her husband didn't contribute anything." Michael said the last comment with disdain, as if the worst thing a man could do was not make money.

"She told you that?"

Again, Michael scratched behind his neck. Ryan wondered what made the man more uncomfortable: the presence of an investigator or disparaging a dead woman.

"Well, she didn't exactly talk to me about it, but I'm guessing she wouldn't have returned to work if her husband had a bunch saved." Michael leaned back and lowered his head, speaking down his nose. "Between us, the guy didn't manage risk right. Trade blew up on him. Cost his bank a hundred mil."

A smile cracked Michael's mouth. Ryan got the sense that the details of Tom Bacon's departure were an open secret on Wall Street, one that traders enjoyed sharing. Given that Tom's wife had just died, Michael's undisguised schadenfreude said something. But was it simply evidence of a competitive personality? Or did it have something to do with Ana?

"I take it that he would have had trouble securing other employment?"

"Losing that kind of cash on a single name would put anyone on the blacklist."

Ryan wrote down *unemployable* beneath the Tom equation. Providing that Michael wasn't exaggerating, he'd just handed Ryan powerful reasons for Ana to be depressed.

"Did Ana quit or did you fire her?"

"I guess I put her on notice." Michael shrugged in a what-you-gonna-do way. "I told her that she couldn't keep taking off. She probably left to avoid needing to explain anything on her record. When she quit, I gave her a sizable severance because I knew that she was going through a difficult time. Came out of my pocket, since I didn't actually fire her."

The boss emphasized the point with a poke at his breast pocket. Ryan thought of a silverback gorilla beating his chest, announcing to everyone in the vicinity *I am the Alpha.*

"And she used that pay to go on vacation . . ."

Michael's lips pursed. The expression was the kind cocky men made when hearing about the misfortunes of others. He stood and extended his hand. "Sorry to cut this short—"

"When did she leave?"

His host's face grew flustered. Ryan guessed he was used to people taking polite brush-offs. "I wouldn't remember. You'd have to check with HR when she picked up her last check."

"Whom should I talk to there?"

"Fernanda can help you." Michael crossed the room and opened the door. "I hope I've been helpful. I've got to prep for an important call."

Ryan pushed himself up from the chair. Michael had given him something. Now he had calls to make too.

6

August 12

Sophia's new daycare lay in the basement of a brick building, directly off the highway. Colors derived from sweets coated the inside walls: cotton candy pink, sour apple green, grape jelly purple, lollipop red. Such artificial brightness had to be jarring for a kid accustomed to the average wood and white Montessori school.

It was not yet seven AM. A few aides sat in a circle, strategizing a game plan for the day. Two kids lay in sleeping bags. Most working parents wouldn't drop their children off for another half hour.

Guilt tugged at my heart more strongly than Sophia's grip on my arm. During the drive, she'd become resigned to spending another day away from home. I'd said that Daddy was busy looking for a new job, though I knew he'd spend most of the day in the man cave, online, with a Scotch in hand. Sophia hadn't fully bought my lie.

She led me into the room. One of the aides, a Jamaican woman named Earlene, acknowledged her with a warm smile. The others kept talking among themselves.

"Mommy, stay with me." Her voice sounded low and scratchy, like a toy running out of batteries. A cold had moved into her throat.

I bent to her level and held her hands. "I wish that I could, sweetheart, but I need to work. You'll play with your friends. Daddy will get you before you know it."

She pulled away and drifted to a row of child-height shelves, where she selected a book before slumping against the bubblegum-colored wall. To Sophia, a book without an accompanying adult was just a series of illustrations.

"Excuse me." The head aide, a heavyset woman named Donna with dyed red hair and a thick South Jersey accent, acknowledged my words with a sideways glance. "I know you have a policy about kids not bringing items from home. But since my daughter comes so early, would it be possible for me to leave her with coloring books? She can put them away when the other kids come."

The woman gestured to the two sleeping toddlers. "Most of the children who come at this time take a nap. We'll start in a bit."

"I know. But my daughter is here now. If she had a coloring book—"

Donna shook her head slowly, as though scolding a young child. "Individual items create fights. It's better that they all have communal toys. It's good for kids to learn to share. Dontcha think?"

I didn't have time to argue. Dr. Seuss's *The Cat in the Hat* lay in Sophia's lap. At least she knew the story. "Sweetheart, Daddy will pick you up this afternoon. You just play and—"

"He was forty minutes late last time," Donna said. "I didn't charge ya, but I can't keep doing that. He said the car broke down." The woman's eyebrows rose, inviting me to join in her disbelief. Two-year-old Maseratis didn't just quit.

"I'm sorry. I'll make sure he's here today at four." I looked away from the annoyed aide to Sophia. I blew her a kiss. "I love you."

My little girl stretched to catch the phantom smooch. She pressed it to her mouth and then tossed back a pucker with a loud smack. I heard it as I hurried out the door.

*

I slipped into my chair at 7:40. Better than 8 AM, when the entire trading desk arrived, but not early enough to beat my boss. I could see Michael's blurry form through the glass wall behind me. He sat at his desk, head tilted to his shoulder. On the phone. He'd answered his own call. Shit.

I logged into his calendar and printed two copies of the day's itinerary: one for him, one for me. I grabbed a yellow highlighter and a light-blue marker from a coffee cup with Sophia's photo printed on the side. Time to categorize the day's meetings: yellow for client facing, blue for internal. Representatives from the Sovereign Wealth Fund of Dubai would arrive at noon. That was an important meeting, potentially worth billions to the hedge fund. I colored it in yellow then underlined it. I made a mental note to remind Michael once he hung up.

I glanced over my shoulder into his office. The desk held papers, but no coffee cup. He was still on the phone. Time to start the morning routine.

Though the office had a fancy coffee maker in the kitchen, Michael didn't like the "motor oil" that came from it. A Starbucks sat across the street from our building. Throngs of commuters made it almost impossible to get a timely coffee—unless one happened to tip the male barista a twenty for his cell number. I dialed Jason on my work line and placed the order that I knew would be waiting for me by the time I got across the street.

The phone still hung off Michael's ear when I approached his door with his coffee, minutes later. He waved me through the frosted glass. I slid my cup onto my desk and grabbed the schedules before entering.

"All right, then. Sounds good. My next appointment is here." His wife, Jessica. I could tell by his tone of voice. Soft and a touch condescending. He spoke to his spouse like a trainer whispering to a wild horse. They'd been married twenty years. I wondered if he'd always spoken to her that way.

Michael smiled at me, a pained, closed-mouth expression that deepened the lines around his mouth and invited me to express similar frustration with the person refusing to free him from the phone. I didn't join in. I'd been the woman on the other end of those calls for far too long.

"You're right," he said. "Send it back. All right. That sounds good. I have to . . ."

He motioned for me to sit. I placed his drink and schedule on the desk and then sat on the fabric chair positioned to face him, my legs crossed. Michael's eye flitted to my exposed knee and the flash of thigh peeking from my navy pencil skirt. I dropped my leg and pressed my feet together, the more ladylike position.

"I know. Send it back then. I have to go. You, too. I have to go. Okay. Bye."

The receiver hit the cradle a little too forcefully. Michael flashed bright, bleached teeth. "Coffee stains don't close deals," he'd said once, "but I can't give up my addictions."

I returned this smile. As bosses went, Michael rated highly. He'd always been pleasant, never shouting for his dry cleaning or lunch, never treating me more like a talking golden retriever than an assistant. Sure, he wanted me at his beck and call for ten hours and available by phone 24-7. But that was the job.

He claimed his coffee. "One day you'll tell me your trick for skipping the line."

"If I revealed all the trade secrets, you might not need an admin."

"You kidding me? I don't know how I ever got on without you." Michael walked around his desk and sat on the edge of it, across from my seat. Navy oxfords landed on either side of my crossed ankles.

"So what do we have today?" He held the schedule but didn't look at it. Michael never took his eyes off me during our meetings. Maintaining eye contact during conversation must have been one of those business school rules.

"Dubai is the main event," I said. "That's at noon."

"What do I need to know?"

I mentally reviewed my brief call with the United Arab Emirates Business Council. "Greet the oldest person in the party first, not the most senior executive. It's considered a sign of respect in Muslim countries. Also, people address each other by their first name with a title. You'll be Mr. Michael. The men you are meeting with will be Mr. Asadel and Mr. Fawwaz. There may be others. I understand that it is not uncommon for unexpected guests to join in. Rick said six people showed up at the last marketing meeting."

"Okay. Got it."

"Shake with the right hand, but I'm sure you knew that one. And let them withdraw their hand first. Oh, and don't ask about the female members of the family."

Michael chuckled. His high cheekbones became more prominent when he laughed. "Don't inquire about the ball and chain. Got it."

"If you want to get personal, ask about their health or their family generally. You can inquire about children and what they're studying. Rick said Mr. Fawwaz has a son attending college at your alma mater."

"Ah, Big Green. I can talk about that."

"Gifts are a common way to break the ice. I know you liked *Blue Ocean Strategy*. I bought a few copies and wrapped them. You can use it to discuss investing in companies with strategic monopolies. That should provide a nice segue into the fund's performance."

Michael's eyebrows arched and he nodded slowly. I'd impressed him. My husband could dismiss administrative assistants as a dime a dozen, but the job couldn't be done right by just anyone capable of picking up a phone and using an online calendar. It required planning, foresight, an ability to anticipate problems before they arose, and plenty of research. I excelled at it. When in work mode, I made sure to be prepared with whatever information my executive might need to complete a task and a plan B, should the task prove insurmountable. I only failed to plan for worst-case scenarios in my personal life.

Michael tapped the schedule in his hand against the side of the desk. "You know, you should come to some of these meetings. Not the Dubai folks, of course. They prefer dealing with men. How about one of the pension funds?"

I struggled to contain my grin. Five months in and I could move up from getting coffee to helping sell the business? What did Tom know? Maybe I could climb the ladder from administrative assistant to marketing or operations. I had a college degree in business management. It could happen.

"That sounds great," I said.

"What's on the docket this week?"

"This week is all sovereign wealth funds. Next Tuesday, you have the Illinois police and fire retirement system."

"What time?"

"Lunch."

"Move it to dinner. We'll take them out and really sell them on our returns." Michael twisted the schedule between his hands until it resembled a rolled up newspaper. He rapped my knee with it as he rose from the desk. "Great work. Let's make it happen."

*

Michael was out of the office for most of the day. I spent the morning moving around the pension fund meeting and preparing background folders on potential clients. He returned just after four o'clock, a satisfied smile spread across his face. Either he'd secured investors or he'd had one too many during his extended lunch.

He swaggered into the office. My cell rang as his hand hit his door. I reached for my phone.

"Ana." Michael waved me inside.

I hit the ignore button without seeing the number and followed him to his desk. "How did it go?"

"A gentleman never tells."

Coy would be the last word anyone would use to describe Michael Smith. It was obvious that he wanted me to beg him a bit. I feigned disappointment. "Come on. Just a few off-the-record details?"

He grinned like he'd caged a canary behind his teeth. "Mr. Faw-waz and I became great friends. He loved the book that—"

My cell's sharp ring cut him off. I glanced through the glass walls. Whoever called really wanted to reach me. I thought of Tom and his drinking. What if something bad had happened? He would never pick Sophia up drunk, would he?

"I'm sorry, may I just see who that is?"

Michael frowned. "Of course."

I hurried to my desk. If the number belonged to my parents, I'd shut off the cell and remind them later not to call during business hours. If I didn't recognize it . . .

A New Jersey area code flashed on the screen. I answered.

"Mrs. Bacon." Donna's nasal voice fizzed through the receiver. "Is your husband picking up Sophia?"

I glanced at the time on my computer. 4:20. He was twenty minutes late. "Yes, he should be. I'm sure he's just running a bit behind."

"We tried calling the number listed for him and your home number. He's not answering either."

Damn Tom. He probably knew that he was running late and didn't want to hear the daycare staff complain. "Okay. I'll call him."

"We have to charge you this time. It's thirty per hour when you don't pay for the extended day beforehand."

The fee was more than double the usual hourly rate. "That much?"

"Well, we have to get one of the aides to stay late because we can't have more than seven kids per adult and it's not part of her usual schedule. So you're paying for someone to stay, just for you. Plus there's a penalty attached, since she has to rearrange her day."

A few hours of extra care would undo my entire workday. I cursed Tom. "I'm sorry. Just let me call my husband."

"We already have to bill this hour, even if he shows."

"I understand. I'll call you right back."

I dialed Tom's cell, hoping to hear the barreling wind that always made conversation unintelligible in the convertible. The call went straight to voicemail. He'd either shut off his phone or let the battery die.

"Everything all right?" Michael shouted from his office. He sat on his desk, waiting for me. I offered an apologetic smile and put up a finger. I dialed home.

The line rang until the voicemail answered. I dialed two more times, praying that Tom had just fallen asleep and would hear the ringer. He'd overslept before, but I'd been able to wake him each time by the second call. If he went straight to the car, he could pick up Sophia before the daycare billed another hour.

After the fourth voicemail answer, I gave up and returned to Michael's office. Tom had probably headed to Sophia's school without his cell, but I couldn't risk another few hours of late charges. We needed my entire check just to keep up with the groceries and minimum credit card payments.

"Michael." I took a deep breath to keep my frustration with my husband from bubbling over into my voice. "I am very sorry to do this, but may I take off early? My husband hasn't picked up our daughter from daycare, and I'm concerned that something may have happened."

He grimaced. "An accident?"

More like a liquor-induced coma. "I hope not. Unfortunately, the daycare can't keep her much later."

Michael inhaled through clenched teeth. "You gotta do what you gotta do."

"Thanks so much. I rescheduled that meeting with the fireman and police pension fund. Research packets are ready to be printed for the rest of the week's meetings. I really appreciate it. I promise it won't happen again."

Michael waved me off. "Don't worry about it. We'll talk tomorrow. I just hope everyone's okay."

I grabbed my purse from my desk and sprinted out the door. I could call Donna on the way. Maybe, with some pleading, she wouldn't dock me for the hour it took to cross the bridge.

7

November 20

Ryan had wasted a whole business day working the phones with little to show for it but a stiff thigh, aggravated from spending so long stuck to a desk chair. The contact number listed on Ana's policy for her parents was out of service. Cold-calling half a dozen New Jersey childcare facilities with "Apple" in the title had yet to locate the right daycare. Tom was not responding to messages. And Robomaids still wouldn't return his calls.

The lack of momentum made him antsy. He bounced his good knee, trying to satisfy his urge to move. Before, he would have run at times like this. Not anymore.

Watching his phone not ring was pointless. He abandoned the device on his desk and slid onto the neighboring bed, stretching his injured leg atop the fluffy comforter. Unicorns were pictured in the center. Angie loved *My Little Pony*. He'd bought the cover thinking it would help her feel at home in his new place, but she hadn't flown out to see him since the move—though he'd visited twice.

He ran his hand across the fabric, petting the blue-winged horse with the rainbow mane. The character was Angie's favorite—or, more likely, her former favorite. She would be on to something new by now.

His thigh pulsed with his heartbeat, despite the full extension. Ryan pulled the bad limb to his chest and pushed up his baggy sweatpants until he could inspect the damage. A dark circle, like a cigar burn only blacker, marked an area just above his knee. A long surgery scar trailed beside it, carving a white line down his tibia to another quarter-sized wound where the bullet had exited.

He massaged the raised skin where the doctors had cut and sewn, feeling lonely and more than a bit sorry for himself. He hadn't been the kind of cop that got shot. Most of the time, his work with the financial crimes unit had involved sitting behind a computer, hunting down identity thieves and money launderers by picking out irregularities in real estate records and tax filings. Half the time, he hadn't even worn his gun.

He should have worn it that day. Checking on a PO box that had been receiving a large number of credit cards just hadn't seemed like a risky decision. Sure, the post office had been in Bedford-Stuyvesant, Brooklyn, but shootings in do-or-die Bed-Stuy were down 66 percent from the drug-fueled heyday that rappers flaunted on the radio. Gentrified Brooklyn didn't do drive-bys.

His partner, Vivienne, had wanted to come with him, but he'd had his fill of the women in his life by that point in the day. He and Leslie had argued the night before over some ridiculousness, and when he'd mentioned the fight to Vivienne, she'd said something cryptic about some wives pushing their husbands because they wanted a shove out the door. He'd told Vivienne that he didn't need a partner to hold his hand while he opened a mailbox.

The statistics hadn't saved him that day. He'd been shot in the most unlikely manner possible: by a woman in broad daylight. Only 13 percent of women even had a firearm. But this twenty-eight-year-old girl with angry-looking acne had aimed a 9 mm Beretta at his torso and blown a hole in his leg. In her hyped up state, she'd mistaken him for a boyfriend that knew about her credit card scheme and wanted to steal her money.

He kneaded the scar tissue, trying to soften its hard, ugly presence. He'd been unlucky, but there was no use sulking. He liked that his new job allowed him to set his own hours. And investigating insurance claims was certainly safer than pissing off organized criminals. Most cases involved checking family health records and calling it a day. The Bacon case was different, though, more like his old life—the one with Leslie and Angie.

Ryan glanced at his desktop computer. He should video call his daughter. At seven, Angie still wasn't great at interacting over the phone for longer than a few minutes. But she'd be better if she could see him. He'd be better if he could see her.

He returned to the desk and opened the Skype application on his computer. A short list of contacts appeared below a search window. Leslie's picture smiled next to her name. Angie didn't have her own account. The sight of his ex-wife kept him from clicking. He hadn't forgiven her for ditching him when he needed her most. Maybe he never would.

He let the cursor rest on the search box and typed a name. Luis Santos, Ana's father. Dozens of people returned. Ryan scanned the listed hometowns for anyone in Brazil. There were plenty, though most of the photos belonged to men far too young to have fathered a thirty-one-year-old woman.

He tried the search again with Ana's mother's name, Beatriz. The list was far shorter. Three names were registered to people living in Brazil. Only one photo showed a woman older than thirty. Ryan double-clicked on the face and sent a message explaining that he was investigating Ana Bacon's case. He sweetened the request for a reply by reminding them that they were also policy beneficiaries and Sophia's secondary guardians.

A static photo of an older woman with a light coffee complexion and tired eyes suddenly dominated his screen. He clicked to accept the call.

"Hello?" Though the woman's voice was shaky, she stressed the *H* sound. The emphasis made clear that the language was not her own.

He introduced himself with a truncated version of the message he'd just sent.

"Yes. We've been waiting to speak with you." Mrs. Santos called over her shoulder. "Luis. *Vem cá. O investigador.*"

Sounds of someone shuffling in the background came through the speakers. A metal chair scraped against tile as Mrs. Santos moved her seat to make room for her husband. When Luis came into view, Ryan knew he had the right couple. Ana had her father's straight nose, though his bridge was slightly crooked, perhaps the result of a break at some point in his life. He had a reddish-brown face framed by curly black hair, far more textured than the straight bob that hung beside his wife's fair cheeks. Together, Ryan could see how they'd produced a woman with Ana's dark, wavy hair and caramel coloring.

"I didn't have a good number for you," Ryan said.

Mr. Santos looked sheepish. "The phone is having problems. We are working with the company."

"You can't let Tom have Sophia," Beatriz blurted. She leaned toward the screen. "He killed our daughter. He will hurt Sophia."

Ryan was thrown by the accusation. Did they blame Tom for their daughter's suicide? "He has an alibi," Ryan said. He remembered the redhead's blush as she embarrassed herself on national television, admitting that she'd been flirting with a married man while the female anchor tut-tutted. "Why do you think he is responsible for Ana's death?"

Beatriz and her husband exchanged a determined look. She stared straight at the camera lens, not at her reflection on screen as so many people did during video calls. "He beat her."

Ryan nodded slowly, giving his brain time to run the relevant data: 25 percent of women were hit by a partner at some point in their lives. Depressed men were more likely to become violent than despondent, and losing a job—not to mention a career—was a prime driver of depression in men. Prior physical assaults also helped explain Ana's suicide. More than a quarter of abused women made attempts on their lives.

However, Ryan reminded himself, Ana's parents had ten million reasons to lie. "How did you know Tom was abusive? Did Ana tell you that Tom hit her?"

An exasperated look passed over Beatriz's face. She pointed at the screen. "My daughter and I were very close. I could tell something was wrong, and she had bruises when she'd call."

"On her face?" Ryan's hand curled into a fist. *Say yes. Say yes.* Facial lacerations, swollen lips, sunglasses worn indoors—such things did not go unnoticed in suburban grocery stores and Wall Street offices. He could get people to corroborate or refute Ana's parents' claims.

Beatriz glanced at her husband. Luis kept his eyes trained on his hands like a chastised child. Was he embarrassed that he hadn't been able to help his daughter? Or ashamed that his wife would make a false accusation against their former son-in-law?

"She told me so," Beatriz said. "She had fingerprints on her arms from where he'd grab her. She had bruises on her stomach. He beat her where people wouldn't see." Tears welled in her eyes. "He wanted her dead."

"Do you think Tom drove Ana to kill herself?"

Beatriz pulled her chin into her neck. "No. Ana would never, *never*, have jumped and left Sophia with him. Never." She frowned. "Why do you think that? She would never."

Luis leaned into the screen. He didn't make eye contact, but Ryan knew that was only because he stared directly at Ryan's face on his monitor. "Ana would not have taken her life. That bastard is to blame."

"He killed her," Beatriz repeated, blinking hard with each word. "He did it."

But he couldn't have. Multiple people had seen Tom at the pool when Ana went overboard. Ryan tried to sound casual. "Did you know about the policy before I called?"

Beatriz's eyes narrowed. "Yes. But that doesn't matter."

"Ana left Tom as the primary guardian. She didn't try to make you the guardian, despite the abuse."

Beatriz now looked at him with bare distaste. If she could have reached through the computer screen and slapped him, Ryan bet that she would have.

"What could she do?" Her hands flew out toward the camera. "What was she supposed to do? Tom is Sophia's biological parent and, and . . ." She stuttered, searching for the right words. Ryan watched her fingertips circle the nook in her thin neck. "Ana was frightened of him. He . . . He punched her in the stomach when she was pregnant."

If lying was a disease, this woman had all the symptoms. She was overanimated and lacked control of her facial movements or volume. Unfortunately for Ryan, he couldn't be sure that her behavior wasn't a result of the underlying circumstances. Severe stress—the kind caused by believing your son-in-law had killed your daughter and now had custody of your grandchild—had similar ticks.

"Luis, if Tom hit Ana before they married, why did she go through with it?"

Beatriz answered for her husband. "Ana was pregnant before they married. What choice did she have?"

Luis's Adam's apple bobbed. For a moment, Ryan thought the man might cry. "It's our fault." He sighed. "She felt guilty. All the money that she'd sent to help us out . . . his money."

Beatriz gave her husband a small approving smile before turning her attention back to the camera. "We plan to challenge the . . ." She turned to her husband. "How do you say . . ."

"Custodianship," Luis said. A lawyer's word. They must have already consulted someone. "You will help us?"

Ryan couldn't settle on a response. On one hand, Tom had seemed more aloof than the typical grieving husband. But that didn't change the fact that he hadn't been with his wife when she'd gone overboard. And Ana's parents had millions of reasons to lie. They knew that if Ana committed suicide, no one would get any money, and they clearly blamed Tom for pushing their daughter over the edge.

Something else troubled Ryan as well: Michael. Ana's boss had never mentioned her having bruises or seeming frightened of her husband. He'd been all too willing to portray Tom as a deadbeat. Somehow Ryan doubted that Michael would have kept quiet about spousal abuse if he'd had reason to suspect any.

"What about Ana's boss?"

Luis's brow furrowed. He looked to his wife and said something in Portuguese. Beatriz shook her head, as if to urge him to stop talking. Her husband continued, becoming more animated with each unintelligible word.

"Sorry to interrupt," Ryan said loudly. "Did you know Michael Smith? Did Ana ever talk about him?"

Beatriz patted her husband's leg. He settled back into his seat, visibly annoyed. She sighed. "Our daughter worked very hard for him."

Luis pointed a finger at the screen. "You check on him too. He's a bad man."

"Because he fired Ana?"

Beatriz shot her husband a silencing look. He ignored her. "You investigate. That man shouldn't get away with what he did."

"What did he do?"

"None of that matters," Beatriz snapped. "The point is that Tom cannot be allowed to raise our grandchild. You have to recommend that we get custody. Tom's to blame."

"But what did Michael do?"

Luis opened his mouth. A glance at his wife's withering expression shut it. "We have to go now." Beatriz sucked in her breath. Tears melted her brown eyes. "Please. I beg you. Don't let Tom hurt our granddaughter too."

The screen went dark.

8

Sophia and I entered the house like cartoon burglars, on the pads of our feet, leaning sideways so as not to open the door wide. I'd told her Daddy was sick and we shouldn't wake him. Really, I just didn't want her interacting with her father in whatever state I would find him.

The late-afternoon sun saturated the house's beige walls in blood-orange light. I scooped Sophia into my arms and then scanned for signs of drunken stupidity: broken glass, scattered clothing, blood splatter. The house's open layout left clear sight lines into the dining room, living room, den, and upstairs hallway. Everything remained in order. No signs of a binge. No Tom.

My enraged heart pounded out the buildup in a techno song. I braced for the drop. Where was my husband? Why hadn't he picked her up?

Sophia nuzzled into my neck. There's a cliché that compares kids to sponges. It's right, but for the wrong reason. Kids don't soak up knowledge; they absorb their parents' emotions. Sophia sopped up my anxiety like it was dirty dishwater.

I cooed in her ear. "You go to your room and play for a bit while Mommy checks to see if Daddy needs anything. Then we'll head out for a slice of pizza."

I crept up the spiral staircase, one arm beneath my daughter's bottom, one hand gripping the railing. Cool air hissed through ceiling vents, electronics hummed beneath the chirps of birds in the backyard. No sound of Tom.

The burnt smell of vacuumed carpet greeted me as we entered Sophia's room. I'd cleaned yesterday. Her puffy duvet lay on the bed like a deflated pastry. I placed Sophia on top of it, and her arm tightened around my neck.

"You have to let go, honey." I tried to keep my voice light, masking my fury at her father for somehow forgetting her. "I need to check on Daddy."

I slipped my head from her noose. Sophia's brown eyes reminded me of a cartoon character. Large. Shivering. TV was made for times like this. Unfortunately, we didn't have one in her room. I handed her an unreadable book, just like in daycare. "You take a rest and I'll be right back."

I walked down the hallway, peeking into the two guest bedrooms between Sophia's room and the master suite. The beds in each remained made, ready for hosting our nonexistent friends and family. I didn't need to check the attached bathrooms. Only college kids passed out beside the toilet after binge drinking. Adults found a way to drag themselves into bed.

The double doors to our bedroom stood shut. I turned the knob and stepped inside. Covers lay in a twisted ball in the center of the king mattress. Pillows hid beneath the bed frame. An empty scotch glass waited beside a business book on the nightstand. *The Brass Ring: Negotiating Without Compromise.* A man's book. The female version would have a different title: *The 50% Solution: How to Reach an Amicable Agreement Without Resentment.*

Tom's phone charger lay on top of the book. His phone didn't. Worry started to overwhelm my anger. I'd assumed Tom would be passed out in one of the bedrooms. What if he'd been in a real accident . . . or not an accident? He'd been depressed. He'd discussed faking his death. Could he have done something crazy? Something we couldn't recover from?

I hurried down the back staircase to the empty kitchen, cursing myself for not paying more attention to our conversation the prior night. I again checked the den. No Tom. The pool? Was it possible to intentionally drown in four feet of water?

I flew down our sloped property to my sanctuary. As I ran, I renewed my religion: *Dear God, please don't let anything else have happened. Please. Please. Please.* Birds screamed warnings of my arrival. A cardinal fled its perch atop a cast iron post. I flung open the gate. A tight vinyl cap stretched over the water. I had activated the automatic pool cover last night. He hadn't removed it.

"Tom? Tom, are you home?" Fear sneaked into my voice as I shouted across the yard and then headed down the outdoor steps to the basement entrance, still calling for my spouse. The playroom remained in its recent state of mild disarray. Plastic food littered the floor near a retro-styled minikitchen, the aftermath of a food fight between imaginary friends. Colored construction paper lay in a loose stack beside the easel. A few stuffed animals spilled from wicker toy baskets.

The basement guest room remained as untouched as always. The attached bathroom looked undisturbed. I continued my search into the subgrade portions of the basement where the light from the playroom's sliding glass door didn't reach.

My husband's lair beckoned, a windowless, soundproofed bar and theater room behind a heavy, barn-style door. I entered and flipped the switch, praying for the light to reveal my man passed out on a recliner in front of the projector screen. Pot lights revealed a half-empty, floor-to-ceiling wine fridge and vacant black leather chairs.

Nerves made me twist the gold band on my finger, what was left of my wedding jewelry. I'd hawked the engagement ring to pay the mortgage after Tom had been unemployed for 180 days. If I had known we'd default on the house anyway, I would have saved it to pay off the credit cards.

Had he gone out? Where could he go, though, without any money? And what had he gone out to do?

I ran back out into the yard and around the house to the far garage. Tom kept his car on the left side of the house, away from the used Camry that I now drove, as though he feared depreciation by association. I keyed in the garage code: 0505. Not a birthday or an anniversary. The number didn't mean anything to us, Tom had explained. No robber would guess it.

The door opened with a loud crack. A motor whirred as horizontal sections folded into the garage ceiling. I didn't need to wait for the wall to retract all the way. The cement floor revealed what I needed to know.

He'd taken the Maserati.

9

Ryan hustled across the busy avenue toward the taller of two skyscrapers, trying to cross the street before the walk countdown hit zero. He was headed back to Ana's old office—this time unannounced. He doubted Michael would make time for him again, and he couldn't risk the head of Derivative Capital skirting his calls. Michael had some explaining to do.

Ana's father hated the guy, and Ryan believed he understood why. Michael had fired Ana *because* of the spousal abuse. It fit everything together. Michael had been uncomfortable during their earlier conversation because he'd felt guilty for failing to report the domestic violence and, instead, firing Ana for absenteeism. The job loss would have robbed Ana of whatever power she had held onto in her relationship, making her financially vulnerable and pushing her over the edge emotionally. As a result, Ana's father blamed Michael almost as much as Tom for his daughter's suicide.

Ryan liked the theory. It explained the parents' accusations without calling into question Tom's airtight alibi. Ana's husband had caused her death, but indirectly. And Michael's callous attitude toward the abuse had helped.

He pushed through the revolving glass door and headed to the long security desk flanking the turnstile gates preventing nonemployees from entering. The one snag in his plan was that the security guards didn't *have* to allow him upstairs. His investigator badge didn't convey that kind of authority, at least, not to anyone trained to examine the shiny shape in his wallet.

He sized up the guards, trying to determine whether the older African American woman and middle-aged Hispanic guy sitting behind the desk had the look of former beat cops. The man was too young to have already retired from the force, he decided. The woman could have served, but the warm smile she flashed as he approached lacked the customary suspicion.

He asked for Michael, flashing the "private investigator" badge, purchased off eBay for ten dollars after he'd had to turn in his real one. The glint of metal did the trick. The male guard nodded respectfully and flashed an ID over a sensor to open the gate. The woman picked up her phone. "I'll tell him you're on your way up."

Ryan could hear her announcing him as he walked through the gate. He entered the fourth of six elevators and hit the button for the twenty-eighth floor. When the doors opened, Michael's admin stood directly in front of him, inappropriately dressed as ever in a white button-down tight enough to be a bodysuit. She slipped through the open doors and double tapped the first-floor button.

"Hey, what are you doing?"

"Helping," she hissed.

Ryan snaked around her to the elevator panel, intent on reopening the doors. "I need to talk to Michael."

She stepped in front of him, blocking the buttons. A flowery perfume assailed his nostrils as she drew close. Her shoulder bag bumped into his thigh. "You want to know about Ana, right?"

Tile pressed against Ryan's feet as the elevator began its descent. He tried to read the woman's expression. Her intent look didn't give away what she wanted to tell him, only that he was unlikely to get to Michael until he listened.

"I heard you on the phone last time," she said. "I wanted to talk to you then, but Michael was watching. He's out this week. Bahamas."

Ryan's anger ebbed. Was this a friend of Ana's? "Yes. I'm investigating the case." He deliberately left out why. The woman might not talk to the guy trying to void her pal's life insurance policy. "Did you know her?"

"No." She tilted her head to the side. "But I met her once. And I know what happened from the news. I know she died strangely."

Her word choice heightened Ryan's attention. Most people would have said that they'd heard she'd suffered a terrible accident.

"I thought you should know that she and Michael didn't part on good terms."

"He'd mentioned. He claims he more or less fired her because she left work early often—"

"No." Her face screwed with disgust. "I asked around about her when I first started. You know, see what she'd done wrong so I could avoid getting on Michael's bad side. People didn't have one negative thing to say. But there was something up between her and Michael. She showed up at work, I'm guessing several weeks after she'd already left, and barged into his office. He shut the door when they were talking, so I didn't hear what about, but I could see them through the walls. Michael was angry and she looked really shaken, like she was about to—"

The elevator stopped. As the door opened, the secretary faced front and pressed her lips together, a clear sign that she would not talk where others could overhear. Two suits entered. They chatted to each other as the elevator continued its journey to the lobby.

The secretary waited to resume the conversation until they all had exited the lift and the men were several steps ahead of them. "I talked to HR after she left and they'd had no idea that she'd quit. They'd still been paying her. Our HR head had thought Michael had hired another admin because he'd wanted to transition Ana to a better role or something."

She walked as she talked, high heels clacking on the lobby's marble floor. Ryan struggled to drag his bum leg to the beat of her determined New York stride. "Something was going on between them," she said.

"You think they were having an affair?" Infidelity between coworkers wasn't commonplace, but it wasn't rare. Somewhere between 15 and 41 percent of men cheated, according to studies. About 36 percent of the unfaithful strayed with a coworker.

The secretary strode through the security turnstile. Ryan caught the questioning glance of the guards.

She scanned the crowd exiting into the gray scene outside the building's glass doors and then headed to a corner obscured by a display of orange lilies. "I don't really want to talk here," she whispered as he approached. "And if you tell anyone I said any of this, I'll deny it. This job pays three times what I made for my old accounting firm."

"But their relationship seemed about more than just work?"

"All I know is that Michael was upset and she's his type." She gestured to her half-buttoned shirt. "Busty."

"When I spoke with him, he implied that Mrs. Bacon had been flirtatious," Ryan said. "He seemed uncomfortable with it."

The admin rolled her eyes. "If she was, I'm one hundred percent sure that he reciprocated. Michael's a pig. He told me that part of my job was to make people want to wait for him outside his office. But the clients don't care. It's for him. When I'm not dressed sexy, he says I'm 'lacking initiative.'"

The back of Ryan's neck got hot. If he'd been at his old job, he would have tried to make Smith pay for his sexual harassment. "You don't have to put up with that, you know. You can report him."

She shook her head like a petulant teenager. "No way. He'll just deny it and I'll be out the best paycheck of my life." She again lowered her voice to a whisper. "But I do think that he should be held accountable if he did anything to drive some woman to . . . Well, you know."

"Suicide?"

Her eyes darted around the room as she nodded. "I saw on the news that she was pregnant. He could have knocked her up and then refused to cop to it or something. Divorce would not be cheap for Michael."

Ryan flipped through his mental files. In the United States, more than four hundred thousand paternity tests were taken each year. That meant there were roughly half a million guys who doubted they had fathered their child. Could Ana have feared what Tom would do to her and Sophia if he discovered that he was not the father? Was that why she'd killed herself?

Three men came in through the revolving door. The woman nearly jumped backward. They must have worked in her office. She waited until they had passed through security to resume speaking.

"Anyway," she whispered. "I thought you should know. And I bet if you look into it, Mr. *Initiative* will at least have to stop being such a lech."

The revolving glass door turned again. Ryan sensed the woman was about to hurry through it. He touched her arm. "How can I contact you?"

She dug into her purse and withdrew a business card. "My cell's on this." She slipped the linen stock into his hand and then hurried through the human centrifuge before it stopped rotating. Ryan watched her escape out to the street, knowing he'd never catch her without yelling and drawing unwanted attention. He read the name on the card: *Fernanda Alvarez. Administrative Assistant to Michael Smith.*

He mentally erased his neat little theory. Ana sleeping with her married boss changed everything.

10

August 12

A series of steady beeps drowned out the television. The house security system was warning me about an open door. I shut off the reality-show repeat that I'd half-watched while waiting up for Tom and then stared at the keypad blinking beside my bedroom door. A code, known only to Tom and me, needed to be entered within fifteen seconds. The correct numbers would disarm the system with a doorbell's ding. The wrong numbers would set off screeching alarms—not only in my house, but in police headquarters eight blocks away.

The police would come then, but they hadn't for a missing thirty-four-year-old man. When I'd called headquarters, the desk sergeant had told me to send an e-mail with a recent photo of Tom and the Maserati's license plate. He'd forward it to the local hospitals on the "off chance" something was "actually wrong" and tell the patrolman to watch for the car, but he wouldn't take a report until Tom had been missing for at least a full day.

"Most of the time, guy goes out with his buddies and forgets the hour," he'd said. I hadn't explained that Tom no longer had buddies or the money for a bender—or that he'd mused about faking his death.

I tapped my phone screen. The time showed eleven thirty PM. Was Tom downstairs or was it an opportunistic burglar who'd realized my husband wasn't home? I got up from the bed and took an instinctual step toward Sophia's room. The alarm beeped

57

good-bye. The message on the security pad's LED screen changed from "fault garage" to a request to arm the system.

A breathless rage squashed my relief. Tom hadn't hurt himself. But if he could disable the alarm, he'd been capable of getting to a phone to calm his wife. I readied my body for a fight and watched the door, battling the urge to barrel downstairs and confront my husband.

My mind played devil's advocate to my emotions: the Maserati could have had trouble, as Tom had told the daycare staff the other day. Perhaps it had broken down, leaving him stranded with a dead cell phone. Or maybe he'd suffered an accident and the hospital had just discharged him. Even more likely, he could have driven buzzed to some errand, been arrested, and had just been released from the drunk tank.

I sat on the edge of the bed as the door peeled back. My husband's broad frame filled the space between the dim hallway and our room. He closed the door behind him, slowly, the way I shut Sophia's room after putting her to bed.

"You're home."

He whirled in the darkness. His head turned right and then left. He rubbed his eyes. "Ana? You're awake."

"I couldn't sleep. I was worried something had happened to you."

"I'm a grown man. What could happen to me?" Tom strode past me into our bathroom. He slipped a T-shirt over his head as he walked. I followed him.

My feet hit the cool marble floor. I flicked on the light. He squinted, as if he'd been in blackness for too long. He unbuttoned his shorts. Clothing puddled around his ankles. He stepped from it and then flung open the glass shower door.

I talked to the fault line running down his naked back. "A lot of things could happen. I wasn't sure if you'd been in a car crash or if you'd fallen and hit your head or if you *did* something . . ."

Tom closed himself inside the glass cage. Water blasted from the showerhead. Steam frosted the walls.

"The daycare called me at work," I continued. "I rushed home, thinking the worst."

His face tilted beneath the stream. Water poured over his pectorals and defined stomach, touching him in ways that I hadn't in months.

"Tom. Talk to me."

"I can barely hear you." He gargled the words beneath the waterfall while rubbing his hands back and forth over his face. He grabbed blindly at the shower shelf. Fingers clasped a green bar of deodorant soap.

I cracked the shower door. The mist covered my face like a veil. "Where were you?"

"An old coworker called asking to meet in the city. I ran out without charging my phone and it died." He ran the soap over his chest and stubble, painting on a foamy turtleneck. "I didn't realize the meeting would last so long and then I lost track of time."

A former colleague had finally reached out? I didn't want to demand a name. It would make it seem like I doubted him. "Didn't this person have a phone?"

"I didn't think to ask. I drank too much. Sorry that I didn't get Sophia. I knew that the daycare could keep her and then you could pick her up on the way home."

"They charge way too much for her to stay. I had to come back early."

"No, you didn't."

"I thought something happened to you."

Tom opened his mouth beneath the stream again. He gargled and spat at the bathroom floor. "I'm sorry you were worried. I just lost track of time."

He switched off the water and then opened the door. His hands reached out toward me. I batted them away and folded my arms across my chest.

He exited the shower and strode over to the towel rack, making a trail of wet footprints. "I always get you one."

"I never forget our daughter at daycare and fail to pick up my phone."

"My phone died. I've said I was sorry." His tone didn't contain any contrition.

I didn't care anymore if he thought that I doubted his story. "Who did you even go out with?"

He rubbed the towel over his face as he talked. The fabric muffled the words. "This recruiter I used to work with all the time. I thought it would be a good way to get some leads on a job."

Investment banking was a male-dominated industry. Recruiting was the opposite. More than half of all recruiters were women, and his deliberate avoidance of a pronoun confirmed the gender. "So you got bombed with some bimbo."

Tom scowled. "You are so fucking dismissive, you know that? I met with someone who might be able to help me get a job."

"Well, did she have anything for you?"

"Not right now. But it's a good relationship to keep up."

"Until nearly midnight?"

He picked something from his teeth. Steak? An olive? He frowned at his reflection, or perhaps the realization that whatever he'd dislodged had been visible at least part of the night.

"Look." He finally faced me with a conciliatory expression. "I jumped at the chance to meet an old colleague who might be able to help me find something and I lost track of time. Once I got into the city, she had to postpone for a couple hours because of a client, so I had to hang around. My phone died. She took me out to dinner to apologize for the wait and talk about prospects for me. It can take an hour to get home from the city with traffic. You know that. I was trying to help our—" He made a praying motion that opened up into a plea for sympathy from an unseen chorus. "You know what? Forget it."

He gathered his clothes from the floor. Footprints marked the marble as he marched from the room.

The abrupt end to what had not even approached a proper apology infuriated me. How dare he act self-righteous? "You should sleep downstairs." I didn't want to wake Sophia, but I couldn't control my volume anymore. "I don't want you in our bed."

"Whatever, Ana." He sounded like a spoiled teenager. I'd won the part of nagging mom to his irreverent boy. Cruel casting. I shouldn't have needed to scold him. He should have come home humble, apologetic.

"You know what? You're right. My fault for worrying. I clearly shouldn't have given a crap," I shouted. "It's not like you do anything around here, anyway."

He spun so fast that I feared he'd slip on the wet floor. He advanced toward me. Eyes narrowed. Teeth glinting.

His fist unfurled as it flew toward my face. A pointed finger stopped inches from my nose. I flinched. In our five years together, Tom had never hit me. Before he'd lost his job, he'd never even yelled at me. Things had changed. His career disappointment had spread like a cancer, infecting his brain, altering his personality. I couldn't trust him, especially not after jabbing his ego in its most sensitive area.

"I bought this house. I paid for the cars, the private nursery school, Sophia's lessons." Tom's voice started at a whisper, but it increased in volume with every word, a kettle whistle as the water neared boiling. "The landscapers, the housekeeper, the swim club membership. All while you sat on your ass for *years*."

"Are you kidding me?" I nearly screamed, daring his finger to hit my forehead. "I cared for our child and this home. I worked with the contractors to get it built. I furnished it. I cooked the meals. I cleaned. I ran all your errands. And now I'm working and still doing all of that."

Tom dropped his finger. His hands surrendered at his sides, but his face retained the fight. "You really think any of that—any of what you ever did or do—is worth a million a year?"

"I do as much as you ever did."

"You're delusional."

"You wanted me to stay at home. Now you're throwing it in my face."

"I'm too tired for this, Ana." He headed toward the door. "I'm dead tired."

*

I lay in bed, staring at the ceiling and seething. Tom was some-where in our house, likely passed out in a guest room. I, on the other hand, couldn't settle down and, unlike Tom, actually had work in the morning.

I wanted to wake him just to vent, let the argument end on my terms. Yes, it was good that he'd taken an active step to land a job. But his sudden initiative wasn't an excuse for leaving Sophia. He didn't have to rush into the city without even trying to give me a heads up. My leaving work early looked unprofessional. Didn't he value my job at all? It was the only income we had.

Well, he'd have to value it. He'd need to watch Sophia until I got home from the meeting Tuesday night. Maybe I'd give him a taste of his own medicine and not even tell him why I'd be late.

The phone on my nightstand showed ten minutes to mid-night. My internal clock said six AM. Damp hair made my pil-low cold and sticky. The bath I'd taken to calm down had only succeeded in further waking me, convincing my body that the moonlight sneaking beneath the shades was an illusion.

I couldn't continue to examine the cracked plaster above me. I needed a distraction. It would be an hour later in Sao Paulo, but Brazilians didn't sleep until at least twelve AM. My parents had always been night owls. They'd still be awake.

I grabbed my laptop from the bookcase in the corner and then returned to my bed to open the Skype application. A bubbly sound, like a ringtone underwater, emerged from the computer's speakers. Moments later, my mother's face came into view: almond-shaped eyes the color of coconut husks. Sand-colored skin, lined around the mouth. Stress had aged her, but not stolen her beauty.

"Oi, Mamãe."

"Hi, Ana."

Even my Portuguese hello betrayed that I couldn't speak the language. She knew that all I remembered of her mother tongue was a bunch of Spanish-accented Portuguese words and Brazil-ian sayings. Not my fault. No one's fault, really. My folks just hadn't been around enough in the past two decades to reinforce their teachings.

"I miss you," I said.

Lines deepened on my mother's brow. "Are you okay?"

"Yes. Of course."

Her mouth twisted with disbelief. She always knew when I was lying. "Is everything okay with Tom?"

My parents had enough problems. I wasn't about to get into mine. "We're fine. It's nothing, just *saudade*." One of the few Portuguese words I knew. It lacked direct English translation: homesickness mixed with longing and bittersweet memories, content with yearning for family and the past. Some said the word encapsulated the Brazilian temperament.

Though I knew the term, I couldn't actually relate to the feeling. My past was a blur. Bad events erase good history like fire burning through film. All that remained for me of my childhood were a series of images. The yard behind our two-family house. Bushy lavender plants, purple tips stretching to the sky. My mother bent over them, pruning scissors in her right hand, jean-clad legs spotted with dirt. Black-clad Immigration and Customs Enforcement officers storming through the kitchen to get her, yelling that she held a weapon. Her promising over and over that they'd be back in a little while. *Just a little while.*

I'd spent my teens in a foster home, and though I'd blocked the visuals from my memory, I'd never forget the smell. Burnt hair and old carpet. Ms. Yvette had done weaves in the kitchen to supplement her foster income. I'd split my time between school, a Starbucks job, and babysitting my younger "siblings"—a.k.a. Ms. Yvette's real kids and smaller foster children. I still think she'd volunteered to take me because it had been cheaper than hiring childcare.

My parents had come back twice, each time just as illegitimately as the first. Immigration was on them within months. As far as ICE knew, they were dangerous identity thieves, not people who'd paid taxes for fifteen years, albeit under false social security numbers.

"*Saudade?*" My mother's voice showed that she doubted my explanation.

I forced a smile for her benefit. "How are you and Daddy?"

A halo of orange light surrounded her head, coming from an exposed bulb in the kitchen. Veined ceramic glass had shielded the ceiling light before. Had it broken? "Oh, you know. We're fine. We miss you."

"Do you need anything?" I couldn't afford for her to say yes. I'd sent the last check six months before, maybe even earlier. Tom had not been happy.

My mom shook her head. I knew she wouldn't ask for money outright, even though they had to be hurting. After getting deported, rebuilding their lives in Brazil had been next to impossible. They'd had no money and no documented work experience. My father had done construction for a few years, but it had never paid anywhere close to what he'd made in the States. Now sixty, no one would hire him. My mother still taught English, but she'd lost students to new language schools popping up in the area. There weren't any savings.

"You just worry about you and my beautiful granddaughter," she said. "How is Sophia?"

"Good. I'll call back with her tomorrow."

A shadowed figure entered the kitchen, just visible behind my mother's head. The form angled toward her before hurrying from the room. "Is Daddy there?"

"No. He's sleeping."

Who was in the house then? "I think I just saw him in the kitchen."

"Daddy's tired. He must have just come in for a glass of water."

Too tired to say hi? My mother's smile appeared constructed from a single pane of glass. One wrong word and it would shatter. Light shifted behind her head again. A figure lumbered in the kitchen. I recognized the outline this time: broad shoulders, thin build, a triangle atop a pole. "Daddy. Dad?"

My mother moved closer to the screen, blocking the view behind her. Tracks ran beneath her eyes. Had she been sleeping?

She looked older than I remembered. Older than a week ago. "Daddy's in bed."

"Mom, I just saw him. Why won't you let me talk to him?"

"He doesn't feel well."

"Dad, I see you. What's wrong?"

"Nothing's wrong with him."

"Dad!" I shouted through the monitor. "Daddy, are you okay? Dad!"

"It's fine, Beatriz."

My mother folded into herself at the sound of her name, and my dad's torso came into the picture. He pulled a seat from the dining table and dragged it next to my mother. I still couldn't see his face.

My mom's eyes welled as he sat beside her, reacting not to my dad but to my expression as I saw him. He'd fought and lost. His cheeks were puffed like mushrooms caps. A deep purple bruise overwhelmed his left eye. Bloody scabs crusted in his eyebrow. A blood blister puckered from his lower lip.

"Oh my God, Daddy."

"It looks worse than it is."

"What happened?"

My mother's face shattered. "Oh, Ana," she wailed. "It's the gangs."

"Not real gangs. Young punks." My father crossed his arms, revealing scabbed lines. Defensive wounds.

"With bats and knives," my mom cried. "They demand money from anyone with family in the U.S. They say it's an import tax on the dollars they know we have coming in. We'd paid for years—"

"How much do they want?"

My dad's chin fell. "It's all right, Ana. They know I can't pay."

"Then why are they beating you?" I almost shook the computer screen. How had they not told me that they were being blackmailed? For years? I could have helped before. I had to help now.

"It's okay. They will understand. We don't have it anymore."

I'd confessed Tom's job loss to my parents after he'd been out of work a few months and I'd needed to reduce the amount of money I sent each month. At first, I'd mailed two-thirds the usual amount. A few months later, I was sending half that. They'd never asked when the checks stopped coming. They both knew what it meant.

"Tell me how much."

"A thousand." Tears gurgled in my mother's words. "It was a hundred a month, but we haven't paid in a while and they say there's interest."

I'd once taken eighty thousand dollars from Tom's seven-figure bonus check and bought my parents an apartment. Tom had complained that, in the right investment, the amount could balloon into a healthy retirement savings. But I'd convinced him that the missing money wouldn't mean anything to us. At the time, it hadn't. Now I couldn't imagine how I'd find a spare hundred dollars, let alone a whole thousand.

"I'll get it. When are they coming again?"

"You don't have it," my father said. "And when they want more than a thousand, what do we do? It's better they realize now."

"And what, kill you? It was enough before, right? When are they coming?"

"Next month," my mother mumbled.

My father scowled at her from beneath his swollen eye. "You have to take care of Sophia and Tom right now." His hands reached out toward the screen, toward me. The gesture made me hurt. It had been so long since I'd felt the touch of either of my parents, so long since I'd hugged them. "You have to take care of *your* family."

"I am taking care of my family."

"How will you do it?" My mother couldn't hide her hope.

I didn't know, but I'd find a way. I'd always come up with money before, even when I'd only had a Starbucks job. Now I was working for a multibillion-dollar hedge fund.

"I'll figure something out."

11

November 24

Ryan stood outside a former furniture warehouse off I-95. A plastic banner hanging above a stairway leading to a basement door read, "Appleday, Where Kids Can Play." Each letter was colored differently, as if children with perfect handwriting had constructed the sign.

He knocked, crossing his fingers that his GPS had led him to the correct place. Amazing, the number of daycares with *apple* in the title located in the NYC suburbs. AppleView, AppleSeed, AppleTree, Apple Montessori, Appleday. He'd called no fewer than eight places before getting a harried aide on the line that had remembered Sophia. The woman had referred him to her boss, a lady named Ms. Donna, who hadn't bothered to return his message. Ryan figured showing up would prove more effective than playing phone tag.

He would rather have been confronting Michael about the paternity of Ana's unborn child than interviewing employees at Sophia's old daycare, but he didn't have a choice. Even if he did manage to reach Ana's old boss in the Bahamas, Michael wasn't likely to confirm that he'd been sleeping with his secretary while on vacation with the wife and kids.

In the meantime, he would try to get a better handle on the Bacons' finances by speaking with someone they'd needed to pay regularly, who could also confirm or deny Michael's story that Ana had picked up Sophia often. With luck, one of the daycare workers might even have some insight into whether Ana had seemed stressed or depressed. Afterward, he could gauge Tom's reaction to questions about Ana's working relationship with her former boss.

A broad woman with screaming red hair opened the door. Children's shouts drifted into the cold outside. The woman looked down at Ryan's knees before returning her suspicious gaze to his face. "You're here to drop off?"

"No. Actually, I was—"

"Picking up?" She pulled her chin into her neck. "I don't think we have you on the authorized list."

"No. I called before. I'm here to ask questions about Mrs. Ana Bacon. I understand that her daughter Sophia went here."

The woman's red strands didn't move as she shook her head. Cherry-scented something wafted into the air. Hairspray? "I can't let unauthorized adults inside. It's for the safety of the kids."

Ryan grabbed the door before it could close in his face. "I understand. Could we talk outside? I only need a couple minutes of your time."

"I'm not supposed to leave the children with just two aides. It's too high a ratio for this age group. State rules." The woman's voice sounded nasal and hoarse. Part South Jersey, part smoker. Ryan wished he had a cigarette to offer. He didn't smoke, given that 90 percent of lung cancer fatalities in men stemmed from cigarettes. Folks who avoided cancer sticks, lived more than fifteen miles from a major city, and got their home radon tested were statistically immune from lung disease. Ryan had checked all the boxes.

The aide grimaced at his hand on the door. "If you'll excuse me."

Why couldn't people just invite him in for once? It was cold, damn it.

"Mrs. Bacon had a large insurance policy, and I am trying to figure out if there were any contributing factors to her accident."

The woman stopped trying to shut the door in his face, though she didn't remove her hand from the knob. "If they get this insurance policy, do they have to use it to pay debts?"

Part of the appeal of life insurance was that creditors couldn't easily claim the payments. Owed parties could sue for a portion of benefits if the recipient was a spouse that shared the deceased's debts. But the Bacons had avoided that by designating Sophia as the beneficiary. Ryan scratched the hair at the nape of his neck. "In some cases."

The aide identified herself as Ms. Donna. She stepped out onto the stairs, closing the door behind her. "Mrs. Bacon pulled Sophia midyear. You can't just do that when you sign up for twelve months. You still gotta pay the remainder."

"Were the Bacons good about paying?"

"Well, they paid each month. But like I said, they still owe us for the rest of the year, even if they don't send their kid. We hire aides based on the expected number of children. We can't just fire them when someone drops out, even if there's a tragedy. And they pulled Sophia before anything happened to her mom."

Ryan feigned sympathy. "Seems like the Bacons didn't get the costs involved in running a daycare. I heard that they were often late picking up Sophia as well."

Ms. Donna chewed at her bottom lip. "I only charged them the once. So you think I could apply for some relief if the policy goes through?"

"They were only charged once? I thought Mrs. Bacon was late all the time."

Ms. Donna shook her head. "I don't know where you're getting your information, but that's not right. Usually it was Mr. Bacon who picked up Sophia. Mrs. Bacon just picked her up the one time, the day I had to charge her because she was ninety minutes overdue. Few days later, she called to say she wouldn't send Sophia anymore."

Ryan couldn't see a motive for Ms. Donna not to tell the truth. But he could imagine Michael lying about Ana leaving work early to obscure the fact that he'd fired her after their relationship went sour.

"When did she stop sending Sophia exactly?"

The answer was important. If Fernanda was right and the human resource department hadn't known that Ana had quit, then her old job wouldn't have an accurate date for her departure. Whatever had caused Ana to stop working had happened earlier than the late August day her firm had provided. Ryan needed the *when* to figure out *what*. Whatever had made Ana stop working just might have started her downward spiral to suicide.

Ms. Donna rubbed her reddening nose. Ryan bet she regretted not inviting him in. "August eighteenth. I know because she sent in a check with a note that said 'final daycare payment' through that Tuesday. I haven't cashed it. I don't want Mr. Bacon thinking I'm giving up my claim to the outstanding bill, you know?"

Ryan nodded. "Could I see the check?"

The aide opened the door and stepped back inside. "I got all these kids, I'm not gonna go look for it now. Gimme your number. I'll call with it."

Ryan's numb fingers fumbled with his wallet. He pulled out a business card and slipped it into Ms. Donna's hand. "My fax is on the bottom."

She inspected the print and then waved the card in the air. "All right, I'll call you. Maybe I can get back some of what she owed. It takes months to get kids into an open spot. It's not like we have a wait list."

The door shut. Ryan hustled back up the steps as fast as he could hop, using his good leg and the railing for support. Excitement made him forget his throbbing thigh. Lies were leads, and Ryan had just found one.

12

August 13

I tiptoed down the back stairs, a thief in my own house, careful to avoid the guest room that I'd heard Tom stumble into around two AM. The refrigerator's hum masked the sound of my movements as I crept into the kitchen. I scurried across the first floor to the basement stairs and then descended into enemy territory: Tom's bar.

My husband's wine collection was the only semiliquid possession we had left. I prayed that Tom's liquor store would repurchase the bottles at a discount.

A small duffle scratched at my side. The bag was Christmas party swag: flimsy vinyl stamped with the name of Tom's old firm. It would hold between six and eight bottles. As I approached the back room, I whispered my justifications for planning to fill the sack: Tom's drinking had become a problem. He needed to stop boozing and my parents needed money. Like a stiff drink, the alcohol could make my problems vanish—at least temporarily.

Tom's wine cellar reminded me of a glass shower enclosure. Chrome wine racks attached to metal scaffolding inside. Swan-necked bottles had once graced each grooved space between the metal bars. Now the majority of the unit was empty.

The fridge could lock, but Tom drank far too often to bother turning the key each night. I pulled back the sliding glass door. Cold air pricked my arm. Goosebumps spread on my skin, spurred by fear as much as the change in temperature. How would Tom react if he caught me?

The best vintages rested on the top shelf. I stood on the pads of my feet and tipped a bottle from its cradle with my fingertips. It landed in my palm. Near black glass obscured the wine inside. A stamp, reminiscent of the wax seal royalty used to shut envelopes, caught the glow of the wine shelves' embedded LEDs. A white-and-black label spread across the front of the bottle: Gaja Barbaresco. Italy. 1990.

I knew little about alcohol, other than to trust my husband's recommendations. Wine was Tom's hobby, and he didn't enjoy anything inexpensive. The bottles in the cellar wouldn't warrant storage space if they'd cost less than one hundred dollars. The stuff at the top of the cabinet would be hundreds of dollars.

I placed the Gaja in the duffle and then tipped another bottle into my waiting hand. Silver foil decorated this one's cap. The label showcased two concentric circles that resembled a star in Van Gogh's famous painting. Any label appropriating famous artwork had to be pricey. I scanned the top shelf for another reachable bottle. There was one with a silver etching of a stallion. I stretched. My fingertips grazed the neck. The bottle jostled in the cradle but couldn't be coaxed into my open palm. Without a boost, I risked breaking it, and there was no way I could cart the stepladder from the garage and down the stairs without making a racket loud enough to wake Tom.

The rest of the top shelf remained out of reach. I grabbed half a dozen bottles scattered around the giant fridge, hoping my husband would be less likely to notice random missing bottles than a raided shelf.

Tom hadn't rearmed the alarm when he'd come home. That was good, since turning it off made a steady beeping noise for several seconds. I opened the door and carried the duffle into the garage. The lot went into my Camry's trunk. I'd sell them first thing in the morning, before Tom sauntered into the basement for whatever liquid passed as his breakfast these days.

I crept back up the rear stairs to my bedroom. Tom's snoring echoed from the guest room down the hallway. I slipped beneath the covers and watched the time on my cell change from three thirty to four AM. Sleep remained a dream.

*

The wine store beckoned from behind refurbished factory windows. The modern, industrial look reminded me of Tom's bar/theater room, only five times the size. No wonder he loved this place.

A pleasant ding signaled that customers had arrived. Sophia looked for the source of the sound as I led her into the store. A bewildered expression crossed her face as she undoubtedly tried to understand why I'd told her father that we would run to Payless after dinner to get her measured for new sneakers and then taken her to a liquor store.

"Mommy just needs to run a quick errand," I explained. "It's a surprise for daddy, though, so we can't tell him." Her eyes lit up, excited to be included in a secret—especially one that she believed would make her father happy.

I disliked lying, and I hated myself for involving my daughter in my alibi. But the shoe excuse had been the easiest way to duck out without Tom asking questions. He knew that Sophia needed sneakers. Her toe had made an impression on the roof of her old Stride Rites from bending to fit inside the shoe.

The duffle was squeezed between us, helping silence the clang of bottles brushing against one another. We stepped into a foyer with a little table, where patrons must taste wines. I hovered around it, looking for the owner.

Legs culminating in a push up bra and copper dye job appeared from within a hallway of Napa Valley reds. "Looking for anything in particular today?" The saleswoman gargled her r sounds as though her first language was French. She flashed a large, fake smile at my daughter before frowning at the duffle.

"Actually, yes. I'm looking for the owner. Vincent."

Her smile softened at her boss's name. She could peg me now: wife of a key client seeking to impress her husband with something special, maybe for an anniversary or birthday, stopping by on the way back from her daughter's kiddie soccer practice or, maybe, the gym. The bag and the need to bring my child into a fancy liquor store no longer sounded the alarm.

"Of course. I'll get him. What is your name?"

"Ana Bacon."

"Bacon." Her eyes narrowed, though her smile spread to each ear. "As in bringing home the. Got it."

I recognized the joke as something Tom would say, or had said. He'd always liked that his surname was synonymous with a slang term for money. He brought home the bacon. I could imagine him, glass of wine in hand, casually flirting with this woman. *Yup, I bring home the bacon.*

Maybe she explained why he went so often to the wine store. Jealousy tightened my chest as I followed her to a back room. Sophia's grip closed around my hand. She sensed my emotion again.

I knelt beside her, bottles jangling as I shifted position. "Hey, Mommy just has to give this man a few things and then we will leave, okay? Want to look for animals on the bottles with me?"

She brightened and swung my arm. We walked between ash-gray wooden racks filled with wine. I spotted a fat mallard on Duckhorn Cabernet. I recognized the bottle as one that had often graced the table during dinner. The eighty-dollar red stood just above Sophia's head, not even near the top shelf. "There's a duck."

She followed my pointed finger to the bottle. "It looks like *Make Way for Ducklings.*"

The salesclerk returned with a man who barely met her chin line. He wore a gray suit open to reveal a blue shirt. His Roman nose combined with his black hair, long and gelled into small spikes, served as an ethnic calling card. The Italian smiled upon seeing me, just enough for his top lip to rise above his front teeth.

"You must be Tom's wife." He extended his hand as he approached. The redhead stood at his side, a doting wife, or mistress.

I shook. His grip was firm. He maintained eye contact. "I haven't seen Tommy in a while. How is he doing?"

Tommy? My husband never went by anything so casual. He would have hated the familiarity.

"Fine. Thanks for asking. Could we chat a moment?" I glanced at the young woman. "In private?"

His open smile sank into the closed-mouth version. The girl's toothy grin became even more strained than before.

"Maybe in your office?" I suggested. "I'd hoped you would be interested in purchasing some of Tom's wine collection."

Whatever remained of Vincent's smile faded. "Well, it would depend on what you are selling and whether we already have it in stock, but I'm willing to give a listen."

I held Sophia's hand as we followed him into the back room. He chatted while we walked. "So Tom is getting out of collecting? That's unfortunate. He was always so passionate."

I scanned price tags as we walked: $80, $95, $100, $150, $200, $220. Either the selection here was extraordinary or this guy marked up bottles like a nightclub.

"I've truly missed him coming into the store. He really possessed a sophisticated palate." Vincent didn't need any response from me to keep filling the space between us with hot air. "Not many folks can recognize the difference between a fruit bomb and a wine with layers of flavors: raspberry, oak, blackberry, vanilla. You know, all the different notes. Like a symphony. Tom really had an ear for wine."

I didn't think Tom's palate achieved the sophistication that Vincent applauded, but I had no doubt that my husband knew expensive. I nodded along. All Vincent's praise had probably helped turn Tom into a wine connoisseur—that and the leggy salesclerk. I squeezed my eyes shut, forcing the thoughts from my mind.

Vincent opened the door to a small back room, just big enough for a stainless steel desk, three chairs, and several bookcases stocked with wine. The room smelled like oak barrels, though I couldn't see any.

Vincent settled into a tufted leather chair behind the desk. I put Sophia in a smaller club chair facing his seat and then placed the duffle bag on the table. I withdrew the two most expensive bottles first. With luck, their value would negotiate for me.

"I understand 1990 was a good year for Gaja. It sells for nearly four hundred dollars online. And I saw the Pingus for well over six hundred."

The warmth wafting from Vincent dissipated. He grabbed the neck of the Pingus, tilted the bottle upside down, and rotated it, looking for something in the liquid. He examined the cap.

"The online price includes a significant retail markup." He continued to examine the wine as he spoke. I figured he was checking for color and clarity, though I didn't see how he could discern either through the near-black bottle. "When I buy wine like this, direct from the vineyards, I get dealer discounts that make it much less expensive. Plus, there's the question of how well it's been stored and cared for."

Sophia scanned the wine shelves. She was looking for animals. Thank goodness that game amused her.

I sat on the edge of my chair. Too eager. I forced myself to lean back into the fabric as I tried to convince my mind to adopt the same laid-back demeanor.

"Well, you know Tom." I faked a giggle. "He babied his wine and he certainly took care of these bottles. We have a temperature-controlled wine cellar, custom built by a design firm that did many of the boutique shops in Manhattan. And, of course, the house has a generator, so it never lost power."

Vincent's tongue dragged across his top lip. "I could give you three hundred dollars for the Pingus." He put the bottle in front of me and checked out the other one. "Maybe two hundred dollars for the Gaja. Say five hundred dollars for both."

Half the value. Tom would be furious. "I could do better on eBay."

Vincent shrugged. "You could try. But I doubt it. People would be too worried that they weren't the real deal without inspecting the bottles. You'd be surprised the things people do: take out the corks, fill the bottle with cheap swill, recork it, and try to sell it as the real McCoy."

"These are authentic."

"I don't doubt it." He placed both elbows on the desk. A half smile cracked across his stony face. "You get a read on people in this business. Whom to buy from. Whom to sell to. Who's a repeat customer looking to build a relationship with the store and who is just running in for a quick bottle of anything to bring to a party. You have your kid here. Tom hasn't been in for an age. You strike me as an honest woman trying to sell off her husband's collection for some extra cash."

He grinned, the satisfied expression of a swindler psychic sure he'd convinced his target of his extraordinary abilities. He wasn't *that* good. I was just *that* obvious.

"Unfortunately for you, people won't get any read online." He folded his arms across his chest. "And wine buyers don't trust anyone they can't look in the eye nowadays."

Five hundred beat nothing, but my parents needed a thousand. If he only gave me half the worth of the best bottles, what could I expect for the six midpriced vintages in the bag? It wouldn't be enough. Could I try another wine store? Would the salesman there take me for a con artist?

Vincent removed the other bottles from the bag. He frowned at the labels, forced to look at inferior swill that he'd undoubtedly sold to my husband at more than one hundred dollars a pop. "These are mostly California Cabs. Some decent bottles, sure, but nothing that commands a high price. I get the—"

"Mommy." Sophia tugged my shirt.

"Yes, honey?" I answered her without thinking. A Pavlovian mom. Paying attention to my daughter was a reflex.

A flustered sigh escaped Vincent's lips. Good. He'd enjoyed his monologue too much. Sophia pointed to a high shelf on the bookcase behind Vincent's desk. It only contained one bottle in a glass case. A white equine was etched into the dark glass. "It's a horse," she whispered.

Vincent grinned. "Not just any horse. A ghost horse. Those bottles are very rare. That one is worth more than fifteen hundred dollars."

The silver stallion in Tom's cellar. "We have a bottle of that."

Vincent's body language changed. The cocky trader left. "I didn't sell Tom that."

I settled back into the chair. Time to play my part: Rich housewife helping "rid" her husband of a hobby. "Tom belonged to several wine clubs. What would you pay for a bottle?"

"It depends on the vintage."

"Assume it's good."

"I'd really have to see it."

I collected the Pingus from the far side of the desk and returned it to the duffle. "Okay, then. Thank you for your time."

"I would be interested in the Ghost Horse."

"I understand that one is valuable. Unfortunately, it's not easy to come to liquor stores with my daughter." I slipped the bag's shoulder strap over my arm. "I believe Christie's auction house would send someone to survey the conditions in our cellar. And they might be willing to buy the larger collection, as well."

He held up his hand. Calling my bluff or biting? *Please don't call my bluff.*

"If the Ghost Horse is on the table, I could do, maybe, eight hundred dollars for this lot."

The silver stallion bottle was beyond my reach, literally and figuratively. But if I could get more than a thousand for the bottle, how could I not try?

"Well?" Vincent licked his bottom lip. The man was salivating at the idea of having two of the famed bottles.

"If we make a deal now for these bottles, I'm inclined to return with the Ghost Horse," I said. "Though I'm sure I couldn't part with it for less than a grand."

A checkbook landed on Vincent's desk. "To whom should I make it out?"

13

Ryan drove past the Bacons' French-style McMaison with his headlights off, hoping to spy signs of life in the house before Tom could pretend that no one was at home. The gray day had darkened into evening, raising the risk of a driver clipping his unlit vehicle. Fortunately, the Bacons' house was tucked in the middle of a quiet residential street, the kind of place that forgave bending the rules.

A car sat in the driveway, blocking one of the home's three garages. Ryan sucked in his breath and pressed the brake. Part of him had hoped Tom would be out. He wasn't prepared to confront a grieving widower about his dead wife's possible infidelity. But he needed to know Tom's suspicions about Michael before confronting the guy about hiding the true reason for Ana's departure.

Lights shone through windows beside the front door. A male figure walked through the dining room, toward the kitchen. Ryan parked across the street and limped up the driveway. Tom must have seen his slow approach. He answered the front door before Ryan had a chance to ring the bell.

The extra week of grieving had done little to mar Mr. Bacon's groomed appearance. He was showered, shaved. And if Ryan's chilled nose didn't deceive him, Tom was wearing cologne.

"Mr. Monahan, are you here with news?"

"I have some more questions."

"Oh?"

"Some concerning information has come to light."

Tom scratched his neck as if Ryan's words irritated his skin. "I can't imagine what."

Ryan steeled himself. There was little point easing into this one. "An affair."

A sarcastic smile cracked at the side of Tom's mouth, as if he'd known this conversation was coming. He shook his head. "Well, come on in, I guess."

Tom led the way through the foyer past a grand spiral staircase leading to the second floor to a descending stairwell tucked behind it. Ryan thought he could hear the sound effects of animated characters having accidents on a TV.

"Just eat it, Sophia." A woman's voice clanged like an angry cowbell from the kitchen.

"I don't like beans, Auntie Eve," Sophia whined.

"It's what I made."

Tom froze as he heard the exchange. He waited for a moment, an animal caught by a floodlight. Hearing nothing else, he continued down to the house's lower level. Ryan waited until his feet hit the basement's tile floor before mentioning the female visitor. "Sorry to interrupt when you have guests. Your sister?"

"I don't have siblings. A family friend comes by to help take care of Sophia."

Tom spoke without looking over his shoulder. He led Ryan through a well-organized playroom and past a gym, complete with rubber flooring, treadmill, and a weight machine. He pulled back a metal barn door at the end of it and entered into a dark room.

Ryan followed him inside. A disorienting moment later, blue LEDs revealed a home bar worthy of a bustling Manhattan lounge. A floor-to-ceiling glass wine-storage container with underlit shelving dominated the facing wall. The adjoining back wall featured ceiling-mounted black cabinets flanking long, lit wall shelves for liquor bottles. A zinc-topped bar extended in front of the display. No barstools. Standing room only. The adjoining home theater featured two rows of black leather recliners, mounted atop a carpeted, tiered floor.

"Get you anything?" Tom walked behind the bar. Ryan peered around it to see a back counter with enough stainless steel appliances beneath to rival a top-of-the-line kitchen.

Ryan considered the selection, more for his mental inventory than anything else. Whiskey and cognac bottles dotted the wall shelves, but many were empty, or nearly so. The wine storage container was basically bare. He revised his earlier opinion about the space belonging in a fancy Manhattan club. Tom's bar was going out of business.

"Nothing for me, thanks." Ryan took off his barely lined pea coat and draped it over the back of a theater chair before heading to the standing bar.

Tom pulled the glass stopper from a curved bottle of Crown Royal. He grabbed a short glass from inside a cabinet and poured. Whiskey neat. Not many people had the stomach for that.

"Hope you don't mind." Tom took a long sip. His lips smacked together before finishing his thought. "I think I might need one for this conversation."

Ryan did mind. Alcohol was a contributing factor in more than 40 percent of murders, let alone physical assaults. Hard liquor heightened anger. He would have preferred having a nice, sober conversation within earshot of Tom's "family friend," someone who could make Tom control himself if things got heated.

He pointed to the ceiling, reminding his host of the witnesses in the house. "So, your friend is helping with the cooking?"

Tom lowered the glass to his hip. "You said something about an affair. In case you're getting any ideas, I'm not sleeping with her. She's just a friend. A lot of friends have been coming to help since Ana passed. They're concerned for Sophia."

Tom was already on the defensive. Ryan tried to keep his tone nonconfrontational. "I'd like to talk to Ana's friends. Maybe she would—"

"No." Tom flashed a tight smile. "She didn't come over to be interrogated. I'm talking to you."

Ryan's host took another long sip of whiskey. He leaned on the back counter, a bartender feigning interest in a client. "So let me guess. Someone misinterpreted my relationship with one of our friends and told you that I must have been cheating. And now you think that Ana found out and jumped overboard, thereby violating the suicide clause in her life insurance policy and letting your company off the hook. Am I right?"

"It's not that."

Tom didn't seem to hear him. "I'm telling you, if you go the suicide route, my lawyers will make sure that your company ends up paying double in damages." He looked into his drink and sighed. "First off, I wasn't sleeping around. Second, even if I had been, my wife wouldn't kill herself. She'd never do that to Sophia or her unborn child—not to mention her parents, whom she'd pretty much supported since fourteen. I mean—"

"These rumors are about Ana."

The blue light from the bar highlighted the dark shadows beneath Tom's eyes and the bulge of his brows. He placed his whiskey on the counter. "What?"

"Someone at Ana's old job suggested she might have been seeing her boss."

Ryan watched Tom's face for flickers of rage and recognition, but the man didn't tense up. If anything, he relaxed. His shoulders shook with a chuckle as he reclaimed his whiskey. "Michael's an ass, but he wasn't having an affair with Ana. Though, I'm sure he would have wanted to. Who even is this source of yours? Michael himself?"

"An employee."

"And this employee knew my wife?"

"Not exactly."

He pointed a finger above the rim of his glass. "My wife was loyal." He looked down at the liquor in his glass. A small, sad smile sneaked onto his face.

Ryan examined Tom's stance. Either the man was an excellent actor or he honestly believed it impossible that his wife had slept with her superior. In Ryan's experience, few people could completely cover genuine anger. If Tom knew that Michael had destroyed his marriage and driven his wife to kill herself, there'd be hatred in his eyes or clenched teeth behind his smile, not the resigned expression before him.

Still, Tom's demeanor didn't mean that Ana hadn't had an affair—just that her husband couldn't imagine it.

A yawn swallowed Tom's face. "It's like I've told you and countless other people. She'd been sick all vacation. I left her sleeping on our balcony to go to the pool for a bit and—"

"You swim?" Ryan asked to avoid hearing Tom's impossible explanation for his wife's fall for the umpteenth time. Repetition had a way of turning fabrications into facts. He couldn't risk Tom convincing him of his crazy story.

"What?" Tom looked into his glass. He rotated his wrist, spinning the alcohol inside his tumbler into a cyclone. "No, not really. Ana was the swimmer."

"Ana didn't want to swim?"

"Like I said, she was sick all trip. She wanted to lie down after the beach, so she went back to the room and I went on to the pool."

Ryan caught the inconsistency. "Wait, I thought you went back with her to the room before you went to the pool."

Tom's head snapped up from his drink. "What? Yeah."

"You just said you 'went on to the pool' like she went to the room and you went straight to the sun deck."

He coughed. "No. Look, I'm tired, all right? I *went on* to the pool, after dropping her in the room. She got settled in the lounge chair on our balcony and then I went up to the ninth deck." He rubbed his temple with his free hand. "If I'd just stayed . . ."

Ryan felt suddenly guilty for jumping on Tom's word choice. He was starting to feel bad for judging him so harshly at their first meeting. So what that Tom had remained presentable after his wife's death? Maybe he was someone who needed to go through the motions in order to manage his grief. Getting a haircut and shaving didn't mean the guy wasn't torn up about losing his wife. It didn't make him a jerk. A cocky guy would have thrown a fit at the suggestion that his wife had boinked her boss, maybe even taken a swing at the man doing the suggesting. Tom had remained calm, almost collegial. Ryan couldn't picture the man as a callous wife-beater like Ana's parents claimed.

The thought reminded Ryan of Tom's earlier statement. "You said Ana took care of her parents?"

Tom took a deep breath. "Sure did. Those two were constantly making withdrawals from the bank of Bacon. Even after I stopped working and we had to cut back on the household, they were asking for money."

Household cutbacks. The Bacons did have staff, at least at some point. Ryan reminded himself to keep hassling the house cleaners' voice machine. "You had a nanny and a cleaning service?"

Tom laughed to himself. "I'm sorry. But you're crazy if you think I'm handing out the name of everyone who ever worked for us so you can spread rumors about my wife." He swished the liquor in his glass. "I answered the question about the affair."

"I take it you didn't like Ana's folks?"

Tom took another sip of whiskey and shrugged. "I tried to. I think they took advantage of their daughter and me, refusing to work because it was too easy to guilt Ana into sending cash." He gestured with the glass. "Those people would say anything for money."

"Ana's mother suggested that you got physical with your wife before her death . . ."

Anger darkened Tom's resigned expression. He opened his mouth, as if to say something, and then took a long drink from his glass. When he lowered the tumbler, he again appeared tired and sad. "It's not surprising. Like I said, they'd say anything for money. They wanted their daughter to support them. Now they want Sophia to do it."

He threw back the last of his whiskey and set the glass on the counter. A guttural sound resonated in his throat, as if the liquid had seared his esophagus. "Anyway, my point was that Ana wouldn't have put them through any grief over her." He smacked his lips together. "So we done here?"

"Just one more question." Tom raised both eyebrows, a get-on-with-it expression. "Why did Ana quit?"

Tom's head cocked. "Who told you she quit? Michael?"

"Yes."

Tom snorted.

"So she didn't choose to leave Derivative Capital?"

Tom eyed the open Canadian bourbon, as if debating whether to pour himself another. He picked up the bottle and placed it back on the shelf beside several near-empties. "It was complicated." He walked around the bar and lifted Ryan's coat off the back of the chair. He held it out to him. "But I can assure you, the reasons she left had nothing to do with her fall. That was just an accident."

Tom paused between every other syllable in the last sentence. Ryan accepted his coat, understanding that his host had said all he would on the matter. He slipped on his outerwear as Tom led the way through the playroom toward the stairs. With luck, he'd glimpse the "family friend" before he left, maybe slip her his card.

Ryan heard a sliding door open before he saw it. There was an exit into the backyard. Tom was letting him out the rear door. The female friend would remain a mystery, at least for now.

Ryan mentally cursed as the lock clicked behind him. Tom had given him nothing and again threatened a legal challenge to any suicide-related denial of benefits. There was no way ISI would win a lawsuit with only a stat showing how *extremely* unlikely it was for a sober person to fall off a cruise ship. He needed to show beyond a shadow of doubt that Ana had reasons to want to die. As it was, all he had was that Ana had quit her job to stay with her family during a challenging time for her husband and that the Bacons had money issues. But they weren't destitute. Tom had managed to remain in his multimillion-dollar home. Losing the housekeeper wasn't justification for becoming shark bait.

His feet sunk into melting snow as he rounded the Bacons' house to the front yard. What was he missing?

He pulled out his cell and wallet from his pocket. Fernanda's card was in the front flap. Ana had stopped sending Sophia to daycare after August 18. Maybe she could figure out what had been on Ana and Michael's agenda that week and what had gone wrong.

14

August 14

A crack ran through the bedroom ceiling. Faint, like a fingernail mark on chalkboard, but definitely there. The new house had settled during the past few years and lines snaked across the drywall. The future owners would need to invest in plenty of plaster and paint.

I listened for Tom's breathing to smooth out into the sounds of a deep sleep, all the while fighting my eyelids back. It had been a long day. Michael had decided to take a family cruise to the Bahamas, at the insistence of his wife. There'd been islands to research, reservations to secure, pets to board, entertainment options to vet. Michael, of course, had insisted that I plan it all. He couldn't "trust the wife to keep the schedule straight."

Gauzy linen crumpled on top of my legs. My husband slept on top of the bedding, too hot from the lack of a blasting air conditioner, and too withdrawn from our recent argument, to join me beneath the sheets.

After an exhausting fifteen minutes, Tom's breathing settled into a long, nasal whistle. I freed myself from beneath the sheet and slid from the bed. My parents still needed two hundred more dollars to keep the gangs at bay, and I had a dozen ideas of how to use the additional eight hundred from the Ghost Horse.

My first stop was Sophia's room. I'd figured out a more portable solution to accessing the wine fridge's top shelf than the stepladder: the wooden stool Sophia used to reach the sink. The extra foot would be enough to grab the neck of the Ghost Horse, and it only weighed a couple pounds or so.

I crept into my daughter's dark bedroom. My familiarity was better than night vision. Often, I put away her clean clothes after getting her to sleep. I guessed most parents did. Children probably got the idea that monsters lived in the closet from fuzzy glimpses of moms putting away the laundry past midnight.

The stepstool stood against the vanity in Sophia's adjoining bathroom. I snatched it and slipped back into the hallway. Again, I tried to think like a burglar as I descended the main staircase to the first floor and then turned toward the basement stairs. Don't turn on the light until there's no chance of it spreading to the upper hallway. Step carefully. Move quickly.

A light in the man cave threatened like an intruder. Tom had left it on. Was he trying to run up the electricity bill? How hard was it to flip a switch after leaving a room? I strode to the LED-lit wine storage unit. Blue light encased the bottles. At least LEDs were energy efficient.

I placed the stepstool at the foot of the enclosure and slid back the glass door. The Ghost Horse beckoned on the top shelf. As soon as my palm wrapped around the bottle, I sensed a problem. The bottle was lighter than an empty milk carton. A full wine bottle should have weight to it.

"I drank it."

I nearly fell off the stool as I whirled around. Tom stood in the opening to the room. His frame filled the exit.

Evidence of my intended theft stuck to my hand. I began stuttering. "T—Tom. I thought you were asleep."

His hips rolled as he walked toward me, a cat stalking a mouse. "Drank it ages ago. You did too. Remember? We were celebrating my promotion to managing director. I kept the bottle because it looked good on the shelf." He shook his head, disappointed or disgusted. "I didn't drink the Pingus though. And I'd been saving that Gaja for a something special."

"I needed to sell them."

"To whom?" He scowled. "Vincent?"

He stopped inches from my perch. His bottom lip pulled above his top teeth. "Do you even know how much those bottles were worth?"

"Vincent gave me eight hundred." A cold sweat broke out on my body like a fever rash. I blamed guilt. I did not fear my husband. "We needed the money."

"To pay what?" The words shot from his mouth and ricocheted off of the high ceiling. "What bill could you possibly pay off with eight hundred bucks? The twelve thousand monthly mortgage, on a house that the bank will take by the end of the year? The last four months of car payments? The maxed-out credit cards with the ten-K limits?"

Thanks to the stepstool, we were eye to eye. His pupils loomed large, reflecting the fridge's blue light, a lightning strike in a dark sky. My lower lids grew heavy with restrained tears.

"Gangs are threatening my parents' lives. They nearly put my father in the hosp—"

"Your parents? Again?" Tom threw up his hands. They landed on his hair and curled into fists. He raked his fingers down his face. "We can't keep a roof over our heads, and you're still sending cash to your parents?"

"They'd been paying off these men, and when I stopped sending money—"

"I don't care about your parents' situation." Tom's hands clasped into a hammer of locked fingers. He beat the air with each point. "Let me explain our situation. We are worse than poor. We don't just have no money, we have negative money." His hands broke apart. A finger hit the center of his forehead, right between his brows. "The debt is up to our fucking eyeballs."

"They were going to kill my dad."

Tom threw his hands into the air. "Ana, I'm not heartless. But there's always some tragedy with those two, and they always make it seem bigger than it is so you will keep them on the gravy train. And that train has long left the station. I can't support them anymore. Babe, I can't even support us. Don't you understand? We are reeling from the biggest financial crisis in a lifetime. Thousands of traders lost their jobs. New jobs are not out there. And even if they were there, they're not open for me. All that risk I took, which was wonderful when the billions rolled in, now, it's this black mark. We are losing our house, our cars—"

"You didn't see the bruises. They had bats."

His hands pulled down his cheeks. A red line followed his fingernails. He'd cut himself. "I am drowning and you keep dragging me further under."

Pity for my husband stabbed at my insides. I cauterized the cuts with anger. This argument wasn't about his struggle to find work. It was about exchanging a bottle of wine for my parents' safety. He was upset because he hadn't drunk it. "So I'm supposed to let you pour thousands of dollars' worth of wine down your throat while my parents suffer?" I shouted. "They're in *real* danger. We can do without wine."

"It's not just—" Tom wiped his hand over his mouth. He shoulders sagged. "We can do without everything, right, Ana? Maybe you can even do without me? It's not like you need my permission."

This time, my sympathy pains stayed sharp. The job loss had been emasculating. And rather than treat him as a spouse worthy of respect, I'd gone behind his back to sell his stuff, as though he didn't matter at all.

I stepped down from the ladder. Once on the ground, he towered over me. But my actions, not my height, made me feel small. I'd betrayed my husband. And why? The alcohol was not the only way to get money for my folks. I worked for a multibillion-dollar hedge fund. Surely I could ask Michael for a salary advance. Selling Tom's liquor had never been my only option.

"I'm sorry." I extended the empty bottle out to him. "I panicked."

He took the Ghost Horse and stepped around me to slide the bottle back into its holster. Without my anger and fear, all I had left was grief: for my parents, for my husband, for me. A sob burned in my throat. I swallowed it with another apology. "I should have talked to you."

Tom looked at me with his oceanic eyes, made bluer by the light of the bar. "When did you stop trusting me?"

"I trust you." The lie echoed in the silence. Obviously, if I still trusted my husband, I would have talked to him about my concerns, not broken into his wine cabinet. I hadn't because I believed losing his job had made him depressed and irresponsible. I hadn't thought he'd make the right decision.

"I'm sorry," I said again.

Tom walked over to a wall. He flipped a switch, shutting off the fridge light. Without it, the room became pitch black. His voice pierced through the darkness. "I don't feel like watching anything anymore. You coming to bed?"

"You still want me to?"

Tom brushed my hand as he passed me out the door. "Ana, we can't afford anything—least of all a grudge."

15

November 25

Ryan stood at the base of the Palace Hotel's twin staircase, waiting for a stranger. Robert Bowen, Esq., would be a thin man with silvered hair and an aquiline nose, according to Fernanda. "He looks like a banker," she'd said, voice hissing through his phone receiver, as though she'd called 9-1-1 from inside a closet.

The stage whisper might have been overkill, given that Michael was still out of the office for an extended Thanksgiving vacation. But Fernanda clearly wasn't taking chances. She'd refused to e-mail him Michael's schedule for the week of August 18, insisting that the firm's IT department would track her actions. Instead, she'd phoned him back from her personal number and read off the relevant week's meetings from Michael's archived calendar.

The only engagement that had stood out was a Tuesday evening dinner with the Illinois Police and Fire Retirement Fund. There'd been a note on that entry: "AB attending." Ana Bacon's initials.

Tracking down the fund's investment team had taken a simple web search. Catching the two-man team was more of a challenge. Bowen and his partner were based in Chicago, according to the fund's administrative assistant. Fortunately for Ryan, Bowen was in the city for the next few days interviewing investment managers. After appealing to Bowen's secretary's desire to help expedite an insurance resolution for a motherless child—as if that were his goal—the woman had squeezed in a meeting before her boss's dinner engagement.

Ryan regretted not asking the secretary for a better description or providing one for himself. Bowen would be looking for *a guy in a black pea coat with brownish hair.* In November, that description fit more than half the male population of Manhattan.

He caught a wave out of the corner of his eye. A man with silver streaks and a long nose with a prominent bump on the bridge sat in the neighboring lobby, gesturing for him to approach. He wore a black suit and orange tie, fitting for the upcoming holiday. A navy top coat dangled over his forearm. He was dressed for dinner—and he did look like a banker.

Ryan limped into the lobby, hand extended. "Thanks for meeting, Robert."

"Of course. Call me Bob." The man gave a firm handshake before settling into one of two velvet chairs positioned cater-cornered to the hotel's reception desk. He draped his coat over the chair's fat arm. "Horrible what happened to that young woman. She seemed very sweet."

Ryan settled into the neighboring seat. The velvet sucked in his bottom, urging him to lie back and stay awhile. Good furniture had a way of forcing relaxation. He made himself perch on the edge of the chair. "I understand that you met Ana during a dinner with Michael Smith."

"Yes." Bob pulled his right leg over his bent left knee and wagged the foot. "A final due diligence meeting."

"What was Ana's role?"

Bowen gave a coy smile. "Guess you'd have to ask Michael. She chimed in with some of the marketing numbers, occasionally."

"Did Michael seem to need that?"

"Well, we'd had all that stuff from prior meetings. We were mostly there to get a sense of Michael in a social setting, have one last conversation before closing the deal." He turned up his palms in a guilty manner. "It didn't hurt having her there. She was attractive and pleasant, you know? Maybe Michael thought she'd make dinner a bit more enjoyable for all of us. Three guys talking shop can get tiring pretty quickly."

"So she was eye candy?"

Bob's nose crinkled like a pug. "I wouldn't put it that way. I think she was there to grease the wheels, kind of. She was quite charming." He smiled as if remembering how nice she'd been. "Shame, really."

"Did she charm Michael?"

Bob's cheeks puffed. He exhaled and glanced around the room. "I don't really want to speculate about who was charming whom. Michael's a married guy. She had a wedding band."

Ryan leaned toward Bob until their knees almost touched. He stared at him, creating uncomfortable intimacy for both of them, trying to encourage Bob to say something to break the tension. "But maybe?"

Bob snorted. "Look, she was attractive, nice personality." His mouth curled in a wry smile. "Maybe Michael seemed a bit possessive of her during dinner."

Ryan raised his eyebrows, asking the question with his face rather than using words. Sometimes, physical signals worked better than outright demands for information.

Bob caught the cue. He rubbed the back of his neck, betraying his discomfort. "I don't really know anything, but he sat pretty close to her all night. And he'd wanted her to stay with him rather than walk us out, which made me think he planned on continuing the party after George and I left."

"Any idea where they would have gone?"

"We'd eaten at L'Ange Treize. I've heard that place has a private after-hours lounge for members." Bob pulled his coat into his lap, a signal their meeting was coming to an end. "But again, I don't know that they stuck around. Could be that Michael had other business to discuss and wanted her to lag behind with him a bit. I don't want to cast any aspersions." He stood and shook open his outerwear. "I should get going. I'm expected across town."

Ryan rose, bracing himself for the obligatory handshake. He really hated all the society-required physical demonstrations of false intimacy. "Thanks for taking the time."

"Of course." Bob slipped on his coat. "Look, I know insurance companies have to do their own due diligence, and I respect that." His friendly face firmed into a serious mask. "Still, I hope you give her daughter whatever life insurance she had. Can't be easy growing up without a mother, and the holidays are coming up."

Ryan hadn't thought much of Sophia during his investigation. Bob's short speech brought back the child's image with painful clarity. A third of Americans grew up without their biological fathers, but a childhood without a mom was far more rare and detrimental. Thanksgiving was tomorrow, and the little girl wouldn't have a mom to prepare a meal. Tom didn't seem like the kind of guy who could roast a turkey or bake the fixings. Maybe *Auntie Eve* would make something?

Ryan felt a newfound sheepishness as he watched Bob leave. If he did his job, Sophia wouldn't have much to be thankful for this holiday, or after.

16

Glasses clinked. A blood-red Syrah sloshed over the edge of Michael's goblet onto a snow-white tablecloth. It didn't matter. We celebrated. My boss had successfully wooed the trustees of the Illinois Police and Fire Department Pension Fund with wine, steak, and the firm's five-year average annual ROI of 12 percent. George and Robert had committed three hundred million dollars to the firm. Everyone felt richer, even me.

I intended to ask Michael for an advance against my salary. Not much, just two hundred dollars, the amount I still needed to get the gangs to stop harassing my parents—at least, for a while. The meeting's success made me feel confident he'd okay it. I'd undoubtedly earned a bonus with my performance: flattering the clients so that they would lower their guard and absorb Michael's pitch, providing relevant statistics from my research, adding levity.

Robert, the thinner of the two men, wouldn't stop grinning at me over his wine glass. George sat far back into his chair, hands folded on a generous belly filled with filet mignon. Talk turned to the Bears and the Cubs. I made a steroid joke, comparing the head size of the rival Cardinals' heavy-hitters to sperm whales. Everyone laughed. Chicagoans love any joke at the Cardinals' expense.

The check came. I glimpsed the $1,200 bill, though Michael barely opened the leather folder to slip in his Visa Black Card.

Spend money to make money. Surely, he would reward my work at year-end with the cost of the waiter's tip. What was a couple hundred dollars, a few months early?

Lanterns in the outdoor garden flickered through casement windows behind us, casting tic-tac-toe shadows on the floor and faces. We stood and shook hands for the umpteenth time. Michael wished everyone goodnight.

As Robert and George headed out, my boss tilted his head toward the table, a subtle motion intended to tell me to remain with him in the restaurant. The mother in me urged my body to follow the pension guys outside. It was nearly ten and I needed to return to my sleeping child and impatient husband. But the daughter in me demanded that I stay and ask for the money.

I stood until our guests exited the dining room and then, taking my cue from Michael, followed him to a row of bookshelves lining a back wall. A server stood in front like a palace guard. Michael nodded. The man slipped a key between two books. The wall slid back to reveal a marble staircase. Michael flashed a naughty grin. His white teeth gleamed like polished porcelain. "Now we can celebrate."

We descended the stairs to a speakeasy worthy of *The Great Gatsby*. Lights, dim as candles, highlighted rows of liquor bottles behind an antique-mirrored bar. Ebony club chairs flanked black-lacquered coffee tables. Onyx stone floors ended in a merlot-colored leather bench, surrounded by floor-to-ceiling wine shelves.

I followed Michael through the empty bar to the wine cove. He sat on the bench and patted the seat beside him.

"I didn't know this was here," I said.

"What would you like to drink?"

The bartender approached. Aside from Michael and me, he was the only person in the room.

Michael grinned. "Red, white? Something else?"

"Oh, I wouldn't know. You pick."

"The Hillside select."

The bartender mimed approval before disappearing behind a wall. The scant lighting created dark shadows in all the room's corners and crannies, hiding the true exits. I felt cast in a spy movie. Michael was Bond. That made me a Bond girl. I much preferred the role to that of nagging wife.

"You were great this evening." Michael fixed me with his stare.

My neck grew hot. I shifted my gaze to my reflection in the shiny table. "No. You did everything. I just tried not to get in the way."

Michael's fingers grazed just below my ear. I tensed at the gesture. He just wanted me to look up, but he'd never made any physical contact before. "Don't sell yourself short. Your charm went a long way this evening."

I could feel the blush creep into my cheeks, an alcohol buzz that started in the gut and spread to the head.

"Robert was smitten," Michael went on. "I thought he might ask you out."

I giggled. The wine at dinner, the hidden bar, Michael's attention: it was all too much.

"And can't say I blame him. You are a gorgeous woman. What man doesn't like the company of a beautiful woman?"

The bartender appeared before I could utter an awkward response. He uncorked the bottle. A long pour landed in the glass. Michael sipped and smacked his lips together.

The bartender filled a third of my goblet and brushed the lip of the bottle with a white cloth.

"Leave it," Michael said.

The bartender gave a curt nod before disappearing a second time. Michael raised his cup. Another compliment would cross the line into overt flirting. This was my boss. My married boss. And I was a married mother, not a Bond girl. I had to get home— but not before I asked for that salary advance. My father's health, if not his life, depended on it.

I preempted his toast with one of my own. "To three hundred million dollars more."

A couple sips and then I would mention the money. Michael wouldn't say no. Two hundred dollars meant nothing to him.

Plus, he could take it out of my salary or withhold a bonus at the end of the year. He knew I wouldn't go anywhere.

Michael took a long sip. "To sealing the deal."

I'd barely set the wine down before he was on top of me. A hand snaked up my inner thigh, pushing the skirt of my black sheath toward my navel. Fingers squeezed my breast like a vice.

I gasped for air, and the opening was all he needed. His tongue invaded before colonizing my ear. I pushed against his chest. "I'm married."

He continued nibbling my jugular. "Me too."

"We can't do this."

"We are doing this." He pressed against me, pinning my body to the bench. The hand on my breast traveled down to my thigh.

"No. I can't."

His pupils seemed to consume his eyes. His fingers dug into my hips as he pulled me into his pelvis. I moaned. The sound was completely involuntary, like a cough or a sneeze, an uncontrolled physical response to an outside stimulant. I hadn't been touched in more than a month. My body didn't understand that the hands groping me belonged to a man other than my husband.

Michael mumbled as his mouth enveloped my neck. "The moment I saw you, I thought, this could be trouble. But you were so smart and sexy. I couldn't not hire you." He licked my collarbone. "Besides, I like trouble."

I slammed my palms against his chest. "Michael, we can't do this. Think of your wife."

"I won't."

"My husband is waiting for me."

"Come on. You think Tom thought of you when he bailed on your daughter the other day and you had to rush out of the office? He's an idiot. What kind of dumbass sells forty million in credit protection against an electronics company with a debt-to-asset ratio of spot sixty-five?"

I blanched at the assessment of Tom's job performance. Did everyone on the street think that? When Tom had complained of a "black mark," I'd assumed he'd exaggerated. Was it really true? Was he permanently unemployable?

My shock enabled Michael to better position himself on top of me. I scooted backward, the leather seat burning my skin. Michael grabbed my calves and pulled me back into him.

"Michael, please. It's late. We've both had too much to drink." I pushed against his torso with all my upper body strength. He barely moved. "*Please.*"

His hands went to his crotch. I heard the fly unzip. "You're my administrative assistant. Now be a good girl and administer some assistance."

I slammed my knee as hard as I could in the direction of his balls. No thought, all instinct. The blow landed. Michael rocked backward, cradling his crotch in both palms.

"Bitch," he screamed.

I rolled off the bench and scrambled to my feet. Somewhere, there was an exit from this dungeon. Where had the bartender gone?

"Fucking tease," Michael yelled. "Don't even think of coming back to work."

I pulled my dress down. "You think this is over? I'm going straight to the cops."

Michael smiled wide, teeth bared. "You think anyone will believe you? They'll think you're just some desperate whore looking for a payout after her husband got his ass handed to him. Everyone will think you saw me as easy money."

He tossed my purse at my feet. The impact knocked open the change container in the front, spilling coins on the floor. Michael laughed.

A pathetic sadness shook my extremities. He was right. People didn't believe in coincidences. It would seem too convenient that Tom and I were broke and a megamillionaire had tried to rape me. Moreover, I didn't have the money to hire a lawyer. What attorney would go up against the big guns on Michael's legal team for a he said–she said sexual assault case, on contingency?

"Fuck you." The words trembled in the air, more of a cry than a curse.

Michael sipped his wine. His face was still red from my blow moments before. "Offer no longer on the table."

A lump formed in my throat. I couldn't break down here. The marble staircase sparkled beneath a chandelier. I stumbled toward it.

Michael called after me. "That's right. Get the fuck out."

*

Headlights cast a spotlight on my double front door. Blackness blanketed the windows. Tom had shut off the exterior lights, a passive-aggressive way to tell me that I wasn't welcome home this late.

My hands still trembled on the steering wheel. I wrapped my fingers around the leather ring until my nails pressed into my palms on the other side. I needed to stop sobbing, control myself, and plan what to tell my husband. I had a last paycheck coming to me. I was entitled to unemployment. Like Tom had said, admin jobs were a dime a dozen. I'd find another.

I pressed the electric garage door opener and watched the wall retract. Nerves squelched the tears in my throat. Would Tom blame me? I'd told him that I needed to work late, but I hadn't provided details. Now I'd have to explain how a client meeting—something outside my job description—had gone so horribly wrong. What if Tom didn't believe I'd even been invited to talk to investors? What if he thought I'd courted Michael's attention and gone out to a romantic dinner?

I parked and then sat inside the garage, staring at the dashboard. The clock read eleven fifteen PM. I'd stayed out too late. If only I'd refused that celebratory drink . . .

I couldn't stay in the car forever, even if I wanted to. I opened the door and stepped out. My legs had fallen asleep. A sadistic acupuncturist jabbed at my thighs as I put weight on them. I planted a palm on the Camry's hood for support and leaned over to open the mudroom door.

I slipped my heels off. My bare feet, sweaty from nerves, squeaked against tile. The powder room door was open on my right. I knew I looked awful, but I couldn't clean up and have Tom hear the faucet running. He might wonder if I washed off someone else's scent.

The railing supported my weight as I ascended the back stairs. I rounded the hall to our bedroom. The house was silent. At least Sophia was asleep.

I slipped through the master bedroom door. Tom sat in our king bed, back pressed against oversized, linen pillows, a large book resting in his lap. A scotch glass sat on the nightstand, cradling a sphere of ice.

I wanted to collapse onto the covers, fold into the crook of my husband's arm, and hide. I wanted Tom to make me feel safe and loved. But I could tell by his lowered brow that he didn't plan on providing any such comfort.

"Working pretty late, huh?"

Though the words were plain, his tone could have sliced stone. I shuddered with the death throes of my adrenaline. Tears tumbled down my cheeks.

Tom jumped from the bed. "What happened?" For the first time in months, he didn't sound angry. Anxiety raised the pitch of his voice.

I couldn't look at him. My long hair covered my face as words bubbled out like boiling water in a saucepan. "My boss invited me to a dinner with this pension fund. He said I'd be helpful in feeding him relevant stats. I thought if I went it could help me get more money . . ."

"What happened?" Tom sounded frantic.

"The guys from the pension fund left, and we were in this private bar." My breath came out in staccato gasps, adding a comma after every word. "And the next thing I knew . . . Michael was forcing himself on me."

I chanced a look at my husband. He stared at the weeping mess before him. It seemed he didn't recognize me. Was he shocked that it had happened or that I had let it happen? I had to get it together.

I wiped beneath my eyes with my fists. "I tried to push Michael away, but he was stronger. No one came to help. I had to knee him in the groin to make him stop. Then he fired me." I attempted a deep breath. Oxygen entered my lungs in painful spurts. "I swear, Tom, I've been over it a hundred ways in my head. I didn't do anything to lead him on. I didn't want this. I only went to the meeting because I thought that if I did a good job, he might consider me for a better-paid marketing role or give me an advance against my bonus. He knew we were married."

Tom's chest rose and fell as though he were running. His neck had turned a raw pink. "Did you go to the cops?"

"No. He said they wouldn't believe me. They'd think I targeted him for money because of our financial difficulties."

Tom paced in front of me. A vein protruded from his forehead. He looked as though someone were strangling him—except for the eyes. They remained focused, furious.

The look reminded me of Michael. My body responded to the similarity. A flight instinct shook my limbs, urging me to run. There was nowhere to go. I slumped onto the ground. "I'm so sorry." I blubbered like a hurt child, not even trying to get it together anymore. "I didn't mean for any of this—I'm so sorry. Please don't be angry. I didn't know . . . I thought I was helping us."

Warm palms cupped my biceps. My husband kneeled in front of me. His lips grazed my forehead. "I should never have let you work for that guy," he said. "He had a reputation."

"I'm sorry. I didn't know. I just thought—"

"Sshhh. Don't apologize. There's no need for you to be sorry." Tom cupped my chin. He looked me straight in the eye. "You're beautiful. And he's a bastard who knows my situation, so he thinks he can just take you from me without repercussion."

My husband's chest muffled my sobs. He stroked my hair. "You did good, baby. You didn't let it happen."

I burrowed deeper beneath his arm. He smelled of sweat and sandalwood. He sounded like the man I'd married, the one who'd promised to honor and protect. Kisses fell on my forehead, my cheeks, and finally, my mouth, each one awakening memories of my humanity. I wasn't flesh, but a mother and a wife. I hadn't deserved this.

My husband scooped me into his arms. I hung on his neck as he carried me to our bed. He laid me on the comforter and pushed my hair away from my tear-stained face. His long fingers slipped beneath me, propping me up just enough to pull the zipper on the back of my dress.

I pulled the fabric over my head and removed my bra, eager to free myself of the clothing that smelled of Michael's cologne, wanting my husband to erase the night's memory with his hands.

"Do you want your pajamas?" he asked, though he didn't move toward the closet. Instead, he stared at my body as though it surprised him.

"No. I want you to come to bed."

He pulled down his boxers, leaving them on the floor as he lay down beside me atop the blanket. His thick palm cupped my side, pulling me close to him. The heat from his body enveloped me. His hand slipped from my waist to my hips and then to my thighs, taking my underwear with them.

He kissed me again, more forcefully this time, leaning his weight into me so that I fell onto my back. Lips traced a line from the center of my neck to between my breasts.

Tom made a possessive kind of love, pulling me into him so there was only space for him to move. I granted him the control, partially because I was too exhausted to wrest it and, mostly, because I feared he would lose interest if I gave any direction. With everything that had happened, he needed to be in charge, at least here.

When he finished, he rolled over onto his side, sweaty and satisfied. I leaned over him and kissed his damp cheek, a thank-you for the intimacy and the trust. "I love you," I said.

He petted my head. "Yeah. I love you, too."

Tom hadn't said those words in a long time. He understood their power. "Love" wasn't a signature at the end of an e-mail. It meant we belonged to each other.

I hid the tips of my fingers in the curled hairs on his chest, trying to make the moment last. It was already slipping through my grasp. My thoughts had turned to tomorrow. Going into work and seeing Michael was out of the question, but there'd be exit paperwork, things to do to collect unemployment. Would HR e-mail the necessary documents? I'd never been fired before. The next steps eluded me. And there was still the problem of my parents needing a grand—two hundred more than I had—not to mention our own financial straits. How long could we squat in our home before the bank repossessed it? Where would we go? We didn't have enough savings to put down a month's rent and a month's security.

"What are we going to do?" I mumbled the question into Tom's chest.

He buried his nose into my hair. "Don't worry," he whispered. "I have a plan."

17

November 26

L'Ange Treize looked like a Brooklyn loft owner had hired a
French decorator. The restaurant's casement windows gave it
an industrial vibe, but the sumptuous décor inside screamed
Versailles. Sunlight reflected off large golden plates gracing a
dozen round tables, each one surrounded by carved, oval-backed
chairs. Most of the seats in the restaurant were empty. The few
guests picked at half-finished entrees. Thanksgiving was not a
popular day for lunch in the city.

Ryan thought of the meal he'd force down later: brown rice
and vegetables out of an undoubtedly white takeout box. Chinese
food: the Thanksgiving dinner of new immigrants and friend-
less bachelors. Leslie and Angie would be celebrating at his former in-laws', waiting for his ex-"dad" to bring the turkey in from
the fryer while his former mother-in-law fussed over how much
sugar to stick in the cranberry sauce. He needed to find time
today to call his kid.

He pushed the thought into his brain's "later" pile and
approached the hostess pulpit. A svelte woman with severe features bowed over an open laptop. Behind her, black velvet curtains framed a massive mural. The painting suggested *The Last
Supper* but was done in an impressionist style with soft colors
and hazy lighting. The faces of the disciples had been swapped in
favor of famous French artists. Monet was Jesus, destined to rise
again. Ryan recognized Renoir, Cezanne, Van Gogh, and Degas

as disciples from their famous self-portraits. Gauguin was close to Jesus, reaching for the bread. He'd been cast as Judas.

An unsmiling young woman looked up from her computer. "Unfortunately, sir, we are not seating now. Lunch has just ended. The kitchen closes at two PM today." Her focus returned to the screen, a visual dismissal.

For the umpteenth time since starting Ana's case, Ryan lamented that the badge inside his wallet had the word "private" emblazoned below the seal. His mouth pinched into an apologetic smile and he tilted his head down, compensating for his lack of authority with acted deference. "Apologies for coming in so late on a holiday. Hoping you could help me."

The ghost of a frown on the woman's face became a full-fledged apparition. "We're closing."

Ryan powered through as though she'd uttered something in a strange language. "I'm an investigator looking into a woman's disappearance." He again avoided the four-letter D-word, as his company had yet to formally acknowledge that fact. "I believe a Mrs. Ana Bacon dined here back on August eighteenth, shortly before she went missing. I want to confirm and speak to any staff who would have waited on her that evening."

The woman's lips pressed together. She stared, perhaps trying to shoo him away by the force of her expression. When he didn't move, she began typing into the computer. "Bacon? Spelled like the food?"

"Yes. On August eighteenth."

Keys clattered before ending in the decisive downbeat of the return key. "I'm afraid that name is not in the system. We keep a record of all reservations. Perhaps she didn't eat here."

"The reservation may have been made under her boss's name. Michael Smith, Derivative Capital."

Fingers flew over the keys, followed by a series of enter slaps. "Yes. Mr. Smith is a frequent guest." Her finger stroked the screen, scrolling down. "It looks like he did join us that evening. Party of four. Table eighteen."

"May I speak with whomever served him?"

The woman's tongue protruded from her mouth. She tucked it back inside, blocking it with pressed lips. "Uh. I don't know if I'm supposed to . . ."

Ryan slipped out his wallet. He flashed his PI badge, keeping it in his hand so she couldn't scrutinize the writing across the metal. "I'd really appreciate the help."

Her shoulders sunk like a kid realizing there was no way out of a homework assignment. She took a visible breath. "I'm pretty sure that Harry works table eighteen on Tuesdays. I don't know that he'd remember someone from three months ago, but I guess it doesn't hurt to ask."

Ryan trailed the girl through the near-empty restaurant and into a galley kitchen of blinding white and steel. The cooks were noticeably absent, though several squat men with rubber gloves bent over large basins of dishes. The hostess led him to a college-age kid, standing in the back of the room beside a linen closet. A crisp, white shirt covered his torso, the sleeves rolled up to show skinny elbows. He was in the midst of unfastening a black apron.

"Harry, this man is an investigator. He wants to know about some woman whom you served last summer."

Ryan limped over to the back of the room. "Do you remember waiting on a Michael Smith and Ana Bacon the night of August eighteenth?"

Harry removed his apron and began folding it. "The guy's name sounds familiar." He glanced at the hostess and simpered. "He's the regular, right? Generous tipper? Always ends up downstairs at the bar . . ."

The girl averted her eyes as she tried to maintain a dour expression.

Ryan ignored their silent exchange. "Mrs. Bacon was the woman who fell off the cruise ship a few months ago. Dark hair, big eyes. Maybe you remember her from TV?"

Harry slipped the now folded garment into the closet before turning back to answer the question. "Oh, yeah. When the story came out, I recognized her."

"How did she seem the night that you waited on her?"

"Nothing stood out. If she'd been crying or something, I'd probably remember." He rubbed his hand over his spiky blond hair, as if dusting off the workday. "She and that Smith guy must have been celebrating. He only comes in here to toast deals over dinner. It's his thing. Then he heads to the private bar below." The server again tried to catch the hostess's eye as he smirked.

"Do you remember if he went to the bar that night? And if Ana went with him?"

He whistled. "That's a tall order. You'd have to ask Jake. He bartends there. I'm back and forth between the tables and the kitchen." Harry shut the closet door. "Jakey was smoking out back a minute ago. Probably still there."

Harry pointed to a back door that must have led to an alley behind the kitchen, probably where the restaurant kept its dumpsters. The hostess folded her hands in front of her belly button. "I hope we've been of help." Her words made it clear that, whether or not she had been, she wouldn't be providing any more aid.

Ryan went through the back door and exited into the seasonally appropriate forty-degree weather. After so many days of cold, it felt like spring. He'd even swapped his pea coat for a thin leather jacket. The dirt-speckled snow had finally melted, leaving the asphalt in the alley looking damp but not dirty. The warmth had a downside, though. It had thawed the garbage, releasing the stink of pasta sauce and old fish from the bins behind the restaurant.

Two men in chef's aprons stood in a cloud of smoke beside another man in black suit pants and a matching button-down. Ryan wanted a cigarette, not to puff but to bum as a way to slip into the group. Smoking excused loitering and idle conversation.

One of the chefs, a large man with that scraggly beard popular with the hipster set, eyed Ryan's jaunty approach. He announced his purpose before sidling up to the big guy. "I'm looking for a Jake. Harry said I could find him out here."

Paul Bunyan in an apron glared at him. Ryan itched to pull the badge from his wallet. He forced himself not to. Just because it had impressed the hostess didn't mean that these guys wouldn't balk at talking to a guy with dime-store identification. "I'm investigating a woman's disappearance."

"Oh?" The bearded man slapped the black-shirted boy on the back. "You got the wrong guy," he laughed. "Jakey don't mess with the ladies. A dude disappears . . ."

The bartender chuckled. "Once they're with me, they don't disappear."

Ryan remained near the door. He didn't want to interview this guy in front of all his joking buddies. Jake walked over like a movie star, head held high, casual body language. His defined arms bulged from a tight black shirt that would have looked Jersey Shore, if not for the guy's slender torso and pop star facial hair. Ryan got the feeling that bartending was what this guy did in between casting auditions. Without wannabe Broadway stars, New York's restaurants wouldn't have employees.

The bartender stopped a few feet from Ryan. "You're here about that woman on the cruise ship, right?" Jake slipped a thin black pipe between his lips and inhaled, waiting for an answer. Ryan watched the e-cig glow. He didn't know if those things were any less dangerous than cigarettes for smokers, but he appreciated the lack of secondhand carcinogens.

"Expecting me?"

"Kind of." Jake inhaled again. "I thought when I saw her on the news that someone might want to know about that night."

Ryan pretended to know what he was talking about. "In the bar."

"Yeah, it was kind of crazy." The guy rubbed his tight beard with the fingers not wrapped around his inhaler. His forearm tattoo flexed into view, a black-and-white image of a guitar, melting in Dali-esque fashion. Above it was French script: *L'amour et la folie.* "Love and madness."

"What exactly happened?"

Jake took another drag on the dog whistle. "Well, nothing that I think I had to report to the police, because, you know, two consenting adults . . . or kind of." His free hand went to the back of his neck. The e-cig dangled from the side of a guilty smile.

"Michael comes to the private bar downstairs every other week or so with a pro. The fancy kind. You know, girls with an escort service who are dressed nice, look like catalog models, so you can't tell right off, but they're too young to be all over some geezer."

"Okay." Ryan's mind raced to figure out where Jake was going with his story. "So Ana was all over him and you thought she was a hooker?"

"No. I mean, she wasn't on him at all. But I thought, given his history, maybe she was new or something and didn't get that they'd be doing their thing down there. So when she started screaming—"

"Screaming?"

Jake removed the e-cig and rotated it between his fingers like a nervous baton twirler. "Shortly after I uncorked the bottle and made myself scarce in the back room, I heard her shouting for him to get off of her."

Statistics flooded Ryan's head. One in every four women was the victim of sexual assault. More than 80 percent of the time, the assailant was someone the victim knew. Sexual assault survivors thought about suicide four times as often as the average person.

"Did you see what happened? You didn't go in?"

Jake rubbed a palm over his face. "Well, I didn't mean to be standing in the storeroom holding my dick while some woman was fighting off date rape or whatever. I just thought at first that she was role-playing. I mean, with Smith, they're always hookers. I didn't realize until I saw the news reports that he'd gone after a married woman."

Jake took a drag off his e-cig. "I think she escaped the worst of it. I heard him yelling about his balls, as though she'd taken the shine off his jewels." He pointed with the device. "You know, you should probably ask for the video of that night."

It was against the law to tape people without their knowledge, but establishments did it all the time. As long as the restaurant posted a sign in some prominent yet easily forgotten place, the police were happy for the security cameras to keep running. One never knew when footage could come in handy. "You guys film the bar? The whole thing or just the entrance?"

"I don't know for sure, but I'm supposed to flash the bottle labels at the corner of the room so they're caught on camera. Gretchen, the manager, would know more. I'm sure she still has a record. She keeps things for like six months in case the members dispute bar tabs or don't remember using the club."

Ryan asked Jake a few more follow-up questions, chief among which was if he would tell his story to the real cops when the time came. The bartender promised he would as he handed over a card with a headshot and e-mail.

Just as Ryan pocketed it, he heard the door open behind him. A woman marched out into the alley. The click of her heels shouted her anger.

"Speak of the devil," Jake muttered. He slunk back as his boss stormed over. She flashed a fake, hospitality smile that belied the venom in her voice. "Is there a problem?"

"Not yet." Ryan faced her. "I need to see a tape of the private bar for the night of August eighteenth."

The woman frowned at her employees. "I don't know what you're talking about."

Ryan tilted his head to the side. Did she really plan to play this game with him? "I think you do. And I don't think a restaurant wants to impede any investigation into a missing person."

The manager's hands hit her hips. She leaned on her back leg and gave him a disdainful look. "Who are you, again?"

"I'm investigating Ana Bacon's disappearance."

"Oh. We're always happy to help the police." Her voice dripped with sarcasm. "May I see your badge?"

The satisfied smile in her eyes told Ryan that she knew he wasn't a real cop. Had his leather jacket and khakis given him away? Many detectives went around in monkey suits all day. Ruined it for every other plainclothes cop.

Ryan pulled out his wallet and flipped back the panel to show the metal. The manager held open her palm. He reluctantly held the badge close enough for her to scan the letters.

"You're a private investigator?" Her tone went up at the end, but her expression was triumphant. She wasn't asking.

"I'm with Mrs. Bacon's insurance company."

She looked down her snub nose at him. "Any footage of our guests is taken with their permission for the express purpose of verifying use and consumption of private bar amenities, not for sharing with outside companies."

"A woman is missing."

She feigned concern. "Certainly, if anything we have is pertinent to your investigation, you can come back with a warrant and we'll be happy to assist you. Until then . . ." Her lips pursed, conveying the same message as a raised middle finger. She stared him down for a moment and then called each member of the staff by name, as though shouting for dogs to get back in the house.

"Don't get rid of anything," Ryan warned. "I'll be back with my friends at the NYPD. You don't want to face an obstruction charge."

She nodded, as though patronizing a child. "Well, as I said, till then." She followed her employees back into the restaurant. Ryan heard the door lock.

He exchanged his damn-near-useless badge for the phone in his jacket pocket and hit number two on speed dial. Vivienne Wu answered on the third ring. "Monahan! How's my favorite PI?"

"You don't know any other PIs, Wu."

"Touché. How about this one? How's my favorite ex-partner?"

"Good. But I need your help—and your badge."

18

The insurance agent didn't have a clue. Mr. William Murray stifled a smile as his eyes climbed the spiral staircase to the left of our foyer and then traveled up the taupe wall to the double height ceiling and the hand-carved, wooden chandelier lording over the entrance. I'd designed the whole house to have an understated elegance, like a beautiful, wealthy woman relaxing at home in worn designer jeans and a silk tank. Not intimidating. Still rich.

My deliberate choices were not lost on our visitor. Dollar signs seemed to sparkle in his brown irises as I led him through the kitchen, past Sophia watching *Sesame Street* on the family room television, and up the back stairs to the office. I'd terminated the daycare that morning with a voicemail. No need racking up more debts that we couldn't afford.

William had a young face and dimpled chin beneath a prematurely balding scalp. He looked earnest. Honest. A fat bumblebee unknowingly caught in a glistening spider web. I was the reluctant black widow.

Defrauding an insurance company was wrong, but I'd run out of right options. We hadn't paid the mortgage in months. My salary had covered the minimum payments on our credit cards, but I couldn't charge anything more on them, and now we would default on everything. The bank was already threatening to put the house into foreclosure. The couple thousand left in our checking account wouldn't pay motels for long, and it would be difficult to rent anywhere with our credit shot to hell. It could take months for me to land another job, assuming Michael didn't trash me to other fund managers. And once I was employed, creditors could garnish up to 25 percent of my wages, making it nearly impossible to support my family. On top of all that, my dad's health, if not his life, depended on getting two hundred more dollars before the end of the month.

As Tom said, robbing an insurance company was a near victimless crime. Insurers were like buildings in San Francisco, built to withstand systemic shocks. A five-million-dollar loss wouldn't even register on their Richter scale. And he knew ISI would pay. They'd delivered on his parents' policy after their car crash.

I led William to the office. It sat above the garage like a trilby hat. Beams connected in sharp peaks at the ceiling. Drywall wrapped the corners, adding feltlike softness to the room's sides.

Tom lounged on a charcoal chesterfield beneath a large skylight. Rain pattered on the glass above, adding a film noir soundtrack to the gray-lit setting.

My husband had donned suit pants and a button-down for the meeting, as if planning to head to the office later. His shirt collar lay undone, creating a triangle that pointed to his defined chest and svelte torso. He looked like the kind of man that played recreational softball and jogged on the weekends, a man with a resting heart rate in the low fifties, no history of diabetes, and plenty of disposable income. An insurer's dream.

Tom motioned to a plush armchair on the opposite side of a low, wooden coffee table. "Thanks for seeing us on such short notice." He flashed one of his Wall Street smiles.

William leaned over the table to shake my husband's hand. A business card emerged in his fingers like an ace up his sleeve. He handed it to my husband and settled into the offered seat, dropping several inches lower than Tom's perch on the firm sofa.

"Not a problem." William joined in Tom's conspiratorial smile. "Happy that you called."

I sat beside Tom, erect and silent. The model wife of a politician, ready with my *Yes, dears* and agreeable head bobs.

"Here we are planning a short vacay, first one without our daughter, and I realize we don't have life insurance." Tom bit his bottom lip and shook his head, as if shocked by our oversight. "I mean, we should have gotten a policy years ago, but we definitely can't both get on a plane without any protection."

William folded his hands on his knee. "Accidents are rare. But you're right. They happen. It's certainly wise to have something in place in case of—"

"You don't have to sell me." Tom squeezed my hand. He leaned forward, as if readying a confession. "My parents died in a car accident. If they hadn't had their insurance policy, I would have lost everything. I still feel foolish that I exposed Sophia and my wife to such a risk."

William nodded like numbers rolling in a slot machine. He opened the satchel resting beside his chair.

I patted Tom's knee. Though I knew he was playing a part for the insurance agent, discussing his parents' death had to hurt. He still rarely talked about the crash that claimed their lives, even with me. And he'd never put up anything of theirs in the house, though I knew he had a locked box from his father in his closet.

I felt the need to defend my husband from his own criticism. "Well, it's easy to not think about death, especially in your thirties. I mean, how many people die so young?"

"You'd be surprised." William pulled several folders from his bag and placed them on the coffee table. Each boasted pictures of young couples holding the hands of toddlers. Clever marketing.

"Cancer, motor vehicle accidents, plane crashes, terrorism." William rattled off the leading causes of untimely demise as though he'd pressed play on a tape recorder lodged in his throat. "Thirtysomethings don't die of old age, but there are risks that you need to protect your family from."

Fear mongering: the go-to sales tactic of insurance salesmen and television journalists. Perhaps William wasn't as naïve as he seemed. Good. His attitude lessened my guilt.

"I agree." Tom released my hand and picked up a folder. "That's why I think both my wife and I should take out five million of protection each."

A smile wrinkled at the edge of William's firm expression. He folded it back inside like straightening a piece of paper. "Well, we certainly can offer that kind of protection if you fall in a low-risk category, which you both should." William opened a folder with the company name, Insurance Strategy and Investment. He withdrew a stack of papers. "We would need medical histories, of course, and some family records: parents' health, that kind of thing. But given your ages, I don't foresee any problems. I would recommend a whole life policy. The premiums are higher but you can—"

"No offense, but I think a hedge fund can do a bit better investing the money than the average insurance company. Fewer restrictions." Tom sat back and draped his arm over my shoulders. "My wife and I are really seeking coverage for the unthinkable. I know from my parents that you can't be too careful."

William swallowed the rest of his spiel. He opened another folder and withdrew a smaller stack of documents. He flipped through and pointed to a chart in the center of a page, outlined in blue. "Here is a premium schedule for your age group. This should give you an idea of the payments required to secure coverage."

Five-million-dollar policies weren't in the chart. However, the document did list the cost of a million-dollar policy: $41.80 per month for the average thirty-five-year-old nonsmoker with no known health problems. Tom fit that bill. I rounded my thirty-one years down to the thirty-year-old age bracket: $37 a month.

Five million, multiply by five. About $210 per month for Tom. Another $185 monthly for me. Nearly $400 a month. It would take the last of our savings and ignoring the credit cards and collection notices, but we could swing that for a few months. I had my last check coming from work, and unemployment would kick in—as soon as I got the courage to call human resources and request the paperwork.

The cost would be easier to cover if we didn't need to also pay my policy. But Tom thought buying insurance for only one of us looked too suspicious. After he faked his death, people would ask questions. We needed to make it seem as though we'd both simply done the responsible thing and taken out protection.

Tom glanced at the payment schedule with the same lack of scrutiny that he'd once used for restaurant bills. No need to quibble over a few dollars when you had an endless amount of them. "We really think five is the appropriate number. If anything happened to me, I'd hate for my wife to lose the house or have to live in a radically different style."

"Of course." William pulled out more documents and a pen from his bag. He set them on the coffee table.

"And we would need to have the same policy on my wife. If anything happened to her, there are childcare costs to consider." A wistful smile peeled back his cheeks. "Plus, I don't know what kind of state her death would leave me in. I'd need time to grieve. I doubt I'd be able to return to work, at least not for a while."

William's head bobbed along to Tom's explanation. He waited a beat before gesturing to the documents on the coffee table and beginning his line-by-line breakdown. I tried not to look nervous as we filled out the forms, signing where William said to and answering his questions. *Yes, both my parents are alive. No, I've never had any health problems. No, I'm not on any medications.* I'd stopped birth control several months earlier. Not much point paying twenty-five dollars a month for antipregnancy meds when you practiced forced abstinence. We had unintentionally rolled the dice last night.

As I spoke, I probed the plan that Tom had outlined the night before. He intended to fake a car robbery gone wrong. He would drive through a rough area in Jersey City, after "getting lost" on his way back from a meeting with his recruiter in Manhattan. He'd leave the Maserati, unlocked, beside the Hudson River beneath an underpass, near a particularly notorious housing project. He'd wipe blood on the seat from a superficial, self-inflicted wound and "butt-dial" my voicemail, screaming,

"You can have the car! Just get that gun out of my face." Then he'd disappear, presumably shot and pitched into the river by his assailants.

In reality, he'd buy a bus ticket, cash, to Florida. He'd lay low for a few months in a roadside motel somewhere. After the policy paid off, Sophia and I would fly down to Miami to pick him up and then charter a sailboat to Brazil. Tom was sure that five million dollars would give us access to all kinds of travel perks, including a no-document-required entry at a South American port and fake passports. It couldn't be that hard to sneak into Brazil, he'd said. After all, rafts of undocumented immigrants washed up on Miami's shores all the time. My parents had sneaked into the United States three times and stayed for more than twelve years. Surely getting into Brazil would prove easier.

His scheme was far from foolproof, but it was something. There were details to work out, but first, we needed to secure the insurance policy.

"And what's the contestability period?" The question in Tom's voice broke my train of thought. My husband had a concern about something. I leaned over his shoulder and scanned the text for whatever had grabbed his attention.

"Oh, that's standard," William said. "If something happens within the first two years, the insurance company will investigate the claim. If it finds any misrepresentations, the company can refuse to pay."

"What would constitute a misrepresentation?"

William's eyebrows raised. "Well, if, for example, you had a medical condition that you didn't disclose or a family history of some problem. But since neither of you are even on medication, I'm sure—"

Tom cleared his throat. "Manic depression."

"I'm sorry?" For the first time since entering our home, William looked uncomfortable. He shifted in his seat, trying to lean forward on our sinkhole of an easy chair.

"My father was diagnosed with the condition." Tom scratched his head. A tight smile formed on his face, a fence barring his emotions. "He was kind of an emotional guy. Not sad so much as angry."

I'd never heard my husband describe his father in anything less than favorable terms, though he didn't talk about his parents often. Tom said that life before his folks' accident had become fuzzy. He remembered his mom as doting and involved with his school. His father had always worked and, occasionally, threw the football around. He had a standout memory of a visit to the zoo. And, like me, he remembered every detail of the day things fell apart: the policemen, the accident report, the crushing absence.

William's Adam's apple bobbed. "Usually, family mental health history won't result in a denial unless there's a history of suicide. The company will likely require an additional health evaluation."

Tom leaned back into the chair. "That shouldn't be a problem."

I relaxed along with my husband's body language. If Tom didn't see any more reason for concern, then no need to worry.

"I assume you want each other as the policy beneficiaries?"

"No. Sophia will be the beneficiary of both policies." Tom's voice took on a cement quality.

"I have to caution you that things can get more difficult when a child is a beneficiary," William said. "The money would then need to go to a policy custodian until she comes of age, and sometimes other family members contest the custodian. It's easier to just pick an adult you trust to spend the policy on your daughter's behalf."

Tom cleared his throat. "No. I want it clear that the policy goes to Sophia. My wife and I should each be the custodian in the event of the other's passing. But Sophia will be the beneficiary."

William looked down at his paperwork like a chastised child. We'd gone against his advice, but I knew why. We had debt, more than a million on the house alone, and tens of thousands on the credit cards. If the policy went to me, I might have to use it to pay off mutual creditors. If the money belonged to Sophia, I could declare bankruptcy and retain the entire policy, defrauding my creditors as well as the insurance company. I swallowed my guilt. In for a penny, in for a pound.

"Okay." William scrawled some notes on the document pad in his lap. "Who would you like to be the custodian in the event an accident claims both your lives?"

Confusion spread across Tom's face. I jumped in with the answer. "My parents. They're in Brazil, but they would make sure Sophia is loved." Unlike when my husband spoke, William didn't write anything down. He looked to the man in the relationship.

Tom frowned. "Do we have to have a secondary?"

"Otherwise the court could appoint someone."

My husband didn't say anything. I was surprised that this was even a debate. Sure, Tom had never been comfortable with my parents' dependence on us. But they were good people and they loved their granddaughter, even if they only saw her during weekly Skype calls.

"Tom, there's no one else."

"They're not U.S. citizens," he said.

William came to my rescue. "That should be fine. Because Sophia is the beneficiary, there shouldn't be any issues with international tax laws."

My husband's eyes rolled. "Fine. Beatriz and Luis Santos."

William finally wrote something down. He scanned the document for blank fields. "And who is your secondary beneficiary?"

"We only have one child," I said.

William cleared his throat. "Obviously, the chances are exceedingly low, but, in the rare event that Sophia could not accept the funds because, say, she perished with one of you in a plane crash or car accident, who would you like to receive the benefit?"

"I guess that I should be the secondary on Ana's and she can be the secondary on mine," Tom answered.

William started to write. I didn't care about being Tom's secondary. If my daughter and husband were dead, how would I go on living? But Tom would go on. He'd survived the death of his parents. He would remarry, cutting ties to my "difficult" family.

Without support, they'd end up dead in Brazil while Tom's new wife spent my death benefit.

"Excuse me, William," I said. "I would like my parents listed as secondary beneficiaries on my policy and, come to think of it, I'd like them to also get a bit of my policy. Not much. Maybe a hundred thousand?"

Tom shot me a look out of the corner of his eye. He grumbled my name.

"If I died, you wouldn't even talk to my folks. I'd want them taken care of."

Tom sighed. "Even in death, they'd be on the payroll, huh?"

"My death, my payroll," I quipped.

"Fine." His eyes rolled, again. "Put it down."

"Mommy?" Sophia yelled from downstairs. She needed something.

"I'll just check—"

Tom patted my back. "I think we're all done with your part. I'll take it from here."

19

Ryan watched Vivienne Wu eat, trying to remain focused on the task at hand. His former partner could have been a perfume model. She had flawless skin and features that drew a man in like an intoxicating scent. She also had a badass brain that could write algorithms capable of identifying irregularities in financial transactions and, unfortunately for him, a handsome husband poised to sell his second tech start-up.

She sat across from him at an indoor picnic table, mouth wrapped around a barbeque chicken sandwich, chin bobbing at the appropriate points as he brought her up to speed on Ana's case and why they were in a barbeque restaurant crawling with men in suits protected by paper bibs.

"Wait, so who's Jake?" she asked, swallowing a bite.

Ryan set down his iced tea. He wanted a beer. It was past noon, but he couldn't have his next conversation with alcohol on his breath. "Jake is the bartender from the restaurant."

"All right. I'm with you again."

"So this Jake guy tells me that Ana's boss assaulted her in the private bar and there's a tape, but the restaurant won't give it to me without a warrant."

"Fuck that. Just let me have a talk with the manager, rattle off a bunch of possible charges for not cooperating, mention all our friends at the IRS. Most eateries pay half the kitchen under the table."

Vivienne took another bite of her sandwich. Her elbows rested on the table. The restaurant made up for the locale with the best barbeque in the city, and it encouraged customers to shun standard manners. Ryan loved the way his partner thumbed her nose at conventions. Beautiful and smart, still swore like a sailor. It made her real.

"Anyway, your girl threatens to tell on Michael, that's motive," Vivienne said.

Ryan blinked as though his former partner had slapped him. Michael. Of course! The man had multiple reasons to want Ana dead. Hedge funds relied on the reputation of their chief investment officer. If it had gotten out that Michael had attacked an employee, Derivative Capital could have lost clients and many millions. Plus, Michael had to have feared his wife's reaction and the loss of his personal wealth in a divorce. Not to mention, the guy was an egotistical prick used to paying women to do what he wanted and his secretary had rejected him. Such things sent sociopaths over the edge.

"A hell of a motive." He slurped his drink, washing down the pulled pork he'd inhaled moments before. After swallowing, he cursed himself under his breath. Why hadn't he demanded Michael's alibi during the first interview? He'd been chasing the suicide theory because it was the one that benefitted his company most, and it had blinded him to the suspect right in front of his face.

"A hell of a motive," he repeated.

"Especially if Ana tried to blackmail him," Vivienne added.

"Given the Bacons' apparent financial difficulties, it wouldn't be out of the question. She needed money. He'd mentioned giving her severance."

"I can try to get permission to check his accounts. See if he was withdrawing regular sums to pay her off or if he took out the two-hundred K for the deposit on a hit."

Ryan looked down. He'd missed the murder connection, and now he couldn't even follow up properly thanks to his PI status. "I'd appreciate it, since I no longer have the access."

She chewed. "You miss it?"

Ryan took a long sip of tea and tried to shake his guilt. "I don't miss meth-heads damn near shooting my balls off."

A pained look pinched his partner's face. She set down the sandwich. "I should have gone with you. I'm sorry."

"It was the post office."

"Yeah. I'm quicker on the trigger than you, though."

Ryan rubbed his thigh. The talk of that day intensified the constant throb in the muscle.

"You need to factor crazy into your statistical models," she smiled to soften the criticism. "You think people are rational. We're all just balls of emotion, justifying rash decisions."

He kneaded the muscle through his pants. "Not me."

"I know." Vivienne's face grew suddenly serious. "You know, one thing bothers me. If Michael has so much money, why not just give Ana a lump sum big enough to guarantee her silence for a while? Has to be easier than hiring someone."

Ryan was relieved to get back to the case. "He could have figured Ana would keep returning to the well until her husband got back on his feet, which, according to Michael, wouldn't have been any time soon. And she was pregnant. We won't know until we see the video, but if Michael raped her, the baby might have been his. A baby certainly makes it difficult to tell the wife that nothing happened."

Vivienne reclaimed her lunch. She eyed the remaining quarter of the sandwich with disappointment, as though it had challenged her to finish it and won. "So we're heading to the restaurant."

Ryan grabbed his cell. Vivienne's theory had readjusted his priorities. "Soon. First, we need to see Michael's secretary."

✶

Ryan loitered outside the glass tower housing Derivative Capital and other firms aspiring to become it, waiting for Fernanda to emerge. As it was, folks were eying the man in the leather jacket leaning against the side of the skyscraper. A large security guard had taken a particular interest. The man glowered at him from beside the building's revolving door, as if trying to determine whether he had explosives packed into his pants pockets.

No one eyed Vivienne, though a few men turned to look at her. She didn't acknowledge the attention. For someone like her, the stares of men had to be like sunrays: something that happened in daylight and not worth noticing unless overly hot or oppressive. He wondered whether she'd ever caught him looking.

The revolving door rotated. Fernanda exited the building doing her best impression of an incognito celebrity: full-length black coat, wide brimmed hat, black sunglasses. She stood out for trying not to stand out. Her head moved right and then left, looking for him. He didn't wave. She'd freak. He was obvious enough anyway.

Apparently, she spotted him. She nearly brushed him with her shoulder as she strode ahead. He followed her around the corner of the building and down the block, losing ground thanks to his limp. Vivienne kept better pace, but Fernanda didn't realize the woman was also following her.

Fernanda ducked into a cupcake shop across the street just as Ryan reached the intersection. Vivienne waited for him to cross.

Ryan found Fernanda seated in the back of the shop, head buried in the steam rising from a coffee mug. A box of minicupcakes sat on the table. She'd removed the shades. The gray hat remained, pulled low over her brow as though she was the monochrome version of Carmen Sandiego.

He slipped into a chair across from her. The scent of the shop warmed his insides. It smelled of sugar cookies and hot butter. Fernanda gestured to a box of minicupcakes. "Michael's kids like these. If I bring back a box along with his Starbucks order, he'll think I took the extra time to be thoughtful."

"He's back?"

"Yeah. But not to see you," she said. "At least, not today. It will be too obvious that I talked to you."

Ryan nodded agreement and waved Vivienne over from her post, hovering behind the line of baked-goods buyers. "I want you to meet someone."

Vivienne took his signal and walked to the bench beside him. Fernanda glared at his female companion. "You didn't say there'd be anyone else."

"My partner, Vivienne," Ryan explained. He caught Vivienne smile out of the corner of his eye. "She's with the NYPD."

Fernanda gave a curt nod and turned toward Ryan. "NYPD." She paused between each letter, letting her anger ring out. "You were supposed to ask Michael questions about sleeping with his employees to scare him straight, not freaking get the NYPD involved. If he's arrested, I'm out of a job."

Vivienne answered for him. "We're trying to get to the bottom of a young mom's disappearance. And from where I'm sitting, your boss looks as though he might have had a hand in it. I'd be worried about your safety, not your job."

"My job is my financial security. That is safety." Fernanda turned back to Ryan and gave him a conspiratorial eye roll, as though he, too, should be annoyed. She pushed a couple folded sheets of paper across the table. "You asked what Michael was up to the week Ana was on the cruise. Here you go."

She grabbed the box of cupcakes. "If you get anything on him, I didn't help."

Fernanda hurried out of the shop. Ryan didn't watch her go. The papers in front of him consumed his attention. The first was a printed screenshot of Michael's August calendar. Fernanda had highlighted a row of dates in yellow. *August 28 through 31: "Michael Away."* He'd gone on a vacation the week that Ana was on the cruise.

Ryan handed Vivienne the first page, exposing the one behind it. It was a printed JPEG of an e-mail receipt for something called "luggage forward." Michael had sent his bags to a Miami cruise terminal. The baggage receipt had a ship number and four accompanying words: "Final Destination: Grand Bahama."

Just like Ana.

20

August 22

The letter from the insurance company puffed from the mailbox, blocking the bronze tin from closing. Its thickness obscured the handful of postcard-sized late-payment notices, which I knew the postman had dropped off along with the adjuster's decision. Pretty soon, our creditors would stop mailing and start sending collectors.

I pulled out an ISI package addressed to me and then sifted through the remaining white envelopes for something similar addressed to my husband. Only one other piece of mail bore the insurance company's elaborate stamp. Tom's envelope was a standard A7 size, hardly big enough to hold more than a folded sheet of paper. Could the company have put both our policies in the large package and sent supplemental documents in a letter? Why address one to me and one to Tom?

I sifted through the rest of the mail as I reentered the house. PSE&G had sent a "notice of discontinuance." I hadn't paid the electric bill for the last couple of months, though I had long stopped air conditioning the house. I'd have to send them something or else they'd shut off the power.

"Tom," I shouted up the back stairs. "The insurance letters are here."

Sophia's head popped up from her seat at the kitchen table. She looked around for her father and then, not seeing him, returned to coloring in a well-worn workbook. She'd done the page before. Now she filled in purple over the panda bear's white belly.

I scratched her head as I dumped the mail on the table. "No black and white?"

"Purple is prettier."

"It's purplicious." I quoted the second book in her favorite series. Pinkalicious. Purplicious. Silverlicious. Adding "licious" to the end of any word made it sound sweet. I smiled to myself. We have mail. It's fraudulicious.

My husband thumped up the basement stairs. He wiped sweat off of his forehead. He must have been working out. The basement always remained at a cool seventy-something, regardless of whether we ran the air.

Tom scanned for the mail. "Already?" he asked.

I pointed to the stack beside Sophia's workbook. A greedy smile crept onto my husband's face. He ripped open the thick envelope like a dog tearing at a package of rawhide and began devouring the documents.

It had taken just two business days for the policies to issue. Tom had requested an expedited decision due to our "impending vacation." He'd talked so much about a trip that we'd probably have to book something and cancel it before the charge hit.

"There it is, babe." He slapped the stack of papers with the back of his hand. "Five million on you for the low, low price of a hundred and eighty-five bucks."

Sophia laughed, trying to get in on whatever joke had filled her father with so much glee. "Why you happy, Daddy?"

He patted the top of her head. "Because things are looking up."

What a way to characterize an impending fake death. Sophia would not see the bright side of Daddy's disappearance, even if I told her the secret that he was really in Florida, waiting for us.

Tom continued to examine the policy, pacing as he flipped pages. His smile grew with each line of digested text. My stomach turned. I took a seat beside Sophia.

"Now I just have to make sure that we don't do anything they can argue is negligent. No alcohol, nothing at dinner." He muttered to himself, already thinking about parts of his scheme that I wasn't privy to.

"Does it say anything about you in there?" I asked.

Tom turned back a page. "Nope. That would be in my policy. I'm sure they're identical."

"There was only the one thick envelope."

"Mine will get here tomorrow then." Tom still didn't look up.

"You got a thin envelope."

His forehead became crosshatched. I picked up the mail addressed to him and held it out. My policy landed on the table. He claimed the envelope between my fingertips and withdrew the contents: a single letter.

The smile on his face remained, but his eyes changed. They became fearful. Frantic. "This can't be right."

He'd been denied. My stomach fluttered with the twisted offspring of dread and relief. If Tom couldn't fake his death, we couldn't become criminals. But without that money, what would we do? What would my parents do? I'd wired the eight hundred to my folks, but the gangs might not accept it. They might still punish them for not having the full payment or demand more interest.

"They denied your policy." My voice squeaked as I stated the obvious.

"It doesn't make sense. They said my family has a history of suicide."

"Does it?"

"I don't . . . I . . ." The letter fell to the table. He clasped the back of his neck, as though trying to keep his head up. "I don't know what they're talking about."

"Do you think you can get them to change their mind?"

"They'd just refuse payment later by arguing that I'd killed myself."

I exhaled: part relief, part staving off tears. "Well, it's probably for the best."

Tom grabbed the back of a kitchen chair. His whole body vibrated as though an electric current ran down his back. His legs gave way as he pulled out the seat. He landed on his knees. My husband, former master of the universe, on his knees.

I abandoned my chair to crouch beside him. "It will be okay. We'll get through this."

"I can't believe they denied me."

"It wasn't the best plan, anyway. I'll get another job. We'll move." I was the cheerleader of a football team down fourteen to thirty-five in the fourth quarter. Anyone could hear that I tried to convince myself as much as I did Tom. I'd never rooted for the underdog.

"They didn't cover me." Tom gestured toward the documents on the table. "How could they not cover me? And they covered you."

The words rang in the air like a preacher calling for the choir's response. The insurance company had given me the policy denied to my husband. My life was worth five million dollars. My "death" could save my family. Can I get a Hail Mary?

Sophia stared at her father as though he'd morphed into a monster. "Daddy?"

Her voice triggered something in him. Tom rose from the floor, face suddenly stoic. He began walking from the room, stiff, expressionless, a man about to face a firing squad. For the second time in a month, I feared my husband could hurt himself. His inability to provide was killing him. If he couldn't fix it—if we couldn't fix it—he wouldn't have the strength to go on.

Sophia sensed the change in his behavior. She flung herself on his leg. "Daddy, don't go," she yelled.

He kept walking, powering through her grip on his leg as though he had a purpose that heaven or hell couldn't pull him from. If I didn't do something, my daughter wouldn't have a father. I wouldn't have a husband.

"I'll do it," I said.

The words stopped Tom's death march from the house. "I can't let you. I'll . . ." His body shuddered, an engine sputtering on empty.

"I can do it. We'll cash in my policy."

"How?" He croaked the question. "You don't drive the Maserati. It's stick."

"I'll think of something."

Tom bent to pick up Sophia from around his calves. He held her close against his chest and buried his face in her hair. His shoulders shook. He walked toward me and placed our daughter at my feet. "Thank you," he whispered.

The words didn't convey his gratitude as much as they expressed his faith in me. My husband believed I could pull this off. He thought his administrative assistant wife was capable of tricking a major corporation out of millions of dollars. He trusted that I could save our family.

So I would. Somehow, I'd fake my death—or die trying.

*

The idea came to me in the pool, somewhere between lap ten and lap fifteen. We would take that vacation. Nothing fancy. A weekend jaunt to the Bahamas on a cruise ship departing from Port of Miami, the extreme budget version of the trip I'd recently booked for Michael and his wife. Tom and I would get a nice ocean-view room. We'd swim. Sunbathe. Snorkel in the Caribbean Sea. And on the last evening, soon after the boat departed Grand Bahama Island, just as it passed the smaller landmasses on the map between the Bahamas' main port and Miami Beach, I would fall overboard.

I laid out my idea while in bed with Tom, discussing it as though I were outlining the itinerary of any normal vacation. We would leave within the month, taking advantage of off-season, $99-round-trip specials from New York to Miami. Ships left on short trips to the Bahamas every day. We would book the cheapest one with an ocean-view balcony on the lowest possible floor. During the cruise, I would complain of motion sickness to anyone willing to listen. Then, on the return trip, I would pretend to vomit over the side of the boat and dive into the ocean.

I'd expected Tom to protest my plan, or at least demand more details. Instead, he seized onto my half-cocked mission like a drowning man would clutch a life raft. Within minutes of sharing the scheme, he was chiming in with ways he could play the grieving spouse. He would leave the room to establish an alibi when I fell and then return a half an hour later, giving the boat plenty of time to leave the scene of my "accident." By the time he alerted the crew that I was missing, I'd be halfway back to the Bahamas.

"It's perfect," Tom said, cupping my cheeks in each palm. "You are a genius."

I felt more like a lunatic. I was a very good swimmer, surely good enough to freestyle a few miles. But this trek could be as many as ten miles in the ocean, not a pool in my backyard where every lap ended with a push against the wall.

"Who will watch Sophia?" I asked.

"Can't she come?"

I tried to hide my annoyance. "You don't think it will be traumatic for her to be there while you're screaming that I went overboard to my death?"

Tom rubbed his forehead. "Of course. You're right. We'll get a sitter."

"We can't afford—"

"I have a cousin, Eve."

Tom had never mentioned any family other than an estranged aunt in Maine. Then again, Tom never spoke about his family. His parents' accident and the lonely years afterward had made it too painful a topic.

"She's a lot younger," Tom volunteered. "I knew her as a kid. She lives in New York, must be twenty-two now. I'll reach out."

"Does she even know you?"

"Well enough. She used to idolize me, and she'll probably be happy to spend some time in a nice house with her niece versus a cramped apartment."

"Is she good with kids?"

Tom looked up at the ceiling. "I don't know. Beggars can't be choosers, babe. I'm sure she'll keep Sophia safe. She's family."

Family that I'd never heard of. Family that didn't have any experience with children. I might be willing to jump off a moving cruise ship, but I couldn't just dump my kid with some girl because Tom had known her as a kid.

"I'll introduce you both beforehand. It will be fine." Tom pecked me on the forehead before turning on his side and shutting off the overhead reading lamp.

He had no problem sleeping. My idea had made him more relaxed than I'd seen in months. Within ten minutes, he was snoring. After a restless hour, I left him with his mouth half-open and descended the stairs to the den.

The room huddled between the formal entrance and the staircase, a family pet waiting to greet and intimidate whoever entered the house. Two tufted blue chairs sat in front of built-in bookcases, stocked with college texts and tomes purchased for the color of their covers rather than their content. A zinc-plated writing desk loomed beneath a large window, a masculine gray touch amid the feminine French décor.

Tom's laptop rested on the desk. I settled into the antique captain's chair beside it and opened the computer. I searched "Bahamas maps." The third link showed the Bahamas archipelago, broken and scattered into nearly two dozen pebbles. Red lines traversed between the Miami coast and the islands like air traffic control flight patterns. The map belonged to a cruise company. The lines were ship routes.

Grand Bahamas port lay 106 miles off Miami's sprawling coast, a pinpoint beside a long wavy line of U.S. soil. The Bimini Islands dotted halfway between both landmasses, buoys scattered between the two beaches. I pressed my thumb to the map. The sliver of white on my stubby nail more than covered the distance between the red line and Bimini. I wouldn't need to swim long from the boat to the smaller islands. Maybe three hours. The Caribbean Sea would be bath temperature this time of year. I could do it. Maybe.

The map made me realize a major hurdle in my plan. White, swirling lines curled around Grand Bahama Island before exiting out to the Atlantic Ocean. They indicated the Gulf Stream current. If I fell between the lines, I'd be carried away, up the U.S. coast and out into the vast blue separating the continents. I'd have to plan my dive precisely as the boat passed Bimini's east coast, before it crossed the current's path.

Cruise ships were slow. Michael had told me once that they only traveled about twenty-five miles per hour. It was why he didn't get seasick on big boats and I couldn't book him on anything smaller than an ocean liner. Judging from the map, I'd need to jump about an hour after we set sail to miss the current and be within five to ten miles of the nearest island.

The swim had other obstacles not depicted on the map. The return trip would be in the evening. I'd be in the water at dusk, prime shark hunting hour. I'd also have to survive the "fall" over the ship's railing without debilitating or bloody, predator-attracting injuries.

I searched for "safe fall distance into water." Links hinted at the answers. At about thirteen stories, the water's surface became akin to cement. Below that height, odds of survival greatly improved. Extreme-sports enthusiasts regularly dove from about four stories, or forty feet, without suffering a scratch. To be safe, I'd need to make sure my balcony was no more than four flights up.

Footsteps plodded down the stairs. Tom appeared in the open entrance to the room. Hair stuck to the right side of his forehead. "Hey, why are you up?"

I typed in a new search: Cheap cruise fares, ocean view. "Research."

Tom flew to the computer. He slammed down the top, nearly trapping my hands between the screen and the keyboard. "Are you nuts? Not on my laptop. What if the police search it? They'll see—What did you even look up?"

"Nothing. A map of the Bahamas. Cruise ships."

"Babe, we have to be smart." He tapped two fingers to his temple, an imitation of a gun barrel. "You can't look up stuff here. Otherwise, the insurance company will think we planned it and won't pay."

"Why would insurance adjusters search our computers?"

"Because it's their job. They'll have to make sure your fall is an accident. Go to a library a few towns over or something." Tom pushed the laptop farther back on the desk, out of my reach. "If insurers paid out for every suicide, they'd be bankrupt."

Suicide. A deliberate fall off a cruise ship was akin to jumping off a bridge, and I was desperate enough to consider it. My lips trembled. Tears built behind my eyes. What had I agreed to?

Tom's arms draped over my shoulders. His chin touched the top of my head. "I'm sorry, baby. I'm so sorry. I'm just on edge." He nuzzled my hair as he whispered. "I know how nerve-racking this is. I wish more than anything that I could be the one to do it. You know that, don't you?"

I made an affirmative noise into his bicep.

"I won't let anything happen to you. I promise. We'll get through this."

I tried to control myself. Woman up. Tom had been willing to risk his life for the family. I could do the same. With proper planning, I'd be fine.

"Just picture the prize," Tom said. "Someday soon, we'll sit on the porch of our beach house, drinking caipirinhas. Your mom will be inside, making rice. Your dad will be running with his granddaughter on the sand, maybe flying a kite that we helped her paint earlier that day. Later, we'll all go for a family swim."

I closed my eyes and saw a lost memory. My mother, hair piled atop her head in a loose bun, leaned over a cast iron pot on the apartment's gas stove. Rice was her specialty. Tom had heard me lament over countless dinners that my white rice with onions could never compare with her garlic-rich recipe. I could visualize her shouting from the kitchen for the family to come wash their hands while my father, healthy and safe, carried his granddaughter on his shoulders.

Tom read my mind. "Our daughter deserves to have grandparents. She deserves to have us." His fingers laced and knotted through mine. "This will become our adventure story: what we did to give our daughter a better life. Like your parents' story."

My parents had sneaked into the United States beneath a tarp on a flatbed truck and then walked for two days in the desert between armed Mexican drug dealers to give their future child—me—a better life. If they could do that, surely I could brave a several-mile swim to give Sophia a chance at the childhood I'd always dreamed of, surrounded by family without the need to work at fourteen for food and clothes.

"How long until the policy pays, you think?"

Tom's fingers slipped into my hair and stroked my scalp. "A few months. Maybe half a year."

"I'll need to smuggle myself back in then."

The petting stopped. "You can't come back without documents."

"My parents did."

"And immigration got them."

"Not for fourteen years. I can't leave Sophia for six months."

"I'll be here."

I didn't respond. Though Tom was a father, he wasn't a caretaker. He didn't know how to bathe our daughter, brush her hair, put her to bed. I couldn't just leave her with him, not knowing when I'd be back. Not to mention, what would I do on an island without any papers or money?

"Don't worry," he whispered. "It will be okay. It's only for a little while."

I heard my mother's voice, right before they'd been deported the first time. *It's only a little while.* But it hadn't been.

"Let's go to bed."

I rose from the desk chair. There was no point arguing with Tom. Come hell or high water, I was coming home.

Part II

Adverse selection

The tendency for persons with a higher probability of loss to seek more insurance than those with less risk.

21

Ryan rocked in Vivienne's office chair, anxious for her to cue the video on one of her many computer screens. His former partner had been right about her powers of persuasion. A flash of her badge and a mention of her title on the "financial crimes" unit, and the restaurant manager had volunteered both the security footage and a free meal.

Vivienne clicked a few buttons on her keyboard. A video player took over the center monitor. The image inside was a still of a swanky bar. "You ready?" she asked.

"Action," he said.

The video lacked sound. Silence thickened the air as Ryan watched Ana and Michael walk toward a back booth. The ghost, and maybe her killer. Ryan could understand the bartender's initial confusion. Though Ana and Michael didn't touch, their body language was close, friendly if not amorous. When Michael started kissing Ana's neck, her head tilted back, giving him greater access, as her hand went to his chest to push him away.

A minute in, Ana's lack of consent crystallized. She squirmed, moved Michael's hands from her thighs, pulled down her dress each time he hiked it higher. Whatever she did, her boss came back at her like a mixed-martial-arts fighter, using his weight to pin her beneath him. Just as it seemed he'd won, Ana landed a shot between his legs that doubled him over.

141

Vivienne hit the stop button, freezing on an image of Ana headed toward the stairs. She rapped her knuckles against her desk. "Well, that should convince someone at the prosecutor's office to let me snoop through Mr. Smith's bank transactions."

Ryan felt a twinge of jealousy. He missed anonymously wading through records of a suspect's spending. Whatever info he wanted now, he had to ask for it.

He pressed hard against the chair arm to hoist himself out of the seat. "I'll leave you to it."

Vivienne ejected the external hard drive. She glanced at him sideways, a look that could be flirtatious or wary, depending on the mouth. Her lips didn't offer any clues. "What are you gonna do?"

"I'm going to find out if Ana was really alone when she fell."

★

Ryan sat in his far less impressive home office, eating leftover takeout from a black plastic bowl with toss-away utensils. He'd spent most of his day trying to chase down the person at the cruise line with access to the keycard data for the Bacons' stateroom. SunSeaStar Sails' corporate line had proven about as helpful as Robomaids' answering service. He'd spoken to several operators, each of whom had put him on hold to endless elevator music. Ultimately, he'd talked with a PR flack who'd promised to get his "questions" to the proper person.

Ryan chewed reheated rice and chided himself for not having demanded the info right away. Given Tom's alibi, he just hadn't been thinking murder.

The phone buzzed on the desk like the last gasp of a dying fly. A message on the home screen said he had a new e-mail from a Mr. Scott Groves, ship's counsel. Ryan braced himself for a canned written statement about the Bahamas Maritime Authority ruling. He opened the message:

Dear Mr. Monahan,

I am writing with regard to your investigation of Ana Bacon's fall off her stateroom balcony at 7:28 PM on the evening of August 30, as confirmed by ship security cameras. As I am sure you are aware, the Bahamas Maritime Authority found "no evidence of homicide" or ship negligence. Testimony from crew passengers and from Mrs. Bacon's husband supported the BMA's findings.

Mr. Bacon was observed on the starboard pool deck by fellow passengers at the time ship's cameras later verified Mrs. Bacon's fall. According to Mr. Bacon, his wife had suffered from pregnancy-related nausea and had vomited over the side of the boat earlier that day. Mrs. Bacon had also complained of upset stomach to fellow vacationers. Cruise line investigators believe that her death was accidental, though not in a way that could have been prevented by ship personnel. Posted signs warn passengers to observe caution around railings, and ill vacationers are urged to visit the ship infirmary on the ninth floor.

Ryan drummed his plastic knife against the lid beside his plate. The chances that the e-mail contained anything helpful were decreasing by the sentence. The attorney was wasting words defending against a phantom lawsuit from ISI to recoup paid death benefits.

With regard to your specific request for the recorded entry and exits of the Bacon's stateroom on the date in question, we can provide the following information based on our electronic keycard system: The door was opened with a room key at 6:25 PM and subsequently locked. The lock engaged at 6:58 PM and again at 8:03 PM, indicating that the door was opened at those times from the inside. The door was opened with a room key at 8:05 PM and subsequently locked. The lock engaged again at 8:30 PM. At

8:45 PM, the door was opened by a ship captain's master key. It is important to note that keycards can sometimes fail to properly open a door, leading to multiple lock engagements for the same entry attempt.

The cruise line interviewed all passengers near the Bacons. One couple in the adjacent stateroom was at dinner during Mrs. Bacon's fall and has nothing to add to the investigation. The other neighbor is willing to speak with you, though he has asked that his name not be included in this e-mail, as he is concerned that his information could be forwarded.

We hope this satisfies your requests.

Mr. Groves's contact numbers were listed in a postscript, along with the telephone number for the nameless neighbor. The number had a New York City area code.

Ryan reread the message's penultimate section, pitting the timeline against Tom's prior testimony. Tom and Ana had returned from the day's beach excursion at 6:25 PM. Then, according to Tom, he'd gotten his wife settled on the balcony and headed to the pool, leaving the room at 6:58 PM. The door locked behind him. Thirty minutes later, Ana fell overboard.

Tom had said he returned around 8:00 PM to an empty stateroom. The cruise line evidently believed that he had attempted to open the door at 8:03 PM but wasn't successful until 8:05 PM.

Ryan stirred the Thai food on his plate. What if Tom's key had worked fine? What if he'd opened the door two minutes after his wife's killer had left?

Ryan chewed a thick piece of tofu that tasted of soy and boiled carrots. He liked the theory, but it had a problem. He couldn't explain how the killer had gotten inside the Bacons' stateroom in the first place. The assailant couldn't have slipped past Tom as he was leaving at 6:58 PM. Surely Mr. Bacon would have mentioned seeing a strange attendant.

Ryan set down his plastic utensils. He could think of only one plausible scenario that put a killer in the room with Ana: Tom hadn't returned to the room. Mr. Bacon had lied about seeing his wife sleeping on the balcony. He knew the policy wouldn't pay if it looked as though Ana had jumped, so he'd put his wife on the balcony, recovering from nausea, to add credibility to his accident theory. Maybe part of him even feared that Ana had killed herself and he'd wanted to cover it up.

But Ana *hadn't* committed suicide because, at two minutes to seven, she'd opened the door for her murderer.

22

A finger pressed to disembodied lips on a large white sign. The words for "quiet" in a dozen languages were scattered around like the spray from a firecracker. The library had at least seven posters urging patrons to keep silent. No one listened. Two women behind the checkout desk discussed their families at a volume intended for the hard of hearing. An elderly man shouted into a cell phone. A vacuum ran in a back room. Two kids played hide-and-seek amid the bookcases while their mom read loudly enough to entertain an entire classroom.

Sophia sat at a long desk of computers, coloring book open to the letter *R*. The monitor in front of her reflected a serious face.

"*R*. Ruh. Ruh," I said, opening up a web page.

"Ruh," she repeated.

"Color the pictures on the page that begin with the letter *R*."

I moved my cursor to the search bar and typed in the address supplied by my mother that morning, after I'd sworn that the info was only for a friend's nanny: www.RTT.com. An acronym, she'd explained, for Return Trips Travel Inc. Times had changed. The smugglers had become incorporated.

Sophia tugged on my arm. She pointed to a rabbit in her notebook. Her cheeks puffed from the force of her smile. I beamed back at her. "Right. Rabbit starts with *R*. Can you fill it in with a color beginning with *R*?"

She scanned the five fat magic markers beside the keyboard. Her fingers rested briefly on the purple before shaking her head vigorously. She grabbed the red. "Red. Ruh. Ruh."

A picture of the globe loaded. Red lines arched across the image to the United States' seaboard cities. Bold black text ran across the screen: Come to the Land of the Free. Financing Available. One-Ways Starting at $5,000. Many Trips Available. Employment Opportunities. Aztec Guided Tours, Canadian Wilderness Retreats, Miami Sailing, Caribbean Cruise Passages.

The listed five-thousand-dollar amount had to be the initial required payment. My breath quickened. I'd been unable to get a grand for my parents. How would I possibly scrounge up several thousand dollars?

Sophia's hand moved back and forth across her coloring page. Red zigzags spilled over the rabbit's thick outline. I would have to teach her to color inside the lines. One thing at a time. First letter sounds. We would work on marker control later. *If there was a later . . .*

I pushed the thought from my mind and tousled her dark hair. "Red rabbit is right."

Sophia moved on to a rhino, trying, in vain, to stay within the thick black borders. The point of her tongue protruded above her lower lip in concentration. My diligent little girl. How could I leave her?

The web page had a phone number. I borrowed a blue marker from Sophia's pencil case and printed it on the inside of my wrist. As I did, I made a mental tally of all the cash sources I could tap. My last work check would arrive in the mail soon, two weeks' pay, or two thousand dollars, after taxes. Unemployment would pay something, though surely not three thousand dollars. Where could I get more? Would the coyotes let me pay less upfront and work off a larger amount?

My daughter finished the rhino. She scanned the remaining animals and then pressed the marker's felt tip to a picture down in the corner. A mouse.

"That one doesn't get colored, baby. Only *R* animals, like ruh-rabbit."

Red zigzags, less controlled than the ones filling in the rhino, scrawled across the animal's pointy nose and whiskers.

"No, Soph. That's *M*. Muh-muh-mouse. Like Mommy."

She continued to scribble over the animal's fat body. "It's all *R*."

"Not mouse."

"Look."

A long, hairless tail protruded from the animal's oversized backside. Whiskers stretched nearly to its knees. I hadn't recognized a rat.

*

Sophia skipped on the Newark sidewalk, all the while rotating a lollipop stick in her mouth. The library kept them in a dish by the checkout counter. I couldn't fail to give her one after she'd waited for me to finish researching something without any entertaining pictures.

"Sophia, no skipping. It's a busy sidewalk and the pavement is uneven." I didn't add, *We may not have health insurance since Mommy lost her job.* My tone conveyed the sentiment. She slowed to a walk, still sucking the lollipop.

I searched the sidewalk for a payphone. Few places outside of America's poorest inner cities possessed such relics. Cell phones had eradicated the demand for a box that charged a quarter a minute to place a call while standing on a corner.

I knew that Newark still had stalls. I was accustomed to passing one on the way to the bodega where I wired my parents money at a fraction of the cost of Western Union. The booth was a corroded metal relic covered in peeling stickers advertising unknown bands and taped-up fliers for long-passed street sales. I hoped it still worked. I couldn't risk calling the coyotes on my cell. Tom would kill me.

Sophia spotted it first. Her distance vision could have qualified her as a fighter pilot. *Mom, look at that plane. What? That speck by the skyscraper a mile away?*

We sped walked the remaining block to the metal case. Wadded gum, blackened by dirt, stuck to the inside of the walls. I'd discovered the one place more diseased than a subway public restroom. Sophia's hand gripped mine. I instructed her to keep a tight hold and stand outside.

I slipped in sideways, pulling in my shoulders to avoid touching anything other than the phone. I held the mouthpiece away from my face while pressing the top circle to my ear. There was a dial tone. Four quarters jangled into the machine. I flipped my free arm over to see the number copied from the website. The smugglers had a local area code.

A man answered on the third ring. "Return Trips Travel."

"Hi. I'm calling because I need to get to the U.S. from the Bahamas."

"Do you have the down payment?"

"Mostly." I swallowed. My unpaid salary was less than half the required amount. "Can I work off a larger amount?"

"No. You'll need the entire five before booking your trip."

I looked longingly through the open payphone door. Sophia stood outside, twisting the lollipop in her mouth. When she caught me looking, her nose wrinkled. She grinned.

"I'll get it." I promised Sophia as I spoke. "I have to come home."

23

November 28

Ryan was on his way to Tom's when a call from Vivienne made him turn around and head back over the bridge. The prior night, a prosecutor had given the Financial Crimes Unit authority to sift through Michael's personnel accounts for evidence that he'd been blackmailed or, more precisely, taken action to stop being blackmailed. Vivienne had already found something.

He picked her up outside the precinct. His old stomping ground was a squat gray box on the corner of Fifty-First and Third Avenue. Windows, each coated with gray film to block out prying eyes, covered the facade. The precinct recalled the Bauhaus building, save for the smart-car-sized American flag waving from above the bulletproof glass entrance. Police cars lined the street out front, parked beneath signs that threatened high fines for standing.

Vivienne hovered by a squad car in her long, black coat with a laptop bag slung over her shoulder. A lanky cop with wire-frame glasses hung behind her. She introduced him as David Parish, her new partner.

Ryan tried not to resent his replacement's presence as the guy climbed into the dodge's backseat. Vivienne slid into the navigator's spot and directed him to drive out to the island. He headed to the FDR, trusting that wherever Vivienne wanted him to go was where the investigation needed to take them.

As he drove, she brought him up to speed on the progress of the FCU's Friday night. There'd been two eye-popping expenditures in Michael's records: a fourteen-thousand-dollar check, made out to cash, withdrawn four days before Ana's death, and a twenty-thousand-dollar wire to the Bahamian bank account of a Charles Pinder, made two days after Ana's fall. A web search hadn't revealed any businesses associated with Pinder's name, but a man with the same moniker had served ten years for human smuggling. "Maybe Pinder was more careful with his other crimes," Vivienne said.

Ryan struggled to process the new information and keep his eyes on the road. "So where am I driving to?"

"Michael's house," she said. "He knows we're coming. State attorney thought he deserved the courtesy given his financial clout."

"Course he did," Ryan grumbled.

"Thought you should do the honors, as you'd interviewed him before," Vivienne said.

Twenty-five minutes later, Ryan stood at the gated entrance to a massive Long Island estate. This mansion didn't require a qualifying prefix. A colonial home, it was every bit as large as the Bacons' house but also sat on acres of green. Three dozen blue pines lined the property. A snow-speckled tennis court was just visible behind the gray gables of the attached four-car garage.

Ryan hung back as David rang the guard bell. An accented female voice invited them in through the speaker attached to the automatic gate. Iron bars buzzed open and vanished in a stone wall surrounding the home.

As they ascended the cobblestone driveway, the front door peeled back. A middle-aged man stood in the opening wearing a trust-me gray suit. He identified himself as "Mr. Smith's personal attorney."

Business cards were exchanged. Afterward, Michael's lawyer led them through a grand foyer to a den of sorts: an oak paneled room with a billiard table and a large fireplace, over which hung massive antlers. The room smelled of tanned hide, though there weren't any visible animal skins. Michael lounged just to the right of the hearth in a leather club chair. He glowered at them, a spoiled brat in the principal's office waiting for his parents to speak to the headmaster.

Ryan heard a door close behind him. The lawyer gestured for the group to join Michael in the four additional leather seats, arranged facing their host. As they sat, the lawyer stood between his and Michael's chairs and set the terms of their "voluntary interview." Mr. Smith wanted to be helpful but would refrain from answering unfounded accusations and addressing rumors. Mr. Smith also reserved the right *not* to discuss any *sensitive* personal matters—whatever that meant.

During the drive, Ryan had considered starting with a few softball questions about Ana's flirtatiousness intended to lower Michael's defenses. But the attorney ruined any chance of that. He threw his hardest pitch.

"Did you sexually assault Ana Bacon when she worked for you?"

Michael's jaw dropped. His lawyer patted his shoulder, silencing him before words could emerge.

Vivienne withdrew the laptop from her bag and turned the screen to face the accused. She'd set the video to the most damning part: Michael pinning Ana to the bench.

Michael's tan grayed. "You can't use that. I was at—" Again, the attorney pressed a hand on his shoulder.

"Where did you get that?" The lawyer asked.

"It's the restaurant's security tape."

"It's illegal to record a private dinner."

"The bar has a CCTV monitoring notice," Ryan said. "And your client hasn't answered."

The attorney stepped forward. "Ana Bacon surely isn't making any allegations about my client. This interview is ov—"

"Is that the way you want to play it?" Vivienne stood. "Because sexual assault is the least of the considered charges."

Michael patted the air for his lawyer to sit. When the man settled into his chair, he whispered into his ear. After a beat, the attorney began parroting Michael's defense. "My client didn't assault anyone. His secretary courted his advances, apparently to manipulate him into giving her money, and then viciously turned on him, as evidenced by her behavior on the video."

"Blame the victim," Vivienne muttered, resuming her seat.

"You did give her money, didn't you?" Ryan asked.

Michael again conferred with his lawyer, keeping his hand over his mouth. The attorney gave Michael some signal: a head nod or blink of an eye. Michael answered the question with a single word: "Yes."

"And you gave her this money because she threatened to tell police about you trying to rape her?"

A sly smile parted Michael's lips. He adjusted in his chair. "Nothing like that. It was charity. She was hard up. Depressed. Confused. I felt bad for her."

Vivienne's hands clenched beside Ryan. She must have wanted to pop the guy.

"How much?" Ryan asked.

Michael shrugged and rolled his eyes. "I don't remember. Not much for me."

Ryan was tempted to reveal the fourteen-thousand-dollar check, but he kept his mouth shut. He couldn't alert Michael to the fact that FCU had been digging through his personal accounts—at least not yet.

Vivienne leaned forward, her full mouth pursed. "You expect us to believe that you gave money out of the goodness of your heart to a woman who kneed you in the balls?"

Michael smirked. "I'm a forgiving guy."

"So Ana was hard up. Yet she went to the Bahamas on that money," Ryan said. "Did that make you angry?"

Michael brushed his lawyer's hand off his shoulder. "If I'd suffered financial ruin like the Bacons, I wouldn't go on a cruise." He shrugged. "But the Bahamas is a great place."

"You go often then?"

"Yes. And before you ask, I visited the Bahamas the same weekend Ana disappeared. But I wasn't on the same boat. I was on the Emerald." He crossed his khaki-clad legs and folded his hands over his knee. "Gorgeous vessel."

"But you both went ashore at the same time?"

"I have no idea. My wife and I got off briefly to go shopping somewhere. Our main destination was Paradise Island."

"So you never saw Ana?"

The lawyer cleared his throat. "He's made that clear. Ask another question or we're done."

Ryan exchanged a glance with Vivienne. It was time to go for the jugular. "Who is Charles Pinder?"

Michael's smile vanished. He sat forward in the chair and leaned over to his attorney. Ryan couldn't make out what was said, but the whispers were more vehement. The lawyer nodded along, his expression growing increasingly grave with each bob.

"You searched his financial records," the attorney said.

"We have a subpoena," Vivienne responded.

"Personal and corporate?"

"Just personal."

"My client wasn't notified."

"It's in the mail." Vivienne's new partner piped up. Ryan guessed he was being earnest, but it came out sarcastic, as though the NYPD had never intended to let Michael know that they'd scanned his recent expenditures. By law, they had to. But they had a few days' grace.

Michael stood and walked to the door.

Ryan pressed his hand into the chair arm, helping himself stand quickly on his bad leg. "Who is Charles Pinder?"

Michael flung open the door and stormed out of the room, faster than Ryan would be able to follow.

"This interview is finished," the attorney said.

"Who is he?" Ryan called after Michael. "Is he the man you paid to kill the woman blackmailing you?"

"It's time for you to go." The attorney moved toward the exit. He gestured like a butler for them to head through before him. "All future contact with my client should go through me. He won't answer your calls."

Ryan followed the lawyer to the front entrance. Vivienne and David trailed behind, taking advantage of Ryan's slow gate to survey Michael's home, showing his attorney that they weren't intimidated by his client's money. Once at the entrance, the lawyer again warned them all not to contact Michael directly before shutting the door behind them.

They walked to the car without speaking, aware that Michael might have cameras monitoring the driveway. Vivienne broke the silence after the Dodge had peeled away from the curb. "The mention of Pinder set him off."

"Did it ever," David chimed in from the backseat. Ryan caught him grinning in the rearview, a happy puppy that had caught a scent.

"Where to now?" Vivienne asked.

Ryan shifted to a faster gear. "I think you should meet Ana's husband."

24

August 24

My doppelganger, only younger with pockmarks beneath her makeup, sat at the desk in front of Michael's office. A black cap-sleeve dress, fashioned out of a fabric akin to Ace bandages, wrapped around her slim figure. The neckline cut in a deep V to show slivers of cleavage. In no world did that dress qualify as business attire.

I strode past her. She hopped up just as my hand hit Michael's closed glass door. My ex-boss appeared to focus on his monitor, no doubt scanning my notes on the California Public Employment Retirees Fund. They were his ten thirty meeting. He wasn't expecting me, but I hadn't needed to be on his schedule, thanks to his apparent failure to deactivate my work badge and alert security to my termination.

"Excuse me. If you're the ten thirty, you're going to have to wait. You can't just go in there." The girl was chewing gum. A glance over her shoulder revealed an open Facebook page on her computer screen. Did she even know who CalPERS was? The managers of a $230 billion fund could do whatever they wanted, including show up thirty minutes early for a meeting.

"I'm sure Michael will want to see me."

She stepped to the side. My familiarity indicated that I knew her new boss far better than she did. I deliberately left the door open behind me. The presence of another person in the room stopped Michael from scanning the document in front of him.

He shot up from the chair. Flinty blue eyes met mine. Once again, I owned his attention. "What do you want?"

I thought of Sophia at home with her daddy, missing me as I ran an "important errand." I steeled myself. "What does everyone want? Money."

He dismissed me with a wave. "You're not getting any. As I already—"

"You explained why the police might not believe me." I deliberately spoke too loud. I wanted the whole office to hear: Rick in marketing. Fadi in accounting. Jeremy in legal. All the administrative assistants. I wanted Michael's entire fifty-person office to know that I'd been fired for my integrity, not for insubordination or mistakes or whatever lies he'd spread in my absence. "I'm here to explain why your wife definitely will believe that, as I screamed, you pulled up my—"

He rounded the desk and slammed the door shut behind me. My heart raced, but I planted my legs, refusing to allow my flight instinct takeover. I'd come here for a fight. Michael was going to pay to keep me from singing to his spouse, something to the tune of fifteen thousand dollars, the amount my parents had thrice paid coyotes to smuggle them into the country. The amount was, undoubtedly, less than he spent on a weekend away. It was certainly a bargain compared to the millions he'd lose in a divorce.

He resumed his seat behind the desk and then motioned to the opposite chair with a sweep of his arm, a welcoming gesture performed for anyone peering through the glass walls. I glanced behind me before accepting a seat. My replacement made guilty eye contact. No one else stood in the hallway.

"You really think you can blackmail me?" Michael smiled a wide Jack Nicholson grin that bared his upper teeth all the way to the fangs. "My wife isn't possessive in that way. We have an understanding."

I knew all about the *understandings* that guys like Michael thought they had: keep the wife in a lavish house with fancy clothing and a generous staff, fund her lunches, support her pet projects and charities, and then go do whatever, and whomever, you want. Undoubtedly, some men did have such arrangements. But I highly doubted that my boss had a half-open marriage. Jessica and Michael had married at age twenty-five, before Michael had made it. Rich women did not *understand*.

"You forget that I know your wife. We've talked on the phone often while you avoided her calls." I stared him down, reclaiming the power I'd lost the prior week. "She won't simply accept you trying to bed your secretary, not when she could take half your money in a divorce, maybe even half your firm."

The mirth faded from his expression. "She won't believe you."

"I think she will. I spoke to my husband. You have something of a reputation."

Michael's smirk finally vanished. His arms folded across his chest. "I won't be blackmailed, you little bitch."

The curse brought me back to that night. If I closed my eyes, I would be trapped in that private bar again. I forced myself not to blink. "Then don't think of it as blackmail. Think of it as the settlement of an unlawful termination suit. I worked hard for you: more than ten hours a day, five days a week, some weekends. I never missed a day. I didn't deserve to be fired."

"You had family emergencies."

Was that his official excuse for letting me go? "I left early once, with your permission. And I worked late the following week to make up for it."

Michael mumbled, "Not late enough."

"I think your wife will agree that it was plenty late."

Michael drummed his fingers against his desk. He sighed. "Well, I can't justify not compensating you for services rendered. Pick up your last check from Linda on your way out. She'll make sure it includes earned vacation."

I had a week of unused leave. That added to my days worked would equal just about three thousand. "That's not nearly enough."

Anger darkened Michael's pale skin to a reddish tan. "You listen to me. You'll take what an axed employee gets and not a cent more. You think you'll have a chance to share your allegations with my wife? My attorneys will gag and bind you like a BDSM hooker. And if you think your husband is unemployable now, wait till I get through with him. Believe me."

The threat to Tom erased my fear. Michael had tried to rape me and now he was going after my family.

"No." My voice didn't sound like my own. "You wait till I get through with you. Jessica and I will be having lunch with her half of your money. Your kids will hate you. Believe me."

Michael sneered a response. He didn't look as confident as he had moments before. I leaned over the desk, tempting him to lash out, to strike me right beneath the eye socket in a place that would show up real nice for my meeting with his wife or in a tabloid photograph. "And you don't just have to worry about your wife. After I tell her, I'll tell the media. The financial crisis has vilified Wall Street. Folks are eating up stories about bad bankers. My story will be a Thanksgiving feast come early."

Michael's eyes went wide. "What do you want?"

I wanted enough to keep my house and stay afloat for another year, but there was no way Michael would cough up a hundred thousand dollars, or even twenty thousand. I needed to ask for an amount that wouldn't be noticed missing from Michael's personal accounts. An amount he could "gift" to a needy coworker without explaining anything to his accountant or his spouse.

"Fourteen thousand," I said.

Michael lowered his chin. "Ten, and only because I don't feel like putting my wife through any conversation with a whore."

The name-calling emboldened me. "Fourteen—or my second call after your wife will be to the *Daily News*."

Michael looked at the clock on his desk. We'd argued for five minutes, at least. His big pension fund appointment would be here soon.

"You're not worth it, but my time is." A drawer opened. He slammed a checkbook onto his desk, scrawling the figure across the paper so violently that I thought the pen might puncture the carbon copy beneath. He tore it from the book and slid it across to me. It was made out to cash.

Fourteen thousand dollars. Enough for the initial payment to secure my passage with the coyotes plus something for my family to live off of while we waited for the insurance to pay out. I grabbed the check.

"Now get the fuck out. I have an important meeting." He nodded in the direction of his assistant. She didn't notice. His hand flew to his intercom. "Fernanda, escort Mrs. Bacon to HR. Now. She quit and has to fill out her exit paperwork."

The girl jumped from her chair. She flew to the glass door. It only took her a second to reach it, but I already stood outside. Water churned in my stomach. I needed to vomit. One thing at a time. I swallowed the bile in my throat. First, I had to cash this check.

Fernanda looked at me bug-eyed, unsure of where she'd been instructed to take me. "Linda is down the hall," I said.

25

Ryan opened the Dodge's passenger door and grabbed Vivienne's calf-length coat from the backseat before David could slide it forward. She shivered in the cold but still waved the garment away.

"He's not one for hospitality," Ryan cautioned. He held the coat open so Vivienne could slide her arms in.

The car door shut, announcing that David was joining the conversation. "What do we want with Tom?" David asked.

"I'm hoping he'll clarify the timeline, make it clear that someone else could have been in the room with his wife," Ryan said. "You guys might help him remember things more clearly."

"If he knows we're looking at Michael for his wife's death, he'll want to tell us everything," David said.

Vivienne jostled her arms through the coat sleeves. "Let's not reveal our suspicions right away. We don't want him manufacturing facts."

Ryan led the way down the Bacons' long driveway with David flanking him. Vivienne lingered a few steps behind, apparently checking out the neighborhood. The Wu-Nosek clan could afford the million-plus suburbs. If Vivienne ever had a kid, she might acquire her own starter castle someplace like this, maybe even in this exact town.

A woman's shout followed the bell ring. Ryan thought he recognized the voice. He'd seen a white BMW parked down the block.

Tom answered the door in his jacket. Ryan gave Vivienne an "I-told-you-so" look as the master of the house shut the door behind him.

"Any word on my wife's policy?"

Ryan answered by introducing his companions, emphasizing their titles and task force. Vivienne removed her hand from her pocket to shake hello. She held it out for an awkward moment before Tom decided to make nice.

His face lost color as he shook. "Financial crimes?"

"May we come in?" Vivienne asked.

Tom's lips parted, but a protest didn't emerge. Instead, his breath formed a cloud in front of his face. He opened the door and led them through the foyer and dining room, toward the kitchen.

Ryan's peripheral vision caught a petite woman emerging from a bathroom. She was blonde. Pretty with round blue eyes and high arched brows. Tom turned toward her. "Check on Sophia." The tone ordered.

She hurried up the stairs. Ryan listened to the quick patter on the steps, hoping to hear Sophia call out the woman's name. She seemed too young to be "Eve," the family friend. Ryan put her in her early twenties. Au pair age. Maybe she was a neighbor's live-in nanny, lent out to help the grieving widower.

Tom cleared his throat. "This way."

The white kitchen was as stark as a cleaned-out cupboard. The boxes from Ryan's first meeting were gone, as was the lavender and other feminine touches that had indicated a woman lived in the home. Tom gestured to the chrome bar stools at the island. He moved to the other side of the room, a safe distance away from the cops.

"I don't understand. Why is the NYPD financial crimes unit involved with my wife's insurance benefit? Are you trying to argue now that my wife killed herself to commit insurance fraud? I don't—"

"It's not that." Ryan settled into the barstool and watched Tom's eyes dart from Vivienne to David and back to him. The presence of real police in the house unnerved the guy.

"Did you know that Michael Smith made advances on your wife before her fall?"

Tom's shoulders rose as he took a deep breath. He nodded. "Yes?"

Tom scratched his brow. "Ana told me Michael got drunk and tried to force himself on her after a client meeting. She was pretty upset." He shook his head and then looked up at Ryan. "But not suicide upset, if that's where you're going." Tom gestured at Vivienne and David. "I still don't understand why the NYPD is here."

"Did you and Ana discuss going to the police?" Ryan asked.

"No."

"She didn't want to press charges?"

"Of course she did, but it would have been pointless." Tom's voice raised. His hands landed on his hips. "Michael would have argued it was consensual, and he has a lot of money to help prove his case. He has a lot of money to put me in jail for attacking him." He threw up his hands. "Sometimes, you have to let things go."

He glared at Ryan. "And none of this has anything to do with her death. She wasn't worked up about Michael. She was ill. She fell after vomiting—"

Ryan held up his hand. "With respect, Mr. Bacon, you weren't in the room when she went overboard. You don't know how she fell. You only know that she'd been sick earlier in the trip."

Tom pressed his lips together. He blinked hard as if he didn't like what he was seeing. "It had to be an accident."

In cop work, there was a time to act casual and a time for confession. Ryan's internal clock told him it was fessing-up hour, both for Tom and for him. He'd go first. "I talked to the cruise line. Your room door was opened at 6:58 PM from the inside."

"Right. I left to go to the pool."

"And it was opened again at 8:03 PM—before you entered with your key at 8:05 PM."

Tom's hands hit his hips. "That doesn't make sense."

"It does if someone else was in the room with Ana."

"No one was in the room with Ana."

"Are you sure? Because if you went straight to the pool, instead of dropping her off—"

"No."

"No?"

Tom shook his head at the floor. "No more question and answer until you tell me what the NYPD is doing in my kitchen."

Ryan felt Vivienne sit up straighter beside him. "Mr. Bacon, we're not here because of your wife's policy." Vivienne's voice was gentle and firm, as if she talked to a child. "We are here because we believe Michael Smith may have paid your wife to keep quiet about him sexually assaulting her on the night of August eighteenth. And we are looking into whether or not he took any additional actions."

"What?" The fight had drained from Tom's voice. He sounded surprised. "Paid? No. He gave her a package, some back-owed pay and unused vacation days. Or HR did. She cashed the check."

"Michael admitted to giving her money," Ryan said. "There was a check made out to cash from his account for fourteen thousand."

Tom's cheeks puffed. He released the air with a whooshing sound, like a toilet flush.

"Does that amount seem familiar?" Vivienne asked.

"Ana told me she'd gotten about half that." His eyes rolled to the ceiling. "Knowing her, she probably gave the other half to her parents."

Ryan didn't like the tangent. "Could Ana have let someone in, Tom? Are you sure it was you leaving the room at six fifty-eight? If I check ship cameras, I won't see you at the pool earlier?"

Tom's palm went to his mouth. He wiped at his lips and then squeezed his chin. "This is all a lot to process. I can't do this right now. I need you all to go."

Tom began walking toward the mudroom. Ryan knew there was an exit door out there. He wasn't ready to leave yet.

"When you entered around eight, did you have problems with your key?"

"Not that I remember."

"Then someone left your room right before you got there."
Ryan followed Tom into the mudroom. He could hear Vivienne's
heels clicking behind him. Tom opened the door, letting in the
frigid outdoor air. "If someone else could have been in that room,
we need to know."

Tom dragged his bottom lip beneath his top teeth. His eyes
moved around, as if searching for the right answer on his guests'
faces. Finally, he blinked and pinched the bridge of his nose.
"I went straight to the pool. Ana told me she was going to the
balcony to nap so I figured that she must have been out there,
suffered a bout of nausea. . . ." Tom's head dropped as though it
weighed too much for his neck. He let go of the door. Ryan put his
back against the wood, holding it open for Vivienne and David.
After his partners walked through, Ryan felt fingers dig into
his bicep.

Tom stared at him. Ryan expected watery eyes. Instead, he
was met with a cold fury. "If you find he did anything, you'll let
me know?" The fingers tightened on his arm. Ryan wanted to
wrest his limb away, but sympathy stalled his march out the door.
He knew what Tom was really asking.

He patted Tom's hand, encouraging him to let go of his bicep.
"Your wife's dead. But your daughter needs you."

✶

Vivienne stood in the driveway, black coat flapping in the wind
like a superhero cape. She turned toward the car and made a slow
advance down the asphalt, waiting for Ryan to catch up. David
was already halfway to the Charger, apparently unwilling to keep
pace with a gimp. The door thudded shut behind them. Vivienne
glanced over her shoulder and then leaned into Ryan's ear. "You
get a read on that guy?"

"I thought him odd at first." Ryan rubbed the stubble breaking through his skin. "I don't know, though. Wife dead. Maybe
murdered. It's a lot to process. And given Michael paid that massive sum to a known criminal who—"

"What do the neighbors say about him?"

"I didn't talk to them yet."

Vivienne stopped walking.

Ryan's face flushed. When someone died suspiciously, the cops always talked to next of kin, neighbors, and coworkers, people who would see the person on a daily basis and notice changes in their behavior or in the attitudes of those closest to them—the people with motive. But he was just one investigator, and he'd been chasing the soured affair and suicide theory.

"It's on my list."

Vivienne made a small gesture toward the house next door. "Tomorrow, I'll try to chase down Pinder. You talk to the neighbors."

"The husband has a solid alibi."

"And he lies."

Lies were like mosquitoes. Once you heard one, you could be sure there were others. But Tom's lie had been to deflect suspicion from his wife killing herself. What reason could he have to tell more?

The gleaming federal mansion next door sprawled out toward them, reaching for the Bacons' property. Its side windows had a view of the French home's rear windows and backyard.

With luck, the neighbors would be nosey.

26

August 24

Return Trips Travel operated out of the first floor of Newark row house. A large map of the Americas covered the storefront's picture window. Two Mexican eateries flanked either side of the agency. One offered tapas, the other tacos.

A teenage boy sat on the stoop outside the travel agency. He eyed me as I approached, judging my immigrant status. I was tempted to say something in Portuguese but feared my American accent would stoke his suspicions. Instead, I waited while he assessed my suntanned complexion and dark hair. He scooted to the side, permitting me to enter.

An older man hunched over a large screen laptop behind a tall, white counter. Plastic bins filled with bus schedules, train maps, and what appeared to be customs documents surrounded him. A large fan whirred by his head.

Brown eyes looked over the top of a laptop screen. "How may I help you?"

He had an unplaceable face. No single ethnicity could claim his latte complexion, curly black hair, wide nose, and almond-shaped eyes.

"I called earlier. I'm taking a trip to the Bahamas and need to get back into the country."

He gestured to a row of blue chairs lining the side of the room like the dismal waiting area at the DMV. I sat down, legs sticking to the plastic. I pulled my purse close to my torso. The cash sat in my bag, weighing it down like a tin full of loose change. A little more than thirteen thousand, in hundreds, filled the inside. I'd cashed the check at Michael's bank right after leaving his office.

My travel agent sat beside me. "Do you have your deposit?"

"Yes."

His focus dropped to the leather bag in my lap. My fingertips paused on the zipper. "Five thousand now and then I work off the rest, right?"

"Yes. We have jobs when you get back."

"Doing what?"

"Gender-appropriate work."

My gut twisted at the addition of "gender" to the word "work." I'd assumed from the website that "employment opportunities" meant cleaning or watching kids in an uncertified daycare, something that didn't require a social security number. Gender-appropriate hinted at something more sinister. A massage parlor? Worse?

I pulled my bag closer to my chest, blocking the view of my breasts. "I'm not a prostitute."

The man scooted back in his chair as if I'd sneezed without covering my mouth. "No. No. Women clean, men do construction. You make eighty dollars a day to scrub, say, the bathrooms in four or five big homes. You work with other girls; a bus picks you up."

"How long will it take to pay you back?"

"It depends on how many houses you work in. We take a third each week, like taxes. In five months, most people have paid the remaining ten thousand dollars."

My shoulders relaxed onto the hot plastic behind me. I fiddled with my bag's zipper, still not willing to reveal all the cash inside. This man was a criminal, albeit not the kind that seemed to walk around with a loaded gun. "So how does it work?"

The travel agent leaned sideways in the chair, arm draped over the side. "You go to Grand Bahama Island, as discussed. When you get there, you'll take a sailing tour with our guy. He'll give you a pass for a one-day cruise from Bimini to Miami and an excursion stamp. You'll go to Bimini, get on the ship, act as though you came from Miami and had a nice day on the island. When you disembark, you'll grab a bus back to New Jersey. You start work the day after you return."

"What about immigration?"

The smuggler shrugged. "Immigration officers board the single-day cruises to expedite offloading of passengers. They check documents in the dining areas. Don't go there. Hang out by the pool. No one will come find you."

"Won't the cruise staff realize that I don't belong on the ship?"

"The boats have hundreds of people; they can't remember everyone who got on in Miami. They just assume that if you have a ticket, you had to have boarded in Florida. The tickets are legitimate. Our people are on the boat. One man leaves with all our people's passes and hands them out to our clients." He patted me on the back and gave a friendly, customer-service smile. "Don't worry. We do this all the time."

He'd made it sound so easy. Of course, he didn't know that I needed to jump off a moving cruise ship and swim to the Bimini islands. I unzipped my purse and withdrew a wad of cash, separated from the roughly eight thousand that I planned to use to pay the cruise fares and support my family while we waited for the insurance settlement. I dropped it into the stranger's hand.

He brought the five thousand behind the counter and counted it with the speed of an Atlantic City blackjack dealer. Then he counted it again, holding up each hundred-dollar bill toward a ceiling light. Satisfied, he pulled a safe from below the counter and inserted the money.

Anxiety rushed through me. I'd just paid coyotes to smuggle me back into the country. No turning back now. "What's next?"

"I need your name and a contact number. Then we're all set. You call with your travel date. We'll handle the rest."

I didn't dare use my real name. If something went wrong, I couldn't have them visiting my house to collect. I offered up my mother's middle name and my maiden one. "Camilla de Santos," I said. "I'll need to get back to you with a number."

"You don't have a number?"

"Not one that will work when you bring me back home."

27

November 29

R yan rang the doorbell, feeling underprepared to apply for a loan. The home's architecture was to blame. Tom's neighbor's house reminded him of a bank with its large triangle third story, supported by ionic columns. Even the carport next to the home seemed to obscure a drive-through ATM.

A woman answered. Ryan relaxed as soon as he saw the homeowner's surprised brows and done-up sapphire eyes: Botox Barb from the café. Only that wasn't her real name. He was here to see Dina Marchese.

"Can I help you?"

"Yes." He reintroduced himself. "I believe we met before, at the café in the center of town."

"Oh, right." She tapped her lower lip and then pointed at his chest. "You had recently moved into the neighborhood."

Lies operate under karmic law. They always return in some form or another. "Actually, I came here to work a case. I'm an investigator looking into Ana Bacon's fall off a cruise ship a few months ago. I was hoping to ask her neighbors some questions."

Dina smiled in the way only someone without full use of her facial muscles could and welcomed him inside. She escorted him into a sitting room plastered in ornate molding. A shiny, mahogany piano served as the room's centerpiece. French-styled chaises were positioned around it, upholstered in two-tone pinks and oranges. She sat on one and patted the cushion beside her.

A phone rang. Dina put up a finger and stood. "If you'll excuse me for a minute." She clacked from the room. In her tight black leggings and cropped black leather jacket, she looked like the tarted-up version of Sandra Dee.

Ryan unzipped his coat before sinking into the settee. The position, with his leg angled up, aggravated his injury. He extended his limb out in front of him, keeping the other one bent. The pose announced his discomfort.

Five minutes ticked away before Dina returned. She removed a Bluetooth ear bud as she reentered the room. The sight of him made her frown. "Do you want an ottoman for your leg? I can have one of the girls bring one."

He wondered whom she meant. A vacuum cleaner buzzed in the background. Ryan smelled vinegar. People, undoubtedly female, were cleaning Dina's house.

"No, I'm fine." Ryan forced himself more upright, not wanting his injury to become a topic of conversation. "Did you know the Bacons well?"

"They came to a holiday party or two at the house," Dina said. "So you're investigating whether Ana's death was an accident or . . ."

She trailed off, waiting for Ryan to fill in the details. He wished he could just ask the questions, but only police officers had the luxury of demanding answers without returning info. Private investigators had back-and-forth exchanges.

"I'm with the insurance company. Mrs. Bacon had a policy, and we are looking into the cause of death."

Her voice dropped to an excited whisper. "You think Tom did it, don't you?"

The sudden accusation surprised him. Did she know something about the Bacons' marriage? Had Tom actually abused Ana, as her mother had claimed?

He tried to keep his face expressionless. "Why do you think that?"

Dina sat down beside him, close enough that her foot almost touched his leg. She flashed a coy, nearly flirty smile. "Isn't it always the husband?"

Not informed then, just a watcher of too many investigation shows. "Well, it could be an accident or suicide or . . ." Ryan trailed off. He couldn't mention Michael. "Did Ana seem depressed before she went away?"

Dina leaned in, as if sharing a secret. He could smell orange juice and alcohol on her breath. "Between you and me, I don't see how she could not have been depressed. Husband out of work more than a year. She lost all her household staff. I'm sure she was doing all the cleaning, cooking, and childcare, even after she went back to work." She rolled her eyes. "Believe me, men like Tom don't lift a finger when it comes to the house."

"Did Ana say anything?"

"Well, not to me, and probably not to anyone in the neighborhood. Ana didn't really have local friends yet because her kid hadn't started school. No one knew her. I tried with my parties but . . ." She sighed. "Ana was very reserved. Maybe the wives here intimidated her. You know, she wasn't used to having money."

"Did she and Tom fight about money?"

"What couple doesn't?"

Ana's mother's voice shouted in Ryan's mind. "Did Ana ever have bruises?"

Dina's hand went to her heart in an overacted gesture of sympathy. "Oh. No. Well, not that I saw, but we didn't interact regularly other than a passing wave as she walked the stroller down the street. I never *heard* them fight." She gestured to her ceiling, indicating her large home. "People move here from the city for space, to get some distance from their neighbors. It helps keep arguments behind closed doors."

Dina's house was large, but it wasn't far from the Bacons. She would have heard screaming matches. "So you don't have any particular reason to think that they had marital problems?"

Dina's eyebrows raised. Her forehead remained unmoved. "Other than the women?" She slipped the phone from her pocket. "I probably shouldn't share this, but I took it about three weeks before Ana died. I'd planned to show her because I thought she should know. I'd want to know." She pulled up an image and passed the phone to Ryan. "I never saw her at home without Tom, so I didn't get the chance . . ."

The photo was grainy, but Ryan got the gist. Tom sat in his Maserati convertible with the top down, face turned toward the sidewalk. A woman with orangey-red hair and a long neck leaned into the driver's seat. Dina hadn't gotten a good angle on the woman's face. But she appeared to be kissing him on the side of the mouth.

"That woman works in a wine shop one town over." Dina's painted lips squeezed together in an exaggerated pout. "When I saw him, I just thought his behavior was in poor taste. I mean, doing that where everyone could see him. At least *try* to be discrete. He didn't have to embarrass Ana in front of every neighbor running errands that way in the middle of the day."

Ryan considered the photo again. "Would you send that to me?"

"Sure, if it's helpful. It's not like I can show Ana now."

He rattled off his number. She keyed it in and texted him the image.

Dina sat back into the couch. She looked pleased with herself. Her spy efforts had not gone unrecognized. "And now, of course, there's that girl always coming by to help out." Dina rolled her eyes and snorted. "The sitter."

"Eve?"

"Is that her name?"

"Blond girl?"

Dina nodded. "Probably bottled, but yes. The young one with the BMW."

Ryan linked the face from yesterday with Eve's name. "You think there's something between her and Tom?"

She shook her head as though disappointed with Tom, men in general, or perhaps just Ryan. He detected annoyance in her demeanor, as though Dina had expected more information or insights from an investigator, something juicy that she could tell her friends.

"Of course, I don't know," she said. "But that girl's a bit young to be hanging out with a married man, let alone a single dad. And she's there a lot. From what I hear, Tom can't afford full-time help right now."

Tom had insisted that Eve was just a family friend. Was Dina one of the people "misinterpreting" his relationship with the girl, or did he lie about sleeping with her? Had he slept with the redhead? More than a third of men cheated on their spouse, Ryan reminded himself. That still left roughly two-thirds who didn't—assuming they weren't lying on surveys.

Dina yawned audibly. "Excuse me, I must be more tired that I realized." She clasped her palm over her mouth as if embarrassed. "Charity dinner last night."

The statement sounded like a setup to end a conversation. Ryan had to reengage her interest, encourage her to wrack her brain for new details, things she might not even realize that she'd noticed about her neighbors. "Do you think Ana suspected Tom of being unfaithful?"

A loud bang stopped Dina from answering the question. Ryan turned to see a young woman standing outside the sitting room. A bucket rolled on its side by her feet, spilling soapy water on the marble. She dropped to her knees to clean it up, keeping her face to the ground, a child prepared for a scolding.

"Honestly," Dina muttered.

"*Desculpe.*" The maid mopped up the liquid with a large sponge. "*Desculpe.*"

The word got Ryan's attention. Though he didn't speak Spanish, he'd picked up enough living in the New York suburbs to know that *lo siento* was the way most people apologized. *Desculpe* was another Latin language—and not French. He'd taken that one in high school.

"You'll have to follow that up with white vinegar and a mop," Dina snapped. "Otherwise there'll be spots. And you need to dry it with paper towel. Hold on a second." She shouted the last part as though the woman were hard of hearing and then stormed from the room, presumably to get the proper materials.

Ryan watched the woman clean. Chivalry demanded that he should help, but he didn't want to insult her by doing her job. She had a light-tan complexion and wavy, ash-blond hair, which hid most of her face. She wore thick plastic glasses that made her look like a nerdy high school student, the one that gets the makeover in the movie and ends up with the quarterback.

Dina cleared her throat as she reentered the room. The sound wrested his attention away from the woman kneeling on the floor. She dropped a paper towel roll beside the maid's knees. "I got this service a few months ago at the suggestion of a friend." Dina spoke only to Ryan. "My nanny decided the house was too big for just her." She turned her nose up at the spot on the floor. "But I still don't know about it."

She returned to the couch. "So, we were talking about Tom's philandering . . ."

"Did it seem like Ana might have suspected anything? Maybe she found out and became depressed . . ."

"The couple times I saw them socially, she seemed very much in love. Starry-eyed." Dina sighed. "Poor thing. My guess? She was clueless."

An angry splash punctuated Dina's statement. The maid squeezed the sponge, wringing out a stream of grayish liquid.

"I'll ask around, if that's helpful. There must be someone who took a mommy and me class with her or something." Dina rose from the couch. "Sorry I couldn't be of more help. I do hope Sophia gets her mother's death benefit. From what I hear, Tom's unemployable."

Ryan followed her lead, pushing off the edge of the seat to pull himself upright without transferring his weight to his bad leg. "I appreciate your time."

Dina's heels came dangerously close to the hand of the woman still scrubbing up her mistake. Ryan followed her back into the foyer, feeling more than a little guilty for failing to aid the contrite housecleaner.

The front door opened. He slipped a card from his wallet and held it out to Dina in lieu of a handshake. "If you do remember or hear anything . . ."

Dina gave another pained half-smile. "Of course. And you'll let me know if I'm living next to a, well, you know."

Ryan exited onto Dina's circular driveway. The bumpy cobblestone unbalanced him, slowing his already sluggish gate. Footsteps rushed behind him. He turned to see the maid running from the house. "Wait," she yelled.

Wind billowed in the woman's oversized sweatpants and shirt. "I heard you say about Ana." She spoke with a thick accent, straight off the boat from South America.

"Yes. Did you know the Bacons?"

"I cleaned for dem." She turned the *th* into a strong *d* sound. "Dom is no good."

"Dom?"

"Tom." This time she pronounced it like a native speaker. "Meester Bacon."

"Excuse me?" Dina shouted out of her front door.

"*Desculpe,*" the maid shouted behind her. She whispered to him. "My number."

Ryan pulled out his cell from his jacket pocket. She rattled off ten digits as Dina stormed down the driveway. "What is going on?"

From behind her glasses, the woman's blue eyes pleaded for him not to say anything. Ryan raised a hand in surrender. "My fault. I'd asked if she knew whether the Bacons had a cleaning service. It took a while for her to realize what I'd been talking about given the language barrier."

Dina's eyes narrowed as she tried to make sense of Ryan's lie. After a beat, she shrugged, deciding either that what he'd said made sense or that she didn't care either way. She turned to the housecleaner. "Finish taking care of that spill." Dina moved her hand in a circle, miming the act of scrubbing. *"Por favor,"* she commanded.

"Look into that woman, Eve," the maid whispered. Her accent wasn't as strong when she spoke softly. "And call."

Ryan saved her number on the walk back to his car. He put the contact as "maid." He hadn't gotten her name.

28

Sophia walked across the mall's tile floor, halting after each step to lick an off-kilter scoop of strawberry ice cream. Shopping centers were the poor man's amusement park. They had sweets, rides, video games, even cheap, overstuffed animals if the right vendor was around. Since arriving two hours earlier, we'd ice-skated in a minirink and rode the carousel, and now we topped it all off with Ben & Jerry's. Cost of the day: forty dollars. Memories with my daughter before risking death: priceless.

I slurped a mint chocolate smoothie. For once, I didn't worry about the calories. Swim practice was much better after loading up on sugar and carbohydrates. I'd train again tonight, even though I'd put in more than three hours in the pool yesterday. Seven miles, at least.

Sophia leaned into me as we walked. "Daddy doesn't get ice cream."

Tom was picking up Eve. He'd pitched his cousin last week on the idea of watching Sophia in exchange for a couple hundred bucks and an all-expenses-paid weekend in a quiet, suburban house. Tom had said she'd jumped at the chance to get away from her boy-crazed roommate. She would meet us here at the mall and then, if everything went well—which it had to—head back to the house with us for dinner.

"Daddy will be here soon," I said.

Sophia licked her ice cream. The day had been better without him and she must have sensed it. If he'd come, she would have spent the whole time trying to show off for him while he half-ignored her, and I would have become frustrated by his lack of responsiveness, leading to an argument.

I knelt beside my daughter. Pink ice cream smeared across the tip of her nose and her top lip. I swiped it with my thumb. "You know how much I love you?"

Sophia giggled. "You would become the wind?"

"What?"

She swallowed the last of her ice cream as though she hadn't heard the question. I knew her mind was working. Three-year-olds took time to translate their thoughts. "Like the mommy rabbit," she said finally. "If I became a sailboat, you would become the wind and blow me home."

The Runaway Bunny. I must have read that story to Sophia a hundred times. "You're my home."

She laughed. "Momma, I'm not a house."

"Home is wherever you are, for me."

She didn't understand, but she hugged me anyway. "I so love you, Momma."

We passed a trash bin. She dropped the cone inside, as she'd never liked the cracker texture. I tossed my shake, freeing my hands to pick her up beneath her armpits and swing her around. Her hair flew out behind her. She laughed. I wrapped her in a big bear hug as she came down from her flight. "I will love you forever. No matter what. I love you forever."

Sophia's legs enveloped my torso. "Me too, Momma. Like the wind."

*

Sophia and I waited in the food court. Our chicken nuggets sat on the plastic table, soggy from abandonment in ketchup. The air was irritating my nose. It smelled like a fair on a sweltering day: body odor and boiled hotdogs. In fact, everything was annoying me: the large screen behind Sophia's head, blasting a music video for some teen pop star whose voice mimicked someone mid-coitus. The crowds. The fact that my husband hadn't accounted for traffic when telling me to meet him upstairs by the teriyaki chicken stand.

My daughter fidgeted in her chair. Napkin drawings and memorized bedtime stories could only amuse for so long. "I want to go," she said for the zillionth time.

"If Daddy doesn't come in the next five minutes, we'll leave, okay?"

"He never comes."

Though he'd only missed one pickup, the memory of waiting while all the other daycare kids had disappeared into the arms of their caregivers had stuck with Sophia. One mistake erased months of showing up.

"He just hit traffic, honey."

"I want to go." She kicked the table leg, sending the leftover lunch bouncing across the table.

"I know, but we have to wait for Daddy. Please don't kick the table."

Again, she slammed the toe of her foot into the plastic leg. "I want to go."

Normally, I would have corrected the tantrum, but I didn't want to be at war with my daughter right before she met her babysitter. I needed her to be happy, to remember the experience with Tom's cousin as something wonderful so she wouldn't be frightened to spend three full days with the woman.

Sophia drummed her feet into the table leg. Sugar highs always resulted in an angry crash.

"Sophia." My voice contained a warning. "Please don't."

"I want to go now," she whined.

"What else can we do while we wait for Daddy?"

She pouted as I recounted previously played games: find the letters on signs, again, count the straws, again, make funny faces, again. Nothing appealed. I considered taking her for another walk around the cafeteria in search of something that she shouldn't have on top of ice cream. Bribes were bad but sometimes necessary.

Tom saved me from hating myself later. He exited the elevator and stood off to the side, searching for us. A very young blonde followed behind him. Her tousled California-girl locks swayed as she scanned the room. She was only about five foot three or so, tiny compared to Tom's six foot two. She had a dainty, girlish face. Fine bones. The only feature she shared with my husband was eye color.

"There's Daddy now."

I waved to them as Sophia bolted from her chair in his direction. He stretched out his arms, catching her shoulders before she could take him out at the knees. She gripped his hand and swung it, not noticing the woman beside her father. Tom touched his cousin's arm and pointed to our table. They walked toward us, Sophia pulling her father forward.

I stood for the introductions, hand extended, a large smile on my face. I had to show Sophia that I liked this "Auntie" whom her father hadn't bothered to mention in four years of marriage. As we shook, I pulled her in for a one-armed hug. "So nice to meet a member of Tom's family," I said.

Her eyelashes fluttered. Her smile appeared strained as she examined my face. She wasn't practiced in handling awkward moments. "Yes." She smiled at Tom. "He's kept us away from each other."

My husband looked down his nose at her, an older brother admonishing a fresh kid sister. "Well, you know, you were always so busy with school and we had the baby. And it wasn't like we had a big wedding."

"Justice of the peace and a couple coworkers," I explained.

She giggled, a tinny sound. "No hard feelings at all. I totally get it. Shotgun weddings don't leave much time to plan."

How did she know I'd been pregnant before walking down the aisle? I shot Tom a hard look while maintaining my smile. He should know that I didn't appreciate his sharing our business with near-strangers.

I walked around the table and touched my daughter's shoulder. "Hey, honey, this is Auntie Eve, Daddy's cousin."

She cracked a shy smile. Sophia was not a timid kid, but all preschoolers treat new adults with an extra measure of caution. Eve responded with a cool "Hello."

"Maybe we could all go to the carousel. What do you two think? Sophia loves it, and I'm sure she'd like to ride with Auntie Eve."

Eve looked at Tom for approval. "Is that what you—"

"Sounds great," he said. "Why don't you two lead the way?"

I fished a couple carousel tokens from the change section of my purse and pressed them into Eve's hand. Her fingers wrapped around them. Sophia grasped her fist. She walked forward, taking seriously the command to lead the way.

The merry-go-round beckoned at the end of the food court. The placement was ingenious, providing an obvious reward for parents to dangle so that their children ate something, thereby enabling the mommies and daddies to shop longer. As the menagerie rotated, it played "Pop Goes the Weasel" and other nursery songs. The music blasted through the cafeteria in two-minute spurts, shutting off for sixty seconds in between songs to allow kids to disembark.

Sophia skipped to the beat, jerking Eve's stiff arm. Tom had hinted that Eve might not be good with children. She seemed particularly bad with our daughter. I took a deep breath and tried to convince myself that I was reading too much into her body language. She was just unsure, and young.

Tom hung behind with me. I reached for his hand, but he was too distracted watching our daughter. He looked straight ahead as he spoke. "I booked the trip."

"When?"

"At Eve's. I bought the tickets on her computer."

"Just the flights?"

"The whole shebang." He rubbed the back of his neck. "Wasn't cheap. It's a good thing that you got all that unused leave. They don't always do that."

"Yeah," I said, reaffirming my earlier lie that I'd received eight thousand from Derivative Capital for two weeks of work and three more weeks of unused sick and vacation pay. "How much is the trip?"

"The airline tickets were two hundred dollars each round trip—I couldn't make any of the ninety-nine-dollar flights work with the ship schedules. The cruise is two hundred thirty dollars per person for two nights. All in, we're at roughly a thousand dollars after taxes and fees."

We still had about eight thousand left, given the seven left over from Michael and the grand in the savings in account. We could live on that for six months, as long as we didn't need to pay rent anywhere. Fortunately, foreclosures took a long time.

Sophia and Eve reached the carousel. Tom's cousin looked back at us, apparently for visual permission to enter the line with Sophia. My husband waved her forward. Sophia saw the signal and tugged her first-cousin-once-removed behind a mom with a young boy.

"Her favorite is the panda," I called out.

Eve looked back at me puzzled. I pointed to a panda as it went around. There were only two of them on the carousel. Sophia preferred the one with the pink saddle, but either would do. To get one, they'd have to make a beeline for it. Lots of kids liked pandas. In my mind, whether Eve managed to get one was a test. Could she cater to our daughter for a few days?

Tom and I watched it play out. Eve and Sophia were four groups back from the front of the line. The first group went to the rocking chair. The second group took the unicorn right in front. A bunch of boys scattered. A younger boy took the panda with the purple saddle. Sophia pulled Eve around the carousel, hunting for the remaining panda. A minute later, the rest of the groups had boarded and they still wandered around.

"All aboard," the conductor shouted. "Everyone choose your seat."

"It's there," I heard Sophia shout from somewhere behind the carousel's massive center column.

The merry-go-round began to turn. I waited for Sophia. When she came round, she was smiling atop the pink-saddled panda. Eve had passed my mental test. She'd try to make Sophia happy. What else could I really want from a last-minute babysitter?

Tom continued to watch our daughter and evaluate Eve. Was he as worried as I was?

"So we're headed back home for dinner."

"I need to bring her back."

"I haven't even gotten to talk to her," I said.

Tom continued to watch the carousel go round. "Sophia will be fine."

"But—"

"She has to get back. Roommate's birthday. It was nice of her to agree to come out at all."

"Sophia has barely got to spend any time with her."

"They'll be fine. Look, Sophia likes her." He waved at our daughter, hugging the painted panda, Eve standing by her side. "I'll bring Eve before our flight, so you can show her the lay of the land."

"When are we leaving?"

"Friday."

My vision swam. My gaze retreated from the carousel, unable to watch something spin as the ground shifted beneath my feet. Friday was just three days away.

29

November 30

Ryan sat in his car, two doors down from the Bacon house, waiting for the BMW parked in the driveway to leave. Three hours of breathing the stale air inside the vehicle had coated the car windows with condensation. For the fourth time, he cleared a visibility circle with his wool coat sleeve. He couldn't miss the bimmer backing out of the driveway.

If, of course, Eve ever left. He was beginning to wonder whether Tom's "friend" planned on sleeping over and at what point he'd have to call off his stakeout. He wanted to catch Eve alone. The girl would never confess any affair while Tom stood over her shoulder.

Ryan bounced his good leg to generate warmth, and for something to do. There was no one left to call—not tonight. He'd left the maid a message, and he'd done all he could with the cruise line contacts: setting up an interview with the Bacons' mystery stateroom neighbor for tomorrow at a place called Fun by Design. The still nameless source had suggested the location, and Ryan had little choice but to agree to it, even though it sounded like a nudie bar. Whoever this guy was, he really didn't want anyone seeing him.

Ryan had also tracked down the folks who had told the Bahamian authorities they'd seen Tom at the pool and left them voicemails. Three people had witnessed Tom on the sun deck. The redhead and two guys who remembered an attractive ginger chatting up "the guy on the news." Ryan didn't really want to hear them repeat their alibis for Mr. Bacon, but he had to check off the boxes, particularly with the financial crimes crew working Ana's death as a homicide.

It might not be a complete waste of time. Anyone hired to kill Ana would have been monitoring Mr. and Mrs. Bacon's movements on the ship. It was possible that the murderer had seen Tom on the pool deck and realized that Ana was alone in the room. And if that was the case, it was also conceivable that one of the people who'd noticed Tom would remember seeing someone else checking him out.

The exterior lights of the home flipped on. Ryan clasped the gearshift. The tiny blonde he'd glimpsed before exited a side door. He watched through his peephole as her headlights illuminated the space in front of where he'd parked, behind an overgrown hedge. He waited for Eve to get a hundred feet past the corner stop sign before peeling out behind her.

She made a right onto the main road through town. Ryan guessed she headed toward the highway. As predicted, the BMW led him to the Interstate. He tailed it over the George Washington Bridge and onto I-87 South, toward Queens, maintaining a one to two car-length distance, depending on the traffic.

After forty minutes of driving, the white car exited into Long Island City. Ryan followed, widening the gap between the Dodge and BMW to compensate for the relative lack of street traffic in the outer boroughs. Eve's car passed a glass skyscraper before turning onto a block of two- and three-story brownstones. It slowed down the street, pausing beside a fire hydrant. She was looking for parking.

The car pulled close to the side of an unevenly spaced row of parked cars and angled into a space. Ryan passed Eve and then stopped his car half a block up in front of a townhouse driveway. A sign on a gate threatened to tow anyone who blocked the "egress." The car was visible beyond the gate. It was already ten. Chances were the homeowner wouldn't head out for the night. And if he had to grab his car out of the impound lot, so be it.

He watched Eve in his rearview. She crossed the street and then ascended the steps of a seven-story building. It looked new. Fancy. The kind of place with a doorman. Good. A concierge could call up to "Eve" with a description.

As soon as she went inside, Ryan counted to ten and exited his car. He entered the same building and wished the linebacker of a guard good evening in the cheeriest tone he could manage. "I'm here to see Eve," he said. "So sorry, I forgot her apartment number."

The doorman gave him a once over. He tapped his keyboard. "Eve Dreher? She expecting you?"

Was he being tested? He had no idea if Dreher was really Eve's last name or something the doorman made up to see if this visitor was a stalker. His expression didn't appear suspicious. "I think I just missed her. I'm a bit late."

He glanced back at his computer screen. "She's in 206."

Ryan walked through to the elevator and hit the button for the second floor. He exited into a wide hallway with gray carpet and cream, grass-cloth wallpaper. Eve's apartment was the second on the right. He rapped twice on the door.

A voice called from inside. The door opened a crack, exposing half of the blonde's face to the hallway. Her eyes narrowed. "Are you here for Bethany? Cause she's out."

Ryan guessed the other name belonged to a roommate. "No, actually, I was hoping to talk to you." He spoke fast, trying to get through the whole introduction before Eve's stranger-danger sensors told her to shut the door. She showed a bit more of her face as he supplied his name, title, and the details of the case. "Tom mentioned that you were helping with Sophia and were a family friend."

The door pulled back. "You have to verify that I watched Sophia when they went away or something?"

Close up, Ryan could appreciate Eve's appeal. She looked like the cheerleader in high school that everyone wanted to date.

"Yes. I do," he said.

She invited him inside as though he were from the gas company. *Check the meter, make it snappy.* There was no offer of water or to sit down.

Ryan entered into a tiny living room. Half of the space had been cordoned off with one of those temporary plasterboard walls that single people in New York erected in order to take in illegal roommates. A loveseat, which mimicked a full-fledged couch in the small room, flanked a furry ottoman. A bar-height counter in the kitchen overlooked the main living area. Eve made her way behind the counter. Ryan leaned on the other side.

"So you are helping Tom take care of Sophia?"

"Yeah. I love kids." She nodded like a bobblehead. "And Sophia is such a sweetheart."

"How is Sophia doing?"

Eve tilted her hand in a what-you-gonna-do manner. "Well, I mean, she's *constantly* asking for her mama." She mocked the little girl. "'Is mama comin', Auntie Eve? Can you get her? Can you take her to me?' I've explained she's dead. Tom has. But she just *refuses* to accept it. Will what you want, right?"

"Poor girl," Ryan said.

"Yeah. Sure." Eve shrugged. "But hey, she's young. In a year or two, she might not even remember her mother. I barely remember mine."

The comment was odd for a family friend. "How do you know Tom and Ana?"

"I'm a recruiter. I met Tom through work."

Statistics flashed in Ryan's mind. Though only 36 percent of affairs were with coworkers, more than 60 percent of extramarital relationships started at work. About a third of these "work-related" affairs were with people met at the office, like a recruiter. Ryan reminded himself not to jump to conclusions. Eve had *not* spent the night at Tom's house, after all.

"And you said you watched Sophia while Ana and Tom were away? You guys must be close."

"Well, there wasn't anyone else. Tom's folks are dead." She snorted. "Ana's parents might as well be given that they're in Brazil and have zero to do with Sophia."

"Didn't Ana have friends?"

"Guess not." Eve glanced around the kitchen, as if debating whether to offer him anything, or looking for an exit. Ryan made it easy on her. "May I have a glass of water?"

She filled a glass beneath the kitchen faucet and handed it to Ryan with an expression that warned against becoming comfortable. He took a long sip. "So you and Tom are just friends or . . ."

"Yup, just friends." She smiled. No teeth showed. "More like a cousin. I just really feel bad for him, you know? He was always good to me when he worked. He'd hire people I suggested or, at the very least, agree to interview them—often only as a favor to me. I wanted to return the kindness."

She glanced at the door, undoubtedly wishing she hadn't let a private investigator into her home. "You should really hurry up and give Tom the policy. Things will be much better when he can hire a team of people to take care of Sophia. That way he can really concentrate on grieving and moving on."

Ryan put the glass down. She immediately scooped it up and placed it in the sink. "So you have everything you need, then."

It was more of a statement than a question. Ryan fished his phone from his pocket. He opened the photo that Dina had sent him the prior day and slid the screen across the breakfast bar. "Do you know this woman?"

Eve picked up the phone. Her face changed from guarded to aghast. "Who is this?"

"Apparently another family friend. I was hoping you might know her and how to get in touch with her."

Eve tried to zoom in on the image. She cursed under her breath.

"You sure you don't recognize her?" Ryan asked. "Tom's neighbor says she works for a wine store. She thinks they might have been having an affair."

Eve shook her head and pushed the phone across the counter. Ryan nudged it back in her direction. "No. No, no, no." She grabbed her arms and rocked back and forth a bit, on the verge of having a fit. "No. He wasn't seeing her."

"Because he loved Ana?"

Eve glanced again at the screen waiting on the counter. Ryan repeated his question.

"Yeah. Ana." She pressed her fingers over her eyelids. "No way he was sleeping with this bimbo."

"You're sure you don't know her?"

"I don't know her!" She turned and strode to the door. "I've answered your questions."

Ryan pressed Eve for her number on the way out while giving her his card. She hesitated before supplying her cell with an eye roll that indicated she wouldn't pick up. That was fine. He knew what buttons to push for her to call back.

After the door shut, he lingered for a moment, listening. He only heard the hiss of the heating system. New construction codes and noise ordinances ruined eavesdropping.

He had a feeling that Eve was phoning Tom.

30

The ocean spread out below the balcony, an opaque blue, darker than the blackout curtains in Sophia's room. I couldn't see through to the depths beneath. I couldn't see beyond it. The sea was infinite. Like death.

I covered the thought with a mental stream of positivity. I would survive this. I was a strong swimmer. The balcony was on the fourth floor, extreme sport height. I had studied how to jump. Cliff divers had a system. First, they leapt straight out, ski jump style: hands pressed to sides, toes pointed. After that, they arched their backs, enabling gravity to pull their bodies straight. They always entered feet first. Finally, they extended their arms to keep from falling too deep.

Once I resurfaced, the ship's motion would push me from the boat. Swimmers often avoided large vessels, fearing they would be sucked under. But the phobia wasn't warranted. Cruise ships displaced so much water that a nearby floater was more likely to be sent miles away—or so said an article I'd read at the library. The waves cresting away from the boat's sides toward the horizon confirmed my research.

Watching the sea foam below made my stomach churn. I had the sudden urge to splatter the lifeboat beneath my balcony with the scant contents of my lunch. I hadn't felt much like eating since we'd gotten on the boat. Nerve-related nausea. I'd vomited the morning before we left and then, again, on the plane.

Bile rose into my throat as I looked at the curved hull of the upside-down dinghy, hanging one floor down beneath and to the right of my balcony. I'd need to jump on the left side to avoid slamming into it. The thought of cracking a rib against the life-boat brought the acid up into my mouth. I retched and spat over the side.

"You'll psych yourself out." Tom kissed the top of my head. I took a panting breath and tried to relax into his chest behind me. He was right. No point overthinking the fall. It would be over in less than a second.

The breeze rippled a white sundress against my thighs. I'd dressed up, applied makeup. Tonight would be my last as Ana Bacon. We were going to my farewell dinner. Tomorrow night, I'd jump.

Tom's thumb caressed my cheek. He pecked my lips. "Shall we?"

I stole one more glance at the sunset, trying to settle my swimming stomach. A wave of nausea overtook me. I broke away from my husband and ran through the balcony doors toward the closet-sized bathroom. My right side clenched. I threw back the toilet seat and hurled into the bowl.

*

The dining room was modeled on the Titanic but styled for Vegas. Two staircases spiraled up to an LED-lit platform fit for show girl debutantes. Gold velvet covered the walls. Fortunately, the sunset outside softened the gaudier aspects of the décor. It flooded through staggered picture windows, bathing the room in a hazy glow.

The dying daylight flickered on Tom's face. His blue eyes had melted to a sea-glass shade. "You look beautiful," he said as we waited for the host to take us to our table.

I accepted the compliment, even though I doubted its veracity. I'd cleaned up and reapplied my makeup after getting sick, but no amount of foundation could cover the sallow undertone in my skin.

A tuxedo-clad server escorted us to an empty round table, set for four. Our dining companions arrived before Tom and I picked up the menus. They introduced themselves with the enthusiasm that Yankees like my husband and I could never manage. Dennis and Kim from Atlanta, though she'd grown up in a small Louisiana town whose name I promptly forgot as soon as she'd said it. Both were business consultants. They'd met at work and married a decade ago. Their two boys, nine and six, were staying with Kim's parents. Friday would be their tenth wedding anniversary.

We hadn't asked for any of the information. They'd volunteered everything as soon as we'd said hello, as if filling out a verbal questionnaire. Name, hometown, occupation, reason for trip.

Tom patted my thigh beneath the table. He joined in their mostly one-sided conversation in a way that only I would recognize as poking fun. *Oh, which firm? Nice. I have a friend there, John Smith in accounting. No, I guess you guys wouldn't have many dealings with the pencil pushers, huh?*

I shoved a piece of bread in my mouth to keep from laughing. John Smith? Could he be any more transparent? Tom didn't know a John Smith any more than he knew Pocahontas.

"And what brings you guys on the cruise?" Dennis asked.

Tom and I smiled at each other. "Vacation." Our secret made conversation more fun. We weren't ordinary spouses. We were coconspirators.

"Vacationing from . . ." Kim trailed off. She expected us to fill in our respective occupations and then, presumably, continue with the name game. *Oh, you work for this company? So does my brother-in-law. Small world.*

Unemployment wasn't a good answer. My husband sipped his water in response. I knew he wished for wine. Where was our waiter?

I piped up before Tom's silence could be misconstrued for rudeness. "We haven't taken a trip without our daughter since she was born. Nearly four years. We needed some time with just the two of us. With everything that goes on in life, a distance can develop if you're not careful. You know?"

Kim placed her hand over her husband's. "It is important, isn't it?"

Tom set down his water glass, watching my speech. "If you don't take time to bridge the gap," I said, "you can really end up lost. Sniping. Blaming each other for things. One day you look at your spouse and think, who is this that I married?" I leaned my head onto Tom's shoulder. "We don't want that to happen to us."

Kim and Dennis raised their water glasses. "To not getting lost."

A white-clad cruise employee appeared out of nowhere with a camera. He asked if we wanted a photo. Cruise personnel were always snapping pics in hopes that vacationers would scan through the kiosks at the end of the trip and purchase the shots for an obscene amount.

"Why not?" Kim said.

The man clicked as we clinked glasses. Tom didn't toast. Emotion, raw as a skinned knee, seized his face. He stood from the table. "Bathroom," he mumbled.

By the time he returned, my first course was cold. I caught the scent of whiskey on his breath. The smell turned my stomach and aggravated the heck out of me. He hadn't gone to the restroom. He'd hit up the bar.

I forced myself to hold my tongue. So he'd needed a drink to calm his nerves. Who wouldn't? If I hadn't been so ill, he'd have asked me to join.

I'd ordered in his absence. A crab cake drizzled in an orange tartar sauce decorated the table in front of him. I tried not to look at it. The smell of shellfish was unsettling my stomach. "I figured you'd want the crab."

A smile pinched the corner of his lips. "That's fine. Just what I would have gotten." He glanced at my plate. "You don't like yours?"

Grilled shrimp lay untouched upon a bed of cooked spinach. The sight made my stomach do somersaults. I began coughing. The violence of it threatened to send the bite of shellfish I'd forced down moments ago into my lap.

Tom pointed me in the direction of the bathroom and I ran. Less than a minute later, chewed shrimp floated in the ladies' room toilet. I held the sides of the porcelain bowl as I hurled, trying to get a grip.

When I returned to the table, Kim donned a wary smile. "Seasickness?" she asked in a low tone, leaning forward, as if the answer might embarrass me.

"Must be." Tom sat straighter in his chair, seizing the opportunity to lay the groundwork for my fall. He might have even believed that my latest bathroom trip had been for show. "She's been sick all day. Isn't that right, babe?"

Kim considered my face and then retreated into her seat. "Motion sickness is rare now, because the boats are so big. Are you sure it's not a virus? The last vacation we were on, I caught something. Ruined the whole trip."

Was the flu a better excuse for falling overboard than seasickness? Which reason would an insurance company prefer? "I'm guessing it's just the motion," I said. "I've gotten super sensitive to it suddenly. I was even ill on the plane."

"That happened to me when I was pregnant." Kim fluttered her mascara-coated lashes. Her cheeks puffed into a conspiratorial smile. "Could you be?"

The question turned all eyes on me. I didn't know how to answer without revealing too much truth to perfect strangers. My period was a week or so late, but I'd always had an irregular menstrual cycle. The fact that my monthly visitor would be MIA during a time of intense stress was normal. Besides, celibate people didn't get pregnant. I'd only had intercourse once in the past six months. And although Tom and I hadn't used protection, people didn't get knocked up from a single mistake . . . except, of course, when I'd unintentionally conceived Sophia after a week of spotty birth control consumption.

"I'm sure it's just the motion." I didn't sound sure.

Tom put a hand on my back and stood. "Babe, you want to dance?"

His request tore me away from silly what-ifs. A four-piece band played "You Don't Know Me," the slower Cindy Walker version rather than Ray Charles's jazzier rendition. We walked to a ballroom floor sandwiched between the stairs. My husband pulled me close to his chest. I rested my head against his pectorals and mimicked his two-step, listening to his heart's drum. Only Tom and I swayed in the center of the floor, the bride and groom at the beginning of the wedding reception. I caught our tablemates smiling at us. They weren't the only ones. I could feel the room's eyes on my back. Watching. Admiring.

Would people remember this moment after I died?

*

Tom and I stopped at the ship's convenience store before heading to our stateroom. On the off chance that motion sickness did worsen my nervous stomach, saltines and a Sea-Band could help. He wanted a bottle of whiskey, ostensibly to replace the cheap Jack in the minibar, but, more realistically, to supplement it.

The commissary was near the main dining room on the upper deck, a pantry-sized store stocked with over-the-counter hangover helpers. Acetaminophen. Ibuprofen. Pepto-Bismol. Gatorade. Raw ginger. Something called RU-21. Feminine products lined the shelf beneath the pharmacy. A few pregnancy tests were stacked beside the tampons, all with the same box. *First Response: Rapid Results. The Only Brand That Tells You Six Days Sooner Than Your Missed Period. 99% Accurate.*

Kim's comments made my eyes linger on packaging. I glanced at the price. Maybe once I would have wasted $13.99 to confirm something I already knew, but not now.

I moved on to a snack shelf, selected a box of water crackers, and then wandered around the store in search of the second item on my list. The Dramamine and Sea-Bands ended up right beside the cash register along with a rotating display of condoms. For her. For him. Hot. Cold. Ribbed. Microthin. Scented. Flavored. I laughed to myself. Pleasure cruise.

I grabbed a Sea-Band and waited at the counter while Tom found his Scotch. He paid with the debit card, funded with Michael's money. The bill came to sixty dollars.

Tom cracked the bottle of Glen-something-or-other as soon as my keycard went into our door. He set the cap atop a vertical steamer trunk and headed out to the balcony, apparently not expecting to close the bottle for the rest of the night. I joined him outside. The plastic bag stocked with stomach remedies dangled from my wrist.

The sound of the sea filled my ears, drowning out whatever calypso music may have spilled from the upper decks above. Two Adirondack-style deck chairs lay on the balcony. Tom lounged in one, staring out into the ocean, cradling the Scotch in his palm. The faint scent of alcohol and the day's lack of food made me light-headed. I sat in the free chair and tore into the saltines.

A mouthful later, I tackled the Sea-Band package, ripping open the cardboard to reveal two pink wristbands reminiscent of 1980s dance workout videos. The directions explained that the bands needed to be placed over something called the Nei-Kuan point, an acupressure spot on each wrist located beneath the pointer fingers. Pressure on the area, according to the directions, cured motion sickness and also morning sickness in two-thirds of tested pregnant women. I slipped them on as directed and lay back in the chair, inhaling the salty air and silently counting the stars, waiting for my stomach to settle.

The water undulated beyond, a black, silk sheet covering two lazy lovers. The air felt like a warm water bottle. It was at least eighty-five degrees. What temperature would the ocean be tomorrow? Would it be this dark?

Tom's complaints interrupted my useless train of thought. Spending fifty dollars for a Scotch with such an overly oaky nose was, apparently, an outrage. "All I can taste is wood." He held out the bottle to me. "Try it, see what I'm talking about."

I wouldn't have messed with my recovery for the bottle of Ghost Horse, let alone a sip of something my spouse couldn't stop ragging on. "I'll pass."

Tom frowned at the bottle and took another swig. So this was to be my last night as Ana Bacon? Watching my husband drown his fears in alcohol before I jumped overboard. Not if I could help it. I rose from the chair, fighting off the sleepiness brought on by the sea's white noise. My movement startled Tom. He bolted upright, arms extended, as though he might need to stop me from hurtling over the railing on the wrong evening.

I grasped both his hands and wrapped them around my waist before pressing my lips to his. It took a moment for him to return my passion, as though he were still worried I intended to say good-bye sooner than planned. As we kissed, I pressed my hands into his chest, urging him to return to his chair while I remained standing.

I lifted my dress and quickly removed my thong, a peep show before the main event. Then I untied the halter string behind my head. The sundress fell to my breasts. I wiggled it the rest of the way down while Tom pulled off his clothes.

I'd intended for us to make love on the chair. Tom had other ideas. He picked me up and wrapped my legs around his waist. My thighs pressed against his sides as he slipped his palms beneath my buttocks. His biceps flexed. He lifted and lowered me onto him, like curling weights at the gym.

Heavy weights. After a couple minutes, the strain of supporting my hundred and fifteen pounds on his forearms began to show. His neck and face reddened to a deep sunburnt color. He stepped toward support. The wooden railing pressed into my lower back. I understood Tom's need for additional aid, but I didn't want to be this close to the ship's edge. I lowered a leg, trying to touch the deck boards below. Tom moved faster. He lifted me higher, too close to finishing to realize my danger.

"Tom."

He continued hammering away, bouncing me higher with each thrust. I wrapped my arms around his neck, clasping my hands in a vice behind his head, trying to hold on. He leaned back and banged into me hard. My torso tilted over the edge. "Tom," I screamed.

The deck light in the neighboring cabin turned on. I could see a man slide open the balcony door. Tom finished with a dying moan and placed me back on the deck. His chest rose and fell as though he'd just run a marathon.

I stepped forward until I stood safely in the center of our balcony. "What were you doing?"

"What do you mean?"

"I could have fallen."

Tom pointed to the neighboring cabin and then put the same finger to his lips. Our neighbors' voices penetrated the wall separating our decks. That meant they could hear us.

"I had you the whole time," he whispered.

Had he? His hands had never left my bottom. If I had started to really fall backward, he could have easily grabbed my thighs and pulled me back onto the ship. But he was sweaty. What if I'd slipped from his grasp?

"My butt was above the balcony."

He draped his arm around my shoulders and squeezed me to his side. "No, it wasn't. Your weight was pitched forward, babe, and your hands were around my neck. You weren't going to fall." He scooped his boxers from the floor and slipped them on. "I'm sorry if I frightened you. I just got caught up. It's been a while."

Ten days had passed since we'd last had intercourse. And given the assault by my boss hours before our last go, that experience hadn't exactly been passionate. Maybe the combination of fear and arousal had made my husband reckless. Or maybe my nerves and the wind had made me sense more danger than I'd actually been in. Still, I didn't want to be outside anymore. I pulled back the sliding balcony door and fell onto our king-sized mattress.

The door didn't close behind me. I looked out to see Tom back in an Adirondack chair. He stared out at the sea. The whiskey bottle had returned to his hand.

"Aren't you coming to bed?" I called through the open door.

"You rest up," he said over his shoulder. "I'll be in shortly."

I slipped beneath the sheet and watched him drink. Ultimately, the sound of the waves and my semistarved state trumped my ability to wait up. My last sight before my lids sank toward my cheeks was the shadow of my husband, elbow on the railing, head in one palm, bottle in the other.

31

December 1

Ryan examined the sign shimmering in the afternoon sun. This was the place. Albeit, not the kind of establishment that he had expected.

Fun by Design wasn't a strip club or high-end lounge with poles and no windows. Ryan found himself looking at a window display of carved wooden dolls seated around a dinner table with fine miniature china and a faux, trussed turkey. The shop could have belonged to Geppetto. Old-fashioned marionettes hung by strings on wall hooks. Elaborate wooden puzzles and sculptures lined the shelves. Ryan didn't see anything plastic. Nothing with Mattel or Playskool stamped on the side.

A toy store was a strange place to meet a man whose name he didn't even know. Ryan scanned the shop for a dude with dark hair and a blue shirt, the description the contact had given. A sales clerk with gauged earrings stretching his lobes checked his phone behind a counter. A skinny woman in tight jeans and one of those fabric baby carriers bent over a pile of wooden kazoos. The infant inside was tied tight to her bosom with a lilac swaddling cloth and tucked between the open sides of her half-zipped puffy jacket.

Ryan hovered by a row of model airplanes. A small, white price tag on one showed a number that he swore was a misprint. Fifty-five dollars for an unpainted wooden airplane with wheels? Surely they meant five dollars and fifty cents.

The bell jangled behind him. A full head of dark hair, spiked high, ducked inside the store. A blue shirt peeked from the center of the new patron's open biker jacket. The man was thin and short, but he carried himself with the swagger of someone much bigger, someone who got laid. A lot.

Suddenly, it dawned on Ryan why his contact hadn't offered a name. He was an actor. He played the heartthrob on some teen TV series. Don. Dan. No. Daniel. That was it. He had two first names, if Ryan remembered correctly. Daniel Matthew. Ryan had never watched his show, but the actor was always on the cover of supermarket checkout magazines, usually with some model on his arm.

Ryan put up his hand, drawing the actor's attention. The man returned a tight-lipped smile and walked casual-like to the same display.

"Apologies about the locale, mate. Nephew's birthday on Saturday." Daniel pointed to the door and lowered his voice. "Probably the only place the paparazzi won't follow me into as well. Manhattan Tiger Moms frighten them off."

Ryan chuckled. The guy had an instant likability and a folksy British accent, if there was such a thing. The ability to be instantly appealing must have been one of those things that separated celebrities from ordinary people. "Thanks for agreeing to meet."

"No problem. Appreciate if you'd keep my name out of it, though. The tabloids would have a field day, me staying next to a woman who fell off a ship."

Ryan could imagine the tacky headlines: *Dying to Meet Daniel? Jumping for His Love.* "I'll keep it quiet, though you might need to submit sealed testimony if you have anything relevant."

The actor grimaced. "All right then. So . . ."

"So you were in the neighboring room?"

"Yeah. I met this girl in Miami and we thought, why not steal away to the Bahamas for the weekend? No one will know." Daniel rolled his eyes. "Murphy's Law, right?"

He joined Ryan at the plane display and selected a blue-and-white one. He checked out the price tag with an overacted version of shock. "Might have picked the wrong place." He put the plane back on its shelf and walked over to a row of trucks. "Anyway, pity what happened to that woman. Young mom and all that."

Ryan followed him to a display of equally expensive mini– motor vehicles. "Did you see anything?"

"I didn't see her fall, but I was out on the balcony a few minutes before the news said she went over. I heard some things."

"Like vomiting?"

The actor arched a single eyebrow, another talent possessed by few other than on screen performers. "No, mate. Nothing like that." Daniel picked up a red fire truck with a ladder attached. He brought the ladder up and down, playing or, more likely, testing the toy's structural integrity. "Boat was going. Maybe it drowned out the sound of someone cooking pavement pizza. But I don't know. I could hear talking."

Daniel turned the truck over and returned it to the shelf. "Isn't there anything in this store that wasn't carved by Tiffany's?" He shook his head. Ryan wasn't in the mood to laugh at any more jokes. He wanted details.

A camera clicked. Ryan turned to see the woman with the baby framing them in a cell phone shot. Daniel flashed a big grin. "My mate's helping me select a present for my nephew Ed's birthday. Mind not posting that? It'll spoil the surprise."

She blushed. "Oh, I'm sorry. I just can't believe it's you."

"How about we pose for a shot, love, and you delete that one?"

The woman nearly bounced on her toes. She made a big show of erasing the former image, jostling the baby against her chest as she did. The child seemed more of a prop in this surreal situation than a real, live human being.

Daniel stood beside her. He draped an arm around her shoulders, took the phone with his free hand, and then extended his arm to take the pic. He turned a shoulder away from the camera so that his face was angled in a three-quarter profile. The woman pulled her chin into her neck as she smiled. Ryan could guess who would look better in the photo.

Daniel clicked and handed back the camera.

"You just made my year," the woman said. Coming from someone who'd made a life within the last few months, the comment sounded odd.

Daniel maintained the big, Hollywood grin. "Who wouldn't want to be photographed with such a beautiful pair of girls?"

The woman laughed—a giddy, teenage sound. "Thank you."

"Better get on with the shopping." He directed his voice at Ryan. "Last time you saw Ed, mate, what was he into?"

"Huh?" Ryan realized as his grunt slipped out that Ed had to be Daniel's nephew and he was supposed to be the man's friend, not a private investigator. "Puppets, maybe?"

The woman fiddled with her phone as she walked from the store. Her pic would undoubtedly be on social media within the next ten minutes. It might end up on TMZ within the hour. *Daniel Matthew Ready for a Baby?* Ryan had witnessed tonight's celebrity gossip in the making.

"Sorry about that." Daniel spoke under his breath. "Acting's like politics. Got to kiss the nippers." His face grew serious. "Now that she's gone, I did want to tell you one thing." He scratched his neck. "Probably should have told the Bahamian police, but there was no way they were going to keep my name out of it. Anything for a quid, right?"

Ryan didn't like how this guy dragged everything out like a bad soap opera episode. He gestured for him to continue.

"There was a man with the woman who fell before she went overboard. I heard a voice."

The words worked like Adderall in Ryan's brain, shutting off the noise about celebrities, fame, and overpriced, imported toys. "You mean like ten minutes before or moments?"

"If the time on the news is right, less than a minute."

"So you heard this man, but you didn't see him at all?"

Daniel gave a sheepish look. "To be frank, the prior night, the dead woman and I guess her husband had been intimate on the balcony. They'd gotten it on right up against the railing and I'd caught some of it, unintentionally. I didn't want to interrupt a second time. All I'd need, you know? Someone blogging that I'm a voyeur. Anyway, when I heard them talking, kind of animated like, I went back inside."

"When did you go inside?"

"It was 7:27. I know because I remember thinking it was a good thing they'd made me go in since I had less than three minutes to make my dinner reservation."

"You sure it was 7:27 when you heard the guy?"

"Yes. Just a minute before the news said she fell."

Ryan felt the hairs prickle on the back of his neck. This was it. Proof that Ana hadn't committed suicide or fallen accidentally. Someone had been in the room with her. But who? Michael? An assassin dressed as a member of the cleaning staff?

Ana had to have known the person or at least thought they had a right to be in the room. She had opened the door for them at 6:58 and spent nearly thirty minutes with them.

"I know I should have come forward sooner. I just kind of convinced myself that it wasn't important, you know?" Daniel rubbed his palm over his spiky hair. "I thought that, since people saw the husband on deck, maybe I imagined it or something. I was happy when you called because I could get this off my chest."

"Did you hear a struggle?"

"No. I would have come forward with something like that. She was just talking with the guy. Not excited or anything. Just a conversation. I heard what the bloke said too . . ."

Daniel trailed off, waiting for some kind of cue. Dramatic pauses were for the stage. The awe of the man's presence had officially worn off.

"Out with it," Ryan said.

Daniel cleared his throat. "He said, 'That was never the plan.'"

32

August 29

Golden rays stretched over the turquoise sea. I thought of Sophia as I watched the sunrise from my balcony, sipping tea. Alone. Was she having a nice time with Eve? Did she miss me?

Through the glass door, I could see Tom facedown on the sheets like the chalk outline at a crime scene. He hadn't come to bed until nearly sunrise. I didn't plan to disturb him. If Tom slept in, I wouldn't need to invent an excuse to leave him on the beach while I checked out a "return trip" sailing excursion.

Warm, citrusy liquid slipped down my throat and tumbled into my gut. I felt better. Aside from a momentary stomach pang spurred from the rancid smell of whatever passed as the in-room coffee, I hadn't suffered any bellyaches. The Sea-Bands around my wrist had to be helping. Or perhaps the view had calmed my nerves. The water beneath the ship was clear and warm looking. Almost still. I could jump into this sea.

My belly grumbled. First, I needed food. I had to consume enough calories for a very long swim. I tiptoed back into the room and grabbed the backpack carrying all my clothes for the weekend. I emptied it onto the desk in the room, leaving only my passport, cruise ticket, room key, and a couple hundred dollars in a Ziploc bag: everything I needed to spend a day at the beach and reboard the boat. I donned my bikini and then slipped a gauzy mesh tunic over it, careful not to disturb anything close to the bed as I dressed. Tom's snore followed me out the door.

In the dining hall, I inhaled pancakes the way a runner loads up on pasta before a big race. After waiting fifteen minutes to be sure the meal would stay down, I squeezed into a full elevator bound for the ship's bowels. The exit was on the second level.

The crew took about an hour to check that all leaving passengers were carrying passports and excursion tickets. Their thoroughness worried me. If my ship checked passengers off a manifest and demanded ID, why wouldn't another boat out of the same port? Could day-cruise ships really be so much more lax than their larger counterparts?

I tried not to think about it as I walked through a metal detector separating the gangplank and the cement dock leading to the mainland. The coyotes had never failed to smuggle my parents in the country. Keeping them there had been the problem.

The road to the island was wide enough for several lanes of car traffic, but there wasn't a single vehicle on it. People, pedal-carriages, and tent stores clogged the artery from the ship to shore. I scanned for anything with a "Return Trips" label. Pedal cart drivers held signs with family names on it. Other men wore caps with the logos of local tourism outfits. They shouted about prices and beaches, each bragging that they alone knew the best spots on the island.

A mahogany-colored man with high cheekbones and a wide smile waved to me from the sidelines. He wore a plain white tee. No logo. "Glass-bottom boat?" The way he drew out the vowels sounded like a song. "Sailing tour?"

"Return Trips Travel?"

He waved me over. "Thirty U.S., take ya to da beach and back to your boat."

"Are you with Return Trips?"

He waved at another woman behind me. "Glass-bottom boat, sailing tours. The best beaches. Thirty dollars."

Panic crept into my chest like cold air. There was no sign of Return Trips Travel anywhere. What if the company didn't exist?

What if the whole thing was a scam and that man in Jersey had just stolen five thousand dollars from me? Could I survive in the Bahamas with the two hundred dollars in my Ziploc bag for a month, let alone six?

I continued walking, feeling more frantic with each step. A hand tapped my back. "Excuse me, miss. You da one searchin' for Return Trips?"

A boy, no older than seventeen, stood behind me. He had darting eyes. His wife-beater tank revealed black tattoos that looked green on his dark complexion.

"Yes. I am."

"Come."

My fear about not seeing my smugglers morphed into terror at dealing with them. Just because they had an office in Newark didn't mean I was dealing with Boy Scouts. I stepped from the young man's reach.

He looked puzzled. "You require a sailin' tour, right?"

"I need to know you're from the agency."

"You talk to Javier?"

I'd never asked the name of the man in Newark. I'd been so focused on not revealing too much of my information that I hadn't asked for any. "What does Javier look like?"

The guy shrugged. "I never met 'im. Come see da boat." He pointed to a mooring beyond the cruise ship terminal. "You'll feel better."

I followed behind, trying to stay in view of the passengers still streaming off my ship. I couldn't spot any sails. When we reached beyond the dock, my guide pointed to a near-black boat shaped like a barracuda with a long, pointy nose. The hull appeared open, a canoe with a steering wheel and instruments where the center bench would have been. Three engines hung off the back.

A man stood behind the wheel, captain's hat on his head, sandy-blond mustache atop his lip. Sunglasses shielded his eyes. The skin on his arms reminded me of a boiled lobster.

The captain's sunburnt whiteness shouldn't have made me feel better, but it did. Bullshit, I knew. Still, I felt myself calming as I followed the tattooed teenager to the safety of someone who looked more like the Skipper on *Gilligan's Island* than my TV-skewed image of a hardened criminal.

The captain looked up from a clipboard. "Name?"

It took a moment to swallow my stock answer. "Camilla de Santos." I spoke with my best impression of my mother's accent, stressing the second to last syllable of every word.

He scanned my face then checked off something with a pencil. Two young men, each wearing the stained, oversized clothing that announced poverty, sat cross-legged on the boat floor next to some straw bags.

"That's three." The captain's accent was Australian. He addressed the man who'd brought me over. "We've five more. Two are coming by boat. Turkish. Another is Jamaican." He made a twisting motion by his head. "Winston Hardie. He'll be on the trolley. Then there's the Chilean family."

My escort nodded. "Okay, boss." He ran toward the cruise ship dock.

The captain extended his hand. I grasped it. Instead of shaking, he gripped my arm and pulled me into the boat. "Hello, miss. You speak English?"

The ground rocked beneath my feet. I struggled to regain my balance. "Yes."

He raised his eyebrows. "You have the American accent. You've been to the States, I take it? Overstayed a visa from—let me guess—Venezuela?"

How could he gather so much from one word? I tried again to mimic my mother's Portuguese-accented English, making my long *e* sound like an *i* vowel and adding a *ch* sound to the letter *t*. "I need to get back," I answered. *I nid chu git back.* "Is there a pass I collect? Where do I meet you in Bimini?"

The captain chuckled. "Bimini is miles away. What are you going to do, swim? Don't worry. We'll wait for the rest of guests and then I'll take you all to Bimini and get you on your U.S. voyage."

The man in Newark had never said that the sailing tour went to Bimini. I'd assumed that the coyotes gave the passes on another island to distance themselves in case anything went wrong. "I can make my own way to Bimini. If you would give me the tickets, I—"

"Why would you have another way to get there?" The captain looked incredulous.

"I took a cruise here and I was going to go to Bimini with my hu—" I stopped myself. Better to say boyfriend. If I had a husband, he would be either getting smuggled in too or applying for my U.S. visa. "My boyfriend. Can't I meet you there?"

"No, sweetheart." He mocked my imitation accent. "You can't *mit mi chere.*"

"Why?"

"Because I get paid per head that exits this boat with one of those little carry-ons." The captain pointed to the straw bags beside my fellow passengers. They looked just like the kind of handwoven totes tourists picked up at local markets. The kind I might have bought myself on a vacation, when I'd had disposable cash. The coyotes had never said anything about a bag.

"What's in it?"

"Never you mind. No one will bother you."

I had to mind. Money? Drugs? Guns? Each one carried a different kind of sentence and made me a different kind of criminal. "I need to know what I'm carrying."

"Go look for yourself."

I picked up the bag. Its flimsy appearance belied its weight. The thing felt as though it contained a gallon of milk, yet nothing lay inside. I turned it upside down. My fingers brushed the outside. Finally, I brought the bag up to my nose like a drug-sniffing dog. My scent glands didn't tell me anything, but the close-up view revealed that the bag wasn't made of straw at all. Each strand was a straw-colored, hollow plastic tube. I could imagine what filled the insides. "Cocaine?"

The captain frowned. He rubbed his index and thumb over his mustache. "Got the trick, did you? No one else will. They've never stopped anyone before."

I put it down. "I can't take it."

"Well, then we have a problem, because then I can't take you. And if I don't take you, I don't get paid."

"Drugs weren't part of the deal."

The smile vanished. The captain stepped toward me. His chest swelled, a puff adder warning of an imminent strike. His top lip retreated further beneath his mustache. "I don't think you heard me. I get paid per head and per bag." A snarl glinted from beneath his mustache. "So everyone on this boat takes a bloody bag."

The men scooted farther to the side of the vessel, away from the advancing skipper. Their movement told me everything I needed to know about the captain. I should be afraid. But I couldn't take the bag. How would I swim with it?

"I'm sorry. I just can't."

"You're sorry?" He licked his bottom lip. A callused hand wrapped around my wrist and wrenched it backward. Pain shot up my arm. "You paid for a one-way ticket to the States. I'm that ticket and these are the travel conditions. And if you don't like it, that's too bad. This isn't American Airlines. I'm the captain and you do what I say. You understand?"

If he sprained my arm, I'd never finish the swim. "Please," I squealed. "I'm not trying to be difficult. I'd planned to jump overboard and swim to Bimini. I need it to look as though I fell off of my ship."

The sunglasses drew closer to my face. I could see the captain's dark eyes behind the lenses. "What kind of trouble are you in?"

"My boyfriend is abusive. He needs to think I died." The lie spat out before fully formulated. Amazing, the things the subconscious could invent under stress.

"So let him think you disappeared."

"He'll never stop looking for me."

"Everyone stops looking. Now sit down." The hand yanked me to the boat floor. My knees hit metal. I pulled away. He let go and watched as I toppled backward.

The boat rocked. I got back on my knees. "Please. There's an insurance policy. I need it to pay so my daughter can have a little money. If I just disappear, she'll get nothing."

The captain bent to stare at me. I looked straight into his sunglasses. He would see the honesty in my eyes. The desperation. He would believe me.

"How much?"

"Um . . . twenty thousand. She's not his. She'll get the money and my aunt in New York will get custody. If he thinks I died, I can be with her and we'll have enough to start over." The lies poured out like water from a tap. "You can pick me up from the water and take me to Bimini this evening. I'll make sure that, when the policy pays, you'll get a bonus."

The captain stood straight. His thick tongue licked the fur above his mouth. Nerves vibrated my whole body. I held on to the boat's metal side and closed my eyes, trying to make the world stop spinning, to steady myself enough to stand.

My head snapped back. The captain's hand was in my hair. Steel pressed against my throat. Sunglasses and the thick blond mustache filled my vision. "I will wait out in the water to meet you at eight. And if you are not swimming toward me, then I'll make sure you are floating facedown later. We have people on every boat."

I feared speaking would cause the knife to nick my jugular. I blinked twice.

He lowered the blade and released my hair. "I'm not waiting around for any bonus. Forget the straw bag." He pointed at me with the steel tip. "You, my lady, seem like a real shopper. You're going to return with a suitcase."

33

December 1

That was never the plan.

The words echoed in Ryan's head along with a litany of questions. What had been the plan? Who had done the planning? Why would the man tell Ana that something had changed before killing her?

Ryan tried to imagine the words emerging from a hit man's mouth. Perhaps Michael's hired killer had initially told Ana that, if she just stopped blackmailing her boss, he'd leave her alone. Then when she'd calmed down, he'd thrown her overboard, making it clear that he'd always intended to kill her.

Whatever the reason for the words, Ryan had to tell Vivienne. Ana had been murdered. There could be no doubt now.

He shuffled behind halting tourists, stuck behind their starry-eyed slowness as they admired New York City in all her holiday finery. Of course, his old precinct had to be located just blocks from where a crystal-encrusted snowflake sparkled over Fifth Avenue, calling shoppers to store windows like that ancient light over Bethlehem. Capitalism, the new Catholicism.

A woman scowled as he walked in front of her mugging for a photo. He pretended not to notice. Wasn't there a rule about giving a cripple a break during the holidays? When he got to the corner, he cut left, freeing himself from the crowds. He limped faster. Vivienne needed to know what the actor had heard. The

214

case wasn't about ISI anymore. A woman had been murdered. He needed justice done.

Ryan hobbled through the precinct entrance to a waiting metal detector. The contents of his pockets fell into a plastic bucket. A baby-faced young man at the information desk asked his name. Ryan didn't recognize the officer, but it didn't surprise him. New recruits got desk duty. He picked out his PI badge from the bucket and dropped Vivienne's name.

The kid directed him to a line of gray, plastic chairs. He sat and people watched, eyeballing the boys in blue as they strode past him to the elevators, their heavy belts weighing on their hips, causing them to walk with a wider stance than most people. Ryan had never belonged with the gun-carrying crowd, though he and Vivienne had clicked. She'd been different.

She came down after a few minutes wearing a black blazer, opened to reveal dark jeggings and a tucked-in tank. Her badge was clipped to her belt. Ryan could see her gun holster peaking from beneath her jacket. He looked over her shoulder. Fortunately, David didn't follow her. Ryan liked working with his partner alone.

"I fear you're going to be disappointed in me." Vivienne's heeled boots struck the linoleum floor. "I haven't called because I don't have anything good."

"Maybe I can cheer you up, then."

They walked south on Third Avenue. A sandwich shop on the corner of Fiftieth made a decent cup of coffee and a much-missed pastrami on rye. They'd always eaten there. He hadn't since quitting the force.

Vivienne buttoned her blazer as she walked beside him. His slow pace made the act fluid, undoubtedly as easy as if she had stood still. The fabric pulled tight over her small breasts. Ryan tried not to notice.

"Don't keep me in suspense. What do you have?"

"The guest in the stateroom next to the Bacons heard Ana talking with a man right before she fell. The guy said something about things not going according to plan."

Vivienne stopped walking to gape at him. "The Bahamian police were sitting on this?"

"Nah. The witness is a celebrity. Daniel Matthew? He didn't come forward before. Afraid of bad press."

Vivienne's face opened with recognition. "He's the guy dating that pop star, what's her name? Millie, Mala?"

"You follow that crap?"

"Doesn't everyone?" She flushed. "Don't judge me. You can't buy eggs without seeing his face."

"Yeah, well, I guess since he was out of his room when Ana fell, the Maritime Authority didn't bother really grilling him. And he didn't want to volunteer what he'd heard for fear that it would damage his image to be associated with a dead woman."

"Real chivalrous guy."

"At least he feels guilty. He said he'd testify."

They passed a Santa Claus ringing a Salvation Army bell at the corner. His alms call was a familiar sound of the season, like commercials to see the Rockettes. Amazing how the Salvation Army managed to get so many folks in red velvet each year when they didn't pay or, at best, offered minimum wage.

He waited until they escaped the ringing to speak again. "How's it going with Michael?"

Vivienne grimaced. "According to the lawyer, wifey will swear that she was with him the whole time and that they only left the boat for a couple hours to go shopping in Grand Bahama before heading to Paradise Island. They gave us a list of shopkeepers that they visited. Calls checked out. But Michael has the money to make sure they would."

"What about Pinder?"

"Nothing promising. Though his bank account is based in the Bahamas, most of the withdrawals are made here. My colleagues in the human trafficking unit say he runs a high-end escort service. Best guess? That twenty thousand was to pay for Michael's date night companions. The bartender said he brought in pros every week or so, right?"

"Shit."

"I know. If I can't find a financial link, I'm going to have to drop the case or, given what you got with this actor guy, hand it back to the FBI, I guess." She threw up a hand. "Not that the bureau showed much interest before."

They reached the restaurant. Ryan pulled back the frosted glass door and held it wide for Vivienne. She strode through without acknowledging his politeness. A woman like her would be used to doors opening.

She got in line to order. He shuffled beside her a moment later, passing the stocky fellow that had managed to reach the queue ahead of him, even though Ryan had been first through the door. As many eateries as there were in Manhattan, the good places always got packed around noon.

He noticed the man looking at him, wondering if he'd cut ahead. Ryan leaned toward his old partner. "So, anything else suspicious in Michael's expenditures?"

"No big withdrawals. But he's a smart guy. He could have been hoarding a few thousand from each ATM visit until he had enough to pay someone. And he probably had cash in his house."

"That's a lot of planning."

"He had a week from when Ana shook him down." She took a step toward the register. "I could go for an iced latte. You want the pastrami, right?"

He was pleased that she remembered his favorite order. "And iced tea. Diet." He patted his stomach, which had rounded since the leg injury. He wasn't fat, but he'd once been built like a brick wall. The leg made exercise difficult.

Vivienne wrinkled her nose. "They make those diet drinks with the fake, cancer-causing sugar, you know?"

"Still better than diabetes."

Vivienne placed their order. They stepped to the side of the counter, allowing the next person to order his lunch choices. Ryan watched his sandwich slide onto a panini press behind the coffee maker. The scent of sizzling deli meat filled the air.

"You given any thought to what I said about the husband?"

Vivienne's half-moon eyes pulled his attention away from lunch. He scratched behind his ear, uncomfortable that he would have to disagree with his partner's instincts. "I know you don't like him, Viv. I didn't at first either. But he's got an alibi. Three people saw him."

"You talk to them?"

"Called them all. Left messages. They're on my agenda for today."

She sucked her teeth. "He's too cool for someone who just lost his wife."

Ryan watched the barista/cashier make Vivienne's coffee. "It seems things weren't going that well for them before. The neighbor's pretty sure that Tom was cheating with a woman from a local wine store. She has a picture that doesn't prove it, but probably would have pissed off his wife. And that girl that is always over helping him out, Eve. Seems to have a major crush. He might be sleeping with her now. She was jealous when I asked her if she knew about the wine store clerk."

Vivienne folded her arms across her chest. "You're going to the wine store, right?"

"It's on the list."

"I'll go with you. Sometimes women can get a better sense about these things."

"What do you mean?"

"Love triangles, sleeping around."

"You don't think I can tell when someone's sleeping around?"

She raised both her eyebrows. "Why did you get divorced?"

The blood rushed to Ryan's head, so fast he felt woozy. "Hey, Leslie wasn't fucking anyone else. She just didn't want to be my nursemaid." Vivienne winced. She swore all the time, but Ryan knew that f-bombs sounded harder coming from him. He watched his language, but when he cursed, he meant it.

Vivienne raised both hands in surrender. "I don't know what Les was or wasn't doing. I'd like to go to the wine store. That's all I'm saying."

He stared at her, hating that they were such good friends that she felt entitled to get personal in a professional conversation, hating that she was probably right. Leslie had hooked up with a new man within a month of moving. It had been too convenient, him being from New Jersey and also needing to relocate to California.

"Like I said, I don't know anything." Vivienne turned her attention to the counter. Her coffee was there. She grabbed for it.

The sandwich arrived in a paper bag. Viv pushed a twenty onto the table. Ryan no longer felt hungry. He had an urge to call Leslie and pick a fight. Not over sleeping with someone—you couldn't accuse an ex of that unless you had some serious proof. Maybe over Angie. Leslie hadn't been getting her to return calls.

He took the paper bag and his iced tea. "Thanks. I'll let you get back to it."

Vivienne pouted at him. "I shouldn't have implied anything. Your ex just gave me a bored housewife vibe before you got shot." She touched his shoulder. He shrugged off her hand. "It was probably me being jealous. Les took so much of your attention. I didn't think she was appreciative."

Jealous? Ryan had never considered that Vivienne might have had a thing for him when he was married. He pushed away his surprise with more anger. He didn't have any desire to sit across from his ex-partner right now. Again, he gestured with the sandwich bag. "I'll call you about the wine store. Plan on Wednesday."

Vivienne frowned. "Okay. I'll see you then."

✶

Despite the cold stiffening his bad leg, Ryan needed to walk. He went east, toward First Avenue and the river. There was a park there, one of those green spaces that popped up in gentrified neighborhoods along with luxury high-rises. The water would be calming.

He entered the esplanade on Fifty-First Street and descended the stairs to a cobblestone boardwalk. Trees sprouted from brick circles within the walkway. Iron benches lined a wall, facing the water. The cold metal seemed to pierce his suit pants as he sat, slicing into his thighs. He leaned on one butt cheek and stretched his injured leg out in front of him, letting the air numb the pain.

His phone buzzed in his pocket. Ryan checked the screen, half expecting Vivienne's number. He didn't recognize the digits, though the area code was Long Island. He answered with his name and full title for ISI.

"Yeah, I'm returning your call. Ben Harris, one of the guys who saw the husband of the woman who fell."

Ryan covered the receiver with his palm, blocking the wind ricocheting off the water. He thanked Ben for returning the message, buying time to locate his notepad in his pants pocket and the pen in his jacket.

"I got Todd here too, on speaker. We were vacationing together. He's the other witness."

"Not together together," Todd clarified, with a bit of a surfer dude accent. "Bros weekend. Looking for a college-girls-gone-wild type of thing."

"Got it." Ryan had his pen ready now. "So you told authorities that you saw Tom Bacon on the pool deck around seven thirty PM when his wife fell overboard?"

"Yeah. We saw him. Light-brown hair, sunglasses. Medium build. Tight douchebag shorts."

"Old. Probably forty."

Forty? Tom was thirty-four, but he didn't look older than thirty. Did he seem ancient to these guys because they were barely out of college?

"Wouldn't have necessarily noticed him, but he was talking to this fine redhead."

"Fa-oin. Huge rack."

One of them started laughing. "Dude, you know when they say someone has sweet melons? Well, she had cantaloupes."

The other chuckled, a wheezing chortle that belonged on a cartoon character. "Only cantaloupe should start with a *D*. Because she definitely had double *D*s."

"Dude."

Ryan heard hands slap. He cleared his throat, interrupting the useless banter. "You said the guy she was talking to was wearing sunglasses?"

"Yeah. The Bahamas are super sunny."

They didn't get where he was going with his line of questioning. The two probably couldn't intuit much of anything at the moment. If he wasn't mistaken, they'd called him while baked. The accent he'd heard wasn't surfer dude. It was stoner. "But you were still able to recognize the guy as Tom, even though he wore sunglasses. How?"

"Well, it wasn't that hard. I mean, the redhead said she was talking to him and she was staring at his face the whole time."

"And we definitely saw her talking to some guy, for a really long time."

"Girl liked old douches, I guess."

Ryan cursed in his head. Witnesses like these were what was wrong with the criminal justice system. "When you two saw the girl and this guy in the sunglasses, were you sober?"

"What?"

Ryan pulled the phone away from his mouth and dropped an f-bomb in the wind. Harold and Kumar couldn't have made a reliable identification. He took a breath and returned the speaker to his lips. "Had you been drinking?"

"Not much."

"We had better stuff."

"Yeah, boy."

Ryan raised his voice. "Level with me. Would it be a stretch to say that your identification of Tom was mostly based on a hazy image of a beautiful woman speaking to a thirty- to forty-something Caucasian man who may or may not have been Tom, and this woman's insistence that it was that guy?"

"Well, yeah, but why would she lie?"

Ryan told them the police would need to formally interview them and hung up. He stared out at the river rushing past the walkway. The fast-moving current hid the garbage beneath, but it was there. Tires. Plastic bags. Maybe bodies. All lies waiting to surface.

Ryan didn't know why the redhead would fabricate an alibi for Tom. But he was going to find out.

34

August 29

I sat on the beach, pretending to admire the endless jewel-toned sea as I waited for my boat to reopen its door. Milky sand, warm as a baby's bottle and soft as talcum powder, snuggled between my bare thighs and slipped into the crotch of my swimsuit. Warm wind tickled my neck. This was paradise.

I'd never felt so trapped. I'd gone to bed with the devil. Several devils: the captain, the New Jersey smugglers, Michael. And I'd done so because I was no angel. There had to be a way to secure my parents' safety, my husband's sanity, and Sophia's future without sacrificing my life as I knew it. I hadn't looked hard enough. In the wake of losing my job, I'd clung to Tom's promise to make everything return to the way it was when we'd been rich.

Tom's idea of us on easy street in some Brazilian beach house was an illusion. Once I went through with this, nothing would be simple again. I'd be an identity-less, fraud-perpetrating drug smuggler for the rest of my days. Wealth couldn't really be worth life as an underground criminal.

There were alternatives. We could file for bankruptcy and start over on a smaller scale. Tom could switch careers. I could get a job as a business administrator for another firm, one located in a cheaper state, far from the reach of the Newark smugglers. My parents could sell their apartment back to the condo company and use that money to move away to someplace rural where they could live out their retirement on whatever they got for the place, plus whatever little I could afford to send back.

I returned to the boat at five thirty, resolved to call everything off. As dangerous as the captain had seemed with a knife to my throat, he couldn't really hurt me on the ship, not as long as Tom was around as a witness, or as my muscular, six-foot-two bodyguard. And the cruise terminal was crawling with cops. Once I got back home, I'd be protected—at least for a little while. The smugglers didn't even have my real name.

As I shuffled up the gangplank, pain pulsed in my lower abdomen, a wrenching menstrual ache, followed by wetness in my bikini bottom. My period had arrived. Its presence confirmed what I'd already decided; I couldn't go overboard. Jumping into shark-infested waters while smelling of blood would be more insane than any of the crazy things I'd done up to this point.

My cover-up was white. I imagined a red stain swelling on the back of the dress as I watched the ship crew run a stick through my backpack. The man checked each pocket, perhaps not believing that all I'd packed was a towel, Ziploc with a couple hundred cash, and my documents. I hadn't even bothered with sunscreen.

When he finished, I dangled the pack behind me and hurried to the nearest public bathroom, hoping to wipe out any splotch before walking through the whole ship to reach my cabin. I closed the stall door and pulled down my bikini bottom, prepared for a mess. The absence of any red mark surprised me. Aunt Flo was still MIA.

Maybe you are pregnant. The thought nagged at me as I walked to the elevators. I'd had unprotected sex and I *had* been sick in the mornings. It was possible. But now? Didn't the body become less fertile under stress?

I listened to the sloshing of liquid in my stomach, the low grumble of my intestines, trying to sense whether I "felt" pregnant. The elevator ding pulled me back to reality. A woman beside the keypad moved aside to allow me access to the buttons. My finger hesitated above the number four and then struck the nine. I couldn't tell if I was pregnant, but the commissary had plenty of tests. It would be better to know. Tom wouldn't want me jumping overboard, carrying our child. The prospect of a second kid might even snap him out of his depressed state, make him accept responsibility as he had when I'd discovered I was carrying Sophia.

The ship's store was adjacent to the elevator. I removed a precious twenty from the plastic bag and went straight for the shelf of feminine products. Moments later, the cashier handed me four dollars change and a plastic bag with one bottle of water and a cardboard box containing two pee-sticks.

I didn't want Tom hovering over me in our stateroom, dread forming on his face as we awaited the results. Better for me to know first. I locked myself in a tight restroom stall, ripped open one of the packages, and did my business. Afterward, I sat atop the closed toilet seat, watching the test's oval window. A line appeared, indicating that the test was working. After another moment, a faint line showed up next to it. Over the next few minutes, the second line darkened to a baby pink.

I stared at the positive result, breathing in the flowery scent of the air-fresheners that barely masked the underlying smells of bleach and beach. Was this good news or bad news? Was it even accurate?

I drank the water and took the second test. The door outside the bathroom opened and closed several times as I continued to occupy the stall. Faucets ran. Neighboring toilets flushed. I heard it all on some level, a distant soundtrack beneath the speeches I created in my mind and Tom's imagined reactions to them.

Within two minutes of taking the second test, both lines turned a deep magenta. A strange relief washed over me. Tom would have to understand now.

I mouthed the words I would soon repeat to him. "Tom, I can't go through with this. I'm pregnant."

35

December 2

Ryan positioned the cursor on the red dot at the bottom of the video and dragged it along the line to the beginning of the clip. Still shots of the reporter, Tom, and the redhead scrolled past. He hit play for the second time. The video stuttered and then served up a banner ad for cruise travel. The Miami station wasn't hosting a year's worth of old stories for free.

He lay back in his desk chair, waiting for the advertisement to finish. Forty seconds later, the young reporter began laying out details of Ana's accident. She cut to a lengthy quote from Tom explaining his motion sickness theory while looking forlorn. He said "Oh God" every few seconds.

Ryan pulled his cursor past Tom's speech until he saw the alibi witness. Her name was Lena Mclean. She was a willowy woman with fair skin and copper hair that brought out the green in her hazel eyes. Attractive in an almost stereotypical Scottish way. And, he had to admit, the stoners had been right; she did have a substantial chest.

What Lena didn't have was a working telephone number or address. Though he'd left one message for her a few days ago, his subsequent calls had gone to a disconnect recording. The Brooklyn apartment listed as her billing address when she'd bought her cruise tickets was also a dead end. She'd moved a month ago. The landlord didn't know where to.

The doorbell rang. Ryan glanced at the time on his computer screen. Noon exactly. Time to hit the liquor store.

*

Vivienne got the storeowner's attention as soon as she walked through the door. The man handed them cards and asked how he could help in an overly earnest way, making it clear that he understood two cops would want more than Cabernet recommendations.

"We're looking for a woman who works here," Vivienne said.

"Red hair," Ryan added. He pulled out his phone and flashed the screen at the man. Dina's picture didn't show much of the woman's face, only her copper hair and long legs.

Vincent scrutinized the photo. "She's one of our sales reps. What do you want to talk to her about?" His face jumped into a variety of microexpressions: fear, anger, disgust. Cops put this guy on edge.

"We'd rather discuss that with her," Vivienne said. "She in today?"

"Yeah. Yeah. Let me get her."

Vincent disappeared down an aisle of wooden shelves filled with bottles. Ryan took in the décor. The place was well appointed with pricey vintages, and it had a warm, wooden smell that recalled nights around a fire. Ryan guessed it would be the kind of place that would be packed on a Friday night or Saturday afternoon, though thankfully it was free of patrons on this Wednesday.

A woman hurried down an aisle as though there was a fire. Copper hair bounced by her jaw line. Her long legs led to a fitted black dress that contrasted with her fair skin. Vincent hurried behind, dwarfed by his tall companion and outpaced by her stride.

"May I help you?" Her smile showed her top teeth from incisor to incisor, a strained imitation of welcome. Her hazel eyes darted around. Ryan couldn't help but notice her breasts in her tight sweater.

It was the woman from the ship. "Lena Mclean?"

"I'm sorry, do I know you?" Her voice sounded shaky.

Ryan elbowed Vivienne and gave her a hard stare, telling her without words that this woman was no longer just someone Ana's husband may have been screwing. His old partner widened her stance and stepped her right foot back, ready to pull the gun holstered above her waist.

"You were on a cruise ship where a woman, Ana Bacon, went overboard. You told police that you were talking to her husband, Tom Bacon, when she fell."

"Yes. I did." She glanced at Vincent. Her nervous smile turned sheepish. "I ran into him. Crazy coincidence."

"You didn't tell the Bahamian authorities that you knew him," Ryan said.

"Well, I don't know him well. He just bought bottles here."

Vincent glanced at her sideways. Either he knew there was more to her and Tom's relationship or, like Dina, he'd guessed as much. "I have to check on inventory," he said. "Help them with whatever they need, Lena." He strode back down the aisle and entered what appeared to be a back office.

Ryan showed Dina's photo. "Seems like you knew Tom Bacon a bit better than that."

She grabbed at the phone. Ryan pulled back his hand. "A neighbor saw you two together."

She chewed her bottom lip. Her eyes seemed to measure the distance to the exit. "That photo doesn't show anything. It's a French good-bye." She shook her head and giggled. "It's how I say ciao to good customers. I must have been dropping off bottles in his car." She spoke with her hands out, palms open as if to show that she had nothing to hide. "We ran into each other on the cruise, completely by accident, and I talked to him for a bit. I didn't know until later that his wife had that accident."

Vivienne's hands sat on her hips. She had gotten up to speed. A small motion and she'd be brandishing her piece, preventing Lena from bolting.

"That's quite a coincidence." Vivienne exhaled as she spoke. Her tone wasn't exactly sarcastic. Ryan guessed she played good cop.

"Yeah." Lena laughed again, a forced, metallic sound.

"It's an unbelievable coincidence," Ryan said. "Your cruise ship had somewhere between two and three thousand passengers, and it took people from the entire Eastern seaboard."

"Small world." Again, Lena's eyes darted to the doorway.

"Not as small as all that," Ryan said. He considered her slowly, giving her time to realize that she'd been caught in a lie. "What makes logical sense is that you and Tom were more than friends and he decided to bring you on the cruise."

"What? Why would he do that?" She stammered. "He went with his wife."

Vivienne gave Lena a pitying look. "Maybe he figured he'd need an alibi and you could provide it. Not that you would have known that. You were probably as surprised as anyone to find out that his wife was coming."

"Or let me guess." Ryan stepped toward her, using his broad body and height to intimidate the truth out of her. "Tom told you that he would pass the trip off as some kind of finance conference. Then he tells you that Ana found out and he had to pretend as though he'd planned the cruise as a surprise for the both of them, but he'll make sure to make time for you too. Next thing you know, you're hearing that his wife went overboard and he's begging you to say the two of you had been talking the whole time."

Lena stepped back. "We had been talking. Other people saw us."

"The two potheads who saw you who weren't sure about the timeline," Ryan said. "You could have talked to Tom hours before, or to a guy who happened to look like Tom. And now that we've caught you in one lie, we are going to interview everyone on that ship. We'll find out exactly who you were talking to and when."

"I was talking to Tom."

"And when we prove you lied, we won't just charge you with providing a false alibi," Ryan continued. "We'll get you for being an accomplice."

Vivienne flashed a pained smile. "You couldn't have known what he had planned. You were surprised that his wife was on the ship, right? And then, when he told you about his wife's horrible accident, you just wanted to protect him."

Ryan countered Vivienne's faux-friendliness with a glare. "Did he tell you that Ana found out about the two of you and jumped? Did you feel guilty for cheating with a married man? Is that why you lied?"

Lena was trembling. She put a shaky hand on a shelf of wine bottles.

"Lena, you okay?" Vivienne was trying to sound sympathetic. But Ryan could hear the predatory edge in her tone.

Lena's hand slipped from the top of the shelf onto a glass bottle. She stumbled backward, pulling the wine from its holster. The bottle hit the hardwood floor. Lena hopped back as though it might break, but it rolled to her feet instead. She picked it up, hand still vibrating, and repositioned it on the rack.

"This is ridiculous." High notes of hysteria pinged in her voice. Her limbs still trembled. "If you're going to arrest me, do it. If not, leave me alone. I'm sticking to what I said. I ran into Tom—a former customer—on the boat. We talked. I didn't tell the police or reporters the customer part because I didn't want to drag the store name into this. That's what happened. I'm not changing my story."

"But did you really talk at seven thirty, Lena?" Vivienne asked. "Are you sure?"

"I'm done talking to you." She walked around them to the door and held it open, dramatically, as though she'd just caught them stealing.

Ryan shot Vivienne a "what now?" look. He wanted to bring Lena in, but not until he had more information to force her to change her story. It didn't help anyone but Tom's eventual defense attorney to allow Lena to put her lie on the record.

Vivienne handed Lena her card. "You don't want to protect a murderer." She gave her a grave look. "You never know when he'll turn on you."

Lena didn't make eye contact, but she took Vivienne's number.

Ryan scowled at her as he passed. "Call us, Lena," he said. "If we catch Tom lying first, there won't be anything to discuss except your sentence."

Lena looked as though she might cry. Ryan waited a beat to see if it would happen, but she didn't break. Instead, she let the door go. He stopped it just before it hit him in the back.

As Ryan walked to his parked car, he noticed his hands were in fists. He was opening and closing them, like a heartbeat. A desire to squeeze something overwhelmed him. He grabbed his phone from his pocket and rotated it in his hand.

"Do you want to bring in Tom?" Vivienne asked.

"I don't have enough to force the truth out of him. I at least need proof of the affair to put him on the defensive." Ryan looked at his phone. Part of him felt like throwing it in frustration. Instead, he thought of his contacts.

"The maid acted as though she knew he was sleeping around." He opened the car door. Vivienne slid inside the passenger seat. "I'll drop you off. Then I'm going to pay her a visit."

36

August 29

A room service tray sat outside our stateroom. I hadn't even jumped and Tom was spending money as though we had millions in the mail. He would not take my news well.

I used my key and opened the stateroom door. Inside was dark. Tom had drawn the blackout curtains over the balcony doors so that the only light came from the sunset slipping in from the sides of the curtains and the flickering television. My husband sat up in bed, half-naked and sipping from a near-empty water bottle.

"How are you feeling?"

He turned off the TV and patted the bed. "I boozed too hard last night. Nerves."

The perfect segue. My thighs scratched against each other as I walked around to his side of the bed. Before sitting by Tom's feet, I tried to brush some of the sand off the backs of my legs. I intended to sleep in this bed tonight. No point getting it all gritty. "About tonight—"

"Did you test the water at the beach? It's warm, right? Probably a lot warmer than the pool back home. And I was watching earlier. It doesn't seem like there are many waves."

Was he trying to convince himself that I would make it through the swim, or me? I searched his eyes, struggling to find the right words. He seemed to do the same as he waited for me to speak. Finally, I looked away. "Tom, I can't go through with it."

"Ana, you have to." He swung his legs over the side of the bed and scooted down so that his bare side touched my beach cover-up. He held both sides of my face, forcing me to stare into his eyes. "We only have a few thousand in savings and now we've spent all this money to come down here. Are you worried about the swim? You've been training. I know you can do this. If you—"

"I'm pregnant."

Tom withdrew as though I'd told him I had a contagious disease. His expression was a mixture of shock and disbelief. I remembered that look from when I'd revealed that he'd knocked me up the first time. He'd bought the ring the following day. My husband could surprise me.

I pulled out the pregnancy test box from the front pocket of my knapsack. I shook the two capped sticks onto the bed. "I was late and I didn't feel right, so I took these tests after coming back from the beach. All the vomiting has been morning sickness."

He looked afraid. I picked up the tests and held them out to him. "The night after Michael assaulted me, we made love, remember? It's been ten days."

He turned on a reading light and held the tests beneath the lamp, comparing their displays to the picture on the box's cover: the one with the two identical lines and the word "pregnant" beside them. He stared at them for what seemed like an eternity. I tried to bear the silence, let the news sink in without my commentary. My heartbeat drummed in my ears.

Tom's whole body tensed. He set the tests down beneath the light and stared at where they sat on the night table.

I couldn't take it anymore. "Tom, say something."

"Looks like you're pregnant."

"I didn't mean for this to happen. But now there's just no way. Are you okay?"

"It's a shock, but . . ." He rubbed his neck. "You know what? That's great. It stops us from doing something stupid, right?"

Relieved tears blurred my vision. "I was hoping you would see it as a blessing. I think that we should consider it a sign to get our lives in order. As soon as we get back, I'll start looking for a job.

You can too. We don't have to feel confined to New York, or even our current industries. We can look in less expensive housing markets. Maybe Maine? Or Florida? We have degrees, skills . . ."

Tom kissed the top of my head. He rubbed his forehead and then grabbed a pair of khaki shorts from the back of a chair and jostled them over his legs. "I'm going to get myself something for this headache, and then we'll celebrate."

"Are you okay?"

"I will be." A weak smile spread across his mouth. "Be right back."

He opened the door. I glanced at the time on the bedside clock: 6:58 PM. The dining rooms stopped serving dinner at nine. We had plenty of time.

His broad frame filled the doorway. After a few seconds, the lock clicked closed. "You know what?" Tom turned back to face me. "Maybe I'll just relax on the balcony."

He crossed the room to the sliding glass doors and pulled back the curtains, flooding the room with amber light. "It's nice out here," he said, as he stepped out onto our little deck.

He needed time to process everything. "I'll join you in a bit." I sequestered myself in the bathroom and turned on the shower. The sound of the water masked my breathless sobs. I felt as I had after giving birth to Sophia: relieved, excited, scared, brimming with emotion. My husband and I had stood at a precipice, and we'd made the right decision.

I showered, allowing the hot water to rinse the salt, sand, and stress from my body. After washing, I stared at my reflection in the bathroom mirror. The woman who looked back at me was tan and attractive. Confident. Ready to take on the world. In no way ready to die. This baby would be a new beginning for all of us.

I slipped on a blue sundress and then prettied my face with a touch of makeup. I put on sandals. The act of dressing in real clothes intensified my feelings of normalcy.

Tom's voice called from beyond the open balcony door. "Babe, you really should see this view."

I grabbed my knapsack and removed everything except the money. I was ready to head to dinner, toast to a new beginning.

I met Tom on the veranda. His hands wrapped around my waist. "Hey, beautiful."

He pressed his lips to mine, leaving me without air until I opened my mouth, allowing his tongue inside. His hands slipped under my dress. He hoisted me onto his pelvis. Dinner, I guessed, could wait.

We kept kissing as my back pressed against the railing. My backpack hung from my forearm as I fumbled with the button on his pants. I tried to shake off the bag. Before I could, Tom drove his still clothed body between my thighs and lifted me to his chest. His lips went to my neck.

"So I'm going to be a dad again?" He whispered the question in my ear as his fingers dug into my thighs. I rose higher as his lips traveled down my neck to my clavicle and toward my breasts. The wind lifted my hair, adding to the sensuality of the experience. This time, I wasn't afraid. We'd done it before.

"Yes," I moaned, anticipating what would come next.

"That was never the plan."

He thrust my body forward and lifted his hands in surrender. I toppled backward, falling beyond the railing. As I hurtled down to the water, I was aware that the thought, now screaming in my brain, could be my last.

My husband had planned for me to die.

Part III

Death in absentia

The legal declaration of a death despite absence of direct proof of that person's demise, typically made after an individual has been missing for an extended period of time, often seven years. Such declarations may be made sooner if the missing person was involved in a presumably lethal accident before disappearing, such as a plane crash.

37

December 3

Ryan climbed the narrow staircase of a three-story townhouse in Newark, following behind a doughy woman with a light step. The boards beneath his feet groaned as he leaned on the banister and took a heaving breath. A fifty-year-old was beating him up the stairs. He had to figure out how to exercise with his injury.

"How do you know Camilla?"

It was the second time she'd asked since she'd opened the door. Ryan guessed that she didn't like letting strange men into her illegal boarding house, at least not past seven o'clock. But she'd allowed him in anyway. Never knew where your next paying customer might come from.

"She's helping me," he repeated.

"With . . ."

"A person we both know."

The woman stopped climbing. She pressed herself against the wall. "She's through there."

His arm brushed the landlady's shoulder as he continued up the last few steps to the converted attic room. The stairs ended in an open door. The maid's large, black-rimmed glasses balanced askew on her nose, overwhelming her delicate face and hiding her blue eyes.

"Thanks for agreeing to meet."

She stepped back from the doorjamb. "I was happy you called." The "you" came out like *chew*, but the rest of her speech was near flawless. Ryan wondered how long she'd been in the States. The room didn't appear lived in. She had scarcely more furniture than a full bed, made up with a faded floral comforter, and a dresser. No photos that he could see. No television. Nothing on the stark, white walls. The place smelled musty, like a closet kept closed.

The door shut behind him. Camilla's mouth tightened as she gestured to the bed. "There's no other place to sit."

"That's all right," Ryan remained standing. "So you knew Ana well?"

"Very. I cleaned for her and watched Sophia."

Ryan thought he heard a catch in her voice as she said the little girl's name, a pause filled with longing. It must be difficult to care for someone else's kids and then leave them. Often, when both parents worked, the nannies did more child-rearing than the parents.

"Did you work with them a long time?"

"Since Sophia was a baby."

Sophia was three. Camilla's length of time in the country explained her near lack of an accent, save for certain stubborn words. "And Mrs. Bacon was home with you?"

Camilla crossed to the bed and sat, eyes trained on the hands in her lap. "I . . . I worked more when she went back."

"How often?"

"A lot."

"Every day?"

"Sometimes."

"But Sophia had daycare . . ."

It wasn't uncommon for affluent stay-at-home moms to have help during the week. But it was uncommon for a family to pay a nanny and a daycare, particularly when the father had been home, unemployed.

Camilla backtracked. "I'm sorry. Not every day." Her fingers traced her clavicle. When she noticed Ryan watching her movements, her hand retreated back to her lap. "I cleaned once a week and watched Sophia for a few hours in between daycare and when Mrs. Bacon came home."

"Tom didn't watch Sophia?"

"He was busy." Her restless hand went to the edges of her blond hair. She twisted the strands into a frayed rope. "Anyway, I wanted to tell you about Eve. Tom was seeing her."

The woman's nervous twitches and lack of eye contact screamed "liar." But it also denoted stress. An undocumented immigrant might be highly anxious talking to someone who looked and sounded like a cop.

"You saw Tom and Eve together?"

"Yes."

"When?"

She closed her eyes, as though scanning through an internal calendar. Ryan examined her clothing as she stalled. Drawstring sweatpants hung off her body, making it difficult to discern her actual size. Judging from the sharp angles of her face, Ryan guessed she was pretty thin. The pale-blue T-shirt she wore was boxy and faded.

"Right before they let me go." Camilla said, finally. "Maybe just before Ana lost her job. Eve stopped by before Ana came home from work. Tom told her that she shouldn't have come to the house and needed to leave. I heard him when I was in the kitchen with Sophia. She said that she wanted them to be together. They kissed."

"You saw them kiss?"

"Like lovers. On the mouth."

"Did you tell Mrs. Bacon?"

She wound her hair into a tighter coil. "No. Tom threatened me. He said he'd hurt me if I said anything. He'd say I stole. Get me deported."

"Do you think Ana suspected anything?"

"They were discrete and Ana was working so hard. When I saw the news reports of Ana's death, I knew Eve and Tom had something to do with it."

She made eye contact when she said the last part. All traces of her accent were gone. Her mouth remained open in a pleading expression.

"Why did you think that?"

"Because Tom wanted to move on with Eve."

Ryan's brain served up a statistic. Only 3 percent of married men left their partner and married their lovers. Most of the time, if the marriage failed, the extramarital relationship also broke up. "You heard Tom say he would leave Ana?"

Camilla traced the prominent bones in her swan neck. "No. But he was mean to her. He wanted out."

Ana's parents' accusations came back to him. "Did he abuse her?"

"He got physical."

"In front of you?"

She shook her head. "I saw bruises."

"Where?"

"Where men usually hit women."

Ryan didn't have statistics for that. There weren't spots that men aimed for, though there were places more apt to bruise.

"I don't know." Camilla rubbed her left ring finger with her right thumb as though trying to remove the skin atop her knuckles. "Forearms, I guess? Cheeks. She covered it with makeup."

"Did he hit Sophia?"

Camilla blinked as though the thought hadn't occurred to her before. She dropped her chin lower, shielding her face with her long, blond hair. "I don't know. Without Ana there now, anything could be happening."

Camilla stood from the bed. She walked straight to Ryan and grabbed his hand. Instinctively, he recoiled from the contact, but she didn't let go. "Please. I know what I'm talking about. Eve just wants Tom, and he wants money. Sophia is not safe with them."

Ryan looked into her eyes. They were a marine blue rimmed with a near navy hue, the same color as Dina's arresting shade, though perhaps not as bright. Dark pupils pierced through the color like coals at the base of a fire.

He stepped back, trying to free himself from the raw emotion that surrounded the woman. She released his hand. It retreated into his pocket, fumbling for his cell. He scrolled through his photos for the one Dina sent. "Did you ever see this woman?"

She took the phone. Disgust wrinkled her brow. "The clerk from the wine store."

"Did she come by the house too?"

"Not that I know of."

"Then how did you see her?"

She looked away from him. "I went to that wine store once."

Ryan recalled the high-end décor in Vincent's wine store, the stickers on the bottles. A woman renting a room like this could not afford anything in such a place. Camilla seemed to read his expression. "I was . . . I was with a friend."

"Tom?"

Tom had been cheating with one woman, maybe two. Why not take out the nanny also? Even with the oversized glasses and overprocessed hair, Camilla was attractive. She'd been home alone with him while Ana was out. He was a good-looking guy. American. A way to get her papers. He could have promised to make her legal and then dumped her for Eve, explaining why she wanted to create problems for them.

Her mouth dropped open. "No way. No. Never. I loved Sophia. And Ana. I would have never."

The horror in her face seemed genuine. Ryan patted the air, urging her to calm down. "I had to ask," he said.

She drew closer to him. Ryan could smell vinegar on her skin, something apple scented, whatever was on Dina's floors. "Please. Look into Tom and Eve. They must have wanted to get rid of Ana. Tom knew the insurance world. He had a policy from his parents. He knew Ana would qualify for a large benefit."

"He'd received a benefit before?"

"Yes. From ISI. That's why he chose them again. He got it as a teenager, after his mom and dad died in a car accident."

"Ana told you this?"

"Yes."

"But you weren't working for her then?"

Again, Camilla closed her eyes, as if trying to remember. "She was my friend. We talked after I left. She thought that they didn't have much money and it didn't make sense to pay insurance right now, but Tom wouldn't listen."

She pressed her lips together, struggling to contain tears. "Please. They set Ana up to die. I know it. They could hurt Sophia. You have to do something."

"Will you make a statement about the affair?"

"I . . . I . . ." She pulled both hands through her hair. "I don't have papers or proof that I worked for them. It was off the books. But I'll make whatever statement I need to."

"Okay, then." Ryan reached for the door handle. She stopped him.

"What will you do?"

Arrest Tom. The words were on the tip of his tongue, but Ryan couldn't say them. He no longer had the authority. And even if he turned over everything to the FBI, it wouldn't be enough for them to secure a conviction against Mr. Bacon. It might not even be enough to charge him. Unconfirmed affair rumors, spousal abuse allegations, Ana's death benefit, the testimony of hearing a male voice in the room with Ana before her fall, even the evidence that Tom's alibi witnesses had lied or guessed—none of it put Tom in the room with Ana. Ryan's witnesses were too easy to take apart. Even if the actor identified Tom's voice, he would be accused of playing hero and inventing the story for publicity. Ana's parents' motives would be called into question because they stood to control their daughter's insurance benefit with Tom gone. And Camilla was undocumented. Jurors respected law, order, and civic duty. They didn't trust the word of people skirting the system.

Tom's side had the stronger case. There wasn't any physical evidence that he'd pushed Ana overboard. His alibi witness was standing by her story and she had an excuse for her lie—protecting her employer. Moreover, the Bahamian authorities had already ruled there was no evidence of homicide.

Yet Ryan knew in his gut that Tom had killed his wife. The affair, the fall, and the statistics all pointed to the husband.

"What will you do?" Camilla repeated.

Ryan looked straight into her pleading eyes. He thought of Sophia, a little girl just a few years younger than his daughter, being raised by her mother's killers, kept as an ATM for Ana's life insurance policy.

"I'm going to make sure Tom pays for murdering his wife."

38

Time slowed as my body fought the fall. My feet kicked. I threw my arms out and felt something metal hit my right palm. My fingers wrapped around it, propelled more by life-saving instinct than any conscious decision to hold on. I grasped the lip of an overturned lifeboat. I jerked to a halt, believing for a moment that I'd be miraculously saved from the depths below, that I could grip the dinghy until my rescue.

But my hand slipped a moment later, weighed down by the backpack still dangling from my forearm. My feet broke my fall. They entered the water fractions of a second before the sea swallowed my head. Too late, I realized that I needed to hold out my arms like the articles had instructed. I pushed my limbs out into the water as gravity continued to pull me to the bottom of the ocean.

Pressure built in my skull. Panic set in. I needed to pop my ears. I screamed beneath the water. The yell cleared my head but spent my oxygen. I kicked and pulled the water behind me, swimming a vertical breaststroke. *Air. Please, God. Air.*

My head broke above the water. Oxygen and sea spray entered my nose. I choked. I gasped.

My sandals and backpack had wriggled off during my frantic struggle to the surface. The knapsack floated on the water in front of me. I swam to it. The money inside was a lifeline. Waves created by the ship buffeted my head as I treaded water with my legs and opened the bag's main compartment. I grabbed the Ziploc with the money, puffed air into it, and sealed it tight. I shoved my makeshift floatation device into the band of my bra, beneath my sundress. It bobbed there, helping keep me afloat as my backpack sank below the surface.

The boat moved forward. I yelled after it as waves pushed me away from the ship's roaring engines. My eyes burned with salt water. I treaded water in the ship's frothy wake, trying to wave to passengers. No lifeboats lowered. No hail of floatation devices rained down. The boat continued to advance.

Only Tom had seen me fall, and he wouldn't tell anyone until it was too late. I was ill-prepared to survive a multimile swim to Bimini. I didn't have my goggles or my swimsuit, just underwear and a sundress that would do little but create drag. I needed to reach the captain.

Land lay behind me. The smugglers' boat would be somewhere between the ship and the shore, waiting for me to arrive at eight. I'd fallen sometime after seven. I took a deep breath and ducked beneath the water, swimming where the waves couldn't continually push me off course.

The current was strong. It pulled me out to sea as I tried to swim toward the shrinking Bimini coastline, hopefully in the path of the cigarette boat. Fighting the tide exhausted me, mentally more than physically. Despair began to slow my stroke. I'd never make it. How could my husband do this to me? How long had he wanted me gone?

I imagined Sophia, crying for me, her stupid mommy who had invented a ridiculous plan with her murderous father. If he'd thrown me overboard, pregnant, God only knew what he'd do to her. I kicked harder. Pulled harder. I'd trained. I could do this. Stretch, pull down, pull back, rotate, breathe. Repeat.

The cruise ship appeared little bigger than a motorboat on the ocean now. Where was the captain? I kept moving, trying, in vain, to stay within sight of the shore where a passing boat might see me. Gradually, the sky darkened to a sailor's blue. Stars peeked from the edges of a navy sky. It felt as though I'd fought the current for hours.

A light suddenly flickered on the ocean. A search light? The cruise ship? Too small for either. A flashlight.

"It's our little mermaid." The captain's Australian accent. A motor started. The boat floated nearly on top of me. Hands grabbed my arms and yanked me from the water like a hooked fish. I fell into the hull.

A palm pushed my head to a soft, fleshy ground. "Stay low." The accent belonged to the teenager from the morning. The ground below me was made up of human beings, packed side by side like bodies in a mass grave. Silent, but not dead. The human floor undulated with heavy breaths. Faux straw bags piled on top of the bodies. Scratchy, woven plastic covered my legs.

The engines suddenly cut off. The man beneath me wheezed. I rolled to his side, giving him room to lift his head for fresh air. Men splashed from the shore into the water. Darkness covered faces. The strangers pulled the boat onto a beach overrun with palm trees.

Music wafted from somewhere on my left. I turned toward the sound. A straw bag slipped from atop my neck where it had rested like a bridle. Tropical shrubs and the surrounding blackness obscured my view of the music source. Colored lights flickered above the trees.

Fingers clenched my upper arms. I flew onto the beach. My knees hit a sharp mix of crushed seashells and sand. The particles dug into my palms as I pushed myself to a standing position.

"Stan' up. Get up. Get up. Come ashore."

People wobbled through the water onto land. We huddled on the beach, a flock of lost sheep surrounded by dogs, unsure what the men herding us did to stragglers. I moved to the center of the group for warmth. The night air was an ice bath compared to the hot tub ocean. I hadn't noticed the cold when lying atop a live body, covered in bags. Now it clawed my exposed arms and legs.

I pulled my thighs together for warmth. My wet sundress clung to my body, showing the odd bulge of the inflated plastic bag in my bra. I lowered my head so that my sopping hair covered my front and adjusted the Ziploc, letting out the air so that my money lay flat against my chest.

With the people unloaded, the men tossed straw bags onto the shore. The smugglers shoved them into our hands. A woman and daughter each put one over their shoulder like pocketbooks. The men held them at their stomachs, unaccustomed to carrying purses, let alone ones filled with contraband.

I held a bag in my hand. Perhaps the captain had changed his mind and I didn't have to bring in anything extra. The totes were well made. Unless someone knew to look for drugs inside them, I doubted anyone would suspect.

The captain's white hat shone in the starlight. He talked with another man. A finger wagged in my direction. A tall man dropped a duffle at my feet. The whites of his eyes glowed with anger. He turned to the captain. "Why she wet?" I recognized the man's heavy patois from reggae songs on the radio.

"I fell in the water," I volunteered, wringing out the bottom of my dress.

"She'll dry on the boat," the captain said. He chuckled. "What do you think of the accent?"

I hadn't thought to affect my mom's speech patterns. The tall man smiled. His teeth glinted beneath the colored lights sparkling in the trees. He reclaimed the straw bag and gestured to the duffle. "Oh, yeah. That's yours."

*

My new ship stretched the length of one dock. It reminded me of a lifeguard buoy, red on the bottom with white lettering. A pool glittered on deck beneath colored lanterns. The sight renewed the energy I'd lost from the swim and tramping through a mile of overgrown shrubs back to the docks.

My dress had dried some during the walk. It no longer appeared as though I'd swum in it—more like I'd slipped it over a sopping bathing suit. I hoped it was dry enough not to stand out.

When our group got to the edge of the mooring, the men stopped. The Jamaican motioned for me to step out of the line and pointed to the duffle cradled in my arms. "Open it."

I did as instructed. A pair of black flip-flops, the kind spas gave out for free, was inside. The man instructed me to put them on while he explained the next steps. I couldn't help thinking how the shoes would have saved my feet during the painful walk across the uncombed, shell-crushed beach minutes before.

"A few shirts in dere and da novelties dem—for if dey search ya, which dey won't. If dey ask questions, chat 'em up. Your accent's as good as green card."

He pulled a laminated slip of paper from his back pocket and a folded form, creased straight down the middle. "Dis here's da pass. Customs officers will be on da boat. Just don't go to dem. Avoid da dining halls and pools. That's where dey make da rounds."

He grabbed my right hand, licked the back of his own hand, flipped mine upside down, and then pressed them together. I retrieved my slimed extremity. A faint dolphin stamp lay beneath my middle finger. "Dat dere da stamp da ship give on da dolphin excursion. Tell dem how ya just love da dolphins. You pet da dolphins. Your best friend name Bluey. Got it?"

"Bluey?"

He chuckled. White teeth gleamed in the darkness. "Bluey da big jumper. Dolphin shoot straight out da water."

"Bluey. Got it."

"When you go ashore, a man will find ya and offer a taxi ride. He'll have a Return Trips hat and a green shirt. Got dat? A green shirt."

"Green shirt."

"Give him da duffel, den tell 'im which bus ya want."

The other smugglers appeared to give versions of the same talk in my cotravelers' native languages. I didn't wait for them to finish, having gotten permission to go from the man in charge of me. It wouldn't be good to be seen with too many people. Cruise personnel might notice all the new faces.

I jogged to the ship, slowed by the duffle jostling against my thigh. It weighed as much as a dozen straw bags. How many years in prison for twenty kilos of coke? Ten years? Twenty? A year per kilogram?

Adrenaline kept me from breaking down about Tom. He'd tried to kill me. My husband. But that didn't matter now. I needed to get home.

I tried to put my faith in the criminals. If I were caught, the smugglers wouldn't get their goods and my man in New Jersey wouldn't get the other half of my ticket. This was their business. They knew what they were doing. I needed to act natural. I filed into a line of vacationers, identifiable by the garish color combinations on their sundresses and Bermuda shorts. Canvas beach bags hung from some shoulders. Other passengers carried small purses. I was the only one with a stuffed duffle.

Sailors in white shirts and red pants stood at the entrance to a metal ramp leading to the ship's second story. They each held two devices. One scanned tickets. The other shined a black light on the back of passengers' hands.

A sailor shouted to have our tickets out. He didn't say anything about ID. A white couple in front of me held slips of paper that matched mine. They chatted in British accents about diving in a sunken ship. The woman appeared to have a green stamp of what once was a boat on her hand, though I could only make out the sail.

Waves of nausea washed over me with each step I took toward the gangplank. What if my ticket was fake? Would I be arrested for trying to board the ship, or would I just be sent away? What if they searched my bag? Should I tell these people what had happened to me? My husband had thrown me overboard. He'd wanted me dead. He thought I was dead. He'd hated me . . . maybe for years.

I pushed the thoughts out of my mind, trying to focus on the task at hand. I couldn't confess. The smugglers were right behind me. They said they knew people on the boats.

The British couple extended their hands to the man with the scanner, royalty allowing a peasant to kiss the rings. Stamps glowed beneath the black light. The ship employee asked the woman to open her purse.

"I didn't shop," she protested.

"I must check, ma'am."

Run. Run. Run. My thighs tensed. At least ten people stood behind me, between the gangplank's rails. I'd have to push around them. I could hide in the forest surrounding the beach. But if I ran, how would I get to Sophia? What would Tom do to his daughter without me there?

A flashlight investigated the passenger's bag. The cruise employee reached two fingers inside. A starfish emerged from the satchel, snared by the diligent inspector. "I'm afraid this must go. You can't bring back living things."

The woman didn't put up much of a fight. Her husband extended a willing palm for the starfish and then threw it in the water. It created a small splash when it entered the ocean before disappearing into nothing. Was that what I had done?

The scanner beeped as it passed over the couple's tickets. The inspector nodded them through. I took their place and extended the hand with the stamp.

The black light flashed. A bright blue dolphin, blurred by the transfer, blazed on my skin. Before the man could say anything, I handed him the ticket. If it didn't work, there would be no reason to risk him searching the duffle. I would run. Dump the bag. Try to talk to the Bahamian police. I could tell them how Tom had pushed me over and explain that I needed to get back to my daughter. We'd be penniless, but she'd be safe—unless Tom convinced the cops I had tried to disappear. He was such a good liar. I'd believed he'd loved me.

The scanner beeped. The duffle dangled from my shoulder, bumping between my left arm and my side. "How was the dolphin tour?" he asked.

"Bluey was amazing." The words came out in a high-pitched, rehearsed manner. "He shot straight out of the water."

The man didn't seem to notice my distress. He waved me through. "Enjoy your return trip." His eyes smiled as he said the name of the human trafficking organization, but he didn't wink. Did he work with the smugglers? He hadn't checked my bag.

The cruise ship employee moved on to the next man. Invisible eyes stalked me as I ascended carpeted stairs. The coyotes were everywhere. I didn't know whom to trust.

A lit sign pointed to a bathroom down the hall. I changed course and burst through the entrance. Beige stone, freckled with specks of gold and brown, covered the walls and floor. Four sinks lined a black granite counter. A stall door opened. The girl from the smuggler's boat entered into the sink area, mom following close behind. The mother gave me a knowing smile and then moved to the faucet. I joined them. I removed the duffle from around my shoulder and placed it between my feet.

My reflection reminded me of an old rag pulled from the wash cycle. The salt water had pasted together the strands of my hair. My skin appeared ashen. I rinsed my face over and over. Each pass with my hands restored some color to my cheeks. I dipped my head into the basin, rinsing and finger-combing my matted mop until I resembled an unkempt tourist rather than a shipwreck victim.

As I tried to look normal, a sharp pain stabbed my stomach. I panted to keep from fainting or vomiting. It didn't help. I grabbed the bag and threw myself into a stall just as the contents of my breakfast reached my throat. Kneeling on the duffle, I heaved over the toilet. Intense cramps threatened to tear my body in two. I feared losing control of my bowels. I pulled myself onto the toilet seat.

Thick clots stained my panties. I tore a piece of toilet paper off the roll and wiped at them. The tissue absorbed the blood, as cramps continued to reverberate through my body. When they subsided, I flushed, pulled my underwear back up, and waited. I expected tears, to bawl over my miscarriage, my marriage, my murderous husband, my misplaced love. None came. Fury burned in my belly, lighting up every nerve ending, forcing me to cup my hand over my mouth to muffle my enraged scream.

I would return to my baby. And once Sophia was safe, I would make Tom suffer.

39

Eve was the key. Ryan needed to turn her against Tom.

He was thinking of how to do it as he sifted through one of three file boxes in an empty cubicle at ISI's Manhattan headquarters. The computer system showed that Tom had received a two-million-dollar benefit, but the details of the early 1992 judgment hadn't been digitized. Ryan was just about done searching through *B* cases from April of that year. He'd search May next.

Whatever he found could strengthen the argument that Tom had planned for Ana to die. Still, what he really needed was Eve. She was young, jealous. He would play into her insecurities, recounting his conversation with Lena, minus her denials, making Eve believe that Tom had played her all along, used her for babysitting. Better yet, he would have Vivienne do it. Eve already knew Tom might have slept with Lena. But hearing how Tom had brought his other lover on vacation while sticking her—the second choice—with the kid would be excruciating coming from an intimidatingly attractive woman. Eve would have to give Tom up, if only not to be shamed by her peer.

He dialed Eve for the fourth or fifth time as he continued flipping through files. As before, his call went straight to a curt recording. This time, he couldn't leave a message. The mailbox was full.

Ryan told himself that it didn't matter. He'd already left Eve several enticing messages, hinting about knowledge of Tom's many affairs. He'd give her a day. If she still didn't get back to him, he and Vivienne could show up at her door. Maybe Vivienne could even bring her into the precinct. ISI was based in Manhattan, and murder for insurance fraud was a financial crime if there ever was one.

He pushed aside the current file box and took the lid off the neighboring one. The scent of stale paper filled his nostrils. He pulled out the first manila file. "BA-Judgment, May 5, 1992."

Ryan opened the folder. The front page had Tom's last name in the right-hand corner. He scanned through the parents' information. What he wanted were the death certificates and the all-important investigator's report.

The coroner's forms were attached. Garrick and Margrit Bacon had both died on the same day, but not from the same circumstances. Garrick's cause of death was listed as "gunshot, self-inflicted." His wife's was carbon monoxide poisoning. In the section for contributory causes, the coroner had elaborated. Margrit had been found dead in a running car, in a locked garage, beside her shot husband. There were scratches on her heels, indicative of being dragged, and a large hematoma on the back of her head that had caused a concussion and, likely, blackout, prior to her death. The coroner had put in parentheses *"homicide."*

Ryan reread the notes. Tom's folks had died in a murder-suicide, executed three years after the purchase of their respective life insurance policies and one year past the contestability period. Tom had received one million in coverage from each parent.

Camilla had said that Tom's parents died in a car accident. Had Ana lied to her friend to hide Tom's sordid past, or had Tom lied to Ana? Had the police lied to Tom?

Ryan flipped through pages of legal documents for the investigator's notes. The file contained five typed pages from an R. J. Sopko, Police Sgt. Retired. Ryan read as though making sense of a difficult book, getting to the period at the end of the sentence only to start from the beginning again to make certain of its meaning.

The investigator had started with a description of the garage. It could fit two cars and had held enough gas to kill a family of five. The door from the garage to the inside of the house had been locked. The garage bay had been closed. The car key, sans accompanying house keys, had been in the ignition of the Bacons' Mercedes. It was clear to cops that the car had been left running for hours.

Mr. Bacon's gun, a Smith & Wesson .38 Model 12, had been found under the gas pedal, where it had probably fallen after Garrick had shot himself. Bacon's face had been splattered on the interior of the windshield and dash. He'd had gunshot residue on his hands.

Margrit had a large bruise on the back of her skull, consistent with being punched or thrown against a wall. The investigator speculated that Mr. Bacon, a respected surgeon, had struck his wife. Upon realizing that he'd done potential brain damage, he'd likely decided to kill her and himself.

Where the investigator's report got confusing was the part about Tom. He'd been found on the other side of the house, playing Nintendo games in his bedroom, volume on the TV blasting. The police presence had seemed to surprise the boy. He'd said that he hadn't heard the house phone ringing, the gunshot, or his parents fighting. He hadn't known that he and his mother had been expected at his aunt's home that morning, nor could he understand why his Aunt had called the cops.

Sopko said the boy didn't cry when informed of his parents' deaths. He'd blinked. Nodded. Said he understood "he would be taken care of."

The investigator had speculated that Tom was in shock. He'd also written that the volume of the game indicated that Tom had, in fact, heard his parents arguing and retreated to his room to avoid becoming involved. Tom's maternal aunt had said that Garrick often hit both his wife and his son. Margrit had been planning to leave and live with her sister, potentially for good. They'd been due to arrive that morning.

Sopko ended his commentary with a note of concern for Tom. When he'd been found in his room, he'd had bloody scratches on his neck and forearms. Though Tom had explained the marks as the result of wrestling with neighborhood kids, there'd been skin under his mother's nails.

"Although the boy's aunt is adamant that her sister was a saint," Sopko wrote, "it seems clear that the boy suffered at his mother's hands as well, which could complicate attachment issues with his new guardian and policy custodian."

Why would a mother scratch her son on the neck? Attempted strangulation? Or to stop him from banging her head against a wall after she threatened to leave his father and blow up his violent but financially comfortable existence?

It was just a hunch. Ryan would never be able to prove Tom had been involved in his parents' deaths. But the theory felt good in his gut. It sat right with the statistics that showed men who killed their wives before committing suicide often took out their kids as well. It fit with the murderer Tom had become.

Ryan thought of Eve. She was young. Jealous. And she couldn't know whom she was dealing with.

He needed to get her to turn on Tom, before Tom turned on her.

40

August 30

Streetlamps pierced the grime covering the bus windows as we idled in turnpike traffic. The passengers sat up and shifted in their chairs, antsy to stand now that we were in our destination state. My rowmate's cell flashed fifteen minutes till midnight. Almost home . . . though it would never be home again.

I'd made it out of the cruise terminal without incident. A drug-sniffing dog hadn't checked my luggage. No officer had unzipped my bags. I'd just walked straight outside and met a Lincoln Town Car driver in the promised Return Trips cap who had collected our group, inspected our bags, and then dropped us at the bus station. Before the man drove away, he'd handed us each an envelope with names of houses in Newark that rented rooms and instructions on how to report for work on Monday.

Fatigue weighed on my body. All told, I'd been on the bus for nearly twenty-three and a half hours, awake for almost all of it. Somewhere between Florida and North Carolina, I'd managed to drift off for a while, only to wake, gasping, as our hulking driver stood over me to say that I had to get off if I wanted a chance to grab anything off of McDonald's Dollar Menu. In my half-asleep state, I'd mistaken him for Tom.

After two more hours of watching the bus roll past I-95's repetitive greenery, we pulled up in front of a busy terminal: Newark Penn Station. Passengers, tired and creaky from the bad night's sleep, stood from stained fabric seats and shuffled outside. A trapped wave of BO released as I rose. The skin around my thighs burned from too many hours marinating in ocean salt and sweat. I'd never needed a shower so badly.

I held my envelope tight to my chest and then patted my breast to ensure that my money was still tucked into my bra. My fingers brushed the plastic bag's edge. I folded in the corners of the Ziploc as I followed the crowd out into the night.

The exterior of the Newark transportation hub resembled an industrial version of Grand Central, minus the storefronts. Fortunately, like its more famous counterpart, it, too, had a line of waiting taxis. I was soon seated behind a driver who quoted me fifty dollars to travel the twenty-one miles to my home. I accepted the price. My suburb didn't have a train station. After paying him, I would have just over a hundred left, enough for one of the rental places where Sophia and I could camp. But not enough cash for food and everything else.

My wallet was at home, tucked into my underwear drawer in my closet. I'd need to include it in the bag that I would pack. The daily limit on my debit card was five hundred dollars. With luck, I'd be able to make two withdrawals before Tom drained the account.

As the taxi traveled up I-95, I planned how to get Sophia out of the house. I was sure only Eve would be inside. Tom had scheduled our return flights for late Monday, aware that the cruise would be delayed by search-and-recovery efforts and that he would be detained to answer questions. With luck, she'd be sleeping and wouldn't have heard about my so-called accident. I didn't want to explain anything to her or for her to be able to tell Tom that I'd made it back.

I needed to slip my daughter out of the house and get someplace safe. Someplace where Tom couldn't find me. Once I had my child and some rest, I could think about what to tell police and how to get the coyotes off my back. But not until then. Too much had happened. I hadn't been able to sufficiently process my husband's attempt on my life and the smugglers' threats. I was running on adrenaline, reacting more than anticipating. Tom was a planner.

I asked the driver to drop me off at the corner so that his cab's lights wouldn't pass in front of the house. I knew that the precaution might prove pointless. The house was designed to wake occupants when someone entered. Before I stepped foot in the mudroom, I had to open the garage door, a noisy affair that rattled the floorboards in my room. I also needed to open the interior door to the garage, which would, at best, send a small alert to the alarm system that it was ajar and, at worst, start the ringing countdown to calling the cops.

I hurried to the house and keyed in the garage door code, ducking beneath the door before it retracted more than a few feet. I sent it back down as soon as I stepped inside. I found myself praying as my hand hit the mudroom door. We always left it unlocked, since the garage door was never left open, but Eve might be extra cautious in an unfamiliar house. The knob turned. A bell dinged once as I stepped inside. Eve hadn't armed the system. Maybe she'd worried that she would forget the code and end up having to explain her presence to the police.

I shut the door and crept up the back stairs. My room was dark, but the door was open. I slipped inside, half expecting to see Eve and Sophia asleep in my bed. My daughter would go to my room if she'd had trouble sleeping, and it was all too easy to pass out when lying beside a kid in the dark for twenty minutes.

The bed was made, just as I'd left it. I slipped into my closet and grabbed a large bag from overhead. I shoved in underwear, leggings, T-shirts, socks—whatever I could grab quickly. A pair of bulky, bleach-stained maternity sweatpants that I still wore to scrub the house went inside too. Cleaning would be my job soon. Most importantly, I grabbed my wallet and cell phone. Both went into the bag's front pocket.

I cradled the tote as I walked swiftly past Eve's guest room to Sophia. Stars greeted me as I entered my daughter's room. Sophia's sky nightlight projected thousands of pinpoints onto the ceiling. She hadn't used it in a while. Her form huddled beneath the covers, despite the heat in the house. For the first time, she wasn't sprawled on her back.

Longing consumed me. I wanted to gather my child into my arms and rock her back and forth as though she were a newborn. I wanted to hold her to my chest and run. But she would need clothes. Once she woke, I'd have a difficult time keeping her quiet and going through her closet.

I grabbed several dresses and stuffed them in the bag along with underwear and socks from her drawers. All packed, I approached my sleeping child. I pulled the covers to her waist and whispered in her ear. "Soph, it's Mommy. I need you to wake up."

She murmured, still in a deep sleep. I lifted her head and shoulders into my arm, prepared to carry her out if she didn't stir. "Baby, it's Mommy. I'm going to take you to the car now, okay?"

Sophia brought her hands to her eyes and rubbed. "Mommy?"

The sound of her voice threatened to shatter the adrenaline wall that had kept me alive for the past forty-eight hours. "Yes, baby. It's me." I kept my voice low. "We have to go the car, okay? And we have to be quiet so we don't wake Auntie Eve."

She wrapped her arms around my neck and buried her head in my bosom. I breathed in her scent. A sob escaped me. I couldn't cry here. We had to get out.

I swung the bag to my back and scooped her into my arms. All the weight made my footsteps thud as I navigated down the main staircase. I carried Sophia across the foyer, through the dining room and butler's pantry.

"Okay, Sophia," I whispered, setting her down on the mud-room's tile floor. "Get your shoes."

She hunted for her sneakers while I grabbed the car keys from a tin atop a built-in bench. I reached my hand out to her. "All right, let's go."

"I can't find them."

I scanned for her shoes, any shoes. Nothing lay on the floor. Maybe in the closet?

Footsteps ran down the back stair. I reached for Sophia's hand, trying to pull my daughter toward me. I grasped air.

"Hey," a voice yelled. "Who's there?"

Eve stood on the bottom step, looking half frightened, half ready to fight. She wore a pajama shirt topped by a large cardigan, weighed down by bulky pockets. Her blond hair frizzed on top. Her eyelids were puffy beneath her highly arched brows.

"Hey, Eve. It's Ana. Sorry for waking you."

"Ana?" Her eyes were bloodshot. "You're here?" She walked into the mudroom and stood, her body between us and the exit. "Oh my God." She shook her head, horrified. "There have been stories on the news saying you fell overboard. I thought the worst. I tried calling Tom, but he doesn't get service, and the cruise line wouldn't say anything."

"Yeah. It's a misunderstanding." I faked a large yawn as I stepped toward my daughter and gripped her hand. "Feel free to go back to bed or to take off. You must want to get back to Queens."

"Wait, where are you going?"

I had no idea. I kept my voice light, as though I planned on coming right back. "Just out to the car."

She kneeled down to Sophia's level. "Oh. Okay, then. Well, I guess I'll pack up. I'll miss you." She adopted the high-pitched, syrupy tone of teenage babysitters. She opened her arms wide. "Can I get a hug?"

The good-bye was so normal that Sophia opened her arms. Eve enveloped her little body and ripped her from my grasp before I could react. With one hand, she reached into her pocket. Something long and black emerged. It pressed against the back of Sophia's head.

"I just can't let you go, Soph," Eve said.

I froze, afraid that any movement on my part could startle her into pulling the trigger. My mind raced, struggling to understand why my daughter's babysitter was holding a gun to her head. Where would she have gotten a gun? Why would Tom's cousin care if I took my daughter? She didn't know Tom had tried to kill—

Of course she did! Tom had never introduced me to his cousin before because he had never had one. He'd had a girlfriend—one he'd planned to murder me for.

Eve pressed Sophia against her chest and picked her up. She still held the gun at my daughter's head. Sophia tried to wrest free.

"Mommy?"

"Sophia, it's okay. Just stay still for a minute." I tried to rid the desperation from my voice. "Mommy's right here."

My girl continued to struggle. Eve pushed the back of her head with the gun barrel. "Listen to your mother."

"Sophia, don't worry. I'm not going anywhere. Just stay still." I pleaded with Eve. "You don't want my daughter. Just let us leave."

"I don't want her?" Eve scoffed. "She's a multimillion-dollar baby. Without Sophia, there's no money." She placed a big smacking kiss on the side of Sophia's head. "This little gold mine is the center of our new happy family."

"Listen to me, Eve. You don't need Sophia. If you let me take her, I'll just disappear and the policy will pay."

"Wow." She laughed again. A harsh, false giggle. "You really are as stupid as Tom says. You think the insurance company won't check to make sure he has custody of the beneficiary? Or is it that you think I don't know that your first move will be to take her to Brazil so your parents can get the money?"

She continued talking. I didn't hear the words. I only saw her footsteps, backtracking toward the stairs with my daughter trapped against her chest and the steel pressed against my baby's temple. Every muscle in my body ached to leap on top of Eve and rip her hands from my child. But she had the power. One shot and my little girl was gone. I needed to get the gun off Sophia and onto me.

"There won't be any money if you don't give her to me. I'll reveal my existence to police. And if you fire that—" My voice broke. I couldn't name the weapon. My daughter was sleepy. She'd never seen a gun. There was still a chance she didn't know

what was pointed at her head. "If you do it, you'll alert the whole neighborhood. Cops will be here in minutes. You'll end up in jail. But if you let me take her—"

"You're not taking her!" Eve screamed. "God, you're like a roach. Why couldn't you just drown?"

"Why don't you shoot me, then?" I said, keeping my tone level so as to not startle her. One shot might kill me, but the police would come. They'd take Sophia away. The police would have to figure out that Tom had plotted with his girlfriend to kill me. They'd take my daughter to my parents. "Come on, take a shot at me."

"Shut up. Shut up." The gun trembled in Eve's hand, but it didn't waver from Sophia's temple. She sat on the stair, pulling my daughter down with her. Sophia whimpered and again tried to turn around. Eve turned her to face me and then pulled Sophia back to her chest, blocking my daughter from running with the weight of her arm and the metal at her temple.

I forced a smile. "Everything is going to be okay, baby. Okay? It will be fine."

"That's right," Eve said, her voice assuming that cloying, condescending tone that she reserved for talking to my daughter. "Auntie Eve is just telling Mommy how things are going to go. Mommy is going to leave, and in return, I promise to keep you safe. And Mommy believes me because she knows you have a lot of money coming to you and we need you here to collect it. Okay?" Eve jostled the gun against my daughter's head. "Okay?"

Sophia whimpered.

"Okay. Okay," I said.

"After the policy pays, Soph, you'll get a nice, new nanny, and later, we'll send you to a great boarding school. Someplace far away. Maybe there you'd even be able to see Mommy. As long as she pretends to be someone else."

Eve's hand moved from my kid's chest to her chin. She clasped it and turned her head so that the gun pressed against my daughter's forehead. The sight of my kid staring down the barrel robbed me of my fight. Tears swam in my eyes.

She doesn't know what a gun looks like, I thought. *She won't know what it is. Please, God, don't let her realize.*

"If Mommy ever reveals her existence," Eve continued, "the policy will become void and we won't be able to take care of you anymore. I'll have to take you to the soundproof basement to watch a movie—a very sad movie that your Mommy doesn't want you to see."

"Please." My voice cracked. "Stop pointing that at her."

"Then leave," Eve commanded, as though she were shouting at a dog. "Go play dead."

I opened the side door beside the garage, leading outside. Eve flinched as the bell dinged. Her movement stopped my heart.

"Say good-bye to Mommy," she said to Sophia.

Tears tumbled down my daughter's cheeks, but she didn't wail or scream. She sensed the danger.

The side door locked behind me. I watched through the transom window as Eve put the gun back into her pocket and led my child toward the alarm system. She armed it with Tom's code. Afterward, she led my baby up the back stairs, to Sophia's hideout beneath the covers.

My body shuddered with rage and sadness. Hopelessness. I had no choice. To keep my daughter alive, I would have to stay dead.

41

December 4

Ryan pressed the accelerator to the rubber mat. The revelation about Tom's past cast Eve's refusal to return his calls in a new light. Maybe she wasn't avoiding him. Maybe she, like the other women in Tom's past, had become expendable.

He called Vivienne while weaving in and out of the light traffic heading to the outer boroughs, bringing her up to date on Camilla's testimony and Tom's history. She agreed to meet him at Eve's apartment. Her backup was a favor. With Michael out of the picture, she wasn't on the case, nor would she be unless he could convince a prosecutor that Tom had killed his wife for the insurance benefit.

It took him fifty minutes to get to Eve's, with traffic. He pulled up to a major crime scene. Police cars lined the street in front of Eve's building. Most of them were marked. Blue-and-white was bad. It meant that whatever had happened no longer required discretion.

He saw Vivienne as he approached the building. She stood on the landing, just outside the building's front doors. Her arms were folded around her small torso.

"We were too late," she said, her face grim.

Ryan's gut clenched. "Where is she?"

Vivienne jerked her head toward the building's entrance, and together they went inside, passing the large doorman on the way to the elevator.

Upstairs, the door to Eve's apartment hung open. Ryan got a whiff of fresh blood and fireworks. The smell left a metallic taste on his tongue.

The victim lay sprawled on the loveseat. From the neck down, she appeared normal. Pretty. Her shapely legs stretched out in front of her, extending from underneath a royal-blue dress that flared around her thighs. Above the neck was a disaster. Her head, or what was left of it, hung over the back of the chair. There was a large hole in her temple. Brain fragments stained her blond hair red.

The sight of the wound sent Ryan's leg pulsing. He winced at the memory of his own injury, his thigh peeled back and exposed like the back of Eve's skull.

Vivienne's partner, David, stood in front of the body, talking to a man in rubber gloves. The medical examiner. Ryan sidled up next to him, tearing his eyes away from Eve's ruined face.

"Gunshot to the head, close range," said David. "Her fingerprints on the trigger. The weapon's registered to her." David turned to his partner. "The television had been blasting when the cops first came in, masking the sound of any gunshot. Her roommate found her." He pointed to the coffee table. "There was a suicide note."

Vivienne acknowledged David's report with a nod. She looked at Ryan.

"Note is bullshit." Ryan rubbed his nose. The smell was getting to him. "Pretty young women don't shoot themselves."

David made a face. Ryan ignored it. Politically correct or not, it was true. Young women who killed themselves took pills or, in rare cases, inhaled toxic fumes from the car. The ones intent on dying more dramatically slit their wrists. The profile for female suicide by shooting victims was different: middle-aged, married, and often significantly overweight, which made poisoning more difficult because of the required quantity of medicine.

"The note was addressed to her parents," David said. "It was filled with the usual relationship drama. She fell for a married man and couldn't bear the thought of living without him. He doesn't want her." David looked at three uniforms hovering by the desk. "They've probably bagged it."

"Has anyone called her folks yet?" Ryan asked.

"Local detectives did an hour ago, right after they reported to the scene." David said. "The parents were surprised, but not entirely shocked. She's been on and off psych meds for years. Borderline personality disorder."

Ryan shook his head. Tom knew how to pick his victims. "No way she shot herself."

David pointed to two plainclothes cops standing in the kitchen. "They talked to the roommate."

Vivienne walked over to the detectives. Ryan didn't follow. His ears filled with the sound of his own heartbeat, blocking out Vivienne's questions. He wanted out of here. Blood and guts weren't in his job description. Besides, he didn't need to hear detectives talk about planned handwriting analysis or gunshot residue or prints. Tom wasn't an idiot. He would have worn gloves when he forced Eve's hand to hold the gun and put it to her temple. He would have had a gun on her when she wrote the note.

The only question Ryan had was what had Tom done with Sophia while killing Eve? Had he left her with Lena? Was Lena at the house now, ready to provide Tom with another false alibi? Was Lena next on his list?

Vivienne was waving him over. His leg throbbed with remembered pain as he limped over to her. "I told the guys that you were the one calling the cell and brought them up to speed on the Bacon case." She gestured to the detectives. "Your apartment was going to be their next stop."

The two men eyed him as though he hadn't been fully crossed off the suspect list. One carried a notepad in his hand. Ryan pointed to it. "You guys have to track down a woman named Lena Mclean. She works at a wine store in Fort Lee, New Jersey, called the Wine Thief. She was also seeing Tom. My guess is that he was dumping the victim for Lena. Eve didn't take kindly to it, maybe threatened to talk to me about Tom wife's death, and . . ." Ryan trailed off. He didn't need to state the obvious.

The detective scrawled as Ryan spoke. "She might be in danger. He'll want her to either provide him with an alibi or disappear."

"What about Tom?" The detective addressed his question to Vivienne. "You have enough to book him on his wife's death?"

"Like I said, the body is in the Atlantic Ocean." Vivienne coughed. The smell had to be getting to her too. "All we've got is a shaky alibi, abuse allegations, and motive. And now the violent death of the woman that Ana's friend says was seeing Tom and might have known something about him plotting his wife's death."

"It's got to be enough probable cause for an arrest," Ryan said. "And either way, we don't have time to gather more. We've got to get to him before he kills anyone else."

42

December 4

A white minivan swerved in front of a brick mansion, ready to collect the women shivering at the curb beside trash bags full of cleaning supplies and take us to our sixth house of the day. I loved and loathed the appearance of the car. For the past four months, it had transported me to and from my old neighborhood, dropping me at one lavish home after another until it dumped me back at the Newark row house where I rented a room. Without the vehicle, I wouldn't be able to scrub toilets and wipe hair from bathroom drains for ten hours. But I also wouldn't be able to see my daughter.

The side of the van featured a cartoon decal of the robot maid in *The Jetsons*. A tagline scrawled across the sliding door read, "Robomaids: Out with the Dirt, in with the Sparkle." When I first saw the vehicle outside my apartment window, more than three months ago, I'd felt this weird sense of déjà vu. It was the same car that had made the rounds in my old town, heading from house to house with its brigade of women, Swiffers over their shoulders like old-fashioned muskets. I thought it strange, and somehow fitting, that I'd now be one of the nameless servants sweeping through town. Part of me had always felt that way.

The van's sliding door opened. I filed in along with six other women. We scrunched inside, our thighs touching, butt cheeks raised off the seats to make more room. Nobody wore safety belts. Our gear went on the floor: paper towel rolls, scrub brushes, brooms, buckets, mops. The van's interior smelled like a hospital, all bleach and musty linens.

I squeezed between a broad woman and a girl with dark-brown hair, bleached at the ends. They smiled at me and then turned away. Both women spoke Spanish, some English. I wasn't letting on that I was fluent in English, lest it raise questions about my identity and how I'd ended up in debt to coyotes. To my coworkers, I was near mute. I think they believed me pathologically shy, or dumb.

The van traveled east, up the hill toward my old street, a block marked by large homes and landscaped properties, all maintained by immigrants. My familiar road welcomed like a wet doormat. It was Friday. The worst and best day of the week.

Dina's house was cleaned on Sunday, Wednesday, and Friday afternoons. Hers was the one home where I had a chance of being recognized. I feared her calling the cops, negating my death benefit and pushing Eve to retaliate against my child. But it was also at Dina's that I could watch out the window for a glimpse of my baby.

As the van turned onto my block, my body hardened into cheap armor. I needed to endure this. As long as I stayed "dead," Eve and Tom had to keep Sophia as healthy and happy as possible. If they abused her, my parents could get custody and control the money.

The driver slowed as she passed the stucco exterior of my French-styled château before pulling into my former neighbors' massive home. Dina had built nearly to the property line. Sophia's bedroom window looked straight into her master bathroom, a fact that had always made me pull her curtains closed.

The woman closest to the door slid it open. I grabbed a bucket, mop, and a milk jug filled with a mixture of white vinegar and baking soda. I stepped outside, feet from my former front door.

We passed columns worthy of the Lincoln Memorial and stood in Dina's covered archway waiting for her to invite us inside. Memories of a different time flashed before me. A

Christmas party. Tom in a velvet blazer. Mistletoe dangling above marble floors. A kiss. Laughter. Manhattans on silver trays passing above my pregnant belly. I'd never fit in here.

The lead woman rang the doorbell a second time. I dropped my gaze to my canvas sneakers, purchased from a convenience store along with blond hair dye and the oversized reading glasses that hid my sometimes faux-blue eyes. Dina had countless boxes of disposable colored contacts beneath the sink in her master bath. I'd taken a twelve pack the day I'd heard her going on about an insurance investigator. I'd needed a better disguise than glasses and dyed hair, especially once I'd agreed to meet with him in person. Had he recognized me, I would have surely been charged with attempted fraud and lost my insurance for Sophia's safety.

I focused my eyes on the floor as the mistress of the mansion opened the door for us. I recognized her sky-high Jimmy Choo boots. Stilettos ruined floors, yet Dina still stomped around her house in heels.

I shuffled into the foyer behind the other women. We all removed our shoes and set them at the edge of the gray-veined marble floor. Dina said something about starting upstairs and then clacked into the living room.

I headed to the first bathroom, cleaning supplies in hand. Dina's master bathroom reminded me of an overdecorated vanilla birthday cake, all cream and curved lines. A vanity ran alongside one whole wall of the room. The mirror above it had to be at least twelve feet long. Toiletries were scattered atop the counter: retinol, bronzer, blush, antiaging eye serum, and a box of Dina's signature eye color.

I caught the reflection of my daughter's bedroom in the mirror. Sophia was sitting on her floor, having a tea party with a circle of stuffed animals. The backside of her curtains framed her play, as though I were watching a silent film in a movie theater. I touched her reflection in the glass. Her image was only about the size of my thumb. I wanted to wave to her, to open the window and try to talk, but I couldn't. If Eve saw, she might flee with Sophia to somewhere I'd never find them.

Tears streaked the cheeks of the unfamiliar blonde in the mirror. The woman weeping in front of me was gaunt with goofy glasses perched on jutting cheekbones, a nerdy heroin addict. My bangs, which had once defined my look, had completely grown out, elongating my face. The blond hair made my skin tone somehow darker. I looked more ethnic as a towhead, and younger.

I told my reflection that my kid was okay. But I couldn't convince myself. Even if Tom and Eve were trying to be model parents, Sophia would not feel loved—not by those two. As good a liar as Tom was, he'd never been able to fake emotion with her. She'd always seen through him. It was why she'd tried so hard to make his feelings genuine. If I couldn't get her away from them, all that rejection would rub her emotions raw until she had scar tissue, until she was as numb and unfeeling as her father.

I wiped my face and tried to concentrate on my work: filling the bucket with water, pouring capfuls of cleaning solution inside. I would rescue my daughter. The insurance investigator was looking into my claims that Tom and Eve had caused my death. My parents had told him that Tom had abused me—a lie, but not a big one considering he'd thrown me off a moving cruise ship. The PI would have to see that Tom couldn't be Sophia's custodian and recommend that my parents get custody. Once he did, everything would be fine. Sophia would be able to keep her identity and her money. My parents would send for me. We'd be happy.

If the insurance investigator didn't come through, I'd have to, somehow, kidnap my kid. Life would be hard for Sophia without documents, but still better than any existence with a sociopath.

A phone rang in the bedroom, a piercing buzz that could be heard all over the house. Dina had left her cell on her dresser. Heels clopped upstairs. My old neighbor always sounded like a trotting pony.

I tried to disappear into the background, appear to be little more than a freestanding human mop. In the neighboring room, the phone stopped ringing. Through the bathroom's open door,

I could see that Dina had put the Bluetooth device in her ear and was sitting on her bed with the television remote in her hand.

"Yeah. I know. I'm putting it on now. ABC?" She sounded excited. Nervous. Had she heard more about Tom? Dina loved gossip. She'd apparently figured out that my husband had been cheating when I'd had no clue.

The television shouted to life. A male anchor spoke with a grave voice:

A young woman, shot dead earlier today in her Long Island City, Queens, home. Police are calling the death of Eve Dreher, a twenty-four-year-old financial recruitment specialist, suspicious.

"That's her," Dina shouted. "That's the woman I was telling you about."

I squinted to see the image on the television without stepping into the neighboring bedroom. A static photo of Eve, probably from a work ID, dominated the screen. I'd have recognized her anywhere. The monster who'd held a gun to my child's head.

My breath caught in my chest. Tom had killed Eve. That couldn't have been his plan. Something had to have changed. Maybe the cops were after him. Maybe she'd betrayed him. If he was on the run, what would he do with Sophia?

I darted from the bathroom, past Dina who was shouting something after me about the mop, past my coworkers downstairs. Out the door. Dampness from the snow-flecked lawn seeped into my socks as I made a mad dash across the side yard.

I stood beneath my daughter's closed bedroom window and shouted for her. If she would just come outside, I could take her away. I had saved what little of my earnings hadn't gone to the coyotes or rent. We could get a bus ticket to the middle of the country somewhere. We could hide.

"Sophia." The cold air carried my voice from her window. "Sophia."

The image of her from moments before came back to me. She was sitting on the floor. From her vantage point, all she could see was Dina's roof.

I flew around the house to the front door. I had no choice. I had to confront my husband.

I rang the doorbell. No one answered. I went to the side door and began pounding on the glass. Tom opened the door with a smile, as though he was expecting someone else. "Did you forget—"

His mouth hung open upon seeing me. It closed with a scowl. "I was wondering when you would turn up."

"The police know you killed Eve," I lied. "It's over. Let me have Sophia."

He grabbed my forearm and yanked me inside the mudroom. The door slammed behind me. I pulled away from him and scanned for weapons.

"I think we're overdue for a civil conversation." His voice was steady, but his eyes—those blue-gray irises that I'd once fallen in love with—they were as stony as ever. How had I ever gazed into those eyes and not seen the lack of soul behind them?

I followed Tom into my former dream kitchen, stripped bare of my personal touches. The whiteness reminded me of a hospital. He walked over to the sink and leaned against the counter. I stood on the other side of the island, as far as possible from my husband and as close as I could get to the open dining room. Just beyond the concrete table was the foyer and the stairs leading to Sophia's bedroom.

"I assume you've come with some sort of proposal . . ."

I hadn't had time to work out a bargaining plan, but I knew the key was to offer him money. "Give me Sophia, Tom, and I'll stay dead. You can still claim to be her custodian. You'll have the cash, I'll have our daughter. We'll both win."

He chuckled at my words.

"It's the only way you'll get the money," I said. "There's no policy if I come forward."

He continued snickering. "I don't have to do anything. You fell overboard while I was on the pool deck." He sighed with overacted drama. "Such a stupid way to die, really, but Darwinism does have a way of taking care of problems."

The insult didn't sting. He'd always seen me as the idiot wife. And clearly, I had been. I'd been married to a sociopath for years without knowing it. "The cops will figure out the truth," I said. "They must already be on your trail, since you killed Eve."

He stuck out his bottom lip in a mock pout. "Shame but . . ." He sighed. "Eve was problematic. Not like Lena. She really loves me, and she feels so guilty that you found out about our affair and jumped. She would never say I wasn't at the pool with her." He smiled. "Guilt and love. The way to a woman's heart. Right, babe?"

Had that been what kept me tied to Tom all those years? I winced away the thought. He was a master manipulator. I couldn't let him control this conversation. "The cops know about you and Eve. They're going to be coming for you. Leave Sophia with me."

"What do they know? That I was sleeping with an obsessed young woman." Tom looked at his fingernails, as though admiring their cleanliness, or examining them for blood. "I'll concede that. After all, it's why she blew her head off. She had a history of being unstable. Jealous." He shook his head, as though scolding her ghost. "She wanted me all to herself. So selfish. Not like my wife. You've been so good to stay hidden. Always putting other people first. Thinking of Sophia's future. Her safety."

I caught the threat in his tone. "I have no reason to hide if Sophia is in danger. Let me take her. You don't want her."

"Of course I do. She's my daughter."

I took a step back toward the dining room. "You don't love her."

"Well, it's true I can't love like you can. I can't sacrifice. If there wasn't money to take care of her, I . . ." He exhaled, mimicking a small explosion. I continued to step backward. "But as long as there are ample funds to go around, I want her well taken care of. I'm not my father."

"You're not a father at all," I shouted. "You're barely human."

I turned and ran up the main staircase to Sophia's room. Footsteps didn't follow me. Tom wouldn't let us get away that easy. Did he plan to climb up the back staircase and surprise us? I couldn't think of his intentions. My adrenaline had one purpose, to get my daughter.

I burst through her door and scooped her into my arms. She gripped my neck and nestled into me, understanding that now was not the time for explanations or tears. She absorbed my silence, my fear. I prayed not my pain.

I hurried down the stairs, one hand on the banister, the other on my daughter's back. Though my heart hammered in my chest and the blood pounded in my head, I could hear Tom coming down the back stairs. Whatever he'd gone up for, it hadn't been for Sophia.

"Stop right there, Ana." His voice sliced through the air. I froze at the bottom step, a deer in front of a Mack truck. Tom stood in the dining room, both hands extended in front of his face. A gun was wedged between his fists. The barrel pointed at my chest—at my child, wrapped around my torso like a shield.

I kept my eyes on the gun as I shifted Sophia to my side, out of the direct line of fire. The gun wasn't the same one that Eve had used. This weapon barely looked real. It was old, more like a prop out of an eighties western than anything I'd seen on recent television. A walnut barrel peaked above Tom's knuckles.

"Come downstairs, dear," Tom said. "We're going for a family drive."

I could imagine where my husband would take us: a wooded area, perhaps one of the hunting grounds in nearby Rockland County where the sound of gunfire wouldn't raise suspicions. He wouldn't need to spend much time hiding my body. I was already dead. No one would be looking for me.

"If you shoot that, the neighbors will come running."

He shrugged. "And I'll have to tell them all about defending my daughter from a strange intruder. Of course, I'd rather not explain that—or do this in front of Sophia."

A strange clarity erased all my other emotions. Tom was going to succeed this time. He would kill me. The best I could hope for was to make sure Sophia didn't see.

I crouched to set her on the step. "I love you." Emotion choked in my throat yet, somehow, I controlled my sobs. "No matter what happens, know that your mommy loves you so, so much."

Sophia's eyelashes fluttered against my cheek. I inhaled her strawberry shampoo and the unnamable scent that I would forever recognize as my little girl. She cried on my shoulder. Her arms still clung to my neck. When I began peeling her hands apart, she clawed at my skin. "Mommy," she howled. "Mommy, no."

"I need you to go back to your room."

Sophia shook her head. I patted her back and stood. "Please, baby, back to your room." She continued shaking her head as she took a retreating step up the stairs. Her lips pressed together, opened and closed, silently calling my name.

Tom's voice rang out in the rafters. "Sophia, stay right there." His tone threatened. She'd be hearing that tone for the rest of her childhood.

I turned toward Tom and his gun. "I'm coming. You don't need our daughter."

My voice caught on the word "our." Tom didn't deserve any claim to the little girl on the steps. But I needed him to remember that she was part of his legacy. Even he wouldn't want to damage his own flesh and blood.

Tom shifted the gun from my chest to Sophia's little form. "Oh, but I do need her. You behave so much better when the kid's around." He gestured toward the floor with the gun. "Both of you, down the steps. Now!"

The screamed command sent Sophia flying down the stairs. She stood at the bottom, shaking, confused. I hurried to her side. Tom gestured with the gun toward the kitchen. "You first, babe."

I held Sophia's hand as we walked through the dining room. She clung to my forearm, a sign that she wanted me to pick her up. I ignored it. Though I wouldn't be able to outrun the bullets pointed at the back of my head, maybe I could push Sophia out the side door before we reached the garage. Tom would kill me. But she'd be running to the neighbor's house. She wouldn't witness it.

Tom's footsteps thudded behind me. I didn't need to see the gun to feel its presence or to know that my husband's finger flexed by the trigger. When we reached the kitchen, he ordered us to stop. It took a moment for me to understand the reason. He needed to grab the car keys from the drawer in the island.

I released my daughter's hand. Her free fingers dug into my arm. I wrested away. "Run."

Tom was on her before she took a step. She screamed as he grabbed her thin arm and yanked her toward him. "No, honey. Mommy is confused." The gun was pointed at my head. "She must not have heard me when I said *we*—all of us—are going to the car."

"Please, let her go." Tears bubbled in my words. "Please, Tom."

He pushed her in front of him and pointed the gun at the back of her head with one hand—just like Eve. He was even crazier than his monstrous girlfriend. "If you escape, there's no reason to keep her."

"Please, Tom!" My knees felt weak. If it weren't for the adrenaline, I would collapse on the floor. "Please. Leave her alone."

He fished in the drawer with his free hand. Keys jangled. As he palmed them, he ordered Sophia and me out to the garage. I looked to my side as I walked, tracking the gun held to my baby's head, pleading with my husband to just let her go.

My cries had no effect. Tom's eyes appeared glazed, as though he was not fully aware of his actions. He opened the door to the garage and pushed my back with his free hand. My old Toyota beeped open. The locks popped up.

"Get in the car." He spoke slowly, as though I may be mentally impaired instead of reluctant.

I opened the door. Out of the corner of my eye, I saw Tom's hand recoil with the gun. Metal slammed into my temple. I felt myself fall to the ground. The back of my head hit the concrete floor. Then everything went black.

★

Shouting woke me. My vision blurred as my eyes opened. How long had I been out? Minutes? Hours? Where was I?

The room came into focus, surrounded by fuzzy blackness. Tires and a silver bumper blocked my view. Something was humming. I pressed my hand to the cold floor beneath me, struggling to get a better vantage point. A black exhaust pipe blurred into view. The noise suddenly made sense. Tom had left the car's engine running. He was trying to poison me.

A loud knock sounded from somewhere beyond the garage door. "Police, open up."

I squeezed my eyes shut. My mind played tricks on me, inventing saviors at the gate. Where was Sophia?

My vision swam as I stood. Instinctively, my fingers pressed against my temples, trying to counteract the blinding pressure in my head. "Sophia." Coughs shattered my attempt to scream her name. My heart threatened to explode in my chest. "Sophia!"

I put my hand on the trunk and peered into the rear window. She wasn't inside the car. Of course not. Tom needed her alive.

A coughing fit doubled me over. The air in the garage had to be thick with carbon monoxide. I'd die if I couldn't get out.

I stumbled to the inside door, my limbs heavy with sleep, as though I were dreaming. The knob refused to turn. He'd locked it.

"Mr. Bacon, police. Open up."

Did poisoning cause auditory hallucinations? Or was it possible that the police were really outside the door? I ran my hand along the wall for the garage door opener. I saw it, knocked half off the plaster holster. Wires stuck out from the inside in a broken, jumbled mess.

He'd disabled it. I had to shut off the car.

The poison weighed on my extremities. I leaned on the vehicle as I sidestepped around to the driver's side. The keys were in the ignition. The vehicle's locks were engaged. I grabbed the door handle anyway and pulled, desperation overtaking my good sense. I kicked the car door. Nothing I could do would help. Blood rushed to my ears, blocking out sound. I felt so woozy.

Another coughing fit sent me to my knees. I half-crawled to the garage door and pulled, trying to force it up with the little strength I had left. Lights exploded behind my eyes. The door didn't budge.

A choking sound stifled my sobs. I had to find something to break the door down. An axe? A wrench? All that stuff was in Tom's garage, not mine.

I cursed myself. In my haste to save my child, I hadn't planned. And Tom was a planner. He'd figured out how to get rid of me without alerting the neighbors. He would poison me, put me in the trunk, and dump me somewhere. Then he'd run off with Lena and my daughter.

Tears clouded my already warped vision. Eve had been a monster. Perhaps Lena would be kind. I said a silent prayer for God to protect my child and took in my final view: the stark garage, the Toyota, the red rope dangling from the hinge of the garage door.

A giggle burst from my lips. Manual override.

I stood on my tiptoes and swatted at the cord. My fingers wrapped around it on the third try. I yanked. A switch flipped, though I barely heard it over the coughing fit caused by the added physical exertion. Again, I crouched beside the garage door handle and pulled, using all the strength in my thighs to wrest the door open.

The door rose several feet. Fresh air filled my nostrils, water to the dehydrated. I ducked beneath the door and hobbled outside.

My coughs intensified as I emerged from the gas chamber, forcing my eyes closed. When I could finally open them, I saw two police sedans in my driveway and the investigator's car. I hadn't imagined the voices. Where was Sophia?

The front door hung wide open. I stumbled toward it, still doubled over from the coughs now brought on by the painful invasion of breathable air. I entered my house and scanned for my daughter. An Asian woman and the investigator stood in the foyer, in front of my husband. Tom had untucked his button-down shirt. Such sloppiness wasn't like him. The gun had to be hidden inside his waistband.

The cops turned as I entered. I pointed to my spouse. "He has a gun. He tried to kill me."

Tom's expression morphed from annoyed to angry. Furious. He stepped back into the dining room and reached to his hip.

"Gun. Gun!" The Asian woman's stance changed as she shouted. Her hip angled back and her weapon emerged in one fluid motion.

Tom reacted by withdrawing his own pistol. He pointed it at me, over the shoulder of the investigator standing just in front of my hunched form.

"Put the gun down," the Asian woman shouted.

"It's over, Tom," I said. A strange giddiness had replaced my fear. He wasn't going to get away with it. "You can't shoot me. They know everything."

Tom looked down the gun sight. His finger was on the trigger. "They're here about Eve. Routine." He appealed to the cops. "This woman broke into my house."

"I've been talking to investigator Ryan Monahan for weeks." I directed my words to the private detective though he wouldn't turn to hear them. His attention was on the pistol in my husband's hand. "I came to check on Sophia and he tried to kill me, Ryan."

At the mention of the PI's name, Tom's eyes opened from their focused slits. The woman shouted again for him to drop his weapon. Ryan angled his body in front of the cop, shielding her side while allowing a clear shot over his shoulder.

"Put it down!" the woman shouted.

The terror in Tom's eyes ebbed. He lowered the gun toward his stomach. "This woman is nuts. She broke in."

My fear of being shot was replaced by dread that my sociopath husband would somehow talk his way out of this, maybe make the cops believe that I was a crazy stranger or that I'd faked my death in hopes of taking Sophia away from him without a custody battle. He was such a good liar.

"I've told them everything," I shouted. "Ryan knows what you did on the boat. He knows that you and Eve planned it all for the insurance money. He knows you shot Eve. You can't kill me to shut me up. He already knows everything. It's over. This whole time, you've been the idiot. You've been thinking you were getting away with it while Ryan was gathering evidence I gave him. You're going to rot in prison."

Tom's eyes darted from the female officer to the investigator and me. Resignation flickered on his face, followed by a rage that distorted his features. "You two were playing me this whole time?" The gun began to rise. It went from Tom's hip to his waist to his chest. "Fuck you both."

A bang pierced the air. I shut my eyes, wanting my last sight to be the back of my lids and not a bullet. Smoke and screams overwhelmed my senses.

The hysterical voice was my own. My lids fluttered back. I feared seeing blood on my shirt or Ryan lying in front of me. Instead, Ryan was standing beside the female cop, his arm around her shoulder. My screams died. I stepped toward the dining room.

Blood was splattered on the chandelier. Tom lay beneath, bent backward over the dining table, a quarter-sized hole punctured in the center of his forehead. Cabernet-colored liquid pooled beneath his skull, seeping into the surface. That stain would never come out.

43

December 4

Ryan sat on the Bacons' front steps, head dropped between his knees. The adrenaline coursing through his body had nothing to do except twist his stomach and spike his blood pressure. Sweat rolled down his face, despite the near-freezing temperature outside. He thought he might be sick.

For the second time in his life, he'd found himself in a gun-fight without a weapon. He was furious with the failure of his statistics-educated gut for not alerting him to the possibility that Tom might attack his arresting officers. Tom had acted out of character. Until hours ago, he'd been smart. Careful. The kind of killer who forced suicide notes and made certain he'd had fake alibis in place.

Premeditated murderers didn't get into shootouts with law enforcement. Something had pushed all Tom's buttons, made him lose control. Or rather, someone.

Ryan looked up from the stone beneath him. Steam wafted from the headlights of the police cruisers crowding the driveway. Their light and the glow from the lit-up house illuminated the Bacons' property in the dark, turning it into a strange movie set. At the center of the action was an ambulance with Camilla and the little girl huddled together on a stretcher. The ambulance's open pewter doors framed their picture. Vivienne leaned against the Bacons' garage, beneath the outdoor torches. The detective that had taken his statement moments ago was now taking hers.

She'd be blameless. She'd demanded that Tom drop his weapon multiple times.

Ryan's gaze returned to the maid. She cradled Sophia in her lap. The girl's head was buried in her chest. Someone had draped a blanket over the two of them, which Camilla had turned to mostly cover the child. Two local officers fidgeted beside the vehicle, clearly holding back from getting Camilla and Sophia into the waiting squad cars. They needed to question them separately, and nobody wanted to snatch some poor kid who had lost both parents in the space of four months from the arms of a familiar adult.

Ryan placed his hand on the side of the house for support and stood. He needed to talk to Camilla before she went to the local station. Undocumented immigrants sometimes disappeared after talking to cops.

He limped down the driveway to her huddled figure. Before he could speak, David came running. Though Vivienne's partner was backlit by headlights, Ryan could see the excited expression on his face.

"NYPD picked up Lena at work," David said. "I just got off the phone with them."

"And?"

"They asked her about Tom. Showed her pictures of Eve. She said that Tom had told her Eve was becoming erratic and obsessed with him."

"Of course he told her that."

Ryan continued toward Camilla. He might not get another chance to talk to her.

David's hand landed on his shoulder. "Wait, your company will like this." A smile spread across his overearnest face. He spoke too loud for Ryan's liking, as though he wanted all the cops to listen in. "Lena admitted that she wasn't talking to Tom on the boat when his wife died. She'd hung out with him earlier in the day while Ana was at the beach by herself. The potheads *did* mix up the time. Lena claims that she lied because Tom told her that he'd confessed the affair to his wife and she'd jumped. Lena didn't want to be vilified in the news."

Camilla knew Ryan was coming for her. He could see her in the ambulance lights, tracking him from behind those ridiculous glasses. Her expression was pained. "Thanks, David," he coughed. "I'll take the statement under advisement."

He nodded to the local cops as he passed and then sat on the edge of the open ambulance, feet still planted on the asphalt. Camilla blinked acknowledgement.

"Soph," she whispered into the blanket, "I have to talk to this man." She looked up at the female cop, now hovering nearby. "She didn't see anything."

The woman gave an apologetic smile and reached into the vehicle for the girl. "We still have to ask her some questions." Her voice became high and Mary Poppins-esque. "Would you like some hot cocoa? I think we have some."

The girl nuzzled into the sitter's chest.

Camilla cooed into her ear. She brushed her cheek with her fingertips until the girl looked up. "I'll be right there." She tapped her chest. "I'm your Auntie Camilla. Okay? I won't let anything happen to you. I'll come right away. Okay? Auntie Camilla will come right away, like I always did when I watched you."

The girl nodded. Camilla carried Sophia to the edge of the ambulance and passed her through the open doors to the female cop. "Auntie's a term of endearment." She seemed to volunteer the information to answer the woman's confused expression. "She's been through a lot. She wants her mom."

Camilla joined Ryan on the ambulance floor. Tears tumbled down her cheeks as she watched the woman take Sophia away.

"What will happen to Sophia? Will she go to Ana's parents?"

"In time. She'll probably spend a couple weeks in a foster home while the authorities work out how to get her to Brazil."

The sitter bit her bottom lip. Her eyes welled. "I'd gladly take her. But I don't have any documents."

Ryan understood her dilemma. If Camilla had overstayed a visa and left the country, the United States might bar her entry for ten years. "Ana's parents can come get her."

She stared into her lap. "They don't have money."

A flush of guilt heated Ryan's face. He'd introduced himself to Camilla as someone investigating her former employer's death. He'd never made it clear that he was working for an insurance company. "Ana had a substantial death benefit. Sophia will get a lot of money. And with Tom dead, it will go to Ana's parents to take care of their granddaughter."

She swiped at her eyes again. The tears fell so fast that she had to lift her glasses to wipe them before putting them on again. "But I heard that cop say there's a woman claiming Ana jumped."

"Tom told the women in his life a lot of things, most of it untrue." Ryan knocked the ambulance's metal floor, giving his still jittery hands something to do other than shake. "Tom killed Eve. He didn't do that to cover up allegations that his wife jumped overboard. Ana didn't plan to be murdered and it was her policy. The company will have to pay the base amount."

Sobs broke Camilla's voice. She wiped her eyes on the blanket and then tried to put the thin, blue fleece over her shoulders. He took the corner from her and helped drape it over her back.

"How did you know that Tom had a gun?"

Camilla sucked in her breath. "I saw on the news that Eve was dead. The anchor called it suspicious. It made me fear that Tom was going crazy and could hurt Sophia. I came over and he invited me inside. He was so . . . calm." She shuddered. "And . . . I lost it. I told him that the police must know he killed Eve and Ana, and it was just a matter of time before you guys came for him. Next thing I knew, he had a gun. I woke up, trapped in the garage with the car running, keys locked inside."

Ryan nodded slowly. Tom had tried to kill Camilla the same way he'd murdered his mother. Why not, since he'd gotten away with it before?

Camilla's breath came out in thin puffs of condensation.

"I'd come to save Sophia and I put her in more danger. I'm horrible. What if he . . ."

Ryan draped an arm around her shoulder. "Sophia will be okay."

"How does a kid get over this?" She lifted her large glasses to wipe her face. Her watery eyes were big and familiar—and brown. They looked like Sophia's.

Camilla's head dropped back into her open palms.

"Lies." Ryan touched his fingers to her chin, encouraging her to look up again. "She's not even four. Memory can be ephemeral at this age. There's no need to traumatize her with the truth. She didn't see Tom get shot. Way I see it, she doesn't need anyone explaining anything other than her parents died in an accident."

Camilla held her head up. She stared at the house, lit up like Christmas by the crime scene investigators inside. Tom's body was just visible through the front windows, splayed across the dining room table.

"Lie," she whispered. "I can do that."

Ryan looked into her determined brown eyes. He bet that she could.

44

December 24

Sophia would be home for Christmas.

She skipped beside me, her bouncy motion sending the child-sized suitcase careening from one side to the other on the terminal's iridescent floor. A smile sparkled on her diamond-shaped face. She was taking her first plane ride to see her grand-parents for the first time. They loved her, and they lived by the beach. It would be warm there since Brazil's summers coincided with the United States' winters. And, per tradition, she would wear a white dress and spend New Year's Eve splashing in the water. It was all so exciting.

She didn't grasp that I couldn't come with her, or that I'd packed all her things in a massive suitcase because she wouldn't be coming back—at least, not for fifteen years.

I'd tried explaining, but my near-four-year-old still possessed a toddler's conviction that she could will whatever she wanted. After all, she'd wished for me to come home—even after her father had told her I was dead—and I'd appeared. So far, she hadn't asked about her daddy.

I guided Sophia onto the rubber strip of a moving walkway. Skipping burned a ton of energy and our gate was at the far end of the terminal. When she hopped aboard, another wave of delight washed over her face. "It's moving, Mommy!"

I winced at the name. Just three weeks had passed since Investigator Monahan had filed his report recommending that the policy pay out to my parents. My folks had yet to receive a dime. The insurer was waiting for the official police report on my death to mail the check. Monahan had assured me that the case was filed as a homicide, on the recommendation of the NYPD's financial crimes task force, but I still feared that ISI would hire another detective to refute the finding. For all I knew, someone was watching me right now, looking for similarities between the blond woman escorting Sophia to the airport and photographs of my former self.

"Soph, remember when you get on the plane, there will be a nice woman to help you. She's called a flight attendant. I'll introduce you when we get to the gate. She will let you watch movies and wait with you at the terminal until Grandpa and Grandma come to get you."

Sophia's eyes grew wide. I silently prayed that she could keep the tears at bay. I couldn't break down here.

"But you're coming?" Her voice sounded so small.

I took her little hand in mine and swung it to keep the mood light. I needed to pretend that saying good-bye to my child, after just getting her back, wasn't shredding my insides. "I have to work for a little bit so you guys have what you need until a big check comes in," I said. "Then Grandma and Grandpa will send for me."

Sophia's bottom lip trembled.

"Here's an idea. Do you want to learn how to say Grandpa and Grandma in Portuguese?"

The conveyor belt deposited us back on the tile floor. Blue carpet and rows of black chairs filled each side of the room. Just beyond them, a wall of iron and glass gazed out onto the runway. The blue tail of Sophia's plane was just visible.

My heart lodged in my throat. I cleared it as I marched my kid toward her departure gate.

"It's *vovô* and *vovó*," I said. "Vo-voh is Grandpa. And Vo-vah is Grandma. But want to know something funny? They're spelled the same. They just have a different strange symbol above the vowel. You're going to learn all about those."

Sophia's nose wrinkled. She didn't spell in English yet, let alone Portuguese. My words were pointless. I was talking to keep from thinking, to keep from feeling. "*Vovô* and *vovó*," I repeated. "Grandpa and Grandma. You try."

"Vo." Her voice lacked any of her prior excitement.

"Vo-vah. Grandma. Try again."

"I want you to come." Tears shone in her brown eyes. I needed to keep it together.

I crouched to her level and hugged her little body tight to my chest. "I will. I promise. So soon." I kissed her forehead. "I love you so much. It won't be like last time. I'll be there really soon."

Could I keep that promise? In truth, I had no idea how long the policy would take to pay out or how difficult it would be to arrange my entry into Brazil. What I did know was that my daughter would be safe, loved, and thanks to me sending a few hundred U.S. dollars a month, financially secure. Right now, that would have to be enough.

By the time we reached the gate, boarding had started. The line entering the plane sent a jolt of panic through my body and started my eyes watering. I wiped away the tears with the back of my hand and, as promised, introduced Sophia to the flight attendant: a friendly woman with bright eyes and hair swept back into a neat ponytail behind a blue pillbox hat.

I dropped to my knees and, again, hugged Sophia as though I wished to squeeze all the air from her body, trying to etch every detail of my child into my memory. I needed to remember this: her strawberry-scented hair, her dark, curious eyes, her fair skin, the shape of her narrow shoulders and thin arms. My Sophia.

Eventually, the stewardess tapped my shoulder. Sophia had a flight to catch.

My little girl was brave. She only cried a little. All the newness surrounding her was sufficient distraction.

I stood at the gate until the plane backed onto the runway. Then I hurried back to the center of the terminal where I could better view the flights taking off. From behind the window, I could still hear the rush of jet engines. The sound of escape.

I sobbed as I watched flight after flight arch into a rose-colored sky. My daughter sat on one of those planes, destined for a better life—a life she would have because of me, in spite of her father.

A germ of pride sprouted in my belly and swelled to my chest. My husband had underestimated me. I had beaten him while officially dead. If I could do that, I could do anything.

I was definitely worth more alive.

Acknowledgments

I'd like to thank my daughters: Elleanor and Olivia. Being their mother has been the greatest gift and source of inspiration. Every day, they make me strive to be a better, stronger person worthy of calling herself their mother.

Thanks also to my husband, Brett, who bears absolutely NO resemblance to Tom Bacon. I am blessed to be married to such a hardworking, generous, witty man. Also, thanks to my dog Westley who lets me pet him endlessly while writing the more tense scenes.

Much gratitude to my amazing agent, Paula Munier, who in addition to selling my work lets me bounce ideas off of her, suggests changes, and makes sure I don't embarrass myself by sending out anything before it's ready. She's a lifesaver.

Thanks very much to the wonderful team at Crooked Lane: Matt, Dan, Nike, Sarah, and Heather. A writer couldn't want for a more dedicated, thoughtful group. Thanks also to Dana, Julia, Amanda, and Meryl for all the marketing support.

I am very fortunate to have a family that not only reads my work but shouts about it from the rooftops: Mom, Dad, Tara, and James. Thank you. I am incredibly blessed to have such great, supportive siblings. My sister is a force. Thanks also to my grandmothers, Madaline Holahan and Gloria Fidee. Both of you are such an inspiration as women, and your support has helped make me the person I am today. Thanks to my late grandfather, James Holahan, who inspired me to write in the first place. I think you would have been proud of this one.

Thanks to Denize, who helped me with the Portuguese language and Brazil research in the book and is a great sounding board.

Many, many, many thank-yous to all the wonderful friends and extended family members that have supported and shared my books: Linda, Erika, Harry, Saundra, Gabby, Madeline, Elaine, Paul, Julie, Megan, Cassidy, Philip, Oona, Sharon, Philip G., Nino, Tamiko, Soroya, Garth, Cheryl, Margot, Shana, Karin, Lisa, Jen, Galit, Gia, Shelley, Mina, Karly, Nadine, Lauren, Dara, Linda K., Shuni, Ken, Tom, Paul M., Marisa, Zakiya, Dennis, Fabrizio, Stacy, Dyandra, Liz, Jessica, Signian, Janice, Cecilia, Fran, Andrew, Junior, Latin, Kim, George, Missy, Nicole, Chris, Jamie, Margie, Elizabeth. Your support means the world.

Last, but always first, thanks to God:

> "In the day-to-day trenches of adult life, there is actually no such thing as atheism. There is no such thing as not worshipping. Everybody worships. The only choice we get is *what* to worship."
>
> —David Foster Wallace, "This Is Water"